ANNE RICE & CHRISTOPHER RICE

RAMSES
THE DAMNED
THE REIGN OF OSIRIS

Anne Rice is the author of thirty-seven books, including the Vampire Chronicles and the Lives of the Mayfair Witches book series. She lives in Southern California.

www.annerice.com

Christopher Rice published four *New York Times* bestselling novels before the age of thirty and has been twice nominated for the Bram Stoker Award. Together with his best friend and producing partner, *New York Times* bestselling novelist Eric Shaw Quinn, he runs the production company Dinner Partners. Among other projects, they produce TDPS, a video and podcast network, which can be found at www.TheDinnerPartyShow.com.

www.christopherricebooks.com

RAMSES THE DAMNED

THE REIGN OF OSIRIS

RAMSES THE DAMNED

THE REIGN OF OSIRIS

Anne Rice &
Christopher Rice

ANCHOR BOOKS
A Division of Penguin Random House LLC
New York

AN ANCHOR BOOKS ORIGINAL, FEBRUARY 2022

Library of Congress Cataloging-in-Publication Data
Names: Rice, Anne, author. | Rice, Christopher, author.
Title: Ramses the damned : the reign of Osiris /
Anne Rice, Christopher Rice.
Description: First edition. | New York : Anchor Books, a division of
Penguin Random House LLC, 2022.
Identifiers: LCCN 2021020563 (print) | LCCN 2021020564 (ebook)
Subjects: LCSH: Ramses II, King of Egypt—Fiction. | Cleopatra,
Queen of Egypt, –30 B.C.—Fiction. | GSAFD: Biographical fiction. |
Science fiction. | Suspense fiction.
Classification: LCC PS3568.I265 R37 2022 (print) |
LCC PS3568.I265 (ebook) | DDC 813/.54—dc23
LC record available at https://lccn.loc.gov/2021020563
LC ebook record available at https://lccn.loc.gov/2021020564

Anchor Books Trade Paperback ISBN: 978-1-101-97033-1
eBook ISBN: 978-1-101-97049-2

Book design by Steve Walker

www.anchorbooks.com

Printed in the United States of America
10 9 8 7 6 5 4 3 2 1

Anne and Christopher dedicate this book to the memory of their beloved cousin Allen Daviau, a brilliant artist and cinematographer who was lost to COVID-19.

A king's lot: to do good and be damned.

—MARCUS AURELIUS

RAMSES THE DAMNED

THE REIGN OF OSIRIS

July 1914: Russia

With hatred for Saint Petersburg burning in his heart, Nikolai Vasilev hurried along the edges of the humid city's narrow
canals, following the shadows as he raced to a meeting that
would change the world forever. Now that he'd left the city's
grand boulevards, he allowed excitement to quicken his steps.

On the glittering Nevsky Prospect he'd passed bejeweled
ladies on their way to the opera, battled his desire to sneer at
the preening fops who accompanied them like strutting dolls.
Curse them all! They thought themselves the proud custodians
of Russia's window to the world, but they were germs, agents
of Europe's stain. And they'd rewritten the history of this city
to fit their delusions of grandeur.

Peter the Great had not summoned Petersburg from these
swamps as a magician might with his bare hands; he had raged
it from them, and at the cost of tens of thousands of lives. And
now the magazine editors and the godless artists who gathered
here ridiculed those who refused to exalt the city's grotesque
seductions as the shimmers thrown off by a nation's crown
jewel. Exhorted them to take off their "Slavophile nappies" and
embrace its ghastly fusion of Russian and European as something wholly unique and therefore wholly Russian!

Curse them! Curse their lies! Curse their betrayal of the true

Muscovite spirit that had risen, lionlike, to make order out of the ashes left by Mongols, erecting glittering fields of onion-domed temples where before there had been only savagery and death.

Russia's window to the world? Never! Petersburg was an open wound, through which the infection of Europe had poured with terrible speed, weakening all within. Even the feckless and doddering Tsar Nicholas II, who now bowed before Europe's nations like a serf, had retreated from its borders to the palaces at Tsarskoe Selo.

And now, as if to make the injustice complete, Europe was on the eve of war. Soon his beloved Russia would be drawn into the storm. A colossus called unjustly into action on behalf of the very Western nations who knew not its true grandeur or its depths, whose liberal democracies sought to weaken the tsar's connection to God.

But in one gloved hand, Nikolai carried a case containing two stones that would end this cataclysm for good. They were the key to a more powerful weapon than all the siege cannons of the Germans.

He wore another of these stones from his neck, concealed beneath his coat. Polished and amber hued but still rough-hewn and bearing the marks of the ancient burial site from which it had been recovered. It hung from a gold chain he'd taken care to tuck between the soft linen of his dress shirt and the thicker cotton of his undershirt so that its miraculous power wouldn't suddenly fire into action against the heat of his flesh.

And there was heat in his flesh, to be sure. Some of it called forth by the long, draping coat he'd worn on this hot summer night to conceal the stone's hard lump, but also by the heat of excitement and anticipation.

If all went as planned, soon Nikolai's father would allow them to act.

To unleash the secret they'd guarded for years now, and on

behalf of the Russia they loved. The true Russia. The Russia of Moscow, the Russia of tsars who did not bow miserably before the delusions of the French and the pretensions of the English.

Nikolai turned a corner, and at last the spire of the Peter and Paul Cathedral came into view, rising across a river of black water that seemed unnaturally still and mirrorlike on this summer night. Its gilded cupola shined, crowned by an angel. A fitting meeting place, this one. But a stone's throw from the old garrison that had given this city its one, true meaning before Peter the Great had fallen prey to the delusion of a thousand European artifices. Great tsars, tsars who had truly embodied Russia's strength, were buried within, and it was for their ghosts that Nikolai did this now.

He saw the shadows he was hoping for before he crossed the street. Anton, a great bear of a man with a lion's mane of hair partly tamed by his bowler hat, and Andrei, shorter than Anton but barrel chested. These were good soldiers and strong men, men whose steady gazes concealed cunning and strategic minds. Men with whom Nikolai had defended the city gates of Tianjin from the Boxer rebels who'd sought to stop the march of Russia's railways through China. But for what? Nikolai wondered now. To merely set the stage for Nicholas II's terrible defeat at the hands of the Japanese!

How many humiliations would Russia be forced to endure before its true spirit rose once more to seize its fate?

No more, Nikolai vowed, no more, *and that is why we shall not proceed headlong into this great war to come.*

The men he greeted now could be trusted with the task before them. They fell silent as he opened the case and handed them each a jewel box one might use to encase a lady's diamond necklace. As they studied the stones and little chains curled within, Nikolai studied the men's faces. Looked for signs of raw ambition or reckless wonder or anything else that might distract them from the momentous work at hand.

He saw only cool calculation, and was calmed.

"Once this task is complete, my father will allow us to act, and not a moment too soon," he told them. "But first we must strike down all those with whom the archeologist might have shared the secret." He reached into his jacket pocket, removed the handwritten lists he'd prepared for them both. A list of names only. It would be up to them to do the rest.

Both men read the list carefully.

JULIE STRATFORD
MR. REGINALD RAMSEY
ELLIOTT SAVARELL
ALEX SAVARELL
RANDOLPH STRATFORD
SAMIR IBRAHIM

"First," Nikolai added, "all those who loved Lawrence Stratford must die."

Part I

I

Brogdon Castle

She was no stranger to war.

She had walked the fields of many plagues through the centuries, offered healing and comfort to the mortals who lay dying there.

She had borne witness to the fall of kingdoms, knew well the tastes and scents and sounds that split the air before a world was shattered by an apocalyptic storm.

Bektaten felt those things now. They rode the brisk, ocean winds that swept her long walks atop the sea-facing cliffs. They drummed against the stone walls of the Norman castle she had so recently restored. They rose high above the English Channel, spun off by the thunderheads rolling over the German Empire.

War was coming.

But the reports from her spies throughout the world, her beloved Heralds of the Realms, had convinced her this cataclysm would have no precedent in history, and so her eight thousand years of immortal life could not prepare her for it. Cannons that could turn a battalion of soldiers to a sea of charnel would soon be rolled into battle. Machinery that once defied imaginations would service an interlocking web of conflict unlike any she'd ever seen. All the great nations of Europe would soon be embroiled.

She could feel the coming thunder of it in her unbreakable bones.

And so she retired to her library with its leather-bound volumes containing her ancient journals, where the great mastiffs she had recently rescued watched her attentively from all corners of the stone-walled room. Outside, the Celtic Sea roared against the bases of the cliffs on which her castle stood, but within her citadel she could hear only the drumbeat of war. She lifted her pen to paper and she wrote. She wrote to all the immortals who had so recently been placed under her care. Immortals who'd been rendered so without her consent, but through the power of an elixir she had created thousands of years before.

She wrote to them of the war she feared and the temptations it would place before them all. When she was through, her loyal servants, Enamon and Aktamu, would make all the necessary copies of the letter and see that it was delivered to all of the recipients addressed therein. To Ramses the Great, once Ramses the Damned, and his immortal lover, Julie Stratford. To the dashing and mysterious Elliott Savarell, who she'd yet to meet. And to the American novelist Sibyl Parker and the immortal to whom she was still mysteriously connected, a woman who may well be the risen Cleopatra herself. She wrote to this Cleopatra as well, sweeping aside the question of whether or not she was truly Egypt's last queen reborn, or a fragmented clone residing within her resurrected skin and bones.

Essential to address them all as one, as if they sat collectively before her. For how else to impress upon them that they were an alliance, a council in the making. The first citizens of a new kingdom that must endure within the shadows and gaps of knowledge that defined mortal humanity.

With each stroke of the pen, she tried to summon her wisdom and her experience, hoping it would form a river of strength through the fear that dominated her thoughts.

She knew it was essential to write them, not just as their

queen, but as their compatriot, and so she began by opening
her ancient heart.

*You are my children now, all of you, and given the extent
of all that I must protect here at my citadel atop the
windswept cliffs of Cornwall, you are my subjects too.
And so I share these words with confidence that you will
each place flame to paper once you have absorbed the
contents of this letter so as to conceal from history the
many secrets alluded to within these pages.*

*The events which drew us all unexpectedly together
have reached their conclusion. Saqnos, the prime minister
of my ancient kingdom, who for thousands of years
strived to steal from me the formula for the pure elixir,
has been vanquished, along with his acolytes, the fracti.*

*I grieve Saqnos. I cannot be untruthful about this. He
was once my lover and prime minister before he turned
traitor, before he was lost to his rage over the fact that I
had kept my discovery of the secret to eternal life from
him. But he was one of but a handful of witnesses to
the glory and expanse of Shaktanu, our fallen kingdom,
our ancient world. With him died memories of glittering
palaces now ground to dust by time, great sailing ships
lost to the winds of history, of a forgotten time when
the Sahara, now desert, was dappled with crystalline
pools and glistening rivers and trees that shifted lazily in
temperate winds. These were the gardens of a kingdom
that was spoken of by the ancient world, as Atlantis is
now spoken of by this modern one.*

*But the destruction of Saqnos is but a prologue to
what I wish to share in this letter. For his vile plots have
brought us all together, and now that we are roughly and
newly united, our new burdens commence.*

*Given the power you all possess, I must speak to you
now of the terrible war I believe to be on the wing.*

2

London

They were kind men, these officials from the British Museum. But their presence here in her front parlor stirred painful memories of other agents of that august institution who had tried to force their way into Julie's home months before, all in a frenzied effort to make off with Lawrence Stratford's last, great discovery—the ancient mummy and artifacts her father had unearthed in the hills outside Cairo just before his murder.

Of course, those men hadn't possessed the slightest idea of the true magic and mystery contained within her father's finds. They'd financed the expedition and felt entitled to its end results. And they'd thought it terribly ghastly Julie had insisted on displaying the mummy right here in the front parlor of her family home in Mayfair. And like the world, they'd no idea of the miracle that followed. A miracle wrought by ancient magic and the sun, the very kind of fierce, midday sunlight that filtered through the stained-glass ceiling of the conservatory now, illuminating the empty shelves that had been filled with her father's journals only moments before.

But these were different men standing before her in this moment, gentler men. And she'd invited them here. They'd not come to collect an ancient mummy and its related artifacts, for the occupant of that sarcophagus had, to the eyes of London, mysteriously disappeared. No, these men had come for something far more intimate and personal.

Lawrence Stratford's journals.

"I must say, Miss Stratford, we're most impressed you were able to make a survey of this many volumes so quickly. Especially given recent events." Eyebrow raised, the shorter of the two men studied her.

Ah, there it was again. They were beset by curiosity about the mysterious tale of her betrothal party to an Egyptologist named Mr. Reginald Ramsey. To say nothing of the earlier scandals that had marked Mr. Ramsey's rather mysterious and sudden arrival into London society.

"My father's legacy had been marked by much excitement, that's for sure," she said. "But I didn't read the journals just these past few days. I'd spent much time with them already, so it was short work, removing the ones too personal. Surely you can understand that some of Lawrence's innermost thoughts must not be . . ."

"Oh, of course. Of course, Ms. Stratford."

Both men practically fell all over themselves to agree.

She felt a stab of guilt. Part of what she'd just said was a lie. But hardly a damnable one. In fact, she'd read the entirety of his journals—thirty-five volumes from a lifetime of expeditions to Egypt—in a single day's time. And she'd memorized every word. These were talents afforded her by the same elixir that had changed the color of her eyes to blue, that ensured her tangle of brown curls remained the same length and the same shining luster. That made her flesh and bones all but indestructible. That had given her the gift of eternal life.

But she could not tell these men this.

And she felt grateful for them. Grateful that in this time of conflict and unrest, they would provide a safe and sheltered home for the chronicles of her late father's travels and blazing insights and passions for the ancient world.

They popped open the clasps on their leather cases. With gloved hands they gently placed the stacks of volumes within. It seemed fussy, the amount of care they showed. The journals weren't in danger of falling apart. Indeed, the most recent ones were in such fine condition they served as a painful reminder of how recently Lawrence had been lost. Nothing among them was as ancient as the accounts contained inside the leather-bound volumes the great queen Bektaten guarded in her castle perched on the Cornish coast. But still, the sight of their methodical packing comforted Julie, made her feel as if this was the right choice.

"Even so, that you would take the time to facilitate during this time of trouble," one of the men said.

"Come now, Mr. Starnes," the taller one commanded. "Mustn't sour Ms. Stratford's day with your dire predictions about the troubles on the Continent."

"Forgive my colleague, Ms. Stratford," Starnes said with a smile. "He believes this will be a short war."

"It will be!" the taller man pronounced. "The British declaration is but an ornament, meant to deter the Germans out of any silliness."

"Whether it's short or long," Julie said, "I'm grateful to know these precious items will rest secure within the museum's walls."

Both men beamed at this, the little tension of their disagreement having vaporized. And then there were handshakes and assurances she could come and visit and read through the journals again at any time she liked as soon as the archivists had cataloged them all.

And then they were gone and, with them, much of her father's memories.

She had not been prepared for this, this harsh stab of grief that struck her now as she found herself alone in the double parlor, the empty shelves in the Egyptian Room exposing the

extent of all she'd handed over to strangers. And the sunlight
filtering through the stained-glass window in the conservatory
nearby a reminder of all her father had been deprived of. Poisoned by her scheming, greedy cousin before the true miracle
of his discovery could be revealed to him.

With her heightened senses, she detected movements just
outside the front doors, assumed it was the men from the
museum lingering, perhaps struggling with the weight of the
cases before descending the front steps. Then there was a slight
scrape, and when she returned to the foyer, a white envelope
rested on the little Oriental rug.

In elegant cursive, the names on the envelope read MR.
RAMSEY AND MS. STRATFORD. And on the flap, a wax seal below
the words BROGDON CASTLE.

Her heart thrumming, she tore open the letter. When the
enormity of its contents became clear, she hurried upstairs in
search of the other addressee, the same man who'd torn the
mummy's wrappings from himself in the front parlor of this
very house months before, stepping fully into the sunlight that
had streamed through the conservatory's stained-glass ceiling,
rousing from centuries of slumber.

To Mr. Reginald Ramsey, once Ramses the Great,
and then Ramses the Damned, immortal counselor to
Egypt's ancient rulers. Once a powerful king of that land
yourself, while swelled from the heat of victory in battle
against the Hittites, you stole the elixir from a woman
you dismissed as a mad priestess when you happened
upon her isolated cave during your wanderings. You
stole it without knowledge that this woman was my
companion, and that it was not she who had discovered
this elixir quite by accident, but I who had concocted it
thousands of years before. I repeat these facts here not
to shame you for that long-ago murder of my friend, the

Hittite priestess Marupa. For all you have done with the elixir's power since, in my view, absolves you of the initial heinousness of that crime. You used your immortality not to become an all-powerful tyrant, but to provide wise counsel to kings and queens who might otherwise have placed the ancient world on a path to ruin. You have guarded the elixir's formula from those whose only desire is to destroy or acquire. You have balanced power with wisdom, despite your rash acts.

No, I repeat these facts of history so they might make clear to all the significance of the treaty to which you and I have agreed, a treaty which dictates that you will engage in no more rash acts. I speak specifically of your use of the elixir some months ago to resurrect remains you identified to be those of the last queen to which you gave your counsel, the last queen of Egypt, your former lover, Cleopatra.

Under your alias, Mr. Reginald Ramsey, you have promised me and those to whom you are now intimately connected that you will engage with this modern world, not seek to disrupt it or thwart its natural course of events with your incredible power and strength. Henceforth, your actions will be guided by your thirst for knowledge and experience, and tempered by your love for your immortal companion, Julie Stratford, daughter of the man who accidentally discovered what you assumed would be your final resting place. For reasons which have become clear since our parting a short time ago, I must hold you to this promise now more than ever.

Kinship, Ramses said to himself as he passed the letter's pages to Julie. *Let me feel only kinship with my new queen. Not this roiling anger. Not this sense of being imprisoned through elegant words.*

But it was a struggle.

He'd read the letter several times in its entirety, then reviewed the passage addressed specifically to him once more, hoping his anger would recede. But it did not. And now he gripped the arms of this soft upholstered chair in the bedroom where he and Julie never slept but made love frequently.

There was so much of his life the historians would never know.

Ramses II of Egypt did not die of old age as the biographies claimed. No stela had recorded the truth of those years—that his own son realized his father was not aging as a mortal man should, that the makeup and beards Ramses wore were a ruse, and that whatever the source of this miracle, it posed a threat to his own ascendancy. Not Plutarch, not Herodotus, not the historians of this twentieth century, not a one knew the hours Ramses spent being tortured by his once-loyal offspring as the man furiously demanded the secret to eternal life Ramses had guarded ever since its discovery.

It's theft, he reminded himself.

They would never know the bargain that had saved them all. Ramses would give up the throne, fake his own death with the corpse of an unloved man, and, in return for his son becoming king, he would be allowed to keep secret the source of his immortality.

But there'd been one other condition. Ramses would depart Egypt entirely, so as never to endanger the ruse or his son's throne by lingering in the kingdom's shadows.

Few could understand the loneliness that had overtaken him as he'd traveled the ancient world for the first time. A robed and solitary figure capable of standing strong against the most powerful winds, greeted in small villages as a mystic or a god, revealing little. Listening, learning with a mind expanded by the elixir's magic. New languages, new philosophies, new tribes unknown to him when he was king. He dazzled all he met with

eyes turned bright blue by the elixir's power, but his real identity was unknown to them. He was a traveler of vitality and
strength who never slept and ate almost constantly, but also a
nomad. A wanderer.

During those first journeys, his loneliness had been threaded
through with the wonder and majesty of all the glorious sights
he beheld for the first time: the vast forests of Britannia, islands
of volcanoes and ice in the farthest north. The raw and rolling earth of the very lands that now composed those empires
marching into war. He had touched and tasted and smelled
these lands in their purest form. Had moved among their
ancient peoples. But his only companion had been the knowledge that he walked alone, experienced alone, learned alone, fell
in love with mortals whose light would soon be snuffed out by
time alone.

Only one creature on earth had tasted this depth of solitude
and the isolation it could bring, the great queen Bektaten, so
newly known to them all. And now the author of a letter that
had by turns saddened and enraged him.

For with solitude had come freedom.

When he'd relinquished the double-headed crown to his
traitorous son, the last of his mortal burdens had left him. A
century later, he'd returned to Egypt and placed himself in service to the empire's new rulers, but he had done so on terms of
his own design. The old priests with whom he'd conspired to
keep his secret were all given the same instruction. They might
lead the new pharaoh to him only if the pharaoh sought true
counsel. For any who tried to raise him as an all-powerful war-
rior or weapon, the retribution would be swift. Never again
had he bent his knee to a king, a queen, or a pantheon.

And now, he answered to one who could reduce him to ash
in an instant.

She would be loath to do this, he was sure. She felt the same
kinship to him that he struggled to invigorate now. But her letter, with its forceful language and queenly decrees, made him

feel imprisoned nonetheless. Not in a tomb designed for a long and sunless slumber, a tomb he'd entered of his own volition. Imprisoned in a construct of rules and laws designed without his input or consent.

Julie read aloud, "'And to Julie Stratford, whom I am tempted to address as Young Julie, even though immortality powers you now and forever. I give my utmost support and endorsement to the love you share with Ramses, for I believe it gives Ramses the nourishment and balance he needs to embrace the modern world without disrupting it. But I must caution you not to lose yourself in a slavish devotion to him. What you experienced as a young mortal woman—the murder of your father, Ramses's resurrection, your near death at the hands of a risen Cleopatra—these events resulted in the shattering of your belief system. The immortality the elixir grants you cannot in and of itself replace the beliefs you have lost.

"'No ideology or moral purpose resides within its chemical structure. These you must construct on your own! And you must do so as Ramses's partner, not his possession! I understand there to be a fierceness in you that is more than up to the task I describe. But I fear your passionate desire for Ramses along with a persistent awe over his centuries of lived experience might conspire to trick you into believing you are merely a jewel he has acquired along his centuries of travel. You are not this, and the weight of immortality might crush your spirit should you fall prey to this false and limited sense of self. Your grief for your father continues to ring inside you like a bell rocked by a constantly shifting earth beneath your foundation. Perhaps it is made worse by the terrible knowledge that your father was so cruelly murdered by a relative before he could come to know the true wonder of what he had discovered inside of Ramses's tomb, before he should share in these dazzling adventures you've recently experienced. I do not wish to speak for your soul, but I wish for you to discover yours in full.'"

Julie paused and gave Ramses a seductive smile. "Is this what troubles you? Her fear that I might cling to you like a school-girl? Your precious jewel."

"Read the rest, Julie. Read the rest."

And she did, settling onto his lap. Intoxicating, the smell of perfume radiating from her tailored men's attire. He embraced her, nuzzling against the hot porcelain nape of her neck.

"She fears immortal intervention in the war," Julie finally said. "I understand her concern."

"She addresses us as if we're children with no control of our impulses."

"She doesn't think us weak, Ramses. She thinks the threat is strong. Without precedent. And the temptation to stop it, stronger."

"And so we do what she asks? We sail to America. All to ensure we don't throw out our powerful hands to stop the sol-diers on the march."

"You speak often of Manhattan." She kissed his forehead, tenderly cupped the back of his neck, the gentle slip of her fin-gers against his flesh sending blissful shivers through him. "You couldn't reach the Americas on your ancient travels. They're open to you now."

"I don't wish to intervene in this war. These temptations she describes, they are hers. She endows us with them with-out cause. I've borne witness to many battles and intervened in none. To do so would be to invite chaos."

"I know," Julie whispered.

"I counseled the kings and queens of Egypt for centuries and never once cast the elixir about like a balm. Her words . . . they treat me as if I am new to all this, Julie. An infant in her magical world. If she can share her ancient journals with me, she must allow me to move about the world as I desire."

"I'm not sure if you're aware, but a transatlantic crossing entails a great deal of movement."

"I am. I've crossed the Mediterranean with you twice."

"Well, it's like that, only longer. And on the other side, a brave young nation neither of us has ever seen. Far from this war."

"I'm not disturbed by the destination. I don't wish to journey there atop a tide of the great Bektaten's superiority. That's all."

"Oh, Ramses. Her words describe a potential. A potential in us all. She addresses us as family. Perhaps that's what's disturbing to you. She doesn't treat you like a king or a lone advisor, but a member of an alliance."

"And her comments on your slavish devotion to me? What are your thoughts on this, Young Julie Stratford? Do I treat you like a possession?"

"So long as we possess each other, I see no issue," Julie cooed.

"Ah, how the nuances of the English language allow one to mislead."

Julie smiled before her expression turned serious at whatever she saw in his blue eyes.

"Don't see her as a queen, Ramses," she said. "You've not known family for centuries. It's no surprise you'd recoil from her parenting."

"So she mothers us. I see."

"If anyone has the right to, it's her. And no one else." Julie rose to her feet. "I'll contact Thomas Cook at once and book us passage on the *Lusitania*. It'll give us cause to close the house. I think that's best. Rita and Oscar will be relieved of their duties. With pay, of course. They can stay with their families during this time. Safest for them. Safest for us all."

"You truly fear this war will come to these shores?" Ramses asked.

"I don't know what this war will do. It seems no one does. Not even our great queen Bektaten."

"And so she's a queen again in your eyes," he grumbled.

Julie approached him, gripped the back of his neck, gave him a long, tender kiss. "If you wish not to be treated like a child, stop grumbling like one. Eat and begin your study of America. There are many books in my father's library to guide you."

"And if I don't?"

"Your precious jewel is going to issue you a spanking from which you might never recover."

With that, she nipped at his bottom lip. Irresistible, her little displays of aggression.

He rose, folding her into his arms, before hoisting her off her feet and carrying her to bed.

"There's something else I wish to dine on first," he whispered into her neck, before making short work of her many buttons.

The same club with its lustrous burgundy drapes and its familiar curls of tobacco smoke rising to the brass light fixtures in the dark wood ceiling. The same members, for the most part. Tuxedoed men, some mustached, and most redolent of whatever they swirled gently within their shining cut-crystal rocks glasses. But none had rushed to meet Elliott after his long absence, and there seemed a low intensity to their various conversations that hadn't been present on his last visit.

"I'm sorry, my lord. But I simply cannot, not in this moment," Elliott's solicitor repeated.

The express conducting of business was forbidden here, but still, they'd agreed his solicitor would quietly hand over an envelope containing the tickets Elliott had requested while they made idle conversation.

But it was not to be.

"You believe it's that serious?" Elliott asked.

"There's the matter of what I believe, and then there's what the travel office will do. They simply won't book the trip. They advise strongly against you setting foot on the Continent at this time. I hope you're not cross."

"No, not cross. Just startled is all."

Elliott studied the men all around them, bent lower over their conversation tables than usual. None of the usual laughter, none of the usual scotch-and-brandy-fueled mirth. Each conversation seemed weighted with muted alarm. With his heightened senses, he could hear their words, their whispers. Belgium. Mulhouse. The steely determination of France. It was all talk of the war. If these men did not stand within the corridors of power itself, they dined often with those who did, and the reports they had received were dire.

This explained why he was not barraged with questions about his sudden return.

Lord Rutherford, returned from Europe, I see!

Run out of luck at the gaming tables, have you?

And what's all this strange business about that betrothal party at your Yorkshire estate? They're saying it was all a ghastly illusion!

And then, of course, the typical dazed stares when they realized his eyes had changed color. That he no longer walked with his telltale limp, and no longer relied on a handsome, silver-headed cane.

None of this had greeted him.

"But you were able to see to my wife," Elliott asked.

"Oh, yes, of course. There's no trouble booking Edith passage west. That's the favored direction at the moment. There's no war in the United States."

"But there's no war *here* either."

"Yes, but it's a stone's throw away, sir. I don't presume to lecture. Your connections are surely better than mine. But I'm told the French occupation of Mulhouse is weakening and the Germans have unleashed wicked reprisals against them for their attempt to retake Alsace. There are rumors the British Expeditionary Force has already left for the Continent to aid the French."

"You speak as if Belgium will soon fall to the Germans."

"At this rate, it will, sir."

For a moment, both men sipped absently from their brandy. It would not bring about the pleasant fog of drunkenness Elliott had so often enjoyed as a mortal man, but its flavors were far more rich. At once sweeter and more pungent, an intoxication of taste alone. Having been forever changed by the elixir, he found all was more vivid, more sharply etched across his senses. Including the fear radiating through this gentlemen's club.

"What about the Russians?" Elliott asked. "Surely the Germans fear an advance from the Russians on their eastern flank."

"They're not proceeding as if they do, sir."

Devastating to have his worst suspicions confirmed. Far more devastating than the news that he could not, in good reason, return to the gaming tables of Europe where he'd known such pleasure, where he'd exercised his new abilities to a dazzling extent. Securing winnings that helped restore his family's tattered fortunes, feeding investments in banks both British and American.

And it was his family he thought of now. Not his wife, for he'd already helped her flee to America so she could escape the rumors swirling around the debacle that had been Julie and Ramsey's betrothal party. And theirs was a marriage that had always been defined by understanding, compromise, and distance.

It was his son he thought of now, Alex.

Strange to feel such a deep connection to him, a sudden desire to protect. For they'd always regarded each other almost as polite strangers. Such different animals it was hard to believe they shared blood. But to hear Julie tell it, his son was a changed man, a man changed by his exposure to miraculous experiences and blindly in love with a woman who may well be Egypt's last queen resurrected.

He thanked his stars Britain had no conscription, but should the British forces truly be poised to enter the war on France's behalf, was it possible Alex, wildly emboldened by his time with immortals, might be foolish enough to enlist? For all Elliott knew, his boy was racing off to join the fight now!

Would he be lost to Elliott forever if so? Or would he, while held prisoner in some enemy war camp, be driven so mad by starvation and abuse he'd begin to speak wildly of the immortals who were sure to save him, a rescue squad of ancient kings and queens?

According to his beloved Julie, the Alex he'd known was almost no more. Such a man might be given to reckless heroism. Hopefully, his love for Cleopatra would hold him in place.

But should Elliott see to this as well?

The concern on his solicitor's face pulled Elliott from these racing thoughts.

After concluding the polite conversation required to finish their drinks, they said their goodbyes. Elliott almost missed the sight of the valet approaching him as he went to exit the club.

"Lord Rutherford," the valet said softly, "if you'd excuse me, a letter arrived for you while you were engaged."

Elliott offered thanks, turned the envelope over in his hand, and went suddenly still at the sight of the two words written above the wax seal on the flap: BROGDON CASTLE. He'd yet to visit the place, but the name alone, fueled by the recent tales Julie and Ramses had shared with him, conjured instant mystery and pangs of excitement that felt almost like hunger.

What could it mean that he'd received a letter from this place, from a citadel housing an ancient queen who'd stepped forward from the shadows of history to reveal herself as the architect of the elixir of life?

Was it a formal invitation of some kind?

But when he unfolded its pages, he saw they were thick, their words many, and he found himself reading in a daze even as he walked out into the bright light of a summer afternoon.

And to Elliott Savarell, close friend to Julie Stratford and the only English aristocrat among our new immortal

*band, while I have yet to make your acquaintance, I'm
confident our mutual friend Ramses will soon share with
you the secrets of my castle. I must confess I am impressed
by tales of the vigor with which you have taken to
immortal life. I can only hope that your rediscovery of
the pleasures of youth and your newly heightened senses
bring you great satisfaction at gambling tables across
Europe. I must insist that you take care that your pursuit
of pleasure and the wealth your family requires does
not devolve into a pursuit of mad glory which perverts
your new talents into a form of notoriety which draws
unwanted attention upon us all. For it seems that no
matter your intention, it was your remarkable talents
at the casinos of Monte Carlo that first captured the
attention of my former prime minister's spies, alerting
them to the presence of fresh immortals in this brave new
century, and drawing them ultimately to Ramses and
Julie's betrothal party in their search for the pure elixir.*

*Understand I do not blame you for all that transpired.
I merely present this story as a caution against what our
powers might result in should we not use them with the
wisdom and maturity I'm sure you possess. I ask that at
some point you pay tribute to me here at Brogdon Castle
so that we might feast together and I might come to
experience some of your charm and the modern style your
intimates say you possess.*

*But know this as well. The explanations you have
given your family as to your recent absences might suffice
when it comes to your wife, Edith. But I fear that will
not suffice with your son, Alex, much longer, for he is
now the romantic companion of a woman he knows to be
not only immortal, but the resurrected form of an ancient
and powerful queen. In Cleopatra's arms, your son shall
be drawn ever closer to the center of the mysteries that*

unite us all, and so, at some point, your explanations of
your absences and your abilities will fail to convince.

Make contact with him swiftly where he now resides
with her on the Isle of Skye. I shall leave the methods
and extent to which you share the secrets of your own
experience with your son, but as your queen, I must
command that you heal this rift before it widens. It is
not my desire to meddle in the intimate affairs of fathers
and sons. But we immortals must never sit by idly while
a mortal's informed knowledge of our power makes an
unholy marriage with their animosity or contempt.

And as I said to Ramses upon our first meeting, you
may not feel you need to answer to a queen, but that will
not change the fact that you indeed have one.

By the time he'd finished the letter, and its dazzling addresses of the many members that now made up their immortal band, he'd reached the bank of the Thames.

It was as if his mind had been read by this ancient queen. But Julie and Ramses had made no mention of her possessing such a power. But perhaps truly ancient wisdom had the same effect.

And ultimately, it was his desire to accept her invitation that drove him to his next decision. He would go north to the Isle of Skye, north to his son, to conquer whatever tangle of complications awaited him there. But his reason for doing so was simple.

Only then would he be free to visit Brogdon Castle and bow before the great Bektaten.

3

Isle of Skye

There was only one place Sibyl Parker loved more on the Isle of Skye than her new home, and that was the little village bookshop she'd found on her third day there, where the portly, tenor-voiced owner greeted her every arrival as if she were a visiting queen. An American novelist had moved to the Isle of Skye! When she'd revealed herself to him as *the* Sibyl Parker, teller of adventure tales, her presence in this town had thrilled Mr. Campbell to no end. And it continued to thrill him during each of her subsequent visits. Whenever he noticed her approach down the cobblestone street, he'd rush to put on a pot of tea and prepare his bone-china service, in hopes of charming her into more conversation about a life dedicated to the spinning of stories.

He'd even started to read her books.

Despite proclaiming himself a lover of the classics.

His shop was a delight. Between the always-polished hardwood shelves, windows looked out over the tranquil harbor with its spray of anchored sailing vessels and the fiercely green mountains beyond, windows he often kept open to allow in the cool breezes off the water.

Even better, he accepted entirely her explanation for why she kept ordering so many of her own books.

She needed them for research, of course. In preparation for future novels. Her journey here from Chicago had happened so quickly—that much was true—that she'd not had time to pack hardcovers of all she'd written during her career.

The latter part was a lie, of course. She'd not packed them, because she'd planned to return. Had never thought her journey would take her beyond London, much less to a Norman castle perched on the Cornish coast and then here, to the northern tip of Scotland and all the mysteries that had awaited her amidst these bright green hills. And the books she needed were not preparation for future novels. Rather, they were the key to unlocking the mysterious connection that existed between her and the woman whose visions had first summoned her across the Atlantic, a woman Sibyl was absolutely sure to be Cleopatra herself.

For all the mysteries the great queen Bektaten had illuminated since entering their lives, her ancient wisdom had shed no light on the connection between Sibyl and Cleopatra. A connection that had begun with strange, dreamlike visions that seemed to travel across a current between them, a connection forged when Cleopatra was first roused from death by the elixir of life, and which became steady and constant and even intimate the closer they drew to each other.

Some had claimed Sibyl was, in fact, Cleopatra reborn, but since their coming together, she'd encountered ever more evidence that the connection between them was a complex entanglement requiring sophisticated analysis. Sibyl, it seemed, had indeed received some of Cleopatra's ancient memories. A miraculous fact that suggested memories themselves had a spiritual substance that allowed them to travel through time like little migrant souls. These visions, these fragments of Cleopatra's ancient life, had worked their way into Sibyl's novels. But when Cleopatra read these passages now, they filled yawning gaps in her own memory, and she was able to give them their proper context and foundation. A description of a palace wall, the dance of sunlight across a young boy's face, the overbearing brutish manner of a palace guard; these once-fleeting details, which had appeared to Sibyl as just flashes of creative inspiration, were echoes of Cleopatra's past. And the more Cleopatra consumed them, the more her spirit was restored.

Now, with the arrival of *The Thrall of Hathor* and *The Rage of Karnak*, their collection was almost complete, and Cleopatra would have more pages to rifle through in search of missing fragments of her memory. Of course, she'd howl with laughter when she encountered the historical inaccuracies in Sibyl's work. As Sibyl had explained to her many a time, she'd written to the specifications of aggressive editors, and their repeated claims the market cared not one whit for the historical details. Accordingly, most of her titles were a mishmash of ancient and Ptolemaic Egypt that would make a scholar roar. The goal had been to entertain, more than to educate. But still, the sound of Cleopatra's laughter was music to Sibyl's ears, even when tinged with condescension. She'd been in such despair when Sibyl first found her. And now, it seemed, the greatest of that despair had lifted.

When she graced Mr. Campbell with a hug, he did not go as stiff as death as a British man might. The Scottish, she had learned, were more well suited to her American effusiveness. He complained only that she hadn't finished the tea. But Sibyl knew she must hurry. She could feel a heat in her thighs and she was suddenly short of breath. It could mean only one thing. She must either hurry home or seek shelter and privacy to avoid an embarrassing scene. But no sooner had she set foot outside the bookshop when a familiar voice in her head said, *Come home, Sibyl Parker. You must lie with us.*

Such seduction in the queen's words. The very thought of what Cleopatra proposed would have seemed positively indecent to Sibyl a few months before. But now it seemed utterly natural, a logical consequence of connections revealed. And embraced.

She steered the motorcar Alex Savarell had purchased for them up the winding road that led to their little farmhouse, left it with such haste she forgot to remove the books from the floor of the passenger seat.

Hurry, Sibyl. He is in fine form today, and full of hunger. The very best kind.

The quiet home the three of them had made together was stocked with the finest furnishings she could find in the village, paid for with funds wired from her accounts in the United States. Of course, in various hysterical telegrams her wastrel, drunken brothers had whined and complained about her long absence, and her lack of plans to return. But she'd hired more servants to tend to them and care for their needs and see to it they didn't burn down their family's mansion in a drunken stupor. How dismissive they'd been of her before her sudden departure, even as the income from her "little stories," as they called them, supported their lavish lifestyle as they ran the family business into the ground.

Let them find their own way, for she had no plans to return to them now.

She had a new home.

And a new family, waiting for her in the bedroom in a lake of soft sheets, the sun streaming across their entwined bodies. Cleopatra, honey skinned, her raven hair kissing the pillow, and Alex Savarell, once the dignified aristocrat, now changed into a man altogether more earthly and soulful by the mad passion that had driven him this far north and into Cleopatra's arms.

Into *their* arms.

For Alex exalted the connection that existed between the women he now resided with, so he'd claimed them both as lovers. He rose now to his feet, guided her to the bed, where she fell into the sweet tangle of Cleopatra's arms. Luxuriated in the tender kisses Alex lavished her body with as he undressed her gently, and then the soft feel of Cleopatra's mouth against hers as Alex unleashed his passion on them both with the ravenous, hungry skill of the long repressed and newly unleashed.

Such bliss, such contentment. Not to be claimed, but to be joined.

And in this, their rural paradise of rolling green hills and vast open space and mountains that seemed to radiate wisdom. So very far from all that might prevent the expression of their true spirits. She'd been with men before and had known the tender, loving company of a few women as well. But Sibyl had never experienced eruptions of bliss like the ones that swept her when she was in this bed, where Cleopatra kissed her with a passionate hunger that seemed to both steal Sibyl's breath and then return it to her, infused with magic.

It always ended the same, their eruptions of passion.

Alex and Sibyl would drift off, and Cleopatra, whose immortal nature released her from the need for sleep, would rouse and walk the grounds, or lose herself to study in the house's other rooms, whereupon Sibyl would awake with the gentle words of Cleopatra's reading mind dancing through her own. But when Sibyl woke this time, with Alex's steady, sleeping breaths tickling the back of her neck, the words she heard did not come from a volume of history, or one of her own novels.

Somewhere in the house Cleopatra was reading a letter, and the words seemed bracingly familiar and direct.

Sibyl rose, absorbing each sentence as Cleopatra did.

To the resurrected Cleopatra. I am told by telegram that you have taken up residence in the Isle of Skye with the son of Elliott Savarell as your mortal lover. There you seek to gain a greater understanding of your mysterious connection to our mortal American friend Sibyl Parker. Having been apprised of all the facts of your experience

*since Ramses brought you back to life in the Cairo
Museum, I am of the belief that you are, in fact, the true
Cleopatra and not some pale revenant of her, some ghost
that existed within her ancient bones while the true spirit
was reborn in another.*

*I believe the memories you share with Sibyl and the
degree to which their intensity in Sibyl increased once
you were brought back to life suggest a complex web of
connections between souls living and deceased. Further,
the extent to which your mental confusion has been
healed by companionship with Sibyl has convinced me
that the mysterious implications of bringing the dead
back to life with my elixir are a vast sea we have only
just begun to explore.*

*I forbid further exploration of this sea with new
vessels.*

*So we, this newly united band of immortals, brought
together for the most part against our will, must look to
you as our ship cresting the waves of an uncharted ocean.*

*And for that reason, I offer you, Sibyl, and the young
Alex Savarell, protection and care here at Brogdon Castle
should you desire it, and I request constant appraisals
of your evolving condition. That said, should you ever
resort to the type of senseless taking of life that marked
your awakening in Cairo, the consequences will be
immediate and swift. The secrets contained within
my garden are both terrifying and miraculous, and no
immortal is immune to their power. While you may have
died a queen, I am your queen now, and I shall never
die unless I choose to. All that made clear, I grant you
forgiveness for these crimes, for they were committed
in the wake of being resurrected without your consent,
whereupon you were abandoned to great psychological
torment and confusion. I command you to make good of*

this forgiveness, and never again use your strength for
indiscriminate killing.

When Sibyl entered the room, Cleopatra set the pages of the letter aside.

She rose to the window and its view of gray clouds married to slate seas. Sibyl could feel the woman's despair at the base of her own throat. The envelope rested on the table. She picked it up, studied it, saw her name written on the front and the by-now familiar words on the flap, BROGDON CASTLE.

"Protection," Cleopatra sneered. "She offers us protection. And me forgiveness."

"She is a good and noble being."

"It's a ruse," Cleopatra said. "She summons us so she might destroy me."

"No. No, this isn't so. She believes you are the risen queen Cleopatra. She says so right here."

"How can you be sure? You were with her but a short time."

"She's had ample opportunity to destroy you and she's not taken it. The secrets there are miraculous. And fearsome."

"It was her prime minister who called me *nochtin*, a foul thing raised from death. Not a pure immortal, but a broken vessel, my memories draining into you. A second death even as I lived again."

"They were rivals, enemies. She vanquished him. She would never use such slurs against you! She is gentle and kind. She concedes it. She knows little of your condition. But she believes as I do. As we do. That you are Cleopatra. She exalts you with her words. She doesn't indict you."

"I won't go to her. Ever."

"There's no need. She doesn't command it."

Sibyl went to her, wrapped her arms around her, nuzzled her lips against her slender, olive-skinned neck, delighted in the fact that gooseflesh could break out on immortal, indestructible flesh.

"I will never leave here." Cleopatra turned to Sibyl and fiercely took her face in her hands. Powerful hands that could snap Sibyl's neck if Cleopatra so chose. But Cleopatra spoke gently. "I will never leave you and the restoration you have brought me."

Sibyl yielded to her powerful kiss. How better to assure Cleopatra that she'd made the same vow?

4

London

It was time to poison the plants in the conservatory, and this knowledge broke Julie's heart.

The plant-filled glass room that ran the length of the back of the house had been her father's favorite place for reflection. Here, he'd sit for hours among the ferns and flowers and absorb all that he'd just read in his adjacent study, which he'd dubbed the Egyptian Room, so named for the passion that had animated his scholarship for most of his life.

Since then, Ramses had fed the conservatory's flowers drops of the very elixir that granted him immortal life. She'd assumed they'd live forever, these flowers, and as soon as their unchecked growth aroused too much suspicion, Julie would be forced to drop them one by one into the Thames. But then came a series of events that turned her engagement party into a scene of assassination, and the revelation that there was a substance on earth that could reduce any living organism blessed by the elixir to ash.

Julie now held a tiny vial of this miraculous substance in one hand.

A sprinkling of strangle lily powder into each pot, and the massive ferns and blossoms would suffer a withering death within hours.

But she couldn't bring herself to administer this poison. Not yet.

When she did, she'd have to be careful. Strangle lily worked only when it was ingested or if it pierced the skin of its target. So long as she wore the leather gloves on the table next to her now, she would come to no harm. The powder would need time to bleed down into the soil, time for the plants to consume it and die.

But why kill them now? Why render this home a haunted house before we've truly departed?

It was the servants, she told herself. Not their suspicions, but their loyalty.

With her own two eyes, Julie's housemaid Rita had watched Ramses emerge from the sarcophagus and tear his mummy's wrappings away with both hands. But still, she'd convinced herself he was just a mysterious, mortal Egyptian man Julie's father had smuggled into Britain inside an ancient, gilded coffin. And that was just the beginning. In the months since, Rita and Oscar had explained away all manner of impossibilities about Julie's changed nature, and the peculiar habits of her fiancé, Mr. Reginald Ramsey. Amidst all that, these plants could grow to the size of motorcars, and Rita would find some logical explanation for it all.

But now that Julie and Ramses were to set sail for America in the morning, Julie had decided to close the house as one might a country property.

Of course, they would return. Eventually. But in their absence, she couldn't have Rita or Oscar feeling tethered to this place, for it would be just like Rita to return to the house again and again just to tend to these plants as she might stray kittens on the stoop. Her servants were already racked with guilt over their unexpected vacation.

"For as long as we're gone, you are free of this house, do you understand me? Now both of you hear this. I insist!" she'd told them again and again. "Your salary will continue as always. But you're to tend to your families. Enjoy the hours as you might if you were a person of means."

To this Rita had quipped, "I dare say, miss, if you're paying us this much for doing no work at all, very soon we shall be persons of means."

Most of the furniture in the double parlor was now wrapped in canvas to protect it from dust, but a table here and there had been left exposed so Rita could cover it in glinting silver trays full of sandwiches and beef Wellingtons and dozens of other delights Julie and Ramses could use to feed the constant hunger with which the elixir filled them. All the food they'd been storing, laid out for a final feast before their departure.

And now, the apparently simple matter of these plants.

But still, it felt like a murder to kill them. And there had been so many murders these past few months. And now there would be war.

Again the words of Bektaten's letter returned to her. How piercingly, devastatingly accurate her description of what had happened to Julie's father had been . . . *so cruelly murdered by a relative before he could discover the true wonder of what he had discovered inside of Ramses's tomb, before he should take part in these dazzling adventures you've recently experienced.*

Memories of her father now, dancing all night with her when she was a little girl to the "Morning Papers" waltz coming from the gramophone in the corner of this room. Dancing until he was blissfully exhausted and gasping the words, "No more, Julie. No more." Imagining the joy on his face when he first encountered the mysteries inside of Ramses's tomb, as he tried to make sense of a New Kingdom pharaoh whose scrolls told intimate tales of a queen who'd ruled a thousand years after his death.

Had there been joy on her father's face in those last moments before her cousin Henry poisoned him, all in some desperate attempt to secure funds for his many vices from the coffers of Stratford Shipping? She would never know. Henry was gone now, and could never tell. What she knew too well was how correct Bektaten's assessment was.

It was not just the loss of her father that pained her; it was the knowledge that he'd been taken from life just before he could witness the true miracle of what he'd unearthed in the hills outside Cairo.

Did you know, my dear father? In the moment before my evil cousin ripped you away from us, did you have any sense that you stood on the threshold of a new and wondrous world in which the subjects of your study rose from death and romanced each other across centuries? In which the dusts of history were blown clear by immortal pharaohs, and miracles were made possible by never-before-discovered blossoms picked from inaccessible mountain peaks and deep caverns by an indestructible, wandering queen?

Tears in her eyes now, tears startled onto her cheeks by a harsh knock against the front door.

Quickly, she wiped them away with the back of one hand.

Rita hurried to the front door. There was a brief, whispered exchange, then seconds later, Rita was standing next to her in the Egyptian Room, handing her an envelope.

"From Lord Rutherford, miss," she said.

Julie took it from her with a too-bright smile, whispering several thank-yous in a row as she quickly turned her back to Rita to hide her grief.

Indeed, it was from Elliott. Beloved Elliott, once her father's dearest friend and for a time something more than that. Then, in later and more recent years, the father of the young man Julie had once seemed fated to marry for reasons having nothing to do with love. In immortality, Elliott resonated with an almost-constant restless energy which had resulted in ceaseless travel since Ramses had given him the elixir.

She was surprised he'd been able to remain in one place long enough to write this note.

My Dearest Julie,

Am told by my solicitor you and "Mr. Ramsey" are soon to set sail for America. I hope this note reaches you before you depart. Have received the missive from our newly coronated queen.

Must admit, to read it was bracing. To be so thoroughly addressed, so thoroughly <u>known</u>, by a powerful figure whose acquaintance I've yet to truly make . . . it is a puzzle of sorts. But there is truth in her words, especially as they relate to my son, and so, after much thought I have chosen to bend myself to her will. For now.

I travel north to Scotland. I cannot, in this present moment, imagine the shape of the conversation I am to have with Alex, given all he has experienced and learned during my absence. I nourish a hope that the distance that has always existed between us, the distance I have kept in place, has been shrunk by his entrance into our world by way of Cleopatra's arms. If that's not the case, I remind myself I've met many challenges without a clear vision of what lies ahead. Including this incredible gift we've all been given.

After my meeting, I do indeed plan to pay tribute to our new queen as she has requested. If she is as you have told me of her, she is a figure to whom the word <u>remarkable</u> barely does justice. But after this event, assuming she does not pitch me into some dungeon as punishment for my wild travels, I am unsure of my next direction, but it is very possible I shall join you and Ramses in America. I ask that you cable my solicitor

upon your arrival and inform me of your travel plans so I
might join you. If I am welcome, that is.
　　Wish me luck. With both my son . . . and our "new
queen."

　XO, E

As she read the final lines, she'd laughed under her breath.

As if Elliott, her beloved Elliott, would ever not be welcome among them. And as if, in his current powerful state, he would ever need luck again.

How it had tugged at her heart when he'd left them days before, a dashing romantic figure in search of constant adventure and sensual experience, who couldn't be stopped by even the outbreak of war.

But his suspicions were correct; a more personal war of sorts might await him in this meeting with his son. She'd experienced Alex's anger herself during their last bitter conversation. When he'd discovered the depth of secrets Julie and Ramses and his own father had kept from him about the mysterious Egyptian woman with whom he'd fallen so helplessly in love, he'd pushed her away, expressing a desire to keep Cleopatra cloistered from all that might disrupt her unbalanced mind. But Alex's relationship with Elliott was not marked by the frustrated and thwarted desire that characterized his painful history with Julie, so perhaps his meeting with his father wouldn't be quite as contentious.

Alex had loved Julie once, truly, and she had never loved him, which had broken both their hearts, but in different ways.

She could sense the approach of Ramses.

"So the plants remain," he said.

"I started to, but it feels like a murder."

"Of whom exactly?"

"My father," she whispered.

"So I am not the only one who has been pitched into dark reflections by our departure."

"No. You are not."

"Then our departure rituals are incomplete."

"How so?" she asked.

"We must say a proper goodbye to him."

"At this hour?" she asked.

"When have you ever known me to be stopped by a lock and a gate?"

"Never."

"Off to the cemetery then."

But she didn't follow him to the doorway. Instead, she turned to the unlit coal fireplace and picked up a porcelain basin from her father's collection, which she'd moved to the mantel during a general effort to sprinkle the house with more of his beloved possessions. She set it next to the lone candle in the room.

"But first, Ramses," she said quietly, "we do something else Bektaten asked of us."

Ramses gave her a questioning look.

"Come now," she said softly. "I know you've been carrying it with you ever since it arrived. Reading it again and again with a glower on your face."

As she held out her hand, Ramses extracted the folded pages from his pocket and handed them to her. But in what felt like a moment of hypocrisy, it was Julie who found herself drawn to the letter's words, to its closing passages. For they contained the most specific and sweeping of Bektaten's demands, and she thought it best to familiarize herself with them again before turning them into ash.

And to this new band of immortals I introduce those
who have served me for time immemorial, former
soldiers of Saqnos from the age of Shaktanu, who, upon
realizing they had been granted doses of eternal life from

dwindling reserves by a mad and directionless ruler, put down their arms and abandoned their mad master as Shaktanu fell to ruin.

I speak not of my loyal servants and lovers, Enamon and Aktamu, who greeted those of you who recently visited my castle. These are different men, their former comrades in Shaktanu's army, who over the centuries found their way back to me. In the time since, we established networks of communication which came before the miracles of the telegram and telephone, using parchment in the hands of immortals who could travel without resting and our vast accumulations of wealth to employ networks of mortal spies. Of course, we have now incorporated modern inventions into this system, using them to swiftly chronicle the events of this rapidly changing world. My Heralds of the Realms, I came to call them. Now, these loyal and wise men have divided up the planet into various realms of investigation, study, and documentation. From their far-flung outposts they feed me a constant stream of dispatches containing everything from mortal secrets spoken inside corridors of human power and influence to the shifts of rivers in isolated climes. In letters and coded telegrams, some written in the ancient language of our fallen kingdom, their reports deepen and illuminate the sometimes-frenzied and cursory articles of the newspapers which cross my door. So consumed were all of us by the machinations of Saqnos and his clan that I had allowed the recent dispatches to accumulate unread, and to a dangerous extent. As I write this, I have read them all, along with the reports in the British newspapers, and they bring me now to perhaps the most urgent portion of this letter.

The world is on the verge of a war unlike any the

*lands of this earth have ever seen. It's possible that
by the time this letter reaches you, battles will have
broken out across the European continent, for I am
told by my Heralds that the nation of Belgium is sure
to be devastated by the invading German army as
punishment for its refusal to allow them a clean right-
of-way to invade France. The great empires of Europe
have been brought into an interlocking web of conflict
for which I can find no comparison in my thousands of
years of existence. Machinery that defied imagination
but a few short years ago will be employed in this war,
and the slaughter it will unleash may hollow out the
soul of humanity itself. Those who assert this will be a
short conflict, swiftly brought into check by the shared
commercial interests of the empires in question, are
either blind to the depths of humankind's capacity for
violence and slavish devotion to ideas of empire, or they
deliberately mislead those to whom they speak because
they are arrogantly assured of their own victory and care
little about the true cost. I have borne witness to many
a war throughout history. I have been shaken by the
various symphonies of armies falling into alignment, of
great squadrons of everything from horses to elephants
stomping bravely to battle lines with a force that shakes
the earth underfoot. And yet, never before have I felt
such a terrible thunder in my bones.*

*But I do not write you of this simply to frighten you.
For why should an immortal be frightened of war? You
should be, but not because it poses any true risk to your
life or limb. For you, my immortals, war will bring with
it terrible temptations which must be ignored, especially
by the younger among you. For if you have heard no
other decree of mine contained in these pages, hear this
one, and hear it in your bones just as I now hear the
terrible march to battle.*

There shall be no immortal intervention in the war to come.

You may believe the power and strength afforded you by the elixir might make you uniquely suited to become a savior to broken humanity, but it will not. It is one thing for us to use our energy and our strength to treat the wounds of those afflicted by plague, so long as we never use the elixir as a treatment for mortal disease. For an immortal, such endeavors might be key to our spiritual survival. But war brings with it dark forces and terrible ambitions that might seek to abscond with not only the elixir itself, but the gifts it has given us. Should our natures be revealed to those whose minds are warped by the heat of battle, we might find ourselves embroiled in a second war that could trigger the collapse of humanity itself. And think not for one moment that the gift of immortal life when granted to several grievously wounded soldiers or injured villagers might shift the course of the war itself, for it will not. This will only briefly stanch the wounds you feel after having gazed upon the bloody field of battle, and it will introduce into the maelstrom of rage and loss a concept most human minds cannot accept or fathom, creating only further devastation.

And so, I say again, there shall be no immortal intervention in the war to come. If you violate my command, my judgment will be resolute. For with our new unity comes new responsibility, and any immortal who has lived out at least a century of existence can tell you this.

Your burden is to bear witness, and your responsibility is never to let your powerful hands disrupt the fragile structures of human failures and triumphs that compose history itself.

And so each of you must now travel far from the

*potential fields of battle so as to remove yourself from the
temptations I describe. Each of you may find protections
and comfort here at Brogdon Castle should you desire it,
and should you believe that my nearness might inspire a
certain measure of self-discipline. Here, or in a location
of your choosing, you might also wall yourself off from
the sunlight that sustains us and sink into the type of
deep slumber which sometimes makes the passage of time
bearable for our kind. These things I do not command
specifically. I merely offer them as possible fulfillments of
the larger obedience I require.*

Julie picked up the letter's pages in one hand and the candle
in the other. Above the porcelain bowl, she brought the flame
to Bektaten's words, to the secrets they both alluded to and
described. What a strange paradox, that giving in to this final
instruction felt like a consent to all the others, and that the end
result of this consent was to reduce Bektaten's words to ashes.

Clean and swift.

Those were the key words Nikolai Vasilev had used to
describe the task at hand.

Killing the maid was out of the question then.

After he watched the woman accept the delivery from the
messenger, Anton retreated into the pools of darkness across
the street, watching the shadows that occasionally moved past
the Stratford house's front windows.

His plan was to wait until the lights inside went dim. Then
he would break in and shoot the archeologist's daughter—
easier to think of her that way than by her given name—while
she slept. He'd then quickly make off with some items of value
so the whole affair looked like a robbery.

In fact, the more he considered it, the best plan would be
to let them wake and discover him, so their shooting—on the

staircase or perhaps the landing—didn't resemble the calculated assassination it truly was.

No telling from his vantage point how many were present inside the house, so better to wait until they'd retired for the night, their defenses down, their minds drifting into dreams. Then he'd cause some tumult in the lower rooms that would bring them to him in alarm.

Just then, two men emerged from the house's front door, walking arm in arm in an intimate manner that shocked him. But when they passed under a streetlamp, Anton saw the shorter of the two sported a a lustrous shock of brown curls above an outfit of fine men's clothes. And so it was one man, and a woman who dressed like a man without any apparent fear of the repercussions.

The archeologist's daughter. It had to be.

They wore long dark coats even though the night was fairly warm. This told him they wished to move in relative secrecy through the fog. How, then, to explain the ease and confidence of their stride? It was as if no threat these streets might offer could frighten them.

And where were they headed at this late hour?

He should strike at them now. A bullet in each back, one after the other. And plenty of empty streets through which to escape on foot.

But their dark clothes and the late hour suggested they might be on their way to a secret assignation.

Could they be leading Anton right to some of the other names on the list Cousin Nikolai had given him?

Emboldened by this possibility, Anton followed, careful to keep his booted steps slower and quieter than the ones that had first brought him to this block, and his right hand within easy reach of the split in his coat and the holstered gun within.

5

Approaching Nottingham

Elliott Savarell had lost count of all the burdens from which he'd been so recently released. Once, not so long ago, his hours had been dominated by fears of his family's financial ruin. Now that fear was gone, relieved by heightened senses he'd taken to the gaming tables of Europe. And the secret storehouses of ancient gold he'd been directed to by the same former king of Egypt who'd granted him eternal life.

Once the pain in his hip had been a persistent bother, a nagging reminder of age and mortality. That burden had also been lifted. From the instant he'd taken the first tingling swallow of the elixir. Now his muscles moved with fluid ease, his joints bent without a single crack or pop. Gone too were the burdens of his title, which had never brought with it the wealth needed to maintain its many obligations. But other burdens had replaced them: one mysterious and exciting, the other an adder's nest of anxiety.

As he sat by himself in the first-class dining car, his thoughts were so powerful and vivid they might as well have been a companion occupying the seat across from his. The near-constant hunger the elixir gave him had led him to give a generous tip to the headwaiter so he could be seated before the other passengers. Then came a prompt delivery of some delicious soup, the

remnants of which now trembled in their china bowl from the
train car's steady clacks and rattles.

He could feel the train's motion in his feet, in his calves, in
his thighs. Could feel it with the same intensity that had caused
the soup's bouquet of flavors to blossom across his tongue, each
one in turn. This was the existence the elixir of life offered. All
was heightened; all was vivid. It was not a departure from the
world of the flesh and into the realm of the spirit. For despite
the adventures he'd experienced, he'd seen no glimpse of a true
spirit world. No, the experience of the elixir was one of an
absolute, exalted carnality. In this moment, it made the powerful train car seem like more of a miracle than when he'd ridden
one for the very first time.

As they charged through the dark countryside south of
Nottingham, the soft, golden spill of light from the lamp on
the wall next to him glinted off the silverware, gave a candle-
like glow to the crown molding on the ceiling overhead. Each
table sat two people, one across from the other, in generously
wide seats upholstered in rich shades of brown and gold that
matched the cherrywood walls. On each, an immaculate white
linen tablecloth and silver so polished it gave off mirrorlike
reflections. He was one of only two passengers eating by themselves. The others, couples speaking in low whispers.

A white-gloved hand set a china plate before Elliott, and the
aromas rising from it were so suddenly intoxicating all worries
about his eventual reunion with Alex retreated.

The filet was perfectly cooked; the reds and browns on its
surface as vivid to Elliott's sharpened eyes as a subtle rainbow.
The artfully arranged side of vegetables so green they looked as
if they had been picked just hours before. He could see every
grain of salt and pepper swimming in the meat's simmering
juices.

*Ah, blessed elixir, giver of eternal life, granter of a vision so
clear one can see the very essence of the gift I can never exhaust.*

Indeed, his vision was so clear when Elliott picked up the polished steak knife, in the reflective blade he could see a man intently watching him from several tables away. Dressed in black tie like the other male diners in the cabin, he ate his meal in sluggish, absent bites that said he was having no real experience of the meal at all. Elliott, it seemed, commanded his full attention.

I am being watched.

And this thought, which might have caused alarm when he was mortal, seemed more like a curiosity in this moment.

When the waiter returned to fill his wineglass, Elliott stifled an urge to ask after the attentive stranger. But this was the instinct of a mortal man looking to diffuse a potential threat.

There was precious little that could truly threaten Elliott now, and so he was content to take his time, to absorb all the details he could about the man just as he was the colors, scents, and tastes of his meal.

If he turned to look closer at him, he'd draw too much attention to himself.

Instead, Elliott made short work of his entrée as if he'd detected nothing amiss.

Bektaten, he thought as he ate. *Has Bektaten sent one of her spies after me? Is this one of her beloved Heralds of the Realms?* Thick black hair, a heavy beard, a stout frame; that was the most he'd been able to make out from the knife's reflection. He'd need a better look to see if there was something of the truly ancient about this character.

The waiter returned, but when he went to clear Elliott's dinner plate, Elliott asked him not to just yet and requested he top off his crystal wineglass. The waiter obliged, and once he departed, Elliott rose to his feet.

He gave his watcher a curt, obligatory nod as he walked past his table.

The man nodded in return. But it was a startled spasm, not a gentlemanly greeting.

The man's eyes were brown, not the shade of blue the elixir would have given them had he been immortal. And he looked down at his meal too quickly as Elliott passed. But in her letter Bektaten had explained that her Heralds of the Realms employed networks of mortal spies. Perhaps this man was one, sent after Elliott to ensure his obedience. He doubted it. There was something shifty and unpolished about him, despite his formal dress. Difficult to see a man with his temperament in any kind of service to the powerful figure Ramses and Julie had described.

Elliott drew back the first door between cars, and stepped into the darkness just beyond it.

He pulled the opposite door open, then let it slide shut again without stepping through. During his meal, he'd been able to hear both doors being opened by various arriving passengers, so he wanted his watcher to believe he'd truly passed into the next car. But Elliott did not. Instead, he pressed himself into the shadows and, through the glass panel in the door next to him, watched the man who'd been watching him.

His suspected spy had finished his meal, and Elliott saw for the first time that he was the only diner to refuse wine. So many moments went by without any suspicious movements from him, Elliott became convinced this little charade of his was pointless, and perhaps he'd imagined the whole thing. Perhaps some of his senses were too sharp.

Then, slowly, the man rose to his feet and, with sudden swiftness, moved down the train car in the opposite direction, passing Elliott's table. A man without the elixir's gifts might not have seen it, might not have glimpsed the speed with which the man shook his fist in one quick jerk above Elliott's wineglass as he passed it. A man without the elixir's vision might not have been able to see the tiny little granules drifting down through the Merlot's deep red like a miniature spirit losing corporeal form.

But Elliott saw it all, and it awakened a primal fear in him.

His hands did not shake as they might have when he was a mortal man.

But there was a sudden tension in his jaw. He was grinding his teeth in painful concentration. The elixir had changed his reflexes by endowing this fear with more anger than panic.

Poisoned, he thought. *This man has tried to poison me.*

Before he'd heard tell of Bektaten and after he'd consumed the elixir, the word *poison* would have barely cost him a second thought. He'd been rendered immune to all of them. But since then he'd learned of a queen capable of reducing immortals to ash. Was this her doing? Had she driven him north to Scotland simply to place him on this train? It seemed like lunacy. It fit with nothing he'd already been told about this great figure, who'd allowed Ramses to leave her castle as a friend even though he'd stolen her elixir and slain her companion thousands of years before. If the queen who had devoted so many words to him in her letter had simply wanted him reduced to ash, there were infinitely easier ways of accomplishing that than with this nervous, mortal henchman who'd watched Elliott so closely he gave away the game.

This was something else, and he was determined to find out what.

Elliott returned to his table.

If the man was already making an effort to leave the train, Elliott was wasting time returning to his seat. They'd slowed at various crossings on the journey here, and it was possible he could make a quick jump for it if he was willing to risk a sprained ankle or even a broken arm should the landing not take. But given how intently the man had watched him, Elliott thought it highly likely he would return to see the job completed.

Also possible he hadn't tainted the wine with poison, but a drug intended to sedate Elliott to incapacity. Maybe this was an abduction in the works, not an attempted murder. If any of that was the case, then one thing was delightfully clear—whoever this man was, he had no sense of Elliott's true power. And that gave Elliott an insurmountable advantage.

Come back, my bearded friend. I've much to ask you.

The bearded man returned, approaching Elliott's table, bound for his own, surely. And for the first time, Elliott got a good glimpse of his face. His beard was thick but well trimmed, his jaw strong. Something that might have been a knife's scar emerged from the line of his beard onto his right cheek. Did the beard hide additional wounds? There seemed a malevolent light to the man's eyes. Despite the fact that they had greeted each other with a nod previously, the man made a show of not looking at him, as if, to him, Elliott was not just doomed, but already dead.

Elliott heard the waiter approach the bearded man's table with a polite request regarding dessert. The man gruffly dismissed him. His accent was Russian.

When the departing waiter passed Elliott's table, Elliott rose to his feet, crystal wineglass in hand.

He sat down across from the bearded Russian as if they were old friends. The man reared back slightly, eyes wide. Nostrils flaring before he managed to quickly compose himself.

"Good evening," Elliott said, "I thought since we were the only two dining alone tonight we might keep each other company for a bit."

The man grunted, one eyebrow raised, trying to affect the annoyance of one who'd been slightly inconvenienced by a sudden intrusion. But the tension in his neck muscles gave away the true fear underneath this pretense.

"I'm comfortable dining alone, but thank you." Perfect English, but a thick Russian accent. For the first time, Elliott noticed the threads of a gold chain around the man's neck. They disappeared underneath the collar of the man's tuxedo shirt, and Elliott traced them to a faint, bright lump underneath the fabric. Odd to wear such a chunky piece of jewelry under formal dinner wear. Was it a medal of some sort, or some ostentatious jewel? If so, why keep it hidden?

"But we've already dined, both of us," Elliott said. "I'm Elliott Savarell. And you are?"

The man accepted Elliott's extended hand, giving it a restrained shake, but his gaze was focused on Elliott's wineglass, just inches below their joined hands.

"Expecting someone," the man answered.

"They're late."

"They weren't hungry."

"Or thirsty," Elliott said.

To this, the man across from him said nothing.

"Are you? Thirsty, I mean?" Elliott asked.

Elliott picked up the crystal wineglass and set it closer to the bearded Russian, who was glaring at him now like a snake about to strike. "I don't care for Merlot, but it's the only red they had. Seems a shame to let it go to waste, don't you think?"

All traces of whatever the man had tainted the wine with had been absorbed into the deep red, which shimmered now from the train's rattling.

When one of the man's hands had disappeared under the table, Elliott found himself so thoroughly amused by the idea this fool might try to shoot him that he began to smile. A gunshot would also be a comfort, he realized, for it would be final proof that this strange spy—this would-be assassin—had no connection to the mysterious Bektaten. An immortal sending someone to dispatch another immortal with a gun was a ludicrous thought.

"A pity," Elliott said. "For both of us, perhaps. Or maybe just for you."

And there it was.

Without breaking his gaze with Elliott, the Russian rose from the table.

When the man turned to leave, Elliott reached out and grabbed his nearest arm. "My good, sir," he said, rising to his feet. "Please, let us—"

And then, with swiftness and strength that suggested a skilled fighter and killer, the Russian ripped his arm from Elliott's grip and used his suddenly free hand to seize Elliott's arm in turn, grabbing him and pulling him close. Elliott realized too late that the Russian had expected Elliott to try to stop his departure, had baited Elliott into grabbing him so he could then use Elliott's outstretched arm to pull them together like dancing partners in the train car's aisle. With his other hand, the Russian plunged a blade into the center of Elliott's stomach and drew it sideways through the flesh with a surgeon's skill and precision.

They were nose to nose now, the man's quick butchery concealed between them. But there were soft cries of alarm from some of the other diners at what they thought might be the start of a brawl. "Do not take offense, Lord Rutherford," the Russian whispered. "You are but a stray thread that needs to be trimmed. That's all."

And then the Russian saw no pain in Elliott's eyes, no terrible agonized grimace in his expression. For while the blade had pierced Elliott's skin with a fiery bloom, the initial pain in his gut was being replaced by a rush of tingles that spread throughout his sternum, danced up the sides of his neck, and made a pleasurable dizzying sensation just behind his eyes. Miraculous, instant healing, nerves alight and regenerating from an ancient power. The Russian flinched when he felt one of Elliott's hands seize his knife-holding wrist. So surprised was he by this burst of strength from his victim that he released the knife, allowing Elliott to pull the blade from his stomach. There would be blood on it for sure. His blood. But Elliott stood fully upright and alert, despite suffering a wound that might have disemboweled an ordinary man. The Russian looked to Elliott's gut, seeing only a line of fresh blood staining Elliott's tuxedo shirt; nothing like the eruption his vicious work with the blade should have unleashed.

"I must say, good sir," Elliott whispered, "your table manners leave much to be desired."

And in that moment, Elliott's would-be assassin took the only option left to him.

He ran down the aisle, and despite the wide-eyed stares of the other diners, Elliott pursued.

6

London

This modern city of the dead was like so many others, but Ramses sensed a tension among the inhabitants that was unlike any feeling emanating from the ancient necropolises he'd explored. There was a jumbled diversity to the place: here a field of headstones; there, a small forest of raised mausoleums. But throughout its expanse he could feel the trembling expectations of the modern-day dead. They hoped for complete resurrection, these deceased Christians. In a single, miraculous event at the hands of a returned Christ, and so they hadn't been interred with their possessions or belongings as his ancestors had been. According to the precepts of the religion that now dominated the world, these were but temporary resting places of earth, stone, and shadow. Someday their inhabitants would rise and walk again.

Moving among these hopeful bones, Julie's hand in his, Ramses felt like a thief. For on so many occasions throughout history he'd achieved a version of what those buried and entombed here in Brompton Cemetery hoped to one day achieve, thanks to several swallows of a strange liquid and a precise blow against the cave-dwelling priestess who'd been its guardian.

All of this, it was so different from the rituals of death that defined his mortal youth. The belief that the dead passed into the next realm whole, and so all the earthly possessions you might require there should be entombed with you, along with the incantations and spells required to reanimate your physical body. None of the Egyptian languages he'd ever spoken had a word for soul; he'd watched this concept evolve over the centuries after he left his kingdom, this concept of a vaporous version of self that connected one to higher purpose, a version of self that could depart the flesh, entering some disembodied realm, awaiting reunion with the body or traveling onwards into a vaunted afterlife.

Why, then, had the modern mind, which thought itself so enlightened, broken down the journey of such an unstoppable, disincarnate force into only two simple phases? Earth and heaven, or earth and hell. Why could this twentieth century after Christ not conceive of any additional destinations?

In ancient times, the journeys that might await the dead were believed to be varied and long. The old priests had spoken of more than one realm beyond the earthly one, and more than one presiding god. The complexity of this system led to poor translations and misunderstandings amidst the historians of this modern age. His people had not believed in reincarnation! What a shock it had been to discover how many history tellers believed this now. His ancestors—and for a time, before the elixir changed him forever, Ramses himself—had believed that a life took many journeys, but only one happened in the earthly realm.

Julie paused at the sight of her father's tomb, a tall, imposing mausoleum, taller than Ramses, and surrounded by small trees amidst other tombs of equal height. The Stratford name was emblazoned large across its front door, even though the only child of the man within would never rest inside its stone walls. A head of Anubis, carved from the same stone as the mausoleum, crowned each corner of the tomb's façade.

"You knew his voice, didn't you, Ramses?" The answer was

yes, as Julie well knew, but the sound of the tremor in her voice now pained him greatly. "Before you fully woke, you could hear him, couldn't you? Moving about the tomb. Reading your scrolls. Speaking of your mysteries."

"Yes, Julie. And in his words I heard he was a good and kind man."

And I heard his murder at the hands of your cousin, but I'd not been graced with enough sunlight yet to rise and stop it. I didn't yet have the strength.

"He had the most wonderful voice," Julie said. "It was gentle and thoughtful. I never heard him angry."

I did, Ramses thought. *I heard his anger when he realized your cousin Henry had forced his way into the tomb just to bully Lawrence into signing over Stratford Shipping stock so he could feed his vices with it. But it was justified anger.*

Should Ramses feel some responsibility for Lawrence's death? Had he not unwittingly provided the weapon Henry Stratford had used to fake his uncle's heart attack? For when Ramses had entombed himself centuries before, he'd hidden the elixir inside a wilderness of poisons, and it was one of these poisons the evil Henry had slipped into Lawrence's coffee. But Ramses had also written admonishments and warnings on the wall of the tomb, warnings of a mummy's curse that would strike all who entered.

Of course, he never could have anticipated discovery at the hands of a man like Lawrence Stratford. Could never have conceived of a man like Lawrence Stratford in general. So how could he blame himself now for the terrible deeds of the man's scheming nephew?

Still, the memories of the murder, the terrible choking sounds Lawrence had made as he'd fallen to the floor. The unhurried and businesslike movements of Henry, the cold-blooded killer, before he'd called out with false alarm. Hearing all of it and still being too weak to rise. They tormented him, these memories. The consolation? Rising from his mummy's wrappings to stop

Henry Stratford when he attempted the exact same murder of
Julie here in London only weeks later.

The woman he'd saved released his hand and approached the
mausoleum, and he knew from this small gesture that she did
not want him closely at her side. Agony to watch as she sank to
her knees before the small temple of stone. Agony to hear the
low stuttering of her tears.

I must find a way to help strengthen her, he thought. *For if
there's one thing immortality never frees you from, it's grief.
For you will bear witness to the deaths of so many as you elude
death over time.*

There was something else he might do, and the thought
arrived with startling clarity.

*Punch through the walls of the tomb with your powerful fists,
open the coffin in which Lawrence's remains now rest. Sprinkle
the elixir across the sunken flesh and watch its boiling work defy
the laws of every god of every religion.*

He banished the thought. Felt his every muscle tense at it.

Too reckless, too horrible. A more outright defiance of his
treaty with Bektaten he could not imagine.

No more rash acts . . .

A terrible repeat of the arrogance he'd shown with Cleopatra's remains. And what had become of that? A risen, murderous monster, her sense of self a shattered thing healing in some
places while splitting open in others. Even now, despite Bektaten's assertions, they'd yet to reach a consensus on the true
nature of Cleopatra's soul, her identity. Would she continue to
heal, or would her madness return?

To take such a risk with Julie's own father? It was an abominable thought!

And Julie knew it, which is why, even in her most piercing
episodes of grief, the idea never passed her lips.

No more rash acts . . .

"I did the right thing, bringing him here," Julie said.

"You did."

"It felt selfish, at first. And ghoulish. Like I wanted to clutch his bones to my breast. But it was right to bring him here, wasn't it? Tell me it was right, Ramses."

"You buried him in Egypt when you thought his death was natural. To leave his remains there after you discovered he'd been murdered—it would have been a surrender to the crime that took him."

"Yes," she whispered, but it seemed like she was speaking to Lawrence himself. "Yes, right to bring him here."

She'd not agonized this much over the decision at the time, had arranged it swiftly through the offices of Stratford Shipping as if it were just another matter of business, through a series of cables and telephone calls made as they'd both traveled through Europe in those blissful days after he'd given her the elixir, when they both thought the risen Cleopatra had perished in a fiery accident.

But since then, these moments of self-doubt had surfaced here and there, and it was painful to see one of them deepening her grief for Lawrence in this moment.

"Just a few moments alone with him, if you don't mind," she whispered, suddenly the dignified British woman again. "Just a few moments alone."

"But of course, Julie."

He touched her shoulder gently, then turned to go.

Suddenly, it felt as if the darkness he faced had slugged him in the center of his chest.

The deafening crack reached him second, followed quickly by another.

Dazed, Ramses was knocked backwards off his feet, realizing once he'd hit the ground that what he'd just heard were two gunshots.

Anton had waited as long as he could.

It was the tomb before them that occupied their attention, and they'd never once searched the shadows for any approaching guests, which had convinced him this wasn't some secret meeting.

Mr. Ramsey must have been in possession of some strange tool he'd used to break the lock, for Anton had discovered it in pieces when he'd followed them through the side gate.

So much time had gone by, he risked alerting them to his presence if he waited any longer.

As soon as Mr. Ramsey turned, Anton fired.

He was an expert shot, and his eyes had adjusted to the darkness as he watched them. And from the way their bodies both jerked, he was confident he'd scored direct hits on each. This was cleaner, perhaps, than striking at them in their home. Here, the police might assume they'd snuck into the cemetery after dark to meet with someone nefarious in secret, and had come to a bad end because of it.

But as soon as Anton started towards their bodies, he heard the voice of the archeologist's daughter ring out clear and steady. "What on *earth*?" She did not sound injured. She spoke as if she'd been merely startled by a locomotive's horn. And she was getting to her feet.

So was Mr. Ramsey. He was standing now as if the bullet that had struck him in the center of his chest had only briefly knocked the wind out of him. He was staring at Anton as one might a child who'd touched an artifact in a museum.

"What is this?" Anton whispered before he could stop himself. "What are they?"

Mr. Ramsey was running straight for him; his rageful expression revealed in the patches of moonlight filtering through the branches overhead. Anton fired again, but this time his aim was off thanks to the man's swift approach. Or maybe he'd struck the man again, and again he'd absorbed the bullet with as much impossible ease as he'd taken the first.

How fast Mr. Ramsey came. How powerful and quick his strides. He was practically in flight.

Anton stumbled backwards, his heel catching on the edge of the mausoleum's stoop behind him. His back slammed into its stone façade, and suddenly he was staring upwards at the statue of the archangel Michael that crowned the mausoleum's front wall. It was the size of a grown man, and it raised its sword skyward as if protecting the entombed below. The Luger popped from his grip when he hit the earth, but even as he struggled to get his air back, Anton reached into his shirt and pulled free the amulet around his neck.

Only to avert complete disaster, Cousin Nikolai had told him, *you may only use its power to avert complete disaster and ensure your own protection.*

This was a disaster, indeed.

And so as Mr. Ramsey bore down upon him, Anton closed his fist around the bright amber stone at his neck.

"Who are you?" Mr. Ramsey demanded. "Why did you fire at us?"

The man somehow lifted Anton to his feet with a two-handed grip on the flaps of his coat. Terrified, baffled by the man's incredible strength, Anton sputtered in response. But just then he heard a sound from overhead that combined the crackling of dry autumn leaves with a distant, muffled roll of thunder. And Anton realized he did not need to answer Mr. Ramsey in words.

She'd torn her jacket away to find hot blood staining her dress shirt, but a ferocious tingling radiated through her from a wound that would have caused her agonizing pain had she still been mortal.

The bullet had struck her in the lower back, the impact briefly knocking the wind from her as a hard shove might.

On instinct, she untucked her shirt to finger the wound, felt the skin fusing, like a minor flesh wound that was already weeks old. She'd not suffered an injury this grave after her transformation, and the delicious feeling of the elixir's healing power being suddenly marshaled to full strength brought with it an opiatic rush of pleasure.

And so when she turned to see what had become of Ramses, she thought the healing's drug-like power was causing her to hallucinate.

She had witnessed many impossibilities of late, but none quite like this. All the miracles she'd seen—immortals dissolving to ash, another rendered mortal once more, a pack of hounds so linked to a single human mind they moved like a battalion of well-trained soldiers—involved stunning manipulations of living creatures and beings, and these events had all been caused by the secret blossoms of Bektaten's cloistered garden. But all of these events had used life-forms—plant, animal, immortal.

This was something else entirely.

This was stone coming to life.

For atop the mausoleum against which Ramses had taken their would-be assassin in his grip, the statue of the archangel Michael was lowering the sword it had just held skyward seconds before. A vague amber light emanated from its carved and deeply set eyes. But there were limits to the statue's sudden animation—its thick waves of hair did not suddenly shift or move as an actual person's might, but the limbs did. The statue moved as if muscles and ligaments and joints suddenly resided within its stone. The illumination in its eyes had spread to the rest of its face, so that its entirety now appeared like a stone mask resting atop a bed of lava so hot it was the color of the sun.

Julie was so dazzled by the animation itself, she lost sight of what the statue seemed to be preparing to do.

Having lowered its sword to one side, the archangel Michael bent his stone knees.

It was going to jump from the mausoleum's roof!

"Ramses!" she cried.

Ramses spun just in time to see the archangel, sure-footed and powerful, land on the earth beside him. It shook the ground, this landing, and Julie was astonished by this evidence that even though it now moved with perfect coordination, it remained a thing of solid stone, carrying its great weight with effortless power. While Ramses had just released the assassin's coat, the man had been so weakened by their fight he was wilting down the mausoleum's façade.

The angel swung its sword, a blow that might have decapitated a mortal man, but Ramses raised one arm and seized the stone blade in his grip. They were almost evenly matched in strength, but not quite, and Ramses was able to use his one-handed grip on the sword to drive the angel backwards on its feet. The angel reacted as a normal man might, bending its knees in an attempt to hold its ground. And from the way Ramses grunted with exertion, it seemed the angel was also exerting considerable effort to pull its sword from Ramses's grip.

An agent of the assassin's will, she realized, *the statue has become an agent of the assassin's will.*

Her final clue in this had been the spot of amber light around the fallen assassin's neck that matched perfectly the ghostly illumination of the statue's face, where only the vaguest of expressions pulsed, quick reflexive responses that rapidly gave way to the statue's now terrifyingly mute natural state.

The blade snapped in two in the pressure of Ramses's grip, shattering the link between them. This threw the statue so off-balance it stumbled backwards, its back knocking into the side of a mausoleum. There was a flash of wide-eyed surprise in the angel's eyes, but it left as quickly as it came.

Then it ran at Ramses, the most spectacular thing it had done yet. To react so quickly! And with an aggression and a frustration that seemed so utterly human! She was so stunned, she realized too late that Ramses had been knocked to the ground. Now it was a ghastly wrestling match.

Her first instinct was to leap onto the angel's back and see if she could snap its head off. Would that have any measurable effect? Had this otherworldly process actually endowed a statue with consciousness, with a brain?

No, she realized, *its brain is right there, lying on the ground, bleeding from the blows Ramses inflicted upon him after he fired several shots at us through the dark.*

The assassin's attention was glued to the wrestling match before him; nostrils flaring and mouth agape from his struggle to draw breath. Was he badly injured, or was the effort of masterminding this fight from a remove draining him of energy? It didn't matter.

It had to be stopped.

Catlike and swift, Julie leapt past the spot where Ramses and the statue were fighting like angry gods, bound for the patch of amber light around the assassin's neck.

In an instant, she seized it. His fingers slipped away from under hers; he'd been gripping the light source in one bare hand. When the chain caught on his neck, she tugged hard to break it free. He let out a startled cry, and was silent.

She rose quickly. Even as the light faded from the object dangling from the chain, she saw that it was some sort of amber jewel inside a frame of hammered gold.

There was silence now except for Ramses's haggard breaths.

She turned; she saw her lover still on his back, imprisoned beneath a statue that was entirely rigid again. It had frozen in the last pose it adopted before Julie tore the jewel—the amulet, she realized—from the assassin's neck. One stone arm had punched down into the earth beside Ramses's head and was now lodged there. The other was bent against the earth on the other side of Ramses's head for support. Permanently, it looked like. Nose inches from Ramses's, the statue's face was once more immutable and dark, so suddenly lifeless it would have been impossible to believe what had just happened were it not for the fact that the statue, which had only moments before towered over them on the roof of the mausoleum above, was now frozen in the pose of a fighting man.

Julie assumed Ramses would simply slide out from his new prison. Instead, he reached up with both hands, gripping the statue by its waist and exerting all the immortal power he could summon. The archangel's torso snapped away from the hips with a great cracking sound. Ramses threw it off to one side, leaving the hips and bent legs in place.

If she'd not been holding the incredible source of this event in one hand, they might have thrown their arms around each other, Julie was sure. But instead, the sight of the pendant necklace dangling from Julie's fist transfixed them both as Ramses rose to his feet.

"Who are you?" Ramses cried.

There was no response from the assassin.

They turned to him, and that's when they saw the force with which Julie had ripped the jewel from the assassin had snapped the man's neck. In her desperation to end the attack, she'd forgotten her strength.

"My God, Ramses," Julie whispered. "What is this thing? His flesh did it. He held it in his hand, and when I tore it from his grip, that's when the statue went still."

"Impossible," Ramses whispered.

Strange the tone in Ramses's voice. Not simply astonishment over what had just happened, but a kind of recognition.

"Ramses, do you recognize it?"

He shook his head, reached out for it, then withdrew his fingers at the last second as if he'd forgotten himself before a venomous serpent. She had seen Ramses do many things since his resurrection, but he'd never recoiled from an object as if its power might be greater than his.

"I believe so, yes," Ramses said quietly.

"What is it?"

"I cannot be sure because I've never seen it do something like this."

"Please. Tell me what you know. We must make sense of this. This man sought our deaths."

"But he did not anticipate our strength."

"Didn't he? This statue was quite strong."

"He began with bullets, thinking they would do the trick, and they did not. He did not know what we are, Julie. And this is information. Important information. We must learn who this man is as quickly as we can."

"But, Ramses. This jewel!"

"Julie, there are thousands of years of memories I must sort through to determine if my suspicions are correct. And I do not want to be wrong. Not in this moment. Let us focus on the man and his designs, and then focus on this impossible thing he's brought."

There might have been some wisdom to his answer. But there was something in his tone that silenced her. After his awakening, his memories had returned with stunning clarity, and he'd had no trouble sharing them with her before now and in great detail. She did not believe this excuse and was confident he would admit to its falseness soon.

His reaction to this jewel was not confusion. It was fear.

Ramses searched the man's pockets.

Carefully, Julie picked up her coat and began lowering the pendant by its chain into one of the inner pockets before folding the coat into a bundle. Only this way could the power of an object that frightened an immortal king be insulated from the touch of her flesh.

Suddenly Ramses shot to his feet. Transfixed by a piece of paper he'd discovered in the man's pockets.

Julie moved to him. He did not display the paper to her, but he did not try to conceal it either, and that's when she saw that it was a list of names.

JULIE STRATFORD
MR. REGINALD RAMSEY
ELLIOTT SAVARELL
ALEX SAVARELL
RANDOLPH STRATFORD
SAMIR IBRAHIM

"Oh, Julie," Ramses whispered.

"Ramses . . ."

"We have stopped him. We are at the top of this list and we've stopped him. Take courage in this."

"But what if there are others?" Julie asked. "Others who can do what this man just did? And on Uncle Randolph, Alex, and Samir, bullets will work just fine."

"We alert them immediately," Ramses said. "We act swiftly and do everything we can."

7

Nottingham

The Russian was injured; of this Elliott was sure.

The train had started to slow for a crossing right as the man ran for the break between cars. No doubt that was the reason he'd driven the blade into Elliott's gut when he did. Any later and he'd have lost his planned window of escape.

As it was, he'd leapt from the train when it was still traveling at a fair clip. One leg had gone out from under him upon landing, resulting in a grotesque somersault of sorts from which he'd risen like a stricken airplane with a determined pilot, running across the vast empty field beside the track with one arm clutched to his chest and a bad limp. Elliott, of course, had no trouble leaping from the train as if it were nothing. He landed on both feet and took off after the assassin without missing a step.

Now, the man had vanished into the thick forest that had been his destination, but as soon as Elliott entered the trees in pursuit he saw the forest was not as deep as it first appeared. Its darkness came from a brick wall that ran through the middle of it, and the trees had been planted here to provide privacy for whatever was on the other side. Atop the bricks, Elliott made out a bloody handprint in the moonlight. The Russian's injuries must not have been as bad as he thought. Somehow he'd scaled the wall and dropped down onto the other side.

With barely a missed breath, Elliott did the same, finding himself suddenly at the very tip of what looked like the vast gardens of a sprawling, dark estate. The landscape swelled upwards from where he stood, and he could just see the dark and shuttered top-floor windows of a distant manor house rising above the walls of hedges before him. His surroundings had the makings of a loose hedge maze. He entered it.

The rage with which he'd first pursued the man had turned into a burning curiosity.

You are but a stray thread that needs to be trimmed, he'd whispered with fierce strength.

What could this possibly mean?

Elliott opened his finely attuned senses to the sounds of the night, of the empty garden, of the train they'd both fled chugging off into the distance. From up ahead came the low sounds of strained movement. He followed them into a square garden where what must have been a twelve-foot-tall reproduction of Michelangelo's *David* stood at the center of a lily-pad-dappled pond. An impressive statue, probably concealed here within the hedges due to its formidable nudity. The rustling was closer this time.

Bravely, he stepped forward from the shadows.

"We should discuss this like gentlemen, shouldn't we? It's already clear the weapons at your disposal won't work on me the way you'd like. Why waste more time fighting? If there's something you desire more than my death, let's discuss it."

Just then, a vague, ghostly light emanated from the hedges off to his right. He turned to face it, convinced the man had lit some sort of flame or found an electric light buried within the leaves. Although why he'd give away his position in this way made little sense.

Still, Elliott turned to him.

"I waste no time," the man said. "Your death is all I desire."

In an instant, Elliott was airborne. It had been so many months since he'd felt at the mercy of any physical force, at first he couldn't summon words to describe this sensation. Some gargantuan blow had just struck him, pitching him sideways and off his feet. Gasping, head spinning, pinpricks needling his entire body and then rapidly transforming into the delicious tingles he knew to be the elixir's healing power, Elliott rolled over onto his back and found himself staring up at an ungodly sight, the likes of which defied even his recently expanded imagination.

The statue of the *David* had somehow leapt from its perch in the center of the pond and was standing over Elliott now, chunks of the stone pedestal littering the ground around its massive feet, glaring at Elliott as if he were a fly that had landed on its shoulder. An illumination the color of fierce candlelight, the same golden shade as the light coming from the hedges, etched the statue's classically handsome facial features, as if some preternatural flame were burning within the stone itself.

The statue had come to life. There was no explanation for it. A normal man might have gone mad in this moment, but Elliott had stopped being normal some time ago.

The statue, on the other hand, was preparing to level a terrible blow.

Elliott rolled to one side just in time as the *David*'s fist cratered the soil next to him.

The light, the light in the hedge. Somehow that's caused this. That must be the source.

Elliott ran past one of the giant's massive legs, hoping it was too lumbering a beast to spin quickly in one place. But it was devastatingly coordinated. As it ran towards the spot where Elliott had stopped, its sure-footed steps shook the earth.

Elliott seized one of the large stone chunks the giant had torn free of its pedestal. It was several pounds at least, as big as two newborn babies, and more than any mortal man would be able to lift on his own. But Elliott could lift it easily with a hand gripping each of its jagged ends.

Instead of hurling it at the advancing giant, he marshaled his great strength and sent the rock flying directly towards the spot in the hedges where the amber light still glowed. The giant was close enough to strike now, but Elliott stood his ground to ensure he'd struck his target. The jagged chunk of stone tore into the hedge like a cannonball. There was an eruption of leaves, then a terrible male howl.

Suddenly, miraculously, the advancing statue froze; arms still bent at its sides, one leg still raised behind it in midrun. The illumination in the statue's face faded. And now it looked as if this large, exquisite work of art had somehow been refashioned by giant hands as if it were clay, then deposited in this new and preposterous position. But the statue's weight could not maintain this off-center pose. It keeled over sideways, crashing to the ground onto one of its bent arms, which cracked in several places from the impact.

He wanted nothing more than to study the colossal evidence of this incredible event, to run his hands along the contorted marble, to ponder and reflect on what miraculous aspect of the physical or spiritual world could have accomplished a feat such as this. But there was no time.

Elliott ran to the spot where the rock had torn through the leaves; he could still make out the strange illumination, but it was deeper within the hedge now. It was also fading. As he struggled towards it, he realized the light wasn't within the hedge; it had been knocked clear through to the other side of it. His Russian pursuer was lying flat on his back inside another corridor of the maze. The dying amber light came from a jewel attached to a gold chain he wore around his neck, the same one Elliott had spotted tucked under his shirt when they sat across from each other in the dining car.

The jagged chunk of stone had struck his target squarely in the stomach. The Russian's tremoring hands held to it as if it were a grotesque baby he'd just birthed from his stomach.

Blood streamed from the man's mouth, and the choking sounds he made, combined with the little seizures in his lips, suggested death was near.

"Who are you?" Elliott asked, sinking to his knees. "Why have you done this?"

Glaze eyed, as if he were seeing more darkness than the night had truly made, as if Elliott might have been anyone from his target of earlier to an avenging angel, the Russian struggled to find the source of Elliott's voice, and when he did, his smile revealed a bleeding tongue and teeth smeared dark red.

Elliott gripped one of the man's hands, leaned in close to hear his dying words.

But at the sound of the name that came next from the man's lips, Elliott recoiled, releasing the man's trembling palm, pushed away by the assassin's hideous and terrifying final words and the way in which they befouled the memory of one of the greatest men he'd ever known.

8

London

Away from the windows. That was all Julie could think. Even though the drapes were all drawn, she had to get Uncle Randolph away from the front windows. He was drowsy and confused and had come so quickly from his home down the street that what remained of his auburn hair was an unruly mess when he removed his hat after stepping into the foyer. He was also her father's only brother, the one who'd managed Stratford Shipping for years so her father could explore the world, and she was determined to protect him at all costs.

"Surely, we must notify the police," he said, veering into the front parlor on instinct.

Julie steered him back into the front hallway by his shoulders. "It was just a note, Uncle Randolph. A very disturbing note, but until we're more sure who left it, we should all stick together."

"A list of names, you said?"

"Yes. Come. Rita will have tea for us in the dining room."

And the dining room has no windows looking out onto the street.

What a relief it had been to round the nearest street corner an hour before and not find the house engulfed in flames; more relief when they were met by Rita and Oscar inside, who were unmolested and untroubled. But now the relief was fading, giving way to a protectiveness that made her wish she could usher Randolph into a giant cage and keep him there until the nature of this threat was known.

"And no one saw who left this list?" Randolph eyed the steamer trunks that lined the hallway.

"I'm afraid not, but we'll question the neighbors as soon as we can. For now, you must remain here where it's safe."

"I do appreciate the gesture, Julie, but in all honesty what can you do that the police can't?"

She fought the urge to bark with laughter.

They'd reached the little dining room, which went so rarely used since it was now the habit of her and Ramses to eat almost constantly and all about the house. For more formal meals, they sat at the oval table in the Egyptian Room. But not tonight. Not only was it within sight of the front windows, the conservatory's glass ceiling and walls were only a few feet away. The thought of some hideously animated statue bursting its way through the glass and snapping her uncle's neck before she could stop it was too terrible to contemplate.

After discovering he'd carried no form of identification on his person, they'd squirreled their assassin's body away beneath the floor of a neglected mausoleum with a broken door.

Upon their return, Ramses hurried upstairs, Julie's coat, with the pendant tucked inside, bundled under one arm, leaving Julie to explain the threat to Oscar and Rita without giving too much away. She'd be furious if she discovered he was doing nothing more than contemplating the pendant he seemed so reticent to discuss. That couldn't be the case. They were dividing responsibilities, weren't they? Reacting as best as they could to this evening's shocking events.

Hopefully, he was calling Elliott's new solicitor. Or Brogdon Castle. Preferably both.

Bless Rita for already having brought the tea! The service was set up on the dining room table, giving her perfect cause to steer her uncle into the nearest chair. But she did so with a bit too much force. He let out a startled grunt before realizing his chair was so close to the table his belly practically touched the edge. She would need to be more careful. She had already snapped one man's neck that evening.

Footsteps pounded the stairs.

Ramses rounded the newel post and approached with the impassive expression he'd perfected for public presentations.

"Good evening, Mr. Stratford."

"Well past evening and no longer quite good, I'm afraid. Are you well, Mr. Ramsey?"

"I've just spoken with Lord Rutherford's solicitor. He'll make every effort to reach him."

"Oh, that's good," Randolph said.

"But he rides by rail to Scotland this evening."

"*Elliott?*" Randolph asked. "Scotland? Whatever for?"

"Elliott loves Scotland," Julie lied.

"Well, someone should alert his one true love, France. He's cheating on her, apparently. Honestly! What sends him to Scotland?"

A strong suggestion from an eight-thousand-year-old queen, Julie thought.

"Alex is there," Julie said.

"What?" Randolph cried. "I've known these men my whole life and they've never gone north of Yorkshire. What is happening here? You must tell me at once!" Randolph stood.

Julie gripped his elbows and gazed into his eyes with as much soft power as she could muster. "Randolph, I will share everything I learn as I learn it. But you are the only family I have left. For this reason alone you are most precious to me. So, please. For the time being, do as I ask."

Perhaps it was fatigue that led him to surrender, or maybe the feeling in her words had done the trick. Randolph nodded and sank back down into his chair.

Close behind her now, Ramses said, "I must speak to your guardian privately for a moment, Mr. Stratford."

"Yes, of course," Randolph said quietly.

She followed him past the steamer trunks, and to the foyer.

"You didn't *just* speak to Elliott's solicitor, did you?" she whispered.

"She summons us to Brogdon Castle."

"Bektaten?" He nodded. "We can't bring everyone on that list to Brogdon Castle. That simply won't work."

"She does not summon everyone on the *list* to Brogdon Castle. She summons all the immortals under her care. She says until we know the true nature of this threat we must all gather in one place."

"Samir is in Egypt. His aunt is dying. They're saying German U-boats might soon target British ships. He can't just cross the Mediterranean in this moment. It's out of the question."

"She knows this, and she says she will cable agents of hers in Egypt to place him under their protection. Immediately."

"Her Heralds of the Realms, no doubt?"

"Or something like them. We've only begun to learn the full mysteries of her."

"And what of Randolph? We're to bring him to Brogdon Castle so he can discuss the outbreak of war with the great queen Cleopatra?"

"She's securing rooms at a nearby inn, where she'll place him under immortal guard. And any other mortal we might bring with us who we feel is in danger."

"Rita and Oscar, then. They've been here all night and no doubt that man was watching the house before he followed us."

"Of course, Julie. Of course."

"Elliott . . . on a train . . . with no way to reach him. If more than one pursued him . . . Does she know what this is? Did you speak to Bektaten of this pendant?"

"I did. And she does not."

"Do you?"

Ramses flinched and looked away.

"Ramses, you simply *must* tell me—"

"It looks familiar to me, Julie. This is all I can say with confidence, but I never saw it used to turn statues into warriors, and so anything else I say about it will be speculation and it might be wrong."

"How? How does it look familiar?"

"There was a ritual. At the Temple of Karnak, when I was made pharaoh. The priests performed it for all the kings of my era, and the pendants they used . . . they looked quite similar."

"Pendants, plural. How many?"

"Julie, please. Don't frighten yourself. You must—"

"How many pendants like this one did the priests at the Temple of Karnak use for this ritual?"

There was pain in his eyes, and she saw now why he was reticent to give more details. He thought they would disturb her, especially given the fear she'd just expressed about Elliott being outnumbered and ganged up on by possessors of such an incredible power.

"Ramses, please."

"Five," he whispered. "I remember five."

"Oh, Ramses . . ."

Dread filled her. Dread at the thought of an immortal being overpowered by four warriors of stone commanded by the evil intent of an assassin like the one who'd struck at them that night. At the thought of Elliott being surrounded and pummeled by a collection of forces that seemed to emanate from beyond this world.

"But they were not used for this purpose, so we can't be sure they're the same. And Elliott has our strength. The immortals who will watch over Samir will have this strength. Bektaten has this strength. *You* have this strength!"

"Against four more of these things? Four more warriors of stone?"

"Know this. If others make a move to strike as that man

struck against us, they are also ignorant of our power. This ignorance will throw their plans into disarray. He was hesitant to use the pendant, this assassin. First, he tried bullets, and only when those failed did he unleash this power. The others will show the same hesitancy, and be undone by it." He gripped her face in his powerful hands tenderly. "Whoever has been sent for us, they do not know who we truly are."

There was truth in his words, and it quieted the riot of fear within her.

He kissed her forehead gently and took her into his arms.

"I hope you're right," she whispered. "Be right, Ramses. Please."

Over his shoulder, she saw their trunks lined up and down the hallway.

"Well, at least our bags are packed," she whispered.

"Yes, but it seems we will have to wait to see Manhattan," he said.

9

Cornwall

It was well past dawn as they approached Brogdon Castle, and the Cornish coast was blessed by a cloudless and deep blue sky. But as Julie drove, Ramses did not see the rolling green moor around them, did not smell the salty ocean air; he saw instead the desert sky over Thebes, heard the melodious incantations of the ancient priests as they guided him to a secret chamber deep within the Temple of Karnak. He heard the slip of their sandals over stone floors, and the gentle brush of their white robes across their hairless skin. Followed their glistening bald heads to the place where flickering candlelight and serpentine curls of incense smoke wreathed a colossal statue, its great legs descending into a pit in the earth so that its incredible height could be contained within this narrow chamber where only kings and priests could visit.

Ramses the Great, new king of Upper and Lower Egypt, cast your gaze upon the colossus of Osiris so that his might and strength ensure you never turn your worship to the sun alone, that you reject the heresy of the king who shall not be named.

Covered in gold dust, this statue, so that it shimmered in the flickering light as if it were alive.

But was it truly alive? For as the elder priests gathered on the sides of this shimmering colossus, the amber jewels hanging from their necks glowed as brightly as the one worn by the Russian assassin the night before. But he'd thought it all a trick of his eyes and a product of the wine they'd given him, which he'd assumed had been spiked with a mind-altering tonic. For the benefit of the priests, he'd consented to this ritual. That was all. To indulge the priests and nothing more.

None of it was real; it couldn't have been.

The jostling of the car rattled him.

I need silence and paper and pen, he thought. *I need time to bring forth these memories with greater clarity before I share them aloud.*

They'd just left Oscar, Rita, and Randolph at a country inn with mossy stone walls and a view through a narrow green valley to the wind-tossed sea, and now he and Julie were alone together for the first time since leaving London. They'd made the drive in two cars: Julie's and Randolph's. Randolph had insisted on driving his own, no doubt in an attempt to gain some small measure of control amidst his confusion, and Julie had insisted on riding with him so that there would be an immortal with each group of passengers. They hadn't said so explicitly to the mortals under their care, of course, but Ramses had understood, and so for the journey there, he had ridden with Oscar and Rita. The servants had been so baffled by their sudden transition into precious cargo, they'd seemed ecstatic to have Randolph's needs to attend to once they were all settled into the inn—a return to familiar order. Waiting patiently for their arrival had been Aktamu, one of Bektaten's loyal guards, dressed the gentleman as always, with his round, boyish face and lean muscular body thousands of years old. He was less of a guard than a loving sentinel, who, like his partner Enamon, served Bektaten in all areas, including the sensual.

So much time had elapsed since the fall of Shaktanu, it dazzled Ramses that these two powerful warriors still treated Bektaten as if she were their queen. Further events they'd shared along the road had surely refreshed and deepened this unbreakable bond.

What would his own ancient existence have been if he'd had companions?

You have a companion now, he thought, *and you are angering her.*

With the mortals they'd ferried out of London now under Aktamu's watchful eye, Julie was calmer. But he could feel her tension.

She drove the motorcar as if she were fighting it.

How could he make her understand? It was not a mere cluster of memories he was trying to sort through, but a vast temple of them. Not since discovering Cleopatra's remains had he experienced such a collision between his present and his ancient past, and so the connections his mind was making in this moment were suspect. And Cleopatra he'd seen and touched and quarreled with in the days before he entombed himself for what he thought would be the last time, so that when he was roused in this new century, his memories of her were fresh, like a morning recollection of the pages read by candlelight before drifting off to sleep the night before.

But this was something altogether different. This was a memory from a time before he was immortal, a thousand years before he tasted Cleopatra's lips. So he had to be sure of it before he gave it voice. And if they were all truly to gather now at Bektaten's castle, he had to allow Elliott or whoever else might have encountered an assassin like theirs to share every detail of their experience without being distracted or even directed by his garbled account of a flickering memory from the deep mists of his mortal life.

Drugged, he said, *I was drugged during this ancient ritual. I did not see what I thought I'd seen. I had seen what the priests wanted me to see. Nothing more. Nothing more . . .*

And now he saw the castle and was surprised by how much the sight comforted him.

The upper floors of its proud lone tower appeared above rolling green hills as the narrow country road they traveled began its descent towards the coastal cliffs. The sense of being confined by Bektaten's power evaporated. Her citadel welcomed them now. A refuge and a gathering place during a time of threat.

The headland on which it stood was connected to the mainland by a perilous rope bridge. Holes in the curtain walls surrounding the castle courtyard had been further mended, and a great, lustrous vine now crowned the length of them, rustling vibrantly in the wind off the ocean, but so thick and heavy it seemed no gale could blow it from the stone. It had grown to this fullness in the weeks since they'd left, no doubt fueled by the elixir and possibly other potions from Bektaten's laboratory. Inside those walls was a garden of their queen's most secret and miraculous blooms. He doubted the thick green leaves of this particular vine harbored a momentous power, not when it was so plainly within view. It was ornamentation, and this ornamentation meant Bektaten had continued to make this once-crumbling place her home, one of many in a vast network of castles and manor houses she'd acquired the world over.

As they crossed the rope bridge, the iron doors in the curtain wall opened, and Enamon emerged. His nose broken in a long-ago battle before the elixir rendered his body immutable, he was the more severe and forceful counterpoint to the man who might as well have been his brother even though no blood connected them. No blood tie could carry greater significance than the years of experience Enamon and Aktamu shared. For while their queen had gone into slumber on many occasions, sleeping by her own testament through entire eras, Enamon and Aktamu had not. Their centuries together had been uninterrupted.

Enamon extended his hand to Julie once they'd crossed the

bridge, and into the courtyard he guided them, past the profusion of blossoms. Some as big as human heads; their colors more fierce than any found in a typical English garden of this era.

"And so there has been no attack here," Ramses said.

"None," Enamon answered.

Into the castle now, where the blowing wind off the ocean became a dull howl through vast chambers, where thick Oriental rugs of muted colors covered the polished stone floors, a soft counterpoint to the vibrant gold-and-purple drapes that climbed to the high, rounded ceilings above. The leaded glass in the windows was new, and it sparkled. Everywhere he looked the dimensions of this Norman castle, rounded but still large and designed to inspire awe, were softened by tapestries. From her armory, Bektaten had brought up gilded swords and daggers she'd collected throughout history. They hung now from the stone walls, their polished blades glinting in the sunlight streaming through the soaring windows behind her.

And above the sounds of the wind came a sudden excited panting. Several large dogs were circling Julie's legs, sniffing at her eagerly and gazing up at her with wide, expressive eyes, eyes a sparkling blue thanks to the elixir. Julie was delighted at their presence. Seven in all, Ramses counted. She bowed down and greeted these proud and powerful mastiffs by scratching their chins and allowing them to sniff her neck. Their very presence here was a pleasant and encouraging reminder of the adversaries they'd recently conquered. Before their rescue, these powerful creatures had been trained to menace Julie, part of a plot to take her prisoner. Since then, a blossom from Bektaten's garden had placed them briefly under the control of a single, benevolent human mind, a process that had changed them from fearsome beasts into loving companions.

The rest of the pack did not share in their excitement. They remained in the corner, curled around the legs of the immortal woman who had made this castle her home. Several more rested against the wall beneath the window. But all told, Ramses counted fifteen hounds, and so the pack Bektaten rescued had remained united. Dressed in her preferred swaddling of purple robes, her slender, black arms exposed, and her regal mound of gold-threaded braids fastened back on her head by a golden barrette, their queen approached them now. Several of the dogs followed leisurely, as if mildly perturbed by the interruption of these guests and eager to rest once more at the feet of their mistress wherever she next decided to pause.

The queen's movements were languid and graceful, completely devoid of the quick reflexes that can bedevil a mortal who knows death is a possibility in every instant.

She did not embrace them. Perhaps their relationship was too new for this, but it was also possible embraces were not in her nature, and they'd simply not learned this about her yet. This was the first time they'd been summoned to her castle under circumstances that were not adversarial. Instead, she extended both hands. Ramses took one, Julie the other, and she strengthened her grip while she studied each of them in turn, as if the expressions on their faces were key pieces in their current puzzle and deserved careful observation. Then her attention fell to the jewel box Ramses held in his other hand. Before their departure, he'd transferred the necklace they'd stolen from their would-be assassin into this velvet-lined box, which had contained an old diamond necklace of Julie's mother. Bektaten didn't need to be told this, apparently. From the sudden intensity of her gaze, it was clear she knew exactly what the box now contained.

"I received a cable from Lord Rutherford a few hours ago in response to your call to his solicitor," she said. "He travels by hired car and should be here soon."

"Here?" Julie asked breathlessly. "He's coming here."

"Of course. At my insistence. He wrote in code. *Have*

weathered fisticuffs, but prevailed nicely, he said. *I only wish I'd done a better job of collecting my belongings from the train. I bring an interesting gift regardless."*

An interesting gift, Ramses thought. *Hard not to believe his assassin also wore a necklace of incredible power and, like the man who'd come for him and Julie, had possessed no knowledge of the strength his target would possess.*

"Thank God," Julie whispered, "thank God."

"And Cleopatra?" Ramses asked, the question sending a silence through the great hall.

"There'd been no assault when I reached them, but the journey here from the Isle of Skye by either rail or motorcar would take them more than a day. So I've had them brought another way. Cleopatra, Alex Savarell, and Sibyl Parker travel to us now across the Irish Sea aboard the sailing vessel of an old friend, but it should be some time before they arrive."

"One of your Heralds of the Realms commands this vessel?" Ramses asked.

"You will meet him soon enough."

"Are the seas safe?" Julie asked.

"Not the Mediterranean, I fear. Not for long. But for now, the northern seas might be safe enough, and Osuron of the Baltic is a mariner of unrivaled skill. His vessel is a powerful one."

Osuron, Ramses thought, *a Shaktani name, no doubt.* When she'd allowed him to read her journals, she provided him with a key for deciphering her ancient language. Strange now to realize while those volumes contained so many descriptions of the events she'd witnessed throughout history, they said little of these networks of immortals she'd maintained throughout that time, nothing of these Heralds of the Realms. Her letter was the first time Ramses had seen mention of them. Was it possible her ancient writings were the result of their collective labor, their dispatches, reports, and vast surveillance of an ever-changing world? If so, Bektaten seemed determined not to reveal the personal narratives, the secrets of any immortal besides herself. She was not just their queen, but their guardian as well.

"You fear for all immortals in this moment?" Julie asked.

"I'm unsure. This list you discovered in the assassin's pocket, it's a blend of mortals and immortals, and this confuses me."

"Me," Julie said quietly. "*I* am what those names have in common."

"We mustn't rush to conclusions," Ramses said, knowing he was also justifying his own silence about the ancient ritual that plagued him now. "Not until we've heard Elliott's account."

Julie nodded, but he could tell she wasn't convinced.

"Should we assume other assassins have been dispatched to deal with both Alex and Randolph?" Ramses asked.

"Perhaps it was two, and they divided the list. Look at where they struck. Elliott was on his way to Alex. They might have known this, especially if they'd been following him for a while. And Uncle Randolph lives right down the street from us. Maybe our killer would have gone for him next."

"If we examine these blades of grass in too much detail, the field will consume us." Bektaten turned without asking them to follow. She didn't need to. The great hall's centerpiece was a vast oval card table, large enough to accommodate an entire royal family, and it was covered with a dazzling array of food. Only when Bektaten moved towards these steaming delights did some of the dogs begin sniffing at the delicious aroma around the table's edge.

A single clap from her and the mildly defiant beasts retreated.

"Sit. Eat. And share with me all you experienced," Bektaten said. "And then we shall examine the most important thing we have at our disposal. The necklace and the stone it contains."

"And this man said nothing as he attacked?" Bektaten asked.

Enamon, who had been taking notes in Shaktani through-

out their conversation, had risen to clear the large table of
its empty plates, leaving Ramses and Julie seated before their
queen, who had guided them through their account with gently
specific questions. Soon there would only be one object left on
the table's polished surface—the necklace, which Bektaten had
carefully removed from its velvet-lined box by its gold chain.

"Nothing that I could hear," Julie answered.

"Some frantic whispers as I rushed him," Ramses added.
"But that was all."

"Let us hope Lord Rutherford learned more from his assassin before he prevailed."

Ramses bristled. "Surely you don't blame us for not—"

"Not at all," Bektaten said, one hand raised.

"It's my fault," Julie said quickly. "I grabbed at the necklace
so quickly I . . . broke his neck."

"I cast no blame. We simply must gather every detail we can
to assemble a clear picture of this mystery."

Knowing he was holding back further details, Julie cast
Ramses a stern look.

Ashamed, Ramses averted his eyes.

Not yet, Julie. Not until I'm sure.

"The stone," Bektaten said, clearly having missed this little exchange. "Describe for me the nature of the stone within
the statue itself. The *substance* of it after this possession took
place?" At their thoughtful looks, she added, "Is there a better
word to describe it?"

"I don't think so, no," Julie whispered. "It was a fearsome
and terrible possession, for sure."

"Except for his incredible movements, the statue's stone
seemed to be unchanged," Ramses said.

"But there was the light," Julie added.

"The light in the pendant?" Bektaten asked.

"No, there was a similar light, almost exactly the same color,
emanating from the statue's face."

"But the face made no discernible expression? It did not speak, it did not cry out?"

Ramses and Julie both shook their heads.

"How closely did you observe the assassin while he was orchestrating this?" Bektaten asked.

"Once the real fight started, hardly at all," Ramses said.

"It consumed his attention," Julie said.

"Well, of course it did," Ramses said. "I was wrestling an archangel come to life!"

"No, Ramses," Julie said, sounding perturbed by his sharpness. "I speak of the assassin. It consumed his attention to orchestrate the battle. He looked winded and exhausted. His eyes were wide and he held the stone tightly in one hand."

A silence fell.

Bektaten looked at Ramses and then Julie, thoughtfully considering, he was sure, the ripples of tension that had passed between them throughout this account.

She let out a long sigh, not over the subtle discord between him and Julie, he was sure, but over the extent of the details they'd shared. Gazing at the pendant necklace before her, she rubbed at her chin with one hand, her sapphire eyes wide and attentive. Then, as if she had come to a decision, her focus shifted.

He followed her gaze. The two statues nearby were almost camouflaged by the wall behind them; they were almost the exact same shade of weathered stone. They'd not been present during his last visit, and at first, he thought she'd brought them up from some hidden vault purely to adorn the great hall. One was the angel Gabriel, wings spread, and prostrate before it on one knee, the Virgin Mary. Two pieces of what had probably once been a larger tableau depicting the Annunciation that was so central to the story of Christ.

Bektaten rose, carefully approaching these statues as if considering their worth. Her back to Ramses and Julie, she asked,

"And the minute the pendant was torn from his neck, the connection was broken. The statue became entirely still."

"Entirely still," Julie said, "every trace of what appeared to be life left it instantly. It was just frozen. And Ramses was able to use his strength to break it into—"

"You mean to test it," Ramses said, rising. "Here. With these statues!"

Amused by the alarm in his tone, Bektaten looked at him over one shoulder. "Of course. What else would I do in this moment?"

"Determine who sent the assassins. Plot a course for them. Hurl them to the ground with our strength and demand to know why they've done this. Whatever their motives, they made the terrible mistake of trying to murder immortals, and they should pay the price."

"Who's to say we won't do all of that in time? But as we've already learned, hurling these assassins to the ground with our immortal strength won't reveal much of their motives if it kills them. The manner of interrogation you suggest could use more deliberation and calm."

She was speaking of his manner in general in this moment, he knew, and he found himself at a loss for words.

"You brought these statues here on your travels?" Julie asked.

"No, they were in the vaults below. Cast out like refuse. We plan to restore them. But they should suit our purposes for now."

Before he could stop himself, Ramses said, "And your purpose is to give wild, uncontrollable life to two of the most central figures of the world's now-dominant religion."

Bektaten turned to face them more fully now. That his own anger inspired no anger in her frustrated him further. For with each new sharp word from him, she regarded him with only deeper curiosity. "You believe me cowed by *religion*?" she asked. "I have lived eight thousand years, and no god or angel has come to call upon me. I fear plague and famine and the misery they will bring to the mortals around me, not pantheons of lies that change names and discard dogma every few centuries in some desperate attempt to explain a mystery that expands ever outwards beyond its grasp."

"And so you're willing to desecrate these objects of worship—"

"These objects of worship were lost in a vault. I desecrate nothing, Ramses. I've no desire to destroy them or even harm them, but in this moment, we must use them to good purpose."

"In eight thousand years, have you seen an object that can do what this one can?" Ramses asked.

"You have not, apparently. Is this why you're so disturbed?" To avoid lying outright, Ramses dropped his gaze from hers, even as Julie whispered his name gently under her breath. "Well, the answer is no. I've seen nothing like this object, and therefore we must test it."

"By bringing the angel Gabriel to life?" Ramses asked.

"Is this what you believe you witnessed? You believe the archangel Michael became manifest last night in Brompton Cemetery and tried to lop off your head?" She was silent, but neither of them could answer. "I do not mean to shame you or disagree with your view, or even challenge it. But this is not the tale you've told. You described a miraculous form of puppetry that defies all the known and observable laws of the physical world through which we have moved as mortals and immortals. But if I'm mistaken, if I've misread your account, say so now, and we shall proceed accordingly. I'm not a tyrant seeking to bend you to my every perception. But neither will I cower in the shadows in the face of a baffling assault coupled with an as-yet-inexplicable power. Nor should any of us."

"Very well then," Ramses said quickly. Then, to the surprise of both women, he picked up the pendant by its gold chain and draped it around its neck. He could have sworn he felt a hot surge when it hit the front of his shirt, but that was his mind playing tricks on him, no doubt. "I'll administer this test."

"You'll wear the pendant," Bektaten said quietly. "We'll all administer this test."

Must seem brave now, former king of Egypt, he thought, *must not reveal you now struggle to avoid sharing all you might know of this.*

"I assume we'll do one at a—"

"No, this first." Bektaten pointed to a block of stone that sat before the feet of both statues.

"You wish me to move the stone block?"

"I wish to see if this power can be wielded against something that has no lifelike shape."

Ramses closed his fingers around the jewel. He'd expected a terrible, jarring physical transformation to overtake him when the jewel illuminated within his fingers, but the effect was the opposite. A delicious warmth spread up his arm, down his sides, through his entire body. It was nothing like the needling, eruptive tingles that heralded the elixir's powers of healing. This was a sense of fullness as it deepened his breaths.

But it was familiar, this warmth. Familiar, these sensations, even though he'd last felt them when he was a mortal man. Because this was the real secret that gnawed at him now. Each minute he did not reveal it felt like another, fresh betrayal of those he shared the great hall with.

Five pendants, yes, he told himself, *I remember five pendants. But during this strange ritual, the elder priests placed one around my neck, and I wore it just as the assassin did last night. But I did not believe what I saw, and I blamed what I felt on the wine.*

The statues before him were changing now. They were not vaguely illuminated as the angel's face had been the night before. Their entire bodies appeared to shimmer, as if a second, effervescent version had been slightly loosened from a stone prison.

Ramses the Great, cast your eyes upon Osiris—

The intoxicating sensations the necklace sent through him acted like a balm as a torrent of thoughts ripped through his mind. He had seen this shimmer before, during the ritual. But he'd assumed the colossus of Osiris had only appeared to waver and dance and lose physical form because of the flickering candles filling the temple chamber and the incense smoke and whatever the priests had drugged the wine with.

You do not know they drugged the wine. Why, in the face of all this new information, do you still rush to assume they drugged the wine?

But the statues before him now had none of these deceptive visual accompaniments. They were not treated in gold dust, and bright shafts of sunlight from the cloudless day outside filled the great room with stunning clarity. And yet, the statues before him shimmered just the same.

Oh, Ramses, you fool, he thought, *you great, blundering fool. Thousands of years ago you wore an incalculable power around your neck and you dismissed it as trickery and illusion.*

"Ramses," Bektaten said next to him. "You see something we don't. Describe it to us."

"A shimmer . . . the statues, they're shimmering."

"Not to our eyes, but to yours. Interesting. Try to move the block of stone."

He followed her directions. But since no shimmer radiated from it, he already suspected that it would not be subject to the pendant's power.

The Eye of Osiris, a nagging voice said to him. *You know the name of this thing. It is the Eye of Osiris! And in your arrogance you assumed it could not be real, and now it has been loosed upon the modern world.*

In his mind's eye, he saw the stone block shifting forward

onto one side, slowly rolling towards them. But the stone did not move, and the warmth throughout him was replaced by a gentle peal of nausea.

"Nothing . . . ," he whispered.

"This is telling," Bektaten said. "So it cannot move pure stone. Its power is limited then."

"To statues," Julie said.

"To renderings of life, perhaps. Renderings made by a human hand. And now Mary, Ramses. See what the Blessed Virgin shall do for us."

When he turned his focus on the statue in question, the nausea left altogether. Now it felt as if warm fingers were gently clutching the sides of his neck, stroking the back of his head. While the shimmer radiating from the statue did not radiate that far out from the stone itself, beneath his skin it felt as if he were being embraced by it, and this feeling intensified the more he gave the Blessed Virgin his rapt attention.

Behind him, Julie gasped.

The statue risen slowly from its prostrate position, this weathered, and in some places chipped, statue of the Virgin Mary. It lowered its hands to its sides, its stone dress shifting easily to match the movements of its suddenly pliant limbs.

Bektaten whispered something beside him that was unintelligible. It was in Shaktani, he was sure. A prayer, perhaps. Or maybe a curse. And he knew then that it would always seem new to them, the power of this thing. It would always seem impossible.

Gently, Ramses extended one arm. The statue did the same, as if they were two dinner companions, each trying to urge the other to take a seat at the table first. Then Ramses stilled his arm and only imagined the statue returning its arms to its sides. And it did so. That was all it took. He only had to imagine it, and the statue followed his command.

"You didn't lower your arm," Bektaten said.

"But I imagined the statue doing it."

"And that was enough," she whispered, dazed. "Let go of the pendant."

"But we've just—"

"Release it, Ramses."

Was Bektaten frightened? That couldn't be it, for she walked confidently towards the statue, which was frozen in its new position, standing erect, arms lowered to its sides.

To Ramses's eye, the shimmer had left both statues. The feeling of warmth was gone too. So incredible the experience had been that suddenly his own immortality felt crushingly ordinary by comparison.

Bektaten lifted her fingers to the Blessed Virgin's face, gently grazed the stone cheek with one finger. Perhaps she was showing more respect and care than she might had the statue not just come to life before her eyes.

"Again," Bektaten said.

For a mournful moment, he'd been afraid the sensations wouldn't return when he gripped the jewel for a second time. But they did. Almost instantly. Again, the warmth. Again, the shimmer. Again, the sense of life—even immortal life—upended and redefined.

"Have her menace us," Bektaten said.

Julie let out a soft cry at this. She was no devout Christian, but all the religions of the world held a certain sway over her, and within her was a belief that collectively each faith brushed more sand from a great tablet of truth. The thought of seeing a figure such as the Virgin Mary endowed with behaviors contrary to her mythic character seemed to appall her. But she did not protest.

And her concerns, if Ramses had interpreted them correctly, were all for naught.

Because the statue would not do what he wished it to.

He imagined it sinking down onto its haunches, raising its arms as a bear might, even baring its teeth. But in response to his mental commands, quick pulses of movement traveled through the stone but did not manifest into anything significant. It did not feel like a rejection on the part of the statue, so much as a failure of the pendant's power to find anything within the stone that could give rise to this urge.

Ramses adopted the pose himself. Clownish and ridiculous, but universally menacing, he was sure. From the statue, nothing. He ran towards it, drawing one arm back as if to strike. And from the Blessed Virgin, nothing.

"It won't do it," Julie whispered. "It won't follow a hostile command."

To ensure the connection had not been severed by something else, Ramses took a step back and bowed deeply. Sure enough, the statue followed.

"And so," Bektaten said, "the stone does nothing a collective understanding of its subject does not suggest. Can you control them both at once?"

He tried, but to do so, he realized, he would need some innocuous move, something that did not contradict either of their characters. And shortly he found one. They both lifted one arm, fingers cupped, as if gesturing to the ceiling above.

"Astonishing," Bektaten whispered. "Gabriel, then. The angel Gabriel. See if he will rise and defend the Blessed Virgin."

At the sight of one of the most famous figures in Christendom performing the ancient hand-to-hand combat moves Ramses had once used in battle against the Hittites, Julie rose to her feet and cried out. But Bektaten held her ground, dazzled by the spectacle. The stone angel spinning, throwing its hands back as if it gripped an ancient sword, delivering punches and blows against the open air. The only sounds were the muted howls of ocean wind and the thundering footfalls of the stone angel as it pivoted and struck at nothing. Isolated and amplified, these footfalls turned the rhythm of combat into a lone staccato that seemed both frenzied and momentous.

"Do you tire, Ramses?" Bektaten asked. "Do these moves exhaust you?"

"No. They are effortless. I see them, and he performs them."

"This is . . . most miraculous. Most miraculous indeed."

Ramses let his fingers slip from the jewel, causing the angel Gabriel to freeze in a crouching, fighting stance, one hand balled into a fist above its shoulder.

Then Bektaten instructed him to leave the room, to test whether or not he could manipulate the statues without keeping them in his sight. It was an awkward endeavor, given he could not see the statue's surroundings, but it was indeed possible. Nearness between the statue and the stone was all that was required to make the connection. And not very much of it, for Ramses walked far from the great hall and still the connection was maintained.

When he returned, no one spoke for a long while, as if each of them needed to be sure the statue wouldn't spring back to life of its own accord.

"And so they will not act in a matter contrary to what their sculptor intended," she said. "This is a power that somehow harnesses the essence of what a human hand might leave in stone. It suggests that carvings, renderings of life, have a certain life to themselves that is invisible to all except those who wear this pendant. It is not simply a giant hand that moves them, for if that was the case the rigidity of the stone would rebel. At the very least, we would see dust and particles thrown off as it defied its original form. But this does not happen. Rather, the necklace seizes upon some force that lies dormant within the stone and uses it to briefly change the very bearing of the stone itself."

More silence, more muted howls of ocean wind, as they all absorbed these precise and undeniable, accurate words.

"Never . . . ," she whispered finally, "of all the miracles in my garden, of all I have borne witness to throughout my existence, never have I seen a thing give life to an inanimate substance. I've harvested and blended that which charges life in directions previously unknown, but it always works upon those things which are already endowed with the miracle of creation. I have never encountered a thing which gives the full force of life to a substance which has none."

"Ramses!" Julie's voice was so suddenly stern, he turned to her, startled. "You must tell her."

"Julie, please."

"Ramses, you must. You must tell us everything you know of this—"

"Julie, *no!*"

It shamed him, this shout, this outburst. But he was already ashamed, so what was a bit more?

He stormed from the great hall, bound mindlessly for Bektaten's library and the silence and shelter it might give him. Once he was surrounded by its shelves of leather-bound volumes, he needed time to catch his breath, perhaps because he'd confused his own breathing with the low sounds of panting all around him. He turned, and that's when he saw all fifteen mastiffs had beat him to this quiet room, having made a hasty and silent retreat from the sight of statues that could move on their own. From their positions under tables and behind chairs, they now gazed at him as if also demanding the answers he was not ready to give.

Never, Julie thought, *he's never turned his back to me like that.*

Perhaps once during their trip to Cairo, after he'd returned to the hotel to confess what he'd done to Cleopatra's remains and the chaos it had caused. But then, his shame had taken the form of martyrdom, and he'd confessed his sins in great detail. This defiance, this bullishness—this was something altogether different. If she'd been a mortal woman, it might have wounded her. But instead, she felt only anger.

And now, alone, she'd have to answer Bektaten's questions about this brief, fiery exchange.

"He knows more of this," Bektaten said.

"Yes, but he refuses to share it."

"Once we've all gathered, he will have no choice."

"Of course," Julie said, "I think he knows this. It's what troubles him now."

"What troubles your Ramses is that he no longer leads a solitary existence."

"So I'm his trouble?"

"Not at all. I knew my letter would distress him. There are many immortals like him throughout the world, and he must find his place among us. Isolation allowed him to dole out counsel from behind veils of secrecy while none around him knew his truth, none could question him beyond his comfort. But now he exists with the knowledge that he cannot run from whatever he knows of this pendant and slide the tomb door shut against time as he did when Cleopatra ended her life."

"Because you would not let him?" Julie asked.

"Would you?" Bektaten asked in return.

Outside, a motorcar's sputtering engine made its way to them through the wind.

Enamon appeared down one of the corridors, then passed through the door to the courtyard.

"Elliott?" Julie asked.

"It would be too soon for the others," Bektaten said.

Sure enough, a few moments later, Elliott stepped through the castle's iron door, a dinner jacket draped over one arm, his white tuxedo shirt rumpled, and his bow tie dangling loose. For all intents and purposes, he looked like an aristocrat who'd enjoyed a hard night of drinking at the club with his fellow lords and viscounts, but managed to make his way to a washbasin so he could be mildly presentable in this moment.

She flew to him, wrapped her arms around him. His embrace

felt strong, but limited somehow. When she pulled away, she saw he was being careful with the dinner jacket draped over one arm. She guessed his reason for this before he revealed it. From inside the jacket's pocket he pulled free a necklace almost exactly the same as the one she'd torn from the neck of their assassin. Only the jewel in this one was a somewhat-rougher shape, but it was the same amber color. The gold frame encasing it had the same weathered luster.

"I come bearing gifts," he said. But the seriousness in his tone didn't match the light phrasing.

For a while they all studied the stone, then Enamon pulled the chain from Elliott's fingers. At first, Elliott seemed surprised by the man's forcefulness, but then he gave a conciliatory nod and a slight smile, as if the pendant were a burden and he was grateful to be free of it. For now.

Then his eyes met Bektaten's for the first time.

Such a powerful charge seemed to move between them, Julie was convinced that perhaps this wasn't their first meeting, and they were both realizing this now. When Bektaten extended one hand, just as she'd done to Julie and Ramses when they arrived, Elliott accepted it, bowed, and gently kissed her fingers, a gesture which brought a smile of such unadorned brightness to Bektaten's face that Julie could not tear her eyes from it until it faded into something softer, fascinated. Charmed.

For who wasn't ultimately charmed by Elliott Savarell, Earl of Rutherford. This charm had served him well over the years, especially as his family's finances became more and more strained. Those days were gone now, but perhaps the good graces and wit he'd cultivated during those struggles gave Elliott the tools to seduce an eight-thousand-year-old queen.

"I have heard many good things about you, Lord Rutherford."

"And I have been eager for the chance to show you they are all true, my queen."

A mortal woman might have blushed and clucked, but Bektaten simply took her time withdrawing her hand from Elliott's, as if she thought there might be another few steps to his knight-errant display and it would be rude to cut him short.

But Elliott stood erect, the warmth leaving his expression as he looked from Bektaten to Julie. "Ramses?"

"With my dogs, I presume," Bektaten answered.

"We suffered a similar attack last night," Julie said. "He is . . . sorting through his reaction."

"He is not injured?" Elliott asked.

"Not physically, no," Bektaten answered.

"I see."

"Elliott," Julie said softly, "the man who tried to kill you . . ."

"Dead," he answered. "Quite dead. Russian. He told me not to take his attack personally, this as he drove a blade into my gut."

"What were his words exactly?" Bektaten asked.

" 'You are but a stray thread that needs to be trimmed.' "

It was a callous and dreadful way to speak to someone of their life, but that these words had been spoken to an immortal who'd borne witness to incredible events somehow compounded the insult in Julie's mind, the sheer arrogance and stupidity of the attack.

"And now, I must tell of this necklace—"

"We know what it can do," Julie said. "The man who came for us also wore one, and we took it from him. And . . . there's been some study."

"Study. Oh, well, this is good. I hope."

Bektaten stepped forward. "Lord Rutherford, I would have you tell me everything you experienced last night, but first perhaps you'd like to wash. And eat. There are many clothes here we can provide you with, and then I shall serve you at my table."

"Yes, yes, of course. That would be lovely. But first, I'm

afraid the final words of this assassin might require some urgency."

"He said more?" Julie asked.

"Oh, indeed he did, I'm afraid. And it was quite distressing."

Elliott's sudden struggle to speak made that quite clear. Both women took a step towards him, as if their nearness might guide the charming Earl of Rutherford through his fear. But it took him what felt like another minute to find his voice again.

No comfort to him now, these leather-bound volumes and all the experiences they described. No comfort, this nearness to Bektaten's testimonies, a historical record that stretched beyond any other known to man, which she had shared with him as evidence of the treaty they had made, the healing of old wounds.

Even the great dogs, lazing about the room's cool stone floor, a few occasionally sniffing at his lap and resting their giant heads there while he absently petted them and gazed out the library's single barred window at the churning sea, offered him little comfort and distraction.

Distraction came with the sound of footfalls approaching in the corridor outside. The lovely, floral scent of Julie arrived first, then the angry coil of her presence just inside the doorway.

"You've never walked away from me like that before. You've—"

"I'm sorry, Julie. Truly. You must—"

"No, please. Don't rush into some hasty apology just to silence me."

"I don't wish to silence you, but I ask for silence for myself."

"And you may have it. Until Cleopatra, Alex, and Sibyl arrive. Then we will all gather and we will all share everything we know. Including you. *Everything*, Ramses."

"For me, this will mean admitting to another failure."

"How so?"

"I wore one of these pendants, Julie. Three thousand years ago when I was king. During the ritual. I wore it around my neck and I dismissed what I saw it do as trickery and illusion, and now . . . Now I see that it's been loosed upon the world somehow, and yet I once had it within my grasp as a mortal man. But I dismissed it."

"You were mortal," Julie said. "Your mind, it hadn't been opened—"

"No, Julie. No. I was not this kind of man. I believed in the gods, and I believed I was one step below them. It was the priests I judged. I thought they'd invented this ritual to trick me into believing a god had become manifest before me. To keep me humble and respectful of their power. It was my suspicions about their motives, their agendas . . . what is the word for it now?"

"Cynicism," she said.

"Yes, my cynicism. This is what blinded me to what I held. And don't you understand what this means now? This power, this incredible power, I did nothing to protect it or secure it. I simply left it to the priests with no sense of where and how they housed it, or who else might have contact with it. Do you see, Julie? I've yet to redeem myself before the eyes of our queen for all the mistakes I've made, and now I must admit to another grave error. Cleopatra . . . we still don't grasp the extent of what I've done to her, and she will be here soon and with her all the implications of my terrible error. And yet, before an audience of her and all of you, I'm now compelled to confess that I let this incredible power slip from my grasp. And as a result, it has somehow ended up in the hands of common criminals in the modern world."

"Ramses, you cannot blame yourself for this. Bektaten herself has seen no evidence of this object throughout history, and she's far older than you."

"Because she never wore it or held it, as I did. I had centuries to find it, to protect it, if only I had *believed* in it."

"Ramses, it will serve no one if you place yourself at the center of this."

"My confession will place me at the center of it soon enough."

"No, it won't. It won't, Ramses."

Tears in her eyes now, and they baffled him. More anger he would understand, but this was pain, pure and raw. Only one subject of late had brought her to tears this quickly. So much so that it caused him to forget his own shame and move to her.

"Julie—"

"It was not your name on the lips of the assassin who tried to kill Elliott last night. It was my father's." A stammer in her voice now. He embraced her. If she was not ready for his touch, she'd push him away, no doubt. But she did not. She crumpled into him.

"The last thing the man said to Elliott was . . ."

Her voice choked. Ramses tightened his arms around her, hoping it would give her strength.

"The last thing he said was 'All those who loved Lawrence Stratford must die.'"

10

Brogdon Castle

"Now, tell me of Lawrence Stratford, Lord Rutherford," the queen said.

"Of course, but you must call me Elliott."

It was a delaying tactic, this nicety, for Elliott was having trouble looking into Bektaten's eyes while also providing the detailed accounts she'd been asking of him. The effort was as challenging as trying to decipher the precise outlines of figures within a mosaic that sat behind a vast bank of flickering candles. Despite all Ramses and Julie had told him of her, he was not prepared for the power in Bektaten's presence, the unblinking steadiness of her patient gaze. To say nothing of the fact that his own experience with people whose skin was darker than his own had been shaped by the bigotries and rigid class structures of this age, constructs this immortal seemed to float above, thanks to vast accumulations of wealth, ancient secrets, and hands so powerfully strong they could snap a mortal neck with one quick twist.

It was almost evening. He had accepted her invitation to wash, then been outfitted in smart new clothes by Enamon. Now, he'd fed until the fatigue that had dogged him earlier was vanquished. Even though it was summer, the constant winds off the ocean brought a deep chill with them, and this had called for the lighting of the enormous fireplace in the great hall. As the sky outside darkened, they were bathed by the flicker of flames, he and Bektaten, as Enamon took notes on Elliott's account inside a large leather-bound volume.

Meanwhile, close by, an enormous pack of gorgeous mastiffs watched them attentively. They didn't doze or snore as normal dogs might, for the elixir had released them from the need to sleep. Instead, they watched with humanlike attentiveness as if they were hearing every word spoken in their presence.

"You do not care for your title?" she asked.

"Oh, I wouldn't say that. I just don't have the connection to it I once did. And it came with burdens."

"What of Lawrence's burdens? Did they involve Russian men of ill intent?"

"Not at all. I don't believe Lawrence ever visited Russia in his life. Egypt was his focus always. The time a man of Lawrence's means might have spent traveling the wider world, he spent almost entirely there. In tents. Uncovering history, he called it. Blissfully happy."

"But his family's company, Stratford Shipping, their business connects to many nations."

"Yes, but not through Lawrence. Lawrence wanted nothing to do with the company."

Julie had said as much to Bektaten when Elliott first revealed his assassin's hideous last words. But no doubt, Bektaten wanted to verify these assertions through another.

"Did he have a title as you do?" she asked.

"No, and he would have run from it if he had." She seemed taken by the affection that came into his tone when he said this. "By the standards of our age, he was what you'd call a free spirit."

"I appreciate your sensitivity, Elliott, but I'm well aware of the standards of this age. I did not rise from the tomb only months ago as Ramses did."

"Forgive me."

"There is nothing to forgive. But I want you to be as free in sharing your thoughts of Lawrence with me as Lawrence was in living his life. Put my great age out of your mind if you can. Speak as if we've known each other for some time, you and I."

Impossible, he thought, *impossible to put your great age out of my mind, but I shall try. For you, I will try.* And then there were the challenges that came with any discussion of Lawrence—stabs of grief emerging from vivid memories of a long-ago passion that in retrospect seemed to have been so very pure.

"He thought I was a coward," Elliott finally said.

"How so?" Bektaten asked quietly.

"I moved with the current. Lawrence followed his passions. We spent a summer together in a houseboat on the Nile when we were young, right after we met at Oxford. It was quite wonderful, this summer. But for me it was a holiday. For Lawrence . . . well, it's when he discovered the seeds of all his passions. All his life's work was born during that summer. But I returned to a life in London I did not truly value. Those were his words, at least. That I did not value my life."

"Were they true?" she asked him.

How it devastated him now, this question. How much he wanted to retreat into his thoughts, and waylay this queen with clever turns of phrase. But this would not work, he was sure. She would see through it. And so, in this moment, there was nowhere to hide.

"In part," he finally said. "In part, they were true. I went about my mortal life believing they weren't, and Lawrence, a charmingly obstinate eccentric. And then I met a man named Mr. Reginald Ramsey, and I knew almost instantly there was a great mystery about him. An ancient mystery out of Egypt itself, and I had to know every word of it. To throw myself into the center of it, even if it consumed me. Only then did I realize how right Lawrence had been. When Ramses rose, he embodied all my old passions, the ones I'd suppressed."

Bektaten studied him. What had his tone betrayed that captured her attention now? Had she sensed the hours he and Lawrence had spent shattering each other in the bedroom of that houseboat on the Nile, shattering each other in the way that only two men of equally matched temperaments and strengths can do? If so, no sense of reproach emanated from her, a reminder that she brought with her a timelessness that transcended petty judgments. For her the scriptures of all religions were ephemeral things, fleeting clouds passing over her vivid memories of lost cities.

"You injured him," she said.

"Lawrence? How so?"

"We speak that way to those who've injured us."

"Perhaps." There was a catch in his throat. "I'd always dismissed it as youth. And wine. There was much wine that summer."

"You loved him."

"Indeed."

"We injure those we love."

"It seems so long ago." His face felt flushed, and he hoped he didn't sound as defensive as he felt. "I know someday it won't. Someday centuries will have passed for me, and the time between now and my Oxford years will seem like the blink of an eye. But in this moment, it all seems so distant, those years."

"You once planned to marry Julie to your son," she said. "Was this a way of drawing Lawrence close to you again?"

She said these words so gently, but they arrived like a slap.

There was no accusation in her tone. No condescension. It was as if she were gazing at a painting and remarking on the detail she saw there. Nonetheless, he was blinking back tears. They stunned him, these tears. No, it was her gentle insight that had stunned him. He'd been prepared for strength and a commanding presence, but not this penetrating knowledge. She was not the rambunctious and boisterous Ramses who'd exploded from his tomb thirsty for every sight and marvel in the modern world, and bumbling his way through the rituals of a formal dinner and asking people what Oxford was. Rather, the rivers that moved Bektaten blended the ancient and the modern into perfect solution. Her insightful wisdom could consume him if he let it.

And this means she was probably quite right about the need for me to meet with Alex, he thought, *right to send me to him.*

"Maybe it was," Elliott said. "Maybe so. The whole plan, the whole *scheme,* it seemed so driven by financial pressure. And fear. So much fear. But the thought that the marriage, should it succeed, would draw Lawrence back from Egypt again and again to be near to me . . . I would not say it was not a great comfort."

"You have not grieved for him, Elliott Savarell. The events of your life since his death have been so disruptive, you've not yet grieved for him. You must take the time to do this at some point. We immortals, we have no choice but to make a companion of grief, for of all the things to which we bear witness, none is more frequent than death."

For a while, they did not speak, until Elliott's voice seemed to find him, and not the other way around. "You are a most remarkable being, my queen."

She smiled, lifting one hand gracefully as if she was reticent to accept this compliment, or the boyish enthusiasm with which he'd delivered it. "You will grow accustomed to me in time. To my strange talk and my way of being. It might take centuries, but in time you will grow accustomed to it."

"Not strange," Elliott whispered. "You are thoroughly modern, and yet somehow ancient still. I wish to learn all I can from you."

"You shall."

Elliott had all but forgotten they were also in the presence of Enamon. The man cast a loving gaze upon him now too, as if he was grateful to meet another who shared his adoration and love for the woman he'd long served.

Then came the sound of footsteps too distant and soft to be discernible to mortal ears.

When she rose, so did Elliott, and together they watched Enamon disappear through the castle's iron door to investigate the source.

A moment later, the door opened, but while the man who stepped through bore some similarities to Enamon, he was also markedly different in various ways. The same great, broad-shouldered height, dark skin, and startling blue eyes—three aspects of him that suggested he too might have been a soldier in Bektaten's long-fallen kingdom. But the man's hair was a great mane of dark bristle that appeared permanently shaped by a great and steady wind. A long mustache draped his proud jaw like the flaps of royal banners. A gleaming silver clasp held the thick swell of hair to his head.

He wore a luxurious modification of the navy pea coat, with shining gold buttons, and a thick, lustrous lining of gold and red revealed by its high collar. On his giant feet, little brackets of gold glinted off the toes and heels of his massive leather boots. And the boots were wet. Elliott could tell right away, this was a man, an *immortal,* who spent much of his time at sea. Of course, he did not need these things for warmth or physical comfort. He wore them for his own pleasure, and perhaps in the event that he crossed paths with mortals wherever his nautical journeys took him.

Elliott had no words for the way this man and Bektaten beheld each other in this moment. He was tempted to read pain and love and a dozen other powerful emotions into the silent current passing between them. But it was a connection that crossed so many centuries that to his own newly immortal mind, it might as well have been infinite in its scope, and impossible for him to truly comprehend.

He was sure of one thing. As soon as Bektaten gave her full attention to this new arrival, Elliott felt instantly and childishly jealous.

They approached each other slowly. And when they were within arm's reach of each other, this formidable man of the seas sank to one knee, looked straight at the stone floor suddenly, then slowly raised both arms from his side, his head following their ascent, until he appeared to be gazing at the ceiling. He cupped his hands together, then extended them slowly towards Bektaten, as if they held something only they could see. Then he emitted several quick, brusque words that sounded more like huffs of breath. Shaktani, no doubt. Their ancient language.

Is it the sun? Elliott thought. *Did he just mime giving her the sun?*

He bent forward even farther, extending his cupped hands, now bowing his head so severely he was staring down at the floor again.

Bektaten was rapt. The display, it seemed, had transported her back to those ancient times when her reign had extended over a vast, global empire. Slowly, she kissed her fingers, then used those same fingers to trace a line across the center of both of the man's upturned palms. The man before her rose to his feet. They were face-to-face now, this great mariner and Bektaten. Tenderly, she cupped the back of his neck and brought his cheek to hers so she could kiss it.

A modern addition, this kiss, Elliott thought, *but the rest of it, an eight-thousand-year-old ritual for greeting the monarch of a kingdom now lost.*

They spoke to each other briefly in their ancient language. Perhaps these words were intimate and personal, unconnected to their current crisis. He was sure she'd share them if they were not these things. And indeed, Bektaten soon turned her gaze to Elliott, gesturing to him with one outstretched arm.

"Osuron of the Baltic, I give you Elliott Savarell. He has the title of an English earl, but he prefers we use his given name."

The man extended his hand, and Elliott took it. Osuron did not grace him with the same elaborate bow, but Elliott didn't expect as much. As it was, given the man's size, the small bow he did give seemed utterly gentlemanly.

"It is a pleasure to meet you, sir." His voice was a cross between a whisper and a rumble. He was a man who spoke little, but when he did, there was a graceful restraint.

"Indeed," Elliott answered.

Bektaten said, "In the time of Shaktanu, Osuron oversaw the construction of our great sailing vessels."

So many questions flooded Elliott's mind he was rendered speechless.

Did this man introduce sailing ships capable of crossing vast seas to the first cultures recorded to have used them? Or had he held these secrets with him, allowing humanity to advance without ancient intervention? He would learn these things in time, he was sure, and this prospect delighted him.

"I know it may seem difficult to believe," Bektaten added, "but our empire stretched across much of the world, and the vessels built under Osuron connected it."

"My queen," Elliott said, "with each passing day, I find there's little left I would be hard-pressed to believe."

She smiled, and as with all her smiles, it felt like a blessing.

"Forgive me," Elliott said, "but I must ask after my son."

"He is aboard my vessel with my crew. Along with the American, Sibyl Parker, and . . ."

Osuron could not bring himself to finish the sentence. He looked to Bektaten. Did he need permission to complete the thought, or was he truly unsure of how to describe his third passenger?

Bektaten said, "Cleopatra the Seventh, last queen of Egypt."

Her response was spoken like a firm and guiding command. And so, Elliott realized, Bektaten remained true to the words in her letter. Firm in her conviction that the woman Ramses had raised from death in the Cairo Museum truly was the resurrected version of Egypt's final ruler and not some monstrous, soulless clone. Should they trust her ancient judgment in this, her ancient wisdom? Or was Bektaten, having never used the elixir to raise one from death before, engaging in wishful thinking.

"I ask permission to bring them to land, and to Brogdon Castle," Osuron said.

"Granted," Bektaten answered. But her expression was fixed and grave. "Enamon, bring Ramses and Julie to the great hall. We should all greet our new and final arrivals."

Enamon turned to go.

"Wait," Bektaten said as if something had just occurred to her. "Take the dogs to my chambers, and confine them there."

At first, Elliott thought this was just a social nicety, until he remembered what Ramses and Julie had shared with him of their previous adventure. These dogs had been used to torture Cleopatra before their rescue, and hers. And whatever would result from this arrival, Bektaten would not have the great queen Cleopatra so menaced again.

At the hard clap of his hands, all fifteen dogs rose to their feet and followed Enamon from the great hall with military-like precision. It seemed a miracle to Elliott, the quick obedience and fluid coordination of these proud hounds. A subtle one, perhaps, given what other secrets this castle might hold. But a miracle, nonetheless.

In the silence that followed, he approached Bektaten, who watched Osuron closely as he departed.

"She is afraid," Bektaten finally said.

"Cleopatra."

Bektaten nodded.

"You can sense this?"

"I don't have that power, no. Osuron whispered it to me just now. Three times, she tried to escape the vessel. She believes this is a ruse, a plot to destroy her."

"My queen, in Cairo I saw her do things. I saw her take life."

Her eyes still on the iron door, she raised a hand. "I have been told all of these things. And you read my letter and saw my warning to her. She has lived with two mortals for weeks now. One, she loves. The other, a woman once believed to be her true spirit reborn. And yet she's done no harm to this woman, nor this man, your son. She was resurrected without her consent and abandoned to terrible confusion and torment. Let us grant her the time she needs for her understanding of this world and her place in it to evolve. She is entitled to this."

"Yes, of course," Elliott whispered.

"Until she kills again," Bektaten added.

It would have been easier to lay eyes on her, Ramses realized, if she had appeared broken. If they'd brought her into the castle in chains, and she'd bucked against them like a captive tiger. If her raven hair had been a wild tangle, and she'd carried herself with some semblance of the terror and chaos that marked their last meeting, when she'd hurled herself through a giant window rather than accept his attempt at rescue.

The only thing that made it easy to see her now was that she seemed to have no interest in laying eyes on him at all. Did not even react in the slightest to his and Julie's quiet arrival in the great hall.

Instead, she stood tall and proud. Her eyes ablaze and intent as she took in the castle for the first time, her perfect mouth set in the same quietly furious line it had assumed when he'd first told her Marc Antony would be her undoing. She could radiate anger, filling a room with it without making a sound, and Ramses thought, *If it is not truly her, there is enough of her within this being to carry her name forward into this century. Provided it costs no more lives.*

Cleopatra showed no resistance to the fact that both of her companions stood close to her, each with an arm linked to hers. Had they walked together through the castle door like this, all three of them? Cleopatra, guided and supported by her new lover on one side, and on the other a woman of this modern age so mysteriously connected to her it was impossible not to believe she contained some portion of Cleopatra's soul reborn.

Only Sibyl Parker reacted to Ramses and Julie's arrival. Her face warmed instantly from one of the surges of pure unguarded emotion she often allowed herself, a tendency which he'd come to understand made her distinctly American. She beamed at them now, and Ramses could not help but smile in return. Of the three of them, she looked the most unchanged since Ramses last saw her. Her golden hair was fastened in a loose ponytail to the back of her head; her dress was generous and flowing, but plain and perfect for the long boat ride, he figured. It was a durable canvaslike material, and he could imagine her sitting and reading for hours in it.

And Alex Savarell. Had he ever seen someone so thoroughly changed in such a short time? Gone were all physical traces of the aristocratic gentleman who'd once vied with him for Julie's affection. He looked less like a man who dined at fine London clubs and more like a man who took long walks along windswept cliffs; he wore baggy pants, and his billowing white shirt spilled out of the sleeves of his long heavy coat. Atop his unstyled mop of brown hair sat a soft cap of similar material to the coat. The loose-fitting jacket, the pants, and the cap were all the color of freshly turned earth; the fabric itself run through with little ridges. Corduroy, Julie had told him this kind of fabric was called.

Elliott appeared to be far more stricken by his son's changed state than the hostility emanating from Cleopatra. The very fiber of Elliott's being had been changed, his cells themselves, and yet the outward appearance of his son in this moment made it appear as if his transformation had been the more severe of the two. Indeed, Elliott had not laid eyes on Cleopatra since the fiery explosion they thought had claimed her life, and yet it was now Alex who captured Elliott's full attention.

It seemed to be a standoff, this meeting.

Cleopatra, Alex, and Sibyl stood only steps inside the iron door. Behind them, a tall and powerful immortal who Ramses knew must be Osuron of the Baltic, and then next to him, three other dark-skinned immortals, dressed in a similar manner: heavy mariner's attire with dashes of luxurious fabric and heavy boots. Former soldiers for Shaktanu who'd been rashly given the pure elixir by Bektaten's traitorous prime minister during that man's rageful coup, a man who had not foreseen that an army released from any fear of death would feel no loyalty to a kingdom or a commander, especially a duplicitous and traitorous one. That many of these soldiers would one day find their way back to some measure of service to their ousted queen was a fitting justice. He wanted to know their stories, each and every one. But for now, there was the story he had rewritten.

The story of Cleopatra.

Bektaten was the reason they were all frozen in place, imprisoned by a rigid silence save for the ocean wind. This was her castle, and she had not yet advanced towards her new guests and extended her hand. This meeting, as fraught and tense as it was, was Bektaten's to begin. But she was too caught up in her quiet study of the raven-haired woman before her.

"Will I be given a choice?" Cleopatra asked.

Bektaten did not ask what she meant. She simply raised one eyebrow. And that was enough.

"My execution," Cleopatra continued. "Will I be given a choice? Is there a blossom in your garden that suffocates, and another that drowns? Will you bring me a . . . what do they call it now? A *buffet*. A selection of deaths ranging from the humane to the grotesque."

"Why do you fear this?" Bektaten asked.

"Because I am a *nochtin*." Then, as if she'd been preparing just such a move, her accusatory glare shot to Ramses, who felt himself jerk in spite of his best efforts to remain still. *You did this to me,* her blazing blue eyes seemed to scream at him. She'd ignored him deliberately, reserving her gaze for this moment, so she could use it like a weapon.

Slowly, Bektaten approached Cleopatra, speaking with a clear forcefulness that stilled Cleopatra instantly. "These words are slurs invented by a man I destroyed. They have no place in my castle, and no one here shall use them against you as Saqnos did. What creatures he did raise from death, he did so with a version of the elixir that was corrupted. And so his science means nothing to us now. For thousands of years he suffered from a mad allegiance to his singular agenda, to discover the formula for the pure elixir. For this reason alone, his other explorations and studies were jaundiced, limited. They cannot be trusted today, and they make clear he was not in possession of the mind required to explore the full mystery of one like you." They were almost face-to-face now, two queens, one known to history, the other invisible to it. "Saqnos dashed his life across the rocks beneath this castle when I stole his immortality, a punishment I meted out in part because of the crime he committed against you. Let every rageful word he spoke in your presence be dashed across the rocks with him."

This speech had done its job, it seemed. Ramses could see from the way Alex and Sibyl had shifted their weight they were now supporting more of Cleopatra, which meant she was no longer as rigid. No longer coiled like a serpent.

Bektaten raised one hand, pressed it gently against Cleopatra's cheek.

Ramses was amazed when Cleopatra did not bat it away. Instead, her eyes glistened. Her jaw quivered. Only months before, this face had been a frozen scream in a museum case, preserved by mud. Attached to a ragged collection of flesh and bone. Now it prepared to weep.

"You are not here for an execution," Bektaten said, "you are here for revelations and illumination. You are here so I might protect you, not exterminate you."

And then Bektaten effortlessly slipped into Ptolemaic Greek, a sound that transported Ramses out of this great hall and back to his final hours, his final weeks, his final years as Cleopatra's lover and counselor before the great dark separation that formed a vast sea between then and now. Where the lighthouse at Alexandria swept the rippling waters of the harbor, and amidst vine-dappled streets, he had shared with Cleopatra the secrets of his immortal existence.

"And while you are here, you shall share with me all that the Romans stole from your story. We shall share with each other the great and abiding ache that only we know, the one that comes from holding great power in your hands. You shall describe for me your favorite volumes within the Library of Alexandria, and you shall share with me tales of your lover Julius Caesar, and Marc Antony if you wish. But you may decide which memories are rich and warming and which are too painful to relive. For I too was often called upon to intertwine power and passion in order to rule, and you will find none of the judgments within me that bedevil this modern age. For you shall find in me another queen such as yourself."

Sibyl was crying softly. Were her tears the result of the mysterious connection between her and Cleopatra? Did the emotions Cleopatra felt at hearing Bektaten's words swell within Sibyl like a symphony across a telephone line? Sibyl was a fiercely brilliant woman, but he doubted she spoke Ptolemaic Greek. Had Cleopatra's mind translated these words for her?

There was so much yet to learn about the connection between them, so much that suggested the crime of raising Cleopatra was not quite the abomination he'd first thought. But of course, he'd want to believe this; of course he'd reach for these possibilities in a desperate attempt to absolve himself.

Bektaten gently removed Cleopatra's arm from Alex's and looped it within her own. Alex seemed startled by this and actually reached out for his lover as Bektaten walked her towards the blazing fire. Then, remembering himself, he lowered his arm, embarrassed.

Over one shoulder Bektaten said, "Enamon has prepared a room for each of you. Go there now and rest and soon I shall summon you. But for now, Cleopatra and I shall come to know each other. As only queens can."

This was all Sibyl needed to bound across the great hall and throw herself at Ramses and Julie in a series of big, warm embraces that made the previous tensions seem like a distant memory.

Alex had been pacing and speaking frantically of world events like a man who'd read nothing but newspapers for the last several weeks. And despite the long and exhausting journey he'd taken to reach Brogdon Castle, he'd not paused for even a moment to enjoy the creature comforts of this bedchamber, with its sweeping view of the cliffs and its lustrous and inviting bedding. He was lecturing Elliott now on how the death of Queen Victoria had brought with it an end to a great age of solemnity and somehow this would set the stage for a new and exciting world in which all the radical ideas for which Alex had suddenly found a passion would take root and blossom.

"But, Alex, are you happy?" Elliott asked.

"*Happy?*" Alex shouted the word. "Father, it's as if I've learned the meaning of the word for the first time. It's as if I've been suddenly admitted to this grand and mysterious club I'd been excluded from for so long. And all of you have always been members, haven't you? You and Julie, you were always members. Always stoked by hidden fires that were your true source, your real fuel. And who was I, but dumb, passionless Alex, trying to wrest happiness from convention. You see, I haven't asked this queen for the elixir. Would you like to know why?"

"Of course."

"I don't want to be free of the fear that I will lose all of this. I don't want my passion for Cleopatra to be dimmed in the slightest by the knowledge that we could be together for all time. It will lessen the intensity and the beauty of all that I feel for her now. And under no circumstances would I surrender those feelings. If I have to die someday to truly savor every drop of *her* in this glorious present, then I shall never consume one drop of this precious elixir."

"You are in love," Elliott said.

"Yes, as you have been in love many times, I'm sure."

"Oh, no, my son. Many passions, yes, but not many loves."

"Who was your greatest then?" Alex asked, bright eyed, grinning. Inconceivable. This conversation would have been inconceivable but a month before. He did not discuss his heart with his son. He did not before now believe his son to have much of one. A good thing, he'd always said, for Alex would endure life with far less pain as a result. They had, for almost their entire lives, addressed each other as two gentlemen at the club discussing cricket scores.

Julie was right. Alex was a dramatically changed man, but Elliott wasn't being met by harsh anger, but a complete absence of restraint, of rational thought. This was a wildness that seemed to know no limits.

Let me test it then, Elliott thought. *Let me discover how many limits my son has let go of.*

"Lawrence," Elliott said. "Lawrence Stratford was my great love."

There was a moment, perhaps. A moment of old judgments.

But they passed through Alex's expression in a flicker before he smiled broadly, nodding, pulling great drafts off his cigarette. "Yes, yes, of course," he said as if this were glorious news. "I'd always suspected it. And that's perfect, it's absolutely perfect. We'll bring him back then."

"What?"

"Lawrence. We'll use the elixir to bring him back and then you two can be—"

"Alex, that is enough!"

"Father, this is a new world!"

"Alex, please. Not for a moment do I wish to deny you the happiness you are feeling, especially in light of all I kept from you. But you must not get confused and think that changes in your world are the same as those in the world at large. For they are not. These are different things.

"You are surrounded by miracles and impossibilities, I know. So am I. But a confederacy of secrets protects us, and the larger world does not share in it because it cannot. Ours is an island, Alex. You must not forget this. Think of this new world in which you find yourself as an island, and when we leave it we must learn to move through the world as it exists, not shape it with the magic we've come to know. It's not Edward who has replaced Victoria for us. It is Bektaten. And we must follow her wisdom and her guiding hand."

He expected his son's face to crumble. A crying fit would have been wildly out of character for him a short time ago, but would it be now? In his changed state, in which he seemed to have no skin, and his every thought tore from his lips. But Alex simply smiled gently and nodded, as if he was the one who'd presented Elliott with truths he could not yet accept, and not the other way around.

"We are here, are we not?" Alex said. "And we bring Cleopatra, even though she believed this was a plot to destroy her. But still we came. Don't worry. I haven't completely lost my mind, Father. Just the parts of it I didn't care for very much."

"Rest now, Alex. I'll have them bring you something to eat. And to drink."

Wine. Spirits. Anything to dampen this blazing inferno within you.

Elliott had one foot out of the door when Alex said suddenly, "I only said it because I want you to be happy."

Lawrence, Elliott realized. *He's talking about his abominable idea about Lawrence.*

"Many passions, but only one great love," Alex said. "That doesn't sound like happiness. Certainly not the life I thought you were living for yourself on the Continent after we all left Egypt."

In a mild daze, unsure of where he was headed next—someplace to recover from the shock of this reunion before whatever grand convocation Bektaten planned—he heard the low sounds of human movement from behind a door off to his right. As he approached it, he felt the chill of the ocean just beyond.

Outside was a stone terrace that looked over the star-flecked sea, and there was Bektaten, her purple robes ruffling in the wind, her gaze on the dark horizon. He took up a place next to her. For a while neither spoke; no doubt she was sorting through whatever her meeting with Cleopatra had revealed.

"Do you still believe it's her?" Elliott finally asked. "Do you believe it's truly Cleopatra?"

"I believe the mystery continues to unfold."

Elliott thought this would be the end of it, and that she was gracefully trying to prevent him from accessing her innermost thoughts.

But she spoke again. "I'll need time with her. And Sibyl. Whatever becomes of this discussion and our investigation into this threat, it'll be my cause for keeping them here."

"That will also include my son, I presume."

"Yes."

He nodded, then felt her gaze upon him.

"This is acceptable to you?" she asked.

"It is most acceptable. He could use your guiding hand."

"And not yours?"

"I lack your wisdom."

"Is it wisdom he needs?"

"He needs many things. I can't provide them. In this moment, I'm too afraid."

"Of this threat?"

"No."

"What then?" she asked.

"I fear a mortal mind cannot exist for an extended period of time in the constant company of immortals. This Sibyl Parker, her connection to Cleopatra renders her extraordinary, but my son is an ordinary man trying to reshape his mind to extraordinary events, and I fear the result will be madness."

Bektaten considered this, then spoke. "I will not administer the elixir to him solely to—"

"I don't ask you to," he said sharply.

It was the first time he'd interrupted her, to say nothing of his brusque tone.

"Forgive me," he said quietly.

"Speak. Tell me what you really ask."

"Bring him to heel. Teach him the importance of the secrecy that surrounds all of this, surrounds us. He speaks of all this like a mad zealot who must share with the entire world all the magical things he's seen. That cannot happen. I am new to your world, and even I know this."

Only once these words left his lips did he think he might be dooming his son before this queen. For how well did he know her truly? And had he not just described his own son as a threat to her cloistered existence?

Bektaten turned her attention back to the sea. "There is only one secret that guards the stability of my world, and that is the elixir's formula. That is why my relationship with Ramses is vital now. For he's the only other who knows it. Your son could tell all the newspapers of the globe what he had seen, and none would believe him. So banish all thoughts that I will execute him solely based on this expression of concern."

"Perhaps that's not my main fear—"

"I understand your main fear. I felt your concern as you made this admission. You feared I would execute him to protect my citadels. Well, I would not and I shall not. Just as I shall not give him the elixir to cure what may be temporary madness."

"Will you do it for me then?" he asked. "Will you give him some measure of guidance and instruction to soothe a father's heart?"

"Of course," she answered. "But I must tell you now. You are right, Elliott."

"That he might try to share what he knows?"

"No, you are correct in saying that a mortal who dwells entirely in the presence of those he knows to be immortal does not often thrive. And so your concern for him, it is wise."

Her compliment veiled a troubling diagnosis.

A moment later, he felt her hand on his. "Come. We can wait no longer. Let us begin our discussion of the greater threat before us."

11

And so at last they gathered.

With the fire blazing and the tapestries shifting in the drafts as the fierce ocean winds sought out every crack in the castle walls in a low, moaning chorus, and the sky black and star filled beyond the great hall's soaring windows, this convocation of immortals and their intimates took their seats in the center of the great hall at the large gleaming wooden table with its dazzling arrays of inlaid-pearl designs.

As Ramses pulled back his chair and prepared to join the others, he realized the size and roundness of this table suggested it had been used for this purpose before, but with other immortals. Immortals still unknown to him. And even though he dreaded the admissions he would soon have to make, the layers of significance to this meeting were many, impossible to peel back all at once. Each trembling with excitement.

A miracle to be seated this close to Cleopatra, not in opposition or anger, but in shared deference to a higher authority, as an equal. A miracle to watch Cleopatra's expression drain of its brittle resistance as Bektaten opened this meeting with a careful articulation of the threat before them, to watch Cleopatra come to realize she was neither the source nor at the center of this threat. That she had been brought here to participate. Perhaps even to advise.

And to see Alex Savarell so transformed! The righteous prig who'd baited him with such determination during their trip to Egypt now seemed dazzled by all he beheld, a new man. A boy before wonders. He held to Cleopatra's hand tenderly and occasionally stroked her arm, as if the recent events that had upended his life had taught him how to love, not just to acquire.

Bektaten began with a detailed description of the test they'd conducted with the pendants earlier that day.

Only then did Ramses realize there was no sign of the necklaces. For some reason, their queen had no desire to demonstrate the power of the stones before the eyes of their new arrivals. Perhaps she did not trust all of them to be in the presence of this power—Cleopatra, or maybe Alex, whose mortal mind was still so new to all this. But she described it in great and vivid detail, omitting nothing that Ramses remembered, save for his outburst and flight from the room.

Surely she would direct the room's attention to him next and demand he share all he knew.

Instead, she gestured in Julie's direction and asked her to share all the details of the attack in Brompton Cemetery. And Julie did, in a quiet and clear voice that did not swell with the emotions the memories might have inspired, and Ramses thought it was the focus with which Bektaten had begun this meeting that gave Julie her focus now.

Everyone listened without saying a word.

Ramses studied their faces in turn.

Elliott seemed somehow contented, as if comforted by the confirmation he hadn't hallucinated the attack against him the night before.

Alex shook his head every now and then, his stare unblinking.

Next to him, Cleopatra had raised one eyebrow and sunk her teeth gently into her lower lip as she listened, the same manner she'd affected when receiving long-ago counsel from him that challenged her perceptions.

And then there was Sibyl. Compared with the other expres-

sions around her, her face was aflame with emotion. She seemed
to flinch and recoil with every great blow of the archangel Julie
described, and occasionally one delicate hand traveled to her
mouth as if to contain a small cry.

As for Osuron and his three crew members, the only other
beings at the table as old as Bektaten, they absorbed Julie's
account with attentive eyes, but expressions that seemed
immutable.

Earlier, it had been decided that Enamon would travel to
Aktamu and relieve him of his guard duties over the mortals
they'd assembled at the nearby inn. In this way, Aktamu could
be apprised of all that had happened the night before, and Enamon could watch over Randolph, Rita, and Oscar with a vigi-
lance informed by his new knowledge of the attacks and the
men who'd attempted them. But if their great age had caused
Osuron or his men to absorb this tale of impossibilities stoi-
cally, Aktamu's age had not produced this reaction in him. He
seemed quietly stunned by what he was hearing. And this alone
drove home the magnitude of Ramses's sense of responsibility
in this moment. For Ramses had done little to keep from evil
hands a power that could shock a being eight thousand years
old.

When Julie concluded, Ramses expected to see Bektaten's
fingers gesture in his direction. But again they did not.

Now she pointed to Elliott, who then began to describe his
experience aboard the train the night before. At the news that
the pendant could animate a statue that sounded like a colossus
when compared with the archangel Ramses had brawled with
in the cemetery, Sibyl gasped and Alex sat slowly back in his
chair, one hand finally going to his mouth. In these new poses
of shock, they listened to Elliott's description of having felled
a towering reproduction of Michelangelo's *David* by hurling a
rock into the center of his assassin's stomach.

As he listened, Ramses found himself fiddling with the

scarab ring he wore on his right hand. Rescued from his tomb, this ring, a connection to his past. But now it felt as if it were trying to crawl from his finger.

Once Elliott concluded his account, Bektaten allowed them a long silence so they could absorb the details.

Then, she spoke. "I say to all of you what I said to Ramses and Julie earlier today. There are many miracles in my garden, but none among them can give life to a substance that has no life to begin with. My ancient wisdom does not yield a quick solution to this. Of course, it has placed many tools and weapons at our disposal, and we may use them against this threat, but it does not illuminate a path to the threat's source, I'm afraid."

She regarded each of them in turn before she spoke again. "Never. I have never seen anything like these necklaces and the stones they bear. Nor have I heard tell of anything like them in all my journeys. I've not simply brought you all here to shield you from the threat of these assassins, although that is my purpose in part. I gather us now for a thorough and deliberative reading of the evidence, which we must conduct as one before we decide how to act. In my view, this process now begins with a simple question."

She looked to Julie.

"Julie, the last words of the man who tried to kill Elliott: 'All those who loved Lawrence Stratford must die.' Do you know of anything that might connect your father to these Russian men?"

"Nothing," she answered with confidence. "I know of nothing that connects him to Russia at all. He never traveled there. He felt no great love for it. He dismissed its literature as awash in trivia and descriptions of the idle rich. His passion was for the great civilizations of the ancient world, and the ancient world of that region organized too late to capture his attention. It was tribes of nomads living in isolation across vast and forbidding plains. Egypt. Egypt was his passion."

Ramses was startled to hear of Lawrence Stratford's distaste for the great Russian novelists. He had devoured Tolstoy and Dostoevsky upon his awakening. What Lawrence saw as trivia had offered Ramses crystalline and dazzling views of this new century and the eve of the previous one. Perhaps men like Lawrence only saw great literature as that which transported them to lands starkly unfamiliar, and in his view the Russian rich were too much like the British rich whose conventions he'd fled. To Ramses, the tale of Vronsky's doomed love for Anna Karenina had been cloaked in the same mystery and wonder with which Lawrence had probably viewed Ramses's tomb and the scrolls within.

"Is it possible he crossed paths with these men in Egypt?" Bektaten asked.

"If he did, there's no mention of them in his journals. I read them all after Ramses and I returned from Europe. Some we donated to the British Museum, but I retained the ones that were too personal. But there was nothing. Nothing of Russians. And I read these pages after I'd consumed the elixir, which means my memory was greater. I would remember, Bektaten. I assure you."

"Do we know where they came from?" Sibyl asked quietly. "The necklaces. They're the key to this, aren't they? Perhaps they came from Egypt. Did Lawrence discover them?"

Julie said, "I simply can't see my father discovering something of this magnitude and not being permanently changed by it. He was not a man who believed in magic."

"Yes," Sibyl answered, "but if he didn't know what they were? He could have . . . transferred them to these people and now they're trying to cover up the trail, if you will."

"Sold them, you mean?" Julie asked. "My father didn't sell his discoveries. Occasionally he quarreled with museums and benefactors over how to display them and where they should be taken. He had grave misgivings about removing them from the countries where they were discovered, but the museums that financed his expeditions had final say. But I can't for the life of me see him selling any discovery of his. Ever."

"Sibyl," Bektaten said, "when you suggest these Russians might have been covering up a trail, what do you mean by this?"

"Oh, I'm speculating, of course. As we all know, I have a very vivid imagination. But if I were writing the story, I'd say they plan to do something with this power, something wretched. And so they've tried to wipe out anyone who might know they have it."

"And Lawrence had this knowledge for some reason," Elliott said quietly. "But with Lawrence now gone, they move against anyone he might have shared the secret with when he was alive."

"'Something wretched,'" Bektaten said quietly, pondering this phrase. "And what is the greatest and most wretched thing stretching from the borders of Russia and into France and possibly soon to the seas around us?"

"The war," Elliott said to her, "you believe this is somehow connected to the war?"

"The timing cannot be ignored," Bektaten said.

Julie straightened in her chair, her jaw jutting and defiant suddenly. "I assure you all. My father could not have *kept* this secret to himself. It's inconceivable. When he first found evidence Ramses had lived a thousand years past his recorded death, he immediately began writing of it in his journals. In Latin, of course, so they couldn't be read by anyone. But I can't see him not reacting to the discovery of these necklaces in a similar manner. A jewel with the power to move stone? He could not have stayed silent about such a thing."

"Not stone," Bektaten corrected her, "statues, the power to animate and give the appearance of life to that which has been carved into the shape of life."

"If anything," Elliott added, "it seems to harness the power of the sculptor, not the sculpture."

"Even more so," Julie continued, "the discovery of something like this would have broken all he believed to be true. He would have been bursting with it. Unrecognizable. But his writings on Ramses's tomb were the musings of a man encountering something beyond natural comprehension for the *first* time, not the second. If he'd witnessed something like this before then, the tone of those entries would have been markedly different, I'm sure. At the very least, he would have compared the necklaces to the discoveries in the tomb as he tried to incorporate them both into some larger framework of that which he couldn't easily explain."

"This is just the beginnings of a theory, Julie," Bektaten said. "It does not impugn your father's good character."

Julie bowed her head, seeking to restrain her defensiveness.

But Julie was right. Ramses knew she was right.

Elliott said, "We don't know for sure they're Egyptian. Any theory linking the necklaces to Lawrence rests on this assumption, but we can't—"

"They are," Ramses said. "They are Egyptian."

The room fell silent. So much strength it took to raise his head and behold all the gazes upon him now.

Bektaten, appearing satisfied, sat back into her chair.

Julie gazed at him as if he now bore the burden not just of sharing what he'd withheld, but of clearing her father's name before this council.

With every moment of discussion that cast Lawrence Stratford as a piece, unwitting or not, of some shadowy and nefarious plot, Ramses could no longer endure his own silence. He felt now the same racing heart he'd felt just before the heat of battle. But in this moment, the sword and shield had to be set aside, his flanks exposed to those who surrounded him.

"They are the Eye of Osiris," he said.

To his silence, Bektaten said, "Continue, please, Ramses."

Ramses stood.

"There is no need to stand," Bektaten said. "We must speak as fellows when round this table."

"I don't mean to elevate myself above the proceedings, my queen. I stand so that I won't continue to slouch backwards from the truth I've withheld for too long. I stand to be seen, to reveal, not to dominate."

Bektaten nodded. But he could tell just from this small exchange that his silence on the matter, and his earlier outburst, had tested her patience, and the business of the earlier arrivals had served as a distraction from her irritation.

"When I first saw this necklace last night, I recognized it," Ramses said. "But I could not trust this instinct, you see. You must understand, as I'm sure some of you can, my memories of my mortal life are clouded. It's not just the thousands of years that separate me from it. There's a distinct difference in strength between the memories acquired by a mortal mind, and those we gain after our mind's been bathed in the hot magic of the elixir. These necklaces, they dwelled for me within those misty recesses. And now I realize, yes, my first instinct was correct. I remember them. I wore one myself. Once, briefly. I clutched it in my mortal hand and watched its power work on a statue of such size it dwarfs those used as weapons against us last night."

He expected a flood of questions, but none came. They were too eager for the tale.

"Many of you know during my reign and the reign of many other pharaohs, we held elaborate festivals during the inundation of the Nile. The fields could not be worked, and the restless energy of the people had to be put to use. Statues of the gods were held aloft and carried through the watching crowds, along the Nile at Thebes and into the Temple of Karnak.

"But there was a ritual that took place within the temple

complex that was known only to the priests and the king. It happened once during a king's reign. And during this ritual the necklaces were used. Five in all, four worn by the elder priests who presided, and the fifth placed around the neck of the pharaoh himself. This took place in a private temple, where a pit had been dug so the hidden colossus of Osiris residing there could fit within the narrow walls and beneath the thick ceiling. Upon our arrival, the tale of this colossus was revealed to the king. To me, Ramses the Great, Ramses the Second.

"They did not share the exact year of this statue's creation, only the fantastical elements of its birth. Elements so fantastical even I, who believed in all the gods, dismissed it as invention. You see, there was a purpose to this ritual. An agenda, as it would be called today. The purpose was to instill humility in each and every king before the power of the priests and the temple. And that is why this statue was covered in gold. For it wasn't gold fresh from the mines that bathed its great torso, head, and limbs. This gold, the priests claimed, came from the personal treasures of the heretic king Akhenaten, who had stolen the power of the priests and brought great ruin to Egypt in his mad devotion to a single god.

"And so, when they'd reestablished their hold, the priests of the Temple of Karnak had destroyed and ground the treasures into a fine and glittering dust, so they could anoint a statue of one of the very gods Akhenaten had sought to banish from existence. At the time, you see, this fury at Akhenaten, I believed this to be the only truth in the ritual. I was sure the priests had invented it solely to ensure that never again would a pharaoh seek to rise above, to displace them as Akhenaten had done. I could understand this rage, this hatred for the sun king and the ruin he brought."

As Ramses collected his thoughts, Elliott said softly, "There are some who think Akhenaten wise and misunderstood. A rebel before his time."

"I have read these scholars, and they are fools. They believe his faith in a single god presages their own belief in a single Christian one. From this basic fact, they spin myths around a man who almost destroyed an empire. To speak in the language of these scholars, this is bias writ large, my friend."

He realized for the first time he was discussing ancient Egyptian history in front of another being who had lived through it. "Do you agree with me, my queen? Or did you walk with Akhenaten along the Nile as he shared with you his plans to destroy one capital and replace it with another?"

"I avoided Egypt entirely during his reign," Bektaten answered. "From the accounts I received, one thing was clear. He desired the transformative power of war, but he found no great conflicts on his borders, so he turned that desire within. When his reign was brief, it seemed a mercy."

Relieved he had not stumbled unwittingly into a shadowed corner of Bektaten's history, Ramses continued, "But Akhenaten is incidental to this tale. The priests mentioned him only briefly as they ushered me into this candlelit chamber where the light made the gold dust upon this colossal statue flicker and dance. They spoke of the colossus before us and told a tale of its origins.

"Of the night when they had cowered in the temple from a great storm that swept the desert outside and brought bolts of lightning down upon the nearby cliffs. A tale of how they emerged the next day to discover that the storm itself had somehow carved into the cliff face the colossus before us. That the lightning striking stone had created the statue's great amber eyes, which towered over the morning desert, dazzlingly bright in the clear sunrise. They spoke of how the priests assembled a great team of wagons and men to transport this colossus to a place of temporary shelter until they could determine its true home. But that during this journey, the great statue toppled and fell, smashing the wagons beneath it.

"And the eyes, the great amber eyes, came loose from the statue's face and shattered into fragments on the ground all around them. Most were too small to collect, but five were not. Five were large enough to be held within a single hand. And the priests wailed and wept, believing they had blinded the craftsmanship of the gods themselves. But eventually, those gripping the largest pieces of stone watched the amber come to light in their palms.

"And these five priests heard a voice that filled their heads. And the voice said, 'I am the colossus of Osiris, and you shall make a home for me. Make a home for me in the Temple of Karnak so that all the kings of Egypt might know my presence.' And the statue rose. It rose to its feet, it rose on *their will*, commanded by the power of the priests who held its shattered Eyes in their gripping palms.

"And this, they said, was how the colossus of Osiris arrived within the temple. It *walked*. It walked under the power of the priests themselves, who thereafter guarded these Eyes and claimed to use them only for the purposes of this ritual. Only to bring the god into the presence of the new king."

No suspicion or disbelief on the faces studying him, just wide-eyed fascination all around. "You can see now why I thought this a show. A parade for my benefit, and the benefit of all pharaohs. The entire tale placed a great power in the hands of these priests, you see? A power greater than any the king commanded. And after all they had lost under Akhenaten, they were desperate to maintain such power."

"And how did this power manifest during this ritual?" Bektaten asked. "You wore this stone today and used it upon statues brought up from my vaults. How did this experience differ from what you went through during this ritual long ago?"

Ramses said, "Understand that at the time every aspect of my mortal mind worked to dismiss what I was seeing. I believed the wine the priests gave me to be drugged, and so I believed what I saw next to be a hallucination."

"Yes, but did you hear his voice, Ramses?" Bektaten asked. "Did you hear his voice as the priests claimed to have heard it when they first clutched the fragments of the Eye?"

"Yes."

He did not think Bektaten capable of shock. Perhaps she wasn't. But how else to interpret the sudden stillness that had come over her, the intensity of her expression, a look in which curiosity had been replaced by something colder. Her beliefs of the spiritual nature of the universe were fixed; he knew this from their previous discussions. She dismissed all gods and pantheons as lies, but believed the engine of the human spirit's experience to be a vast and complex cycle of rebirth.

And here he was, telling her he'd once heard the voice of a god.

He felt a sudden fear that she might withdraw from him over this. Perhaps not now, but gradually over time. But these were rash, childish thoughts, he knew.

"Today," she said, "when you wore the stone today, did you hear this voice again?"

"I did not."

"Interesting," she said. "We'll return to this point in a moment, but continue with your account."

"Three thousand years ago, when I gripped the Eye in my hand, as the priests retreated, it appeared as if the colossus of Osiris came to life before me. But it did not leap at me or jump or whirl or do any of the things our attackers made those statues do last night. It would have crushed me underfoot if it had. And in that moment, I had no fear. For I believed my mind had been altered, and what I was seeing a product of the story the priests had poured into my ears. Nothing more."

How many times could he say this before it would stop being a comfort? How many times could he cling to this idea that what he'd witnessed in the temple had been the product of an altered mind, when he, and others, had seen with sober eyes what the Eye of Osiris could do now, in this century? Some measure of it, at least.

He was hesitating, afraid. He'd entered a part of the story for which the present might have few answers, but there was no turning back now.

"Ramses," Elliott said softly, "may I ask a question?"

"Yes, of course."

"The elder priests. The ones who wore the other four fragments of the Eye. Did they continue to hold the necklaces they wore as you held yours?"

"They did not. They dropped their hands and slowly backed away once I clutched the stone at my neck."

"Were they behind you?" Julie asked. "They could have been acting out of your sight."

"They were not. They were behind the colossus, so that I could stand before the statue alone. When they withdrew, I could see their silhouettes. The elder priests lowered their hands, and their stones went dim as mine began to glow."

"And so you can be sure that what happened next was the result of your connection to the Eye of Osiris, and not some puppetry performed by the priests?" Elliott asked.

"I believe so, yes. But what happened next might not be what you are expecting me to say."

"How so?" Bektaten asked. "The statue did not move according to your will?"

"It appeared to move of its own will."

Elliott shifted uncomfortably in his chair, eyes so wide it seemed he was seeing everything Ramses described. Sibyl appeared shocked. Alex looked at Ramses as if he were getting steadily more radiant before his eyes.

"Explain this, please," Bektaten finally said.

"Its great knees bent. One giant arm extended in my direction, its hand, a hand large enough to take me in it if it wished, opened, and the gold dust covering its stone skin shimmered and became something so luminous and effervescent it appeared to reveal another world. A world beyond the chamber, a world beyond the temple. A world beyond *life*.

"And it was then that I heard the god's voice, and it said, 'Know me, Ramses. Know that you will one day stand outside my gates.' And I realized it was the gates I saw, the gates to his realm. The realm of Osiris, the realm of the dead. For it seemed that his very shimmering body was now a window, and through it I saw a great grove of brilliant green trees, pummeled by powerful winds.

"And I knew that these trees were of the very type in which the goddess Isis had concealed and protected the limbs of Osiris's body after he was dismembered by his brother Typhon. But just beyond this grove was a cliff face and within it a set of towering doors of gold and obsidian. And I saw that the brilliant sunlight seemed to come from nowhere, for the skies above these cliffs were black with storm clouds and lightning bolts fired from their great, dark bellies. And again the voice said, 'Know me, Ramses. Know that you will one day stand outside my gates.'"

A sudden crushing silence in this great hall, and Ramses realized this tale had done something fearsome and terrible—it had somehow brought the power of death into a room full of immortals. For if death had a voice, it had spoken to him then.

Bektaten's eyes had left him for the first time since he'd begun the tale. He sensed great distress in her. The presence of this feeling, given how out of character it was, gradually drew the focus of everyone around the table, until she realized she was the one being studied, and slowly sat up taller.

"This grove of trees," she said, "these towering obsidian walls. Were these things you'd seen before? Could they have been plucked from your own mind by this experience?"

"I don't believe so now. But it's possible. I'd heard the Osiris tale throughout my life. Out of all the gods and deities of our kingdom, the story of his origins was packed with incident. It was a full narrative similar to the tale told of Christ today.

Later, the Greeks would rival this with tales of their own pantheon. But in the time of my reign, the tale of Osiris was unique in its complexity. Betrayed by his brother Typhon so that he could steal his wife, Isis. His dismembered body collected by her and protected and sheltered in the great hollow of a tree before it regenerated and was reborn. These were tales we all learned, and so perhaps my mind peopled the grove I saw with the same tree I imagined when I first heard the story. I cannot say for sure."

The room could sense he was not finished.

"What else, Ramses?" Bektaten asked.

"A sound," Ramses said. "A great pulse. At first I thought it a heartbeat. But it was more like breath. Sustained breath. One great inhalation followed by two huffing exhalations in a row."

He demonstrated for them. To his ear, it was a pale imitation of what he remembered.

A new voice broke the silence. Alex, sounding strangely energized as all the others had fallen into a grim silence. "Some god of death he is. You'll never stand outside *his* gates, will you, Ramses?"

Was young Alex Savarell mocking him? No. There was joy in his eyes, as if the thought that Ramses would live forever truly thrilled him now.

"How do we reconcile the differences?" Bektaten asked.

"What do you mean, my queen?" Ramses asked in turn.

"Today, you saw a shimmer from the statues here, but they did not become windows into other realms before your eyes. Today, the statues moved precisely to your will, so long as you willed them to act in a manner consistent with their rendering. Today, you did not hear the voice of a god, nor did you hear this great and powerful breathing. You heard no voices at all, except for mine and Julie's. You were capable of conversing easily with us while you wore and held the Eye. It was nothing like the transportive experience of the ritual you just described. So if they are truly the same objects, how do we reconcile the differences in the experiences they bring? I ask this question of us all."

"The colossus," Julie said quietly.

"Yes?" Bektaten said.

"The Eye, if it was made as the priests claimed, was intended for use with the colossus. That's the other great piece of this. If you use it on an ordinary statue, it's like sending out an electrical current to something that can't truly receive it. Not the way it was intended, at least."

"So it works one magic on a statue made by human hands," Sibyl said breathlessly, "and an altogether-more-momentous magic on a statue created by a god."

A statue created by a god, Ramses thought, and was sure he was not the only one present trying to embrace these words. Had the events of the last two days brought them to a place where they could all fully believe this aspect of the tale told by ancient priests?

"Yes," Ramses said, "this is what I believe. What we've seen is a limited and degraded version of what the Eye of Osiris is truly capable of. And so I must do what I did not three thousand years ago, or in the centuries that followed. I must locate all the Eyes of Osiris *and* the colossus. And if these items are already in evil hands, then I must remove them. Even if it means breaking these hands."

"It's our burden now," Bektaten said, "not just yours."

"Perhaps. And I've made it so."

Bektaten said, "If you are to embark on this mission, Ramses, we must mark some possible path to those who sent these assassins."

Elliott said, "If I may, what our assassins didn't know reveals much. They didn't know we were immortal, that we could easily overpower them. That means they must not know who our dear friend Mr. Reginald Ramsey really is. He's but a name on their list."

"Because of his connection to me," Julie said miserably.

"Perhaps, but this also strongly suggests they know nothing of the elixir, or of the incredible events that had reshaped our lives this past year. I know these might all seem like *absences* of facts, but they're facts in and of themselves, and they can guide us."

"Yes," Bektaten said, nodding. "All this is true."

Invigorated by this approval from their queen, Elliott continued, "If we accept Sibyl's theory that these men are wiping out anyone who might know they possess the Eye of Osiris, then we'd do well to accept Bektaten's suspicion that the timing of these attacks is connected to the war, a war Russia is poised to enter in full with vast deployments of troops. Therefore, I propose these men, or whomever they answered to, plan to use the Eye of Osiris as a weapon of war."

"And perhaps the colossus," Bektaten said, "if they possess it."

"My God," Julie whispered.

After a silence that felt eternal, in which the fire crackled and several of the dogs shifted lazily across the stone floor, Bektaten spoke. "I am told the Germans are now transporting guns to the forts at Liège that are unlike any the world has ever seen. Great metal beasts capable of turning a field of advancing soldiers into a vast sea of charnel."

"This isn't war." It was clear his pronouncement had confused everyone, so Ramses continued, "This isn't war. In war, a man had his sword. In war, the battle was won when the king for the other side fell. Victors were determined by either the persistence or exhaustion of human will. These things contained the battle. But these machines, it's as if man has tried to make a weapon out of thunder and believes he can control the skies. The result will be an unending storm that mercilessly tramples all those sent to battle and any innocents near it."

"And now," Bektaten said, "there might be some faction in this great battle that holds a weapon believed to come from a god."

"Do you believe this?" Ramses asked. "That it came from a god?"

Instead of answering directly, Bektaten said, "I believe the powers I saw demonstrated today cannot be allowed onto the field of battle, or anything close to it. Nor can they be used in the service of political plots or the pursuit of power at large. Immutable assassins, immune to bullets and sword strikes, wielded by humans who can protect themselves at a remove? It must be stopped. At all costs."

A quiet male voice said, "Then stop the war."

When Ramses realized the voice had been Alex's, he wondered if the man had only made this radical suggestion to take the focus off his chastened lover.

"Alex, whatever do you mean?" Elliott finally asked.

"What are the alternatives?" Alex asked. "You've no identifications for these men. You've hidden their bodies, but what does that do? Are you going to pose them for photographs and circulate their pictures through the streets of London like common detectives, all while the wheels of war continue to turn? You speak of a weapon made by a god, and yet you have the hands of gods, each of you. Use them. *Stop* the war!"

"We do not have the hands of gods," Bektaten said quietly, but Ramses could see an anger growing within her unlike any he'd ever witnessed before. "This is mistaken thinking. It implies an inherent moral purpose to the elixir's structure that does not exist. We have hands powered by an incredible strength that comes from an accident of nature. A momentous accident, to be sure. But the only intrinsic purpose to what powers us is what our enduring human intellect endows it with. Only how we choose to view it as moral creatures gives it meaning."

"All of that might be true," Alex continued, "and you can still stop this bloody war!"

"How?" Elliott asked. "Alex, *how*?"

"Tear the tanks apart with your bare hands!" Alex cried,

sounding overjoyed. "Invade the ships before they leave port. Of all the nations embroiled in this, in equal measure. Punch holes through their hulls so that they might sink right there before they can fire on anyone or anything—"

When Alex started rising to his feet, Elliott said, "Alex, please. You must calm yourself!"

"No, no, Father. You sit here, all of you, dithering, as if you are prisoners of things you are not. It's unbearable. It's unbearable to listen to this, knowing what each of you can do."

"*Alex!*" Elliott shouted, rising to his feet to match his son's height.

Undeterred, red-faced, Alex addressed them all. "You can hide in the mists. You can sabotage each and every advancing force. You wouldn't take life, you would just destroy these terrible machines. And with each new discovery of a broken tank or an inexplicable display of your great strength, they would come to realize, all of them, Russian, German, French, Belgian, British, they would all realize there was a force. An invisible, powerful force seeking to thwart this war. And they would see it as the hand of god and they would question their purpose and fall back. They would say among themselves, *Can't you see? Look at this great gun torn to shreds by a force we do not know. It can only mean one thing. One thing, alone. God himself does not want this war.*"

He was crying now, shuddering, a mortal man, a mortal mind, vulnerable to the implications of all they'd discussed in ways the rest of them were not. Pity. Ramses felt great pity for him, and he was not alone, for there were tears in Elliott's eyes too, and Sibyl's; she was sitting erect, gazing at Alex as if at any moment she might leap from her chair and throw her arms around him.

Breathless, tears slipping down his face, Alex stared at each of them in turn. "Why can't you see it?" he whispered. "God himself does not want this war."

Slowly, Cleopatra reached up, caressing Alex's arm gently. Her expression, so cold only a moment before, was full of sympathy. *Love,* Ramses thought. *Was it truly love?* Tenderly she said, "Alex, my darling. Please. Sit with me and be calm." Her voice seemed to command him; he collapsed into his chair, covering his face in an attempt to hide his tears. Cleopatra snaked an arm around his shoulders and brought him close to her.

Elliott was still standing, as if caught now between a desire to embrace his son or bind him in restraints and cart him from the room.

Bektaten raised a hand in his direction, and slowly he sat.

"We mustn't silence young Alex," the queen finally said. "His pain gives voice to the pain within us all. The pain we will continue to feel as we bear witness to this unfolding cataclysm. No war in history has ever been launched by one who could predict its end, for if they knew its end, they would never begin. All wars begin in chaos and delusion. And as immortals, you will see this more clearly than ever.

"I reiterate my invitation to those of you who feel you cannot effectively aid us in our new mission. I will relieve you of this pain with everything at my disposal. This means if some among you wish to slumber through this conflict, as I have slumbered through great conflicts of the past, you may do so beneath this castle and under my protection.

"As for an effort to put a stop to this war, I would be lying before you all if I said I had not entertained these very thoughts myself.

"But the truth remains this: there is no power at our disposal that can stop the force that has created these terrible machines. These acts of sabotage you describe, Alex, would have your desired effect on some men, but not all. The remainder would simply tear themselves apart on the field of battle with their bare hands, or make new constructions of their ferocity. The more likely result, and a terrible one, is that our intervention would be discovered, and by those who could not comprehend or even value the great mystery of us. They would either confine us, or worship us as false gods. Both would be a prison, I assure you.

"Look to the history of Ramses himself if you don't believe me. Look to what his own mortal son did to him upon discovering his secret. Imprisoned him, sought ways to torture him so the elixir's presence and formula would be revealed. Look then to how Ramses embraced the ages. Guarding his secret, dispensing wisdom over power. Even though we never met, my journey was much like his. Only I dispensed healing, and in ways the mortal mind could accept."

A silence and calm had returned to the great table.

"We cannot stop this war," she said, "but we can prevent its marriage to a power that even we, in all our collective wisdom, cannot yet fully explain."

"And there's only one way to begin."

Ramses was as surprised by Julie's interjection as everyone.

Regarding her now, he saw that she seemed to have retreated within, as if in vigorous but concealed debate with herself. She sat rigid, her hands clasped at her chest. When he looked more closely, he saw she was gently kneading the fingers of one hand with the fingers of the other, something she did when her anxiety was slowly giving way to resignation. Her eyes were wide, practically unblinking, it seemed, but they were studying the empty expanse of table before her as if all the other figures around it had turned to vague silhouettes.

"And what is that, Julie?" Bektaten asked softly.

"Alex is correct. We have no easy way of identifying our assassins. No easy way of tracing the steps they took before they reached England. And while I will gladly bring them here for everyone to study, I can tell you confidently my father's journals will be of no use to us. But my father . . ."

Julie fell silent, and at this Elliott sat up, suddenly rigid, his eyes wide. He had heard something in Julie's words, something Ramses had missed. "Julie, no," Elliott whispered.

"What?" Ramses said. "What is this? What do you—"

Staring directly into Bektaten's eyes now, Julie continued, "We've yet to answer the question you posed when we first gathered. What connects my father to these men? Well, given our circumstances, and our powers, there is only one sure way to answer it."

Sibyl let out a soft cry and brought her hand to her mouth.

"Julie . . . ," Ramses said, refusing to believe he was correct in his interpretation of her words.

"We must bring my father back from the dead," Julie said.

12

For as long as she could, Julie had held the words within her. Until they'd caused her heart to thunder.

She thought if she said them quickly, she could leap past her initial revulsion at the idea. Enter the terrifying but also exhilarating suggestion into the record of this great meeting before she lost her confidence entirely.

She'd assumed someone else would see it before she gave voice to it, the terrible inevitability of it. But the longer they went without the idea passing between anyone's lips, the greater her torment became.

It felt like an injustice that she'd had to say it.

Even if it died a quick death as those before her tore the notion to shreds.

No such luck, it seemed, when she regarded their silent faces. No such luck at all.

And so it was. This was her burden.

And that was just, wasn't it?

His remains had been her burden, his tomb had been her burden. His journals and all his belongings sprinkled throughout the home in Mayfair she could not bring herself to part with. His legacy was her burden. And it would remain so for all time because she, Julie Stratford, would remain for all time.

The ones we love become our burdens in death, and this is how we remain connected to them, she realized. *But for immortals, these responsibilities will only lengthen and deepen unless we throw them off in a rage.*

There would be accusatory questions now, of course, she was sure. The belief that she'd proposed this only to stage some reunion with her father, no matter how ghastly and unpredictable the means.

But could they not see it? Their other avenues of investigation had narrowed down to nothing. Before he'd lapsed into his desperate insistence that they stop the war, Alex could see this. The bodies of their assassins had yielded nothing. Elliott could see it too. The ignorance the assassins had displayed as to Ramses's true identity suggested there was nothing else in Ramses's past that connected him to the men themselves. The necklaces, perhaps, but not the men who wore them. And she knew full well, Lawrence's papers would yield nothing.

There was only one well for them to plumb, and it was Lawrence himself.

Just hours before, the idea might have seemed abominable.

It was Cleopatra who'd changed that. She hadn't meant to, but she had. Julie couldn't deny this.

Having sat now for hours in her presence, finding her no longer the hobbling, strained creature Julie had last encountered at her engagement party, seeing her move with fluid grace, assemble quick coherent thoughts: these things had made this idea somehow seem tolerable, if not acceptable.

And Cleopatra was staring at her now with a small, wry smile, as if reading these thoughts.

"And so your eyes slide to me," she said softly, "the risen queen, the revenant Cleopatra, who so recently was but a pile of bones and tattered flesh in a museum case before she was plucked from the great black abyss." Cleopatra studied each of them in turn. Julie did as well and saw that Cleopatra was correct. At Julie's suggestion, the table's focus had shifted to the resurrected queen.

Cleopatra continued, "You wish to hear of the misery I endured, and the wonder I felt after I was hoisted from death without my participation or consent."

"Your misery," Ramses began carefully, "was compounded by my abandonment of you in that moment."

"Perhaps," Cleopatra said, "but no one else among us had endured what you now propose to do to your own father, and so it's my responsibility to advise you."

When no one disagreed with her, Cleopatra nodded gravely and studied her clasped fingers before continuing. Julie braced for venomous words, for some attempt by her old rival to use this moment to torment her. But Cleopatra spoke softly and with new focus.

"I was dead for a thousand years. Your father has been dead only months, so I cannot assume our experience will be replicas. He will not behold the motorcar for the first time. He will not cower before the locomotive. But if he feels what I did, life, his new life, will arrive like the sudden violent jolt of a wagon rousing you from sleep. And instantly he will be beset by an agonizing wash of pain from head to toe. He will have an instant awareness of his own decay. But as soon as this awareness arrives, the pain will turn to a baffling pleasure, and the confusion between the two will be its own torment, for this awareness will not leave.

"A great tingling will sweep his limbs. But the mind will struggle to reconcile the two, and the feeling will be akin to drowning. Not in anything that fills the lungs, but in a substance that clogs all perception like mud. And this struggle itself, it will make a sudden contrast with the blackness that preceded it, and he will realize he has known death, tasted death, luxuriated in death, but his mind will scramble to reject this revelation. And it will flail wildly for every sensory experience in its immediate presence, and it will be able to seize none individually as it gropes for them all, desperately, hungrily. Wildly. And he will feel as if he is being dragged behind some great vessel at sea, fighting the current and the waves and the darkness of the depths below. And he will sense things in the depths. Presences. Awareness other than his own. He will rise with the knowledge that the blackness in which he resided for so long, known only to him now thanks to its sudden absence, was filled by things nameless and vast."

Elliott shot up out of his chair. The rest of them looked to Bektaten to see if she'd order him to sit.

She did not.

He stared into the blazing fire, back to them, his hand to his forehead, hiding his reaction to Cleopatra's account. He was, it seemed, imagining Lawrence, his dear friend, his lover once, enduring all these things just as Cleopatra described them.

Unfazed, the former queen continued, "But no doubt, you will be there to comfort him, to explain to him the momentous change he's undergone. Perhaps this will speed the healing of his mind. I had no such blessing. I stumbled through the streets of an Egypt I did not recognize, menaced by the inventions of the modern world. But he will rise surrounded by the familiar, the comforting. And his bones will not be exposed as mine were. For you will be there to administer more of the elixir to him, as Ramses eventually did to me, when he was finally able to once more lay eyes upon the monster he'd raised.

"But this was just prologue," she said, "as you all well know. I died again and resurrected again, but my memories began to fade, and in their place visions of a woman"—she turned to Sibyl then, and Julie was convinced she might show her some hostility, but instead Cleopatra reached out and laced her fingers in Sibyl's lightly, studying her as if she was a marvel—"visions that seemed to come from nowhere and filled my mind even as my memories of my ancient life faded quickly into blackness.

And if this woman had not suffered her own visions of my existence, if she'd not struck out to find us, to find *me*, I might very well have gone mad, or at least become an empty vessel of memories lost, my sense of self entirely obliterated. It was proximity that healed me."

She gripped Sibyl's hand tightly now as they gazed into each other's eyes. "That, and our union, which brought with it the discovery that my lost memories had become woven through her perception, even if she did not know clearly what they were. Our nearness, our exchanges. They returned them to me; they restored my mind. You all know this, but I walk through it now to remind you of what you may have forgotten in this moment. You may very well not raise just Lawrence Stratford with what you propose to do. You'll awaken his connection to another life, a life that contains elements of his spirit reborn. And the only way to heal Lawrence's mind will be to bring him into union with this life, no matter who they are or where they reside."

Cleopatra reached out with her other hand and gently caressed the side of Sibyl's face, which allowed the woman to kiss the tips of her fingers. Remarkable, the connection between them; it seemed to chase all else from their minds the second they both gave themselves to it.

"Unless," she said, slowly lowering her hand from Sibyl and turning her attention to the table again, "you plan to have our queen destroy him after he's revealed all we need to know."

"Mind your tongue!" Elliott bellowed, whirling from the fireplace. "Mind your tongue, Cleopatra!"

Cleopatra smiled, but it was a strained and tired smile. Quietly, she said, "You did not hold your tongue when you lay with me so soon after my resurrection that my bones were still visible. Don't pull a saintly veil around yourself now, Lord Rutherford. You are no stranger to this. You too saw me shatter that glass case in which my remains had rested. You heard me fill the museum with my howls. Do not shirk your responsibility in this moment."

"And what responsibility is that, pray tell?" Elliott asked.

"Tell her," Cleopatra said, "I have shared what I felt in those moments, but you saw them. Ramses fled. But you saw them. Tell her what you know to be truth. Tell her that, yes, she will hear her father's voice again, but it will arrive with screams."

"You think I only wish to hear his voice again?" Julie snapped. "You think that's the only reason I propose this?"

"No, no," Cleopatra said quietly. "Not at all. I think you are correct. I think we must uncover the secrets your father took to his grave, and until we do the mystery before us will only widen. But you must know full well what you are about to do."

"She's *not* about to do it," Elliott cried, but there was a pleading tone in his voice. It was not a command so much as a question, and the sound of his pain rent Julie's heart. "It's an abominable thought, and we must stop this talk at once. It's . . . it can't be done. It just can't."

"And yet," Bektaten said, "I do not forbid it."

Elliott let out a strained gasp and turned to the fire again.

"I don't command it," Bektaten added, "nor do I forbid it."

And so, Julie realized, she would not be released from this conflict by the dictates of their queen. She'd been partly expecting this but, alas, no such freedom.

"I will supply the vials of the elixir needed for this most sensitive task," Bektaten continued, "provided those who undertake it directly will accept the full consequences of it, and what it might bring. While we must be grateful for Cleopatra's account, no matter how unvarnished, we cannot be sure what Julie proposes will unfold in exactly the same manner. The differences are clear. Lawrence has been gone but a short time. The connection to another life, if it is present, may not be so far advanced. Conversely, we know not what new revelations may be unearthed by this act. Those who can bring themselves to stand in the presence of Lawrence Stratford's resurrection must be willing to contend with them all."

"I will do anything Julie asks of me in this moment," Ramses said, "anything that's asked of me to end this threat, but this is Julie's decision. It must be."

He clasped her hand firmly, and she returned the grip, but her focus had fixed itself upon the man standing before the fire, the one who'd recoiled from this group when its discussions had become too painful for him to endure. Slowly, she rose and moved to him, and when she placed a hand against his back, he did not turn, but he did not flinch or recoil either, and she saw, in the flicker of the fire, a sheen of tears standing in eyes brilliantly blue.

"I will not do it if you cannot do it with us," she said. "For if you cannot bring yourself to stand with us as we raise him, it means I am too blinded to the danger of this. You loved him as much as I did. And I know full well I risk befouling every precious memory of him by whatever we might raise. And if you think that risk unconscionable for yourself, for all that you remember of him, then perhaps I should too."

"Oh, Julie," he whispered, "had I not entertained this thought a thousand times myself."

"Elliott, if you do not stand with us—"

"I will stand with you." He embraced her suddenly and forcefully. "I will stand with you on anything to end this threat."

But as he nuzzled into her soft brown curls, he whispered, "To hear his voice again, Julie. To hear his voice again."

Perhaps his words were detectable to the immortal ears in their presence. If so, there was no reaction from the gathering a few feet away. When they finally parted, Elliott quickly wiping his tears from his cheeks, steadying himself with the quickness of an aristocrat, Bektaten rose to her feet, a sign this convocation was coming to an end on the axis of this decision.

"Osuron and two members of his crew will accompany

you to London to assist you in what lies before you now," she said. "You will not travel until daylight, in the event of further attacks. The three of you"—she turned her attention to Sibyl, Cleopatra, and Alex—"shall remain here with me until significant progress against this threat has been made.

"We've spent too little time together, and as we await reports on the actions Ramses, Julie, and Elliott undertake now, we will come to know each other more fully. For with such a great mystery surrounding us, the shadows must be chased from the mysteries between us, as many already have been by this gathering. But the process continues, our discovery of each other continues. And we shall stand in alliance against whatever strikes at us next. Go now to your rooms, each of you, and rest in the manner you see fit. Take with you my gratitude for all you brought to this most challenging of discussions.

"Come dawn, we shall face this threat anew."

From the tower's balcony, beneath a vault of stars and buffeted by the ocean winds, Ramses felt released from the great weight of all they'd discussed in the great hall below. But he knew it was a temporary relief.

Even with eyes sharpened by the elixir's power, he was having difficulty determining how far along the cliff's edges Elliott and Julie had walked. Arm in arm, they'd left the shadowed rise of the castle behind them. If they were glimpsed by the driver of a motorcar on the nearest road, they'd be mistaken for spirits, no doubt. And perhaps this was fitting, for it was a ghost who walked with them—the ghost of Lawrence Stratford.

They needed this time together, he knew. Even if they spent it in silence, their memory of Lawrence Stratford a living, breathing thing. They might shed themselves of this dangerous idea by the time their walk brought them back to the castle. But he doubted it. He could accept either possibility. Any possibility except the one in which he made this decision on Julie's behalf.

It is the war, Ramses realized, *the war and its possible con-*

nections to these terrible men, which has placed us on this frightening schedule. In another time, they might have found success with an investigation like the one Alex had mocked. Their hands could break open vaults and access all manner of secrets. But in this new age of chaos, it would take too much time. Precious time.

When he heard his scarab ring knocking against the stone, he realized he was drumming his fingers against the terrace wall. Then new sounds joined this light patter.

Bektaten approached.

He waited for her to speak. But instead, she stood next to him at the stone rail, also watching Elliott and Julie become smaller, more-vaporous-looking silhouettes against the dark marriage of night sky and black sea. There was a gentle rustling as she reached into her robes. When Ramses looked down, she had unrolled a narrow velvet belt in which she'd tucked several glass vials. He recognized the familiar glisten of the elixir in six of them. In the other three, a different, darker shade in each. One of those he recognized easily. It was strangle lily powder, capable of reducing an immortal to ash as soon as it was ingested or pierced the skin. The others, he presumed, could have a similar devastating effect.

Her fingers caressed one of the vials containing a sparkling red substance he did not recognize. "Dream rose, I call it," she said. "A puff of it in a mortal's eyes and nose and they're beholden to your every suggestion for hours. A valuable tool to prevent discovery. But one that could lead to terrible abuse. You must not lose hold of it. The other is *sacelum,* with which you are familiar."

Indeed. He'd seen it put to use, but he'd never held a vial of it in solution before. Several threads of the blue-tinted liquid poured along a mortal corpse could dissolve it in a matter of seconds. Inside the vial, it was a darker shade of blue than when it touched mortal flesh.

Ramses nodded, and with one hand gently drew the belt of vials closer to signal his consent.

After a while, she said, "You must be prepared. If you raise something that is beyond control or comprehension, you must be prepared to destroy it, Ramses."

A moment's hesitation, then he signaled his consent by rolling up the velvet gently, careful not to damage the glass vials within, which made soft little clinking sounds as they touched.

"Yes, my queen," he said.

Part II

13

London

She was turning down her father's bed, the bed that had gone untouched since his death.

A mahogany four-poster bed, with a tapestry of ripple-fold brown fabric covering the wall behind the headboard and a tasteful canopy of evenly spaced golden tassels. Her mother's choice, this bed. But her father had loved it and kept it throughout his widowhood, often joking that a man was allowed to conceal his taste for fine, soft things behind the choices of his wife.

For months now, it had been left this way, just as Rita had made it up after he'd departed for Egypt.

Julie removed the duvet cover, gathered it into her arms. She placed it inside the closet, then she folded the top of the comforter down to give a glimpse of the familiar dark sheets underneath. This was what her father had always done, usually an hour before retiring. An hour that would turn to two or three if he lost himself in study again.

As if it were all ordinary, she did these things. As if these were habitual, daily tasks, the turning down of a dead man's bed so that he might be brought back to life within its sheets.

The house had been ghostly quiet upon their return.

It was still quiet, but they'd mostly restored the rooms to

their original state, removing the canvas wrappings they'd swaddled most of the furniture with in preparation for their now-aborted transatlantic crossing. Save for the trunks lining the front hallway. Those had been waiting for them inside the front door like patient house pets, eager for their return.

From downstairs came the gentle thuds of Elliott returning her father's precious artifacts to their shelves in the library, arranging the silver candlesticks her mother had once loved. The two men from Osuron's crew who'd accompanied them were sitting patiently beside the house's front and back doors, silent sentries.

The phonograph, she thought suddenly. *We shall set the phonograph close to the bed and we'll play Chopin's nocturnes, the same songs he listened to in the evenings to relax. We shall greet him with memories, warm familiar memories.*

But how could she be sure these memories would soothe him?

How could she be sure of anything in this moment?

And the answer, of course, was that she could not be. But she could strive to bend every aspect of this effort towards its best possible intention. It's what Elliott was doing in the double parlor now that he'd surrendered himself to the insanity of this. At first it had looked like hesitant pacing until she realized he was moving deliberately, summoning from memory how the house had looked before Lawrence had left on what no one then knew would be his final expedition.

It comforted them both, she knew, this busyness, this focus. This constant movement.

But still, the part of her mind that repeated these thoughts seemed small and fragile. Like the chirping of a bird trying to be heard over steady rain. And the rain was grief and it was fear and a terrible sense that they were about to do the unthinkable, right here in the house where she'd grown up, this little palace of memories.

Pausing at the top of the stairs, she suddenly forgot what she'd intended to do next.

Julie whispered to herself, "If it is not him, then this won't destroy my memories of him. If it is not my father we raise, then it will be as if we haven't done this thing at all."

Before these words could stop their comfort, she descended the stairs, in search of the next small, but somehow monumental, task.

The shattered archangel had not been discovered, it seemed, for its fragments were resting right where Ramses had left them.

Osuron crouched down before the head and torso, studying the angel's stone face as if expecting it to react to his nearness. It did not. The immortal ran his fingers over the stone cheeks, along the jawline, down the chest. A mortal man, trying to process the tale he'd been told of this statue, might have shaken his head in this moment, breath whistling through his teeth. But Osuron studied it silently.

"Unchanged," he finally said, his voice a low rumble. "As you said, the stone is unchanged." Osuron stood. "The assassin. May I see his body?"

"Of course," Ramses said, then guided the man to the tomb with the broken door.

Inside, there was barely room enough for both of them to stand. Ramses removed the stone panels he'd loosened in the floor, where below lay a dirt pit that had perhaps once housed another grave before this tomb had been built atop it. The smell of a fresh death rose to meet them.

As soon as the body of the man was revealed—flat on his back, with something ghastly in the way they'd left his arms at his sides, not folded across his chest—Osuron sank to one knee and studied the corpse through the shadows.

For a while, they remained crouched down over the opening, the two of them, before Osuron reached down and gently touched the man's face with one powerful finger, as if to ensure he wasn't just dead, but also human, possessing ordinary mortal flesh.

"I know what you think now," Ramses said.

"Do you?"

"You think it might be better to raise this man than Lawrence Stratford."

"I am not thinking this, but you are, I see," Osuron said.

"It would not be better."

"I agree."

"His knowledge might be too limited to justify the terrible effort," Ramses said. "For all we know he didn't answer to the true architects of all this, has never spoken to them. That's why he needed a list of targets."

"Perhaps. Perhaps not."

"And we'd be giving great power to an enemy, an adversary. There'd be no good way to restrain him. If he were to throw us off and escape with knowledge of what we'd done, before we could destroy him . . ."

"Yes, Ramses. I know," Osuron said gently. "This is why I did not propose it."

"It's a terrible idea."

"It is. A dreadful one."

When Ramses looked up from the man's corpse, he saw Osuron staring at him. "And yet," the great man said, "if our effort with Lawrence Stratford fails, we may well have to resort to it."

"I know."

"Come," Osuron said, "it's another tomb that calls us now."

They returned the stone panels to the floor, and then the door to the tomb itself, and then they were moving silently through the shadows.

"I'm taken with your crew," Ramses said.

"How so?"

"That ones so old could be so submissive."

"In ones so ancient, submission is but a quiet veil before a cosmos of private thoughts. It's not submission so much as seclusion."

"I see," Ramses said, and it made perfect sense.

And a moment later, the word STRATFORD appeared between the shadowed branches ahead, as if the letters themselves were carved of shadow and not stone.

14

Ramses had left the vials with her, the glistening vials so full of terrible promise, and now Julie laid them on the windowsill.

She'd already filled the bedroom with flickering candles, brought the phonograph up from downstairs, and placed it on the bedside table. All in hopes that the warm and wavering light and the gentle music would conspire to soften the edges of what they were about to do.

Suddenly she realized Elliott was behind her. He'd said her name several times, but she'd only heard him just now.

"Would you like me to stay with you?" he asked when he turned.

"I would like us all here during it," she said.

"Of course, Julie. But as we wait, would you like to be alone?"

How to answer this? It seemed such a small question, suggesting such a small concern.

"I would like to know what gods immortals have, who judges us. Do we truly have no law but Bektaten's, and is it written in any formal way, or does she guide us now on ancient instincts alone? I would like to know what we are truly prepared to raise. I would like so many things in this moment that are beyond my grasp. And I cannot bring myself to saddle you with the terrible burden of obtaining them."

Elliott took her into his arms, tenderly kissed her forehead.

"Were I able to answer these questions, I would take these burdens gladly. But for now, I'm here for your comfort."

"It cannot be only that for you. You loved him. You loved him as much—"

"I know, Julie. But I cannot make that my focus in this moment. You are my focus, and in this I'll find a measure of sanity."

A temporary one, she thought, and was sure he thought this too, but hadn't voiced it.

"Meet them on the steps. Ensure this ghoulish transfer doesn't draw the attention of the neighbors. If we can do any part of this swiftly, make it that one."

"Of course," he whispered.

And then he was gone, and her thoughts such a powerful swirl she could not recall the moment of stepping free from his embrace.

Alone now amidst her father's things, in the bedroom where he'd once slept and dreamed. Alone and braced for what was to come. It comforted her, their agreement to leave Lawrence's coffin within its tomb; open, but empty, as if prepared to receive the terrible consequences of all this should it end in disaster. Should they be forced to seal away the wreckage of this effort, not just from a world that would not understand, but from themselves, its desperate architects.

She moved to the gramophone, and a moment later, the scratchy sound of a Chopin nocturne filled the room: op. 9, no. 2, her father's favorite.

She took one of the vials into her palm, as if it might speak to her, as if it might suddenly flush her gripping palm with warning heat. A message from some divine force known only to immortals, a force that might say, *Do not do this thing, Julie. Do not do this terrible thing.*

She realized then she'd returned to some measure of what she'd felt aboard the ship bound for London when she'd tried to take her life. A sense of rootlessness, a sense of old constructs shattered by all she'd seen and learned. She had never groped for religion during her mortal life, but perhaps she'd taken some of its precepts for granted, even as she refused to wear them on her sleeve. And none of those old teachings seemed capable of guiding her now.

No law but Bektaten's, Julie thought again. *Is that truly how we are to live for all time?* And in this instance, the queen's judgment had seemed almost detached. Vague, even. The responsibility placed squarely in Julie's hands. But the need, the terrible need for information, the terrible need to chart some course to the source of the impossible power that had been used against them, this need was greater than all other fears.

She heard first the low chug of the motorcar's engine and managed, for a fleeting instant, to convince herself it was the music of some ordinary arrival. Perhaps a neighbor. But she could hear no voices or relaxed talk after its doors closed softly.

And when she heard the front door of the house creak on its hinges, it felt then as if her immortal heart had stopped altogether, and she heard a sharp little sound which she realized was the breath she'd been holding leaving her in a little gasp.

And it was then that a voice, a comforting voice that sounded as if it could be her father's, said, *He will be able to accept the momentousness of this. He was prepared to accept the miraculous things he discovered inside of Ramses's tomb, and so he will be able to accept this.*

It had to be true, she told herself. Yes, she knew this was a rushed and frantic attempt to comfort herself in these final agonizing moments of waiting. But it was true.

Her father had devoted his life to ancient wisdom, ancient magic. Throughout everything he'd done had been the same constant driving force. His belief that Egypt had discovered great universal truths, themselves more significant than each and every technological invention of the modern age. He had grave misgivings about the bullish manner in which the empires of Europe asserted themselves as the center of the globe without fully incorporating the spiritual discoveries of the ancient world.

Yes, he was a man who could bring himself to believe in the impossible, she was sure of it, even if the impossible included his own resurrection. So long as Egypt gave birth to it. If the being they were about to raise was truly him, there would be some measure of this within him, and it would guide him and aid him in ways perhaps she and Ramses and Elliott and even Osuron could not.

Then she heard the footsteps on the stairs, and these thoughts withered.

They were careful footsteps. Slow. The footsteps of a strong being carrying something of great consequence in its arms. And the fear was such in that moment she wanted to cry out for them to go faster, but what they carried was fragile bones. Some measure of flesh, for sure, but mostly bones within a body that had gone rigid in death. And so she had no choice but to let them move at the pace which they had decided was the most sacred and the most safe.

Then there was silence, and she realized they had reached the top of the stairs and were waiting now outside the bedroom door.

You must turn, she said, *you must turn now and face this thing you are about to do.*

And it was Elliott she saw first. Elliott who held her gaze with deliberate intensity as he stepped first into the room, holding the door open behind him, the candlelight abstracting emotion in his expression.

And then she saw Ramses.

The weight of what he carried in both arms might have brought a mortal man to his knees. They had wrapped the blanket they'd taken from this very room around her father's corpse like a shroud; a mummy's wrappings, but of French satin. And in his powerful arms, Ramses had carried the rigid corpse up the stairs as if it were a dancing partner. She saw now why it had taken him so much time. It seemed he'd refused help from the other men, for that would have meant carrying her father upstairs by both ends of his body as if he were a wooden plank. And that, it seemed, wouldn't do. Instead, Ramses embraced her father's body. It would be a living thing once more soon, his embrace said, and so even now it required tenderness.

The smell hit her, the smell of death. Her senses went mad with it, and she thought suddenly that all those who have lost someone dear should smell this terrible stench if only for an instant, for it would speed their grieving along its painful course. For it said without equivocation that your loved one had departed, had been replaced by the terrible assault upon the senses that was deeply and profoundly not them. A smell that did not bear any connection to that they'd given off in life.

But was this true? Was there something fundamentally unique to the stench of decay given off by each and every corpse? A smell, perhaps, that their flesh had concealed in life and released only in death? Or was this the earth itself she smelled now, the earth and all the terrible and inevitable work it did on all who vainly walked above it for but a short time.

Gently, Ramses lowered the shrouded corpse to the bed. The heavy blanket was wrapped around it in such a way that it would not come loose if Ramses carried the corpse close to his breast. But now, it had parted ever so slightly, and when Ramses withdrew from the side of the bed, they could all see Lawrence's hands, clasped against a patch of chest.

Pale and somewhat drawn, but not yet fully withered.

He was next to her now, Ramses. Next to her and smelling of her father's death, but perhaps she was mistaken in this, and the smell had so filled the room it seemed to be upon everything now. And she welcomed it, suddenly. Welcomed it because she knew it would propel her past her hesitation and her doubts, for if they could not chase the stench of death from the room, they could chase death itself from the room.

"Julie," he whispered. She was staring at the vial of elixir in her hand.

"We must do it now. We mustn't wait."

"Yes," he said softly, "but to avoid the mistakes of the past, we must apply as much of the elixir as we can all at once. And so we all do it, Julie. Not just you. All four of us at once to different parts of the body."

"Yes, yes, of course." But it was someone else saying these words, someone else giving this answer. Someone else was with these impossible beings who had the strength of gods, and their power to create life.

Ramses moved to the windowsill and collected the remainder of the six vials. He passed one to Elliott and then two to Osuron, before keeping two for himself. There was a chance that Julie's and Elliott's emotions might cause them to lose their grip as they poured, and so it was best to give the bulk of the elixir's volume to steadier hands. Slowly, they all approached the bed; she and Ramses on one side, Elliott and Osuron on the other. Save for the glimpse of her father's hands, the blanket still covered him. And once Ramses had given gentle instructions on who should target which area of the body with their vials, she realized no one had decided who was to remove her father's shroud.

It was her, of course. Who else?

But was it necessary. Must they reveal him in his current form to complete this?

Yes. If every drop of elixir was required for a complete and swift resurrection, they could not allow any of the blanket to soak it up before it touched his remains.

"Julie," Ramses said softly, "would you like me to—"

Before he could finish, she took one edge of the blanket and carefully drew it to one side. Then, without looking at anything she'd just revealed, she did the same to the other, careful to step back from the bed before she beheld what she'd just exposed.

Of course her eyes went to the tiny details first, the seemingly inconsequential ones. The tattered sleeves of the rotting khaki coat, the holes in his linen shirt, the same spoiled-milk color of the mottled skin underneath. Buried in the clothes he'd died in, buried in whatever he'd been working in when Henry poisoned him. It had seemed too ghoulish to have his corpse re-dressed when she'd had his remains collected from their hasty grave in Egypt and brought back to England. The simple wooden coffin had been replaced with something gleaming and grand. But not his clothes. Because never, not once, did she believe she'd lay eyes upon him again in this way.

And then, at last, with the sound of her own deep breaths filling the room, and the watchful eyes of the men close to her like a collective weight upon her limbs, she summoned all her courage and looked to his face. The sound of Chopin in that instant became like a ghostly transmission from another world, where the thing they were about to do, the thing they had already done—removing a corpse from a coffin—was just fantasy.

Sunken eyes; a mouth so lax in death it looked like a grimace. Desiccated lips that had once kissed her; silver hair retreating from the forehead she'd often gently kissed, making the forehead appear unnaturally swollen when really it was just unnaturally exposed.

Not him, she thought as she beheld this creature of death. *Not him. Like the stench he brings with him, this figure is not my father, and I doubt now there is any power on earth that can truly reclaim what death steals.*

And as if in response to these tragic assumptions, her voice emerged strong and resolute. "Now," she said. "We raise him now."

And at this command—for what else could she call it?—each of them uncapped the vials they held and positioned them over the areas of the body Ramses had assigned to them the moment before. Ramses held one clutching fist in the air above Lawrence's head and the other above the man's collapsed throat; Julie, above her father's chest; Elliott, over his waist; and Osuron, standing at the very foot of the bed, was prepared to anoint both of Lawrence's legs.

"Now," Julie whispered.

They all poured at once, tracing the areas of the body.

First came the sound, a sound like oil cooking on a pan. She knew this was the elixir working upon flesh, lifeless flesh. It bubbled and spread, as if it had life itself now, this impossible substance. And then she saw Ramses had set his vials aside. He reached down and smoothed the elixir across the dead limbs with both hands.

He did it this way with Cleopatra, she realized, *and I'd thought it an abomination then. And now we do the same to my father.*

She thought then the candlelight might be deceiving her. She cursed herself for filling this room with it. But her vision was sharp; there was no mistaking what she saw. The once-mottled flesh was regaining a pale luster where it was visible through the tattered linen shirt. The hands that had been clasped against his chest a second before had parted, and the flesh on each finger was filling in. But their pose was still clawlike, as if they were trying to clasp again but some invisible, repulsive force was keeping them apart. They trembled, his hands. Was it the bones in his wrist doing this as they regained thickness? Or was it the veins themselves as they filled?

Or are the hands trying to hold to death itself, and this force, this force we've unleashed, won't allow it?

So fascinated was she by the quiet spectacle of his hands, she'd missed the more momentous development. Ramses now held the back of her father's neck and was feeding the rest of the vial into his lips. At first, she thought it was Ramses who was lifting her father's head off the pillow, for again she'd been distracted. This time by the sight of his silver hair thickening, filling in, sprouting from the once-exposed sweep of his forehead, shimmering in the candlelight. Its original color, but somehow shining with newness, the luster of new life driven through the cracked prism of a life arrested. But it was not Ramses who was raising her father's head. It was her father himself. His lips suckled at the vial Ramses held, nursing from this monumental accident of nature, as their queen had called it.

And these lips were full now; the hollows in his cheeks were gone.

And when his eyes opened, they were the bright blue of an immortal's and full of shining tears.

Of course, he is like an infant in the moment, she thought. *For what is he if not reborn?*

The moans, she realized, had been escaping him for some time, covered up by the lilting piano coming from the gramophone beside the bed.

And then he saw her.

She told herself not to speak, told herself he was too new to this. But she failed.

"Father," she whispered.

No name for the sound that came from him. A howl perhaps, or something closer to the great sound of anguish he'd made when she'd been younger and had wandered too close to the edge of a train station platform while reading a newspaper folded in one hand. A cry of terror but also of deep, visceral pain.

He was scrambling to sit up suddenly, and his actions drove them all back. But it was also Ramses who drove them back, with one arm thrown out in a gesture for all of them to retreat, to give space to whatever wildness this awakening required.

Tears slipped from her father's eyes now, from eyes dry and rotting only seconds before. And it was the sight of her that had done it. That and her single desperate whisper, a whisper that had said, *Come to me. Be with me. Be what you were. Again.*

She wanted to believe it was just the awareness he was suffering, the great awareness of his decay that Cleopatra had described. But he'd healed much more quickly. It seemed they were now past the moment when he'd been tormented by the sense of not being whole.

Ramses was retreating behind her now and gently pushing her forward. It was then that she remembered Ramses was entirely unfamiliar to her father, and the sight of him bedside would be a shock. Her father had never seen what had been under the mummy's wrappings, much less laid eyes upon the king restored.

But as Julie stepped forward, her father recoiled, and she wanted to recoil suddenly too, for it was the very thing Ramses thought her father needed, the familiarity of her, that seemed to be driving her father mad.

"Father, it's me," she whispered.

"Take his hands, Julie," Ramses said.

"He doesn't want—"

"Take his hand."

As she summoned the strength for this, Elliott stepped forward, seizing Lawrence's other hand with swift, precise force. Her father jerked, looked to Elliott with the same wide-eyed terror with which he had just regarded her.

"My dear Lawrence," he said, controlling the tremor in his voice, "you've always been about the journey, haven't you? Well, we can assure you, this is your most momentous one yet."

Bless you, Elliott, she thought. *Bless you and the strength you bring to this.*

She took her father's hand, gripped it with a strength she

hoped matched Elliott's. And now, his frenzied attention divided between them, her father's terror seemed to be softening, turning into something else. But it was nothing she wanted to see. It was not the joy of a reunion. It was terror becoming something closer to despair. His lips were trying to form words, but instead all that came from his mouth was a sibilant *s*, which repeated itself again and again, making a sound like a serpent's hiss. Was it his tongue that was not yet fully restored, or his mind?

And the tears. The flood of tears from his shining blue eyes streaming down his restored face, that was the worst of it in this moment.

"Father, you have suffered something terrible. But you are restored. You've been brought back to London from Egypt. You are in your bedroom, in your home. Your true home. This is real, Father. What you see before you, it is real. Your confusion, it is real. Your pain is real. But we are here to guide you and comfort you and protect you. Any question you have, ask it, and we shall answer it."

The words came from her more easily because he'd begun to return her grip, and it seemed he was able to follow her words, absorb them. Or perhaps it was just the sound of them that captured his attention. Perhaps to him they were just notes like those coming from the gramophone. For there was still great confusion in his gaze.

"Something . . ."

The entire room went still at this, the first spoken word of Lawrence Stratford's new life.

"Yes, Father."

He looked from her to Elliott and back again, and the expression had changed, no doubt, but it wasn't full of the recognition she craved. Rather, the tenor of its despair had shifted. And in a familiar way. He looked poised to make an admission he found shameful.

"Something in the dark," he whispered.

She thought perhaps he was referring to Ramses and Osuron, who'd both retreated into the shadows. But he did not look in their direction. Instead, he looked desperately from Julie to Elliott again, and Julie thought perhaps he did recognize them both, but her father felt this recognition would be meaningless to him unless those gathered around his bed could comprehend the meaning of what he'd just whispered.

Julie was about to attempt just that when Lawrence let out another terrible howl, reared up off the bed, and clawed his way past Elliott to the bedroom door, the shock of his new strength reminding Julie of all they'd just granted her father aside from resurrection.

A great thunder, their footfalls, as they all descended the stairs in pursuit of him. He did not run for the front door, but Osuron's awaiting crew member had braced himself across it just in case. Instead, her father careened into the double parlor, grabbing at every surface he passed. For balance or to assure himself of their solidity, she couldn't tell. And when he found himself in his old library, he spun in place, jaw agape and eyes wide, hands up and trembling as if he thought he could hold back the great flow of images assaulting him.

He doesn't believe it's real, Julie realized. *He believes this is the illusion.*

And so it was partly as Cleopatra said; he was scrambling to reconcile the dark in which he'd dwelled with the bright shocks of this new reality, and it was causing him a profound torment.

It was worse than just darkness, she realized. *There was something in it with him, something he can't shake himself free of now.*

"Father, this is real," she said, advancing on him. Elliott was close to her.

Her father stood behind the upholstered chair in which he'd spent so many hours reading. When he touched its back almost tenderly, she thought it a good sign.

"Father, you must eat and drink. This will help you."

But he was shaking his head slowly, as if no words of hers could help him in this moment. Had there been something too artificial in the way they'd reassembled the room? Or was her father struggling to see it through veils of darkness that clung to him like the tattered remains of the clothes in which he'd been buried?

We must get him out of his clothes, and we must wash him. These things will help him, I'm sure. But she thought herself mad for thinking them. They seemed as petty as the candles and the gramophone. And what peace had these objects brought? None. *Perhaps,* she reasoned, *this would have been even worse without them.*

He went still. It was the sight of the conservatory that did it. Had he noticed the unnatural growth and vividness of the plants within? They were the same ones as when he'd left, but they had been altered just as he had been altered. Was this what held his attention?

Before she realized what had happened, the glass wall of the conservatory had shattered. He'd thrown the chair he'd been holding on to a second earlier, thrown it with an immortal's strength and force, and now the brilliantly colored shards of glass that had filtered the sunlight on so many peaceful afternoons were tumbling into the leaves and pots below, leaving a great yawning mouth that stared into the terrible barrenness of the alley beyond.

"Father, no!" she cried too late.

Despite his new strength, this effort seemed to exhaust him. He had struck out against what he believed to be illusion and heard it explode with substance, solidity, weight. He fell to his knees. Was it from exhaustion or from the realization that glass could shatter here in this realm of the physical; she didn't know. But he had come to some acceptance, some acceptance that this was a different realm than the one from which he'd been pulled by the elixir's power.

And in that realm there had been something with him, she thought, *something in the dark.*

How else to interpret these words?

She hit the floor beside him, took him firmly in her arms.

Let him try to throw her off! Let him try to use his new strength against her. He'd learn instantly that her strength matched his, and by God, she would use every ounce of it to drive his spirit back into his mind the way she'd returned it to his body.

But he wasn't fighting her; he was weeping in her embrace.

Finally, her father lifted his gaze to hers, and without throwing her off, he brought one hand to her face, cupped her cheek gently. With a great surge of relief, she thought this would be the moment recognition broke. But he touched her face as if the substance of her skin was foreign to him, and while there was a desperate, pleading look in his eyes, it said he was still in search of an answer to the questions plaguing him now.

"It's Julie, Father."

He touched her hair now, as if afraid to run his fingers through it, but somehow astonished that the great tangle of brown curls was attached to her head.

"I'm here too, old chum." On one knee next to them, Elliott managed a solicitous smile. But her father's eyes darkened at the sight of him, mustered none of even the limited recognition with which he'd just gazed into her eyes. Upstairs, he'd looked to both of them with mutual terror. But the terror was gone now, and the look he gave Elliott radiated only one thing—a total absence.

Dear God, she realized, *he doesn't remember Elliott.*

She saw the pain of this break across Elliott's face, but he concealed it quickly, and for a while no one spoke.

"Food and drink, then," Elliott said quickly, rising to his feet. "Food and drink."

She wished she could reach out to Elliott in this moment,

and explain to him the recognition she'd just received from her father was limited, and that perhaps his memories of Elliott would return slowly. But they knew full well what Cleopatra's experience had taught them—yawning gaps developed in the memories of the resurrected, and the process required to heal them was laborious and baffling.

Her father was looking into her eyes again, as if he thought she might explain the strange presence of the man who'd just left them. And perhaps she would, and that would be enough. But he was now quiet and still for the first time since they'd raised him, and she would do nothing to disrupt this moment with a single word.

He said little as she washed him. As inappropriate as it seemed, a daughter bathing her own father, who else could she entrust the task to? He still regarded the others with silent suspicion.

And besides, would there not have been moments just like this had he aged and become infirm under her care? Was his infantile dependency on her now not in and of itself a kind of restoration of the mortal life he'd lost?

"I have many of your journals," she said. "We shall have you read them."

Better to do it this way, she thought. *Better to let him connect with the enormity of it gradually, by way of his own words.* She was hopeful just the sight of his own penmanship would further awaken his mind. Bring back the memories more vividly. Elevate him above this monosyllabic numbness that gave no real indication of whether or not he was capable of complex thought. Perhaps his thoughts were ragingly complex, and it was just his speech that was stunted and simple.

She brought him undergarments and one of his old paisley robes she'd not been able to throw away. She turned her back as he stepped from the tub. The time it was taking him to dry himself caused her to look back over one shoulder, and she saw he was doing so with a dazed fascination over his own body. As if each pat of the towel against his damp skin was another reminder that he was once more a solid thing.

He didn't protest as she curved an arm around his waist and guided him down the stairs. His newly restored hair glistened and shined in the electric lights she'd turned on in the library, and she sat with him at the oval table as he read his writings on the miraculous discovery that had changed all of their lives. The writings she'd deemed too personal and too revelatory to donate to the museum. Something about the way in which he read, the way the robe slid loosely off his form, reminded her of the time he'd had a terrible bout of influenza when she was a girl.

But he read intently, his eyes moving smoothly across the page.

And from the front parlor, Elliott, Ramses, and Osuron watched, as if each was ready to be called into action at any moment. As if each man hoped for this and thought it preferable to this terrible waiting. For if Lawrence recalled none of what his writings described, what chance was there he'd recall anything of what might connect him to the Eye of Osiris?

He appeared quietly stunned now, his mad confusion gone.

It was Ramses he'd centered in his gaze. Lawrence raised his hands to his chest, pointed to his own ring finger, then pointed to Ramses. In response, Ramses stepped forward, raising his hand and studying the scarab ring he now wore. And that's when Julie realized her father recognized the ring from inside the tomb. Now it was worn by a proud Egyptian man who stood only paces away, whose very presence confirmed the tale he'd just read.

Julie braced for more horror, for another mad flight from the room. But as Ramses approached Lawrence as cautiously as he might a tiger, Lawrence slipped from the chair and fell to his knees, his eyes filling with tears. And Julie realized connections of all sorts were being made within her father's mind. The tale told by the scrolls was real, he realized. And it suggested an incredible power, a power that had been used to bring him back from death. A power embodied by the former king, who stood above him now, extending one hand in gentle greeting.

Forever she would be grateful for the warmth in Ramses's smile in this moment, for the grace with which he received her father's thunderstruck, childlike awe.

And her father, he kissed Ramses's hand. Her father, who might have bristled at the idea of bowing before the British sovereign, kissed the scarab ring on Ramses's finger.

It has happened, she thought, *no matter what awaits us next, my father has been granted the moment I thought would always be denied him, the moment of standing before a king reborn.*

But Elliott must have been feeling envy. To see Lawrence all but incapacitated by joy before Ramses when he could not recognize Elliott at all. But bravely, he did not turn from the sight.

"Sit, my friend," Ramses said softly. "My new friend, Lawrence Stratford." Lawrence allowed Ramses to guide him back into his chair. "I have you to thank for great adventure and new loves."

Her father didn't speak as Ramses guided him back into his chair, but he didn't take his eyes off Ramses either. And now it was Julie's turn for envy, for there was something more wondrous in his expression than when he'd struggled to say her name and caress her brown curls. Something less tortured and confused. Was his recognition of Ramses more joyous and pure because it was not a memory that had been dragged through death itself?

When Ramses withdrew, Lawrence reached out for him with both arms, like a child wanting to be held. Then, the farther away Ramses grew from him, the more his joy seemed to fade. He lowered his arms, a lost and confused look returning to his eyes. Were all things this temporary in his consciousness? Did it only take Ramses backing away by a few feet for the wonder of this new realization to fade?

He looked at her again, and for an awful moment she thought he'd forgotten who she was.

So she spoke. Gently but forcefully, confident that what he'd read in his journals formed a foundation atop which he could receive the more elaborate portions of the tale. She told him everything from his discovery of Ramses's tomb, to Ramses's awakening in this very room, to their trip to Egypt and the awakening of Cleopatra, and then, the eventual discovery of Bektaten. In fear of confusing him, she omitted the details of Bektaten's ancient battle with Saqnos, and described Shaktanu in only the most passing of terms. What mattered was that it was the elixir's birthplace, its source, and what mattered most was that he gain an understanding of the elixir and its path through history. To him.

If his mind could seize upon this thread, she hoped, he could understand all of it.

He asked no questions, so occasionally she paused, asked him if he could understand, if he needed her to speak more slowly. And she was heartened when he shook his head and raised his hand and twirled his fingers in a gesture for her to continue. A familiar gesture, one he'd made countless times while mortal. Even if he made it more slowly now, and with evident strain. Still, its appearance here encouraged her.

When she arrived at the events of the past few nights, there was no visible change in him, no reaction to her description of stones with the power to move statues.

All those who loved Lawrence Stratford must die.

Not a flinch or a tremor from him as he heard his own name used in this awful way. He'd listened to the whole story in almost-total stillness.

But there was something there, some vague dawning recognition.

He clasped his hands together, and for a terrible moment, she thought perhaps he hadn't heard a word of it. Hadn't absorbed a single line of this incredible, sprawling narrative.

"Father," she asked quietly, "can you think of anything that might connect you to these Russian men?"

As the silence stretched on, she threw a desperate look at Ramses, who'd watched this all from under the archway to the front parlor, as if fighting an urge to interject, but desperate for Julie to have this moment of connection with her father.

The silence continued, grew unbearable, silence except for the papery sound of her father rubbing his hands together. He could either be lost in some struggle to remember, or he could have simply become dazzled by the newness of his own hands. She had no way of knowing. Because there was so much about the man before her that seemed foreign.

Not him, she thought before she could fight the words back. *There is so much before me now that is not him.*

Then he drew a long, slow breath, the gentle sound of which seemed to fill the front parlors.

"A Russian," he whispered.

As if he himself was amazed he'd summoned this response, her father searched their faces for proof he'd said it. And then haltingly, and in a tone that sounded vacant and detached, like a voice in search of a soul, the resurrected form of Lawrence Stratford began to speak, and it said a name, a name Julie had never heard before.

"Dimitri," her father whispered, "Dimitri Vasilev."

15

Lake Ladoga, Russia

On nights like this, when the sky was cloudless and the lake surrounding his palace a mirror for the stars, Dimitri Vasilev could sit for hours upon the cast-iron bench he'd placed right next to the water's edge, listening to the divine whisper of the occasional wind moving through the towering pines, of the gentle kiss of water against the shore at his feet.

This was his island on Lake Ladoga, an island on which he'd built his tribute to the true uncorrupted spirit of his nation, a palace that combined re-creations of Kremlin rooms with details of the multidomed cathedrals that had risen in Muscovy after the terrors wrought by the Mongols. The white stone walls had small windows framed by twisting Solomonic columns, and the roofline overhead was lined with gleaming onion domes in gold and purple. His palace, he had ensured, would be utterly divorced from the grotesque cakelike confections built by his ancestors, crass tributes to Versailles, gleaming intrusions into a land whose true architecture melded the dazzling complexity of the Byzantine with the rounded expanses of the Romanesque into something that was far from European, that was truly and indisputably Russian.

And in danger now of being forever lost.

Because of this, his builders had been shocked when he'd

asked them to transport the reproduction of Étienne Maurice Falconet's *The Bronze Horseman* his grandfather had commissioned to these grounds. But once they saw the statue's new home, they must have realized Peter the Great and his proud horse were prisoners of this island, not its conquerors. The tsar who'd thrown open the doors to the West was now hemmed in by flat white walls styled after the Orthodox monasteries an hour's boat ride away. By day, he was shadowed by the onion domes lining the rooftops overhead. He enjoyed a view of the placid lake, of course, but a narrow one; as if it would be his only escape should the walls that seemed to press in on all sides decide to finally crush him to dust.

Perhaps the builders didn't understand these things at all.

The Vasilev name, the Vasilev fortune, had begun with this long-dead tsar; this was common knowledge. Some rendering of Peter was planted upon each of their family's estates.

But this particular statue, a faithful reproduction of the one that currently stood outside the Hermitage in Saint Petersburg, Dimitri had uprooted from outside a museum his family had founded generations before, an outpost of learning and treasures in vast Siberia's heart. No doubt its absence had left a scar, perhaps inspired talk throughout the city. But places as remote as Tomsk enjoyed as strong a connection to the history of the tsars as they did to the dithering of Saint Petersburg society. And so it was entirely possible its citizens mourned only the departure of the shade the statue had afforded those who passed through the museum square.

So many Europeans saw fit to lecture him on the subject of Russia's size. How it rendered the great country unknowable, as if the enormous expanse of his homeland was somehow unknown to him, Dimitri Vasilev, as well. If they were men of consequence, he lectured them in return—it was not Russia's size that had rendered its towns and cities so scattered, so disconnected, but the muddying of the rivers of belief meant to flow from one to the other. It was not distance that rendered Saint Petersburg and Moscow so wholly separate from the country's vast interior. It was that these cities were being consumed by a preening coterie of European nations who shared one thing in common, aside from their ignorance of Russia's true nature. They believed the will of kings—the will of God—should be subjected to the will of the people. Even though they had no good and true vessel for channeling the wishes of the mob.

It was you who did this. Dimitri had turned to face the statue's shadow. *It was you who opened these doors to the West, laid us bare to these invaders. You, who were arrogant enough to believe you could take only what you desired from Europe. You sacrificed the only thing that could hold us together. And that was God.*

His great-grandfathers, and all the Vasilevs who came before, would deride him as ungrateful for thinking these things, of course.

For wasn't it Peter who'd given them everything? Centuries before, he'd elevated Nikolai Vasilev, for whom Dimitri's own son was now named, without regard for rank, of which the first Nikolai had none, and solely because he'd stumbled across the man's blacksmith shop and his marvelous work within.

Taken with his vitality and his skills, Peter soon after placed the first Nikolai in charge of a failing foundry in Siberia's heart, allowing him to use the wealth he generated there to purchase the deeds to newly discovered mines throughout the Ural Mountains. Mines from which Nikolai, and the Vasilevs who followed, produced not only the weapons needed for Russia's wars but the malachite and silver and other precious stones which came to adorn the palaces of Europe.

Not just Europe, Dimitri remembered, *they adorned our palaces too. They brought the European infections into the glittering halls of Saint Petersburg and Moscow and as far south as the*

Crimea. We, the great Vasilevs, with our wealth and our palaces and our transcendence of rank, were the agents of Europe's stain, disguised as ornament.

Only slowly did his family realize that they had abetted this infection. And it had fallen to Dimitri to be the rightful executor of the consequences.

And now, it was Dimitri's responsibility to put a stop to it before it ended in calamity.

Russia's decay was evident. Their tsar was now a weakened puppet, strong-armed into war alongside the very nations that had diluted his power and the powers of all kings. Nicholas II spent his days henpecked by a spineless, neurotic wife who was herself in thrall to a deranged peasant who thought himself a mystic. A great darkness had been spreading within the royal corridors at Tsarskoe Selo. Everyone knew this. Many thought it lay within the strange spell this Rasputin had cast over the royal family. But Dimitri knew Rasputin was but a symptom of a larger illness.

The Duma. A parliament. An invention of the British that had wormed its way into their politics, its godless supporters emboldened by Russia's humiliating defeat by the Japanese. An insane invention that said the myriad voices of a chaotic and confused people were somehow better at interpreting the will of God than a single tsar. It was sheer madness, this idea; as if God spoke more clearly to hundreds than to one. A weakening of the country that could not be abided by anyone who truly knew its fierce, independent spirit.

Footsteps now, soft but audible above the gusts of wind that moved through the surrounding trees. Sergei, his brother, whose quiet humility soothed his soul. He'd allowed his beard to grow since his arrival here days before, and his long hair draped his angular face; a face that bore the jutting jaw and widely spaced eyes and patrician nose that defined so many of their ancestors' portraits. Portraits that did not hang anywhere on this island, for what Dimitri and his close relatives had undertaken required a break from the delusions of the past.

If your fathers and grandfathers and great-grandfathers could see you now, some might have railed against them. *If they knew what you planned to do.* And to these accusations, Dimitri would have countered, *If they were alive now, if they could see what Russia has become, a country where revolutionaries assassinate tsars even on the eve of being granted more rights, our fathers and grandfathers would join us. They might have acted before now.*

"Nikolai has called," his brother said. "There is no word from our men in Britain."

And for a while, neither man spoke, pondering the implications of this. And this was the thing Dimitri loved most about his brother, that the man allowed him to ponder. He wished he could say as much of his only son. The price of young Nikolai's competence was a constant, bullish demand for quick answers at the precise moment Dimitri required reflection.

"The hunt continues then," Dimitri said. "It was, after all, an extensive list."

"It was," Sergei offered. "It is."

"But no word at all," Dimitri said.

"They've learned things, I'm sure," Dimitri said, "but they're afraid to share them over the wires."

But these words felt hollow; his own voice sounded weak.

Sergei simply nodded.

"And the wires themselves," Sergei offered, "across Europe, they've been cut, destroyed by battle. Perhaps the disruption . . ."

"Yes, Brother," Dimitri said, but he wanted to withdraw now. Before their comforting talk could veer too close to the frightening truth. "I visit Anya now."

When Sergei reached out through the shadows and gripped his arm, Dimitri was surprised.

"Brother, he is on his way now."

"My son?" Dimitri asked, loathing himself for the dread he felt when he spoke these two words.

"And he is angry as before," Sergei said. "He believes if we delay further, then—"

"I'm aware of what he believes."

It was a risk, sending Nikolai's best men in pursuit of so broad a target. And with them, fragments of the Eye. And if the risk did not yield rewards, no doubt his son would hold it against him. But what force on earth could be more powerful than the Eye and those well trained in how to use it? There was none.

But how can you be so sure of this? said a voice in his head that sounded so much like his son's. *How do you know what else the world might hold, when you didn't know something as extraordinary as the Eye could exist until fate blessed your path with it?*

But this was foolishness. His assassins sought the intimates of an ordinary man. Ordinary people, who might be in possession of extraordinary knowledge. Which is why they had to be wiped out before the secret Dimitri sheltered on this island could be unleashed upon the world.

"Go to Anya," Sergei said. "She always soothes you. If Nikolai arrives while you're with her, I'll see to him until morning."

Dimitri brought his brother close to him, kissed him on the forehead.

Sergei understood him. Sergei understood their destiny. He thanked God for his brother. And always would, no matter what was to come.

16

London

"He was mad," Lawrence said again.

Several times he'd said these same words as he attempted to tell the tale. Julie couldn't tell if the details of his memories overwhelmed him, or if he was struggling to call them forth. But these words, this whispered assertion of Dimitri Vasilev's madness, were like a refrain, a chant that gave his mind its only focus.

Dimitri Vasilev. When Lawrence had first said this name, Osuron had clearly recognized it, straightening and stepping away from the wall in a way that drew the attention of everyone present. Even Lawrence, who'd looked up at the giant man's reaction as if it was a sign he'd provided the correct answer to a mathematical equation he'd been struggling through.

"This is a famous name in Russia," Osuron had quickly explained. "A mining family with an immense fortune that dates back to Peter the Great."

Of course he knew this, Julie realized. Osuron, whom Bektaten had introduced as Osuron of the Baltic, the Herald of the Realms whose network of spies covered Russia and its adjacent nations. She'd assumed the queen had enlisted his aid only because of his steamship and his proximity to Cleopatra, Alex, and Sibyl. But now he might aid them in tracking down the architects of this plot.

"Yes," Lawrence had said at this, nodding. "Yes, Dimitri Vasilev . . . Mad."

The details he provided next were scattered, out of sequence. As if his nearness to death had destroyed his concept of linear time.

And for Julie, the challenge was in trying to focus on the emerging facts and details even while her mind put the same question to every gesture, word, and change in tone that came from the man across from her—is this my father speaking now? There were moments when great confusion seemed to overtake him, and the room strained to let the silence pass. And then, more distressingly, moments in which he referred to himself in the third person, as if he were narrating a tale he was watching now for the first time and through smoke-darkened glass.

From what she'd been able to piece together, Lawrence's memories of this man Vasilev came from an expedition that had taken place the year before. She had not been with him and remembered it as having been a disappointment for him. Indeed, she was recalling more details of it than Lawrence seemed able to now.

The British Museum had failed to provide the promised amount of supplies, and so Samir had been forced to make various runs back to Cairo while her father had worked tirelessly and alone at what he'd been sure was a temple platform, but which, after days of excavation, had turned out to be a natural bed of rock. He'd returned home exhausted and defeated and furious with the museum for their broken promises. And with absolutely no mention of this man Vasilev. Either their meeting had seemed insignificant at the time, or it was defined by a great secret.

"Cars," Lawrence said, "he came with so many . . . cars, so many tents. I thought at first he might be the khedive. Or one of his men . . . So regal, so royal, everything he brought."

"I know the name as well," Elliott said gently. "The family's fortunes are vast."

Lawrence nodded. "And he brought this wealth to the desert, and it looked . . . It looked so out of place . . . but he was tired and so all the shining motorcars and rolled-up tents looked wonderful to him."

To him, Julie thought. *To you, Father. You mean to you, don't you? Looked wonderful to you . . .*

"He was on an expedition, like you were?" Julie asked.

"Yes," Lawrence said. "But it was mad."

"How was it mad, Father?"

His eyes shot to hers, and there was vague alarm in them. Was it that she'd referred to him as her father, or was he struggling to remember?

"Father, did he have a stone with him? A stone on a necklace? Perhaps more than one."

"A stone . . ."

"Something he might have called the Eye of Osiris," she added.

And then he went very still. The furrow left his brow.

"The Eye of Osiris," he whispered, nodding.

"He had it with him?" Julie asked.

Lawrence shook his head to correct her, raised a finger into the air as if preparing to speak. There it was again, an old gesture of his, a familiar gesture. But he had to swallow several times and gaze at the floor to summon these vestiges of his mortal behavior. "He did not have it. He had a stela that *told* of it."

A ripple of excitement went through the room. When she looked to Ramses, she saw in his alert expression that they'd just obtained what they needed most; not only a name, but something concrete that connected the weapon their assassins had carried to this name, this Dimitri Vasilev. If they dared describe anything bubbling up from her father's reassembling mind as concrete.

Was it truly enough? Could they cease this difficult interview of her father before long?

At first, this thought came as a relief. Then she realized it would leave them with the far-greater challenge of confronting the true essence of what they'd brought back. Who would care for him, and who would travel on to investigate this Dimitri Vasilev? These were questions they'd yet to tackle, so consumed had they been by the enormity of resurrecting him.

But when she saw Ramses, Elliott, and Osuron staring back at her, she realized they wanted to know more, had to know more. As much as Lawrence could share.

"A stela, you said," Julie continued. "From a temple."

"He'd found only the stela," Lawrence said. "But he was searching for many other things. And he was wrong."

"Wrong about what, Father?"

"The story it told," Lawrence said, "the story on the stela, he'd misinterpreted all of it."

"Dimitri Vasilev?"

"Yes. His translation, it was wrong. What he saw, he saw backwards, and when I corrected him, I saw rage in his eyes."

17

Lake Ladoga, Russia

Inside the palace, Dimitri took his time moving through the warren of rooms, none of which possessed the high ceilings and grotesque climbing gilt that now defined grandeur throughout the world. The great hall was designed after the Palace of Facets at the Kremlin itself, its wide and soaring arches creating a womb-like space close to the floor that soared into high, pointed ceilings overhead. He'd decorated these ceilings with frescoes of the Muscovite victories that had first unified Russia; the walls below were deep red and topped with regal lions in gold leaf.

In the corridors beyond, swaths of deep red Oriental rugs stretched between fat, rounded columns decorated in red-and-white tilework. And on all sides of him, deeply recessed stained-glass windows of mica. By day, they admitted a light so dim as to require candles. These were walls that looked as if God had commanded them to grow from the earth itself. And everywhere the furniture was dark, hardwood. No blinding cascades of furious color. This was the austerity of the Slav, the beauty of the true Russia. A design that dismissed spring and summer as deceptive distractions, that acknowledged cruel inevitable winters as the true architects of the people who belonged on this soil.

Beyond the lockless door to Anya's bedroom, he found his greatest treasure sitting at her dresser table, running a silver-plated brush he'd given her through her long, ink-black hair.

Anya. His beautiful Anya.

Skin darkened from a touch of Mongol blood, dark eyes sultry even when widened by fear. The delicateness of her slender frame belied by long fingers strengthened by the years of labor from which he'd saved her. When she saw him, her eyes radiated a need that soothed his soul. Her innocence had evolved in the years since he'd brought her here. Her dependence on him now as acute as her despair had been then.

Two years she had been here, sheltered from all who might judge her strange and terrible visions. He'd provided her with her own bedroom to allow for the illusion of separateness, of independence. But the first time he lay with her inside these walls she'd shown only a vague sense of surprise, as if her mind had been driven so far from her that his suckling and his thrusting caused it to return only gradually.

She'd looked at him like a father when they'd first arrived, and then, soon after, like a lover, showing greater surrender each time he took her. He'd offered her tutors to teach her how to read, but she'd refused, terrified that whatever she fed into her mind might only strengthen her overwhelming visions. But she'd been allowed other teachers. They'd taught her table manners and posture and left her with the general bearing of an aristocratic lady. And how he treasured the quiet effort she would exert to hold the teacup just so or the fork just right when they dined together. The way a slight furrow to her brow would indicate the concentration required to act like something other than the peasant girl he'd rescued. But for the most part, she was as mute as the beautiful porcelain dolls he'd filled her bedroom with, with their white rounded cheeks and wide staring glass eyes and little tumbles of curly hair under their kerchiefs and frilly caps.

So succulent and inviting she looked in the lace nightgown he'd given her. She wore it now just to pleasure him, he was sure. She turned from the mirror and sank against him, curling her delicate arms around his waist, resting her head against his groin without nervous regard for what she would inevitably stir there with this affection.

"You are gone too long." Her words now sounded focused and calm.

"Just since this morning," he whispered. "Did you enjoy your walk?"

"Yes," she whispered. "They are always peaceful. Come with me one morning," she said, looking up at him suddenly. How it pleasured him, the desperate eagerness in her look. "You will see me at my best. When I'm untroubled and peaceful myself."

"You don't trouble me."

"You'll see that I can make a companion for you."

"We are companions and more already."

"You will see I could be your wife."

So shocking and direct this suggestion that it threw water upon the fire spreading in his loins. The confidence in her words, it startled him silent. She swallowed nervously, troubled by his expression. The bright sheen in her dark eyes might have been tears, but the light here was too dim to tell.

"I do not ask for position or wealth. I ask because in this way I can return the gifts you've given me. It could be a private ceremony, here in the chapel. I never need to see Saint Petersburg or Moscow or to meet your friends in society. I'm content to live here in seclusion with you forever. But if you make me your wife, Dimitri, I can give myself to you more fully."

She reached up for one of his hands, clutched it in hers with strength. A new energy drove these words. A new need. A new fear. "I am getting well, Dimitri," she whispered, and several tears slipped free now. "I am getting well and because of this I can be more fully yours."

His heart broke for her. For all she didn't understand.

He did not need her well.

He simply needed her to be his.

That the ideas had somehow joined in her mind was a sign he'd let her drift for too long. He mustn't reward this behavior, he knew. Anything but a polite retreat would do just that. Besides, he had a far-more-effective tool to use on her than false promises.

When he bent forward and kissed her gently on the forehead, she closed her eyes as if bracing herself against a small but painful blow.

"You place too little value on what you already provide," Dimitri whispered. "Rest, and we shall talk in the morning." And then he withdrew, turning his back on the sight of her arms reaching for him as he left the room.

In his bedroom, right next door, he pulled aside the painting that concealed the peephole into her room. Her arms, which had reached for him a moment before, now rested limply on her lap. She was crying bitterly, silently. Suddenly she turned to the dresser, picked up the silver-plated brush, and slammed it to the table with surprising force. He jumped at the sound. At this private show of aggression.

Yes, he realized, *I've gone far too long.*

He'd relinquished his true hold over her too quickly. Now she was like a surly child roused from a nap too soon. But that she'd roused with this need—marriage!—shocked him to the core. If anything, he'd feared the retreat of her visions would inspire a need for independence, a cold rejection of him. When this had not been the case, he'd allowed her mind more freedom and less torment, even though most of the torments he inflicted on her inspired a grasping, clutching need for his protection that roused a great lusty beast within him. She was his reward; God's reward for having accepted the momentous responsibility of the gift she'd discovered without realizing it. But she'd come to sense he saw her as a possession; a beautiful, precious, and fragile possession. And so she arrogantly, foolishly, sought to replace a wife he'd lost years before, a woman for whom his grief had never resolved.

He did not know who Anya had been before God brought them together, had only heard tales of the young woman her hysterical parents described to him during his first visit to their home. A loyal girl. A good girl. A hard worker who toiled long hours cleaning the Vasilev Academy of Science and History in Tomsk. Well into the night she'd often worked, polishing the display cases and waxing the stone floors, alone amidst the relics the Vasilev fortune had collected from all over the world, all in a grand attempt to make an island of culture and learning of the Siberian outpost.

Now, as he watched her slip under the bedcovers, he pulled the necklace out from his robes and clutched the stone in one hand.

He waited until she dimmed the oil lamp next to her bed, and then, as he'd done so many times before, he filled the room with a low rustling sound, as several of the porcelain dolls slipped from their various perches, their tiny feet meeting the rug in soft little thuds. When she heard them, she sat up in bed, but she did not turn on the lamp. For Anya, this was a familiar sound. As she'd done so many times before, she brought her knees to her chest, wrapped her arms around them, and breathed with great, strained exertion.

But this time she did not hide her eyes, didn't bury her face between her knees. Instead, she watched as the dolls walked across the rug and towards the bed; the childlike innocence in their faces cruelly mismatched with their determined gaits. She watched, and in the moonlight coming through the window, he could see that she was less afraid.

And so, he had them go farther than he ever had before, climbing the bedcovers and crawling onto the comforter, until at least four of them were walking towards her knees.

And that's when the familiar sobs claimed her. She turned to one side, shielding her face with one arm, drawing the covers up over her head. And Dimitri felt regret. Bitter, terrible regret. But he needed to return her to her previous state. Needed to rid her of this childish, desperate need to wed him. She was not well. He would show her this now. She would never be well. And her hunger, her childlike need, had sustained him during these years of plotting and quarrels with his family. He could not let it solidify into an agenda of her own. He'd too much to contend with already.

Anya was his island on this island, and she must always be this. Her touch would heal him from the wounds of his son's scorn, and the memory of an older disdain, disdain from a man who had, for a brief and magical evening, seemed poised to become Dimitri's companion in all this, before that man's suspicion and dismissal had filled Dimitri with shame.

Lawrence Stratford.

Perhaps that had been what he'd truly sent his assassins to destroy. Not just those secrets Lawrence might have shared before his death, but the last vestiges of the look the man had given him when Dimitri came close to revealing his full plan. A look that had said, *I can sense the depths of what lies in you, Dimitri Vasilev, and I believe it to be madness.*

18

1913: Outside Cairo

The Englishman had cut such a fine figure when he'd emerged from his tent at the sound of the little wreck, Dimitri found himself instantly captivated by him. He had all the poise and dignity of an aristocrat. But with the sleeves of his linen shirt rolled up past his elbows and the smudges of dirt across his flushed cheeks and brow, it was clear the man had given himself over to the mysteries of these sands with as much surrender as Dimitri. Clear that, like Dimitri, he was no longer confined by the present borders of nations, fully devoted to the quest for secrets ancient and momentous.

And he'd reacted to their accident with such genuine concern, as if the great expanse in which they all found themselves made them fellow sailors on a great sea with a noble obligation to keep one another afloat.

If Dimitri had not been still so elated by his recent discovery, he might have flown into a rage over his lead driver's carelessness, but as he stepped down from the car he'd been riding in and walked to the head of their motorcade, he saw the cause of the accident.

A back tire on the lead car had been shorn from its rim, probably by the many jutting rocks that studded this road. As a result, the driver had lost control, and the car behind it, the one carrying Dimitri's rugs and oil lamps and all of the other furnishings he'd used to transform his tents into something suitably royal during this long expedition, had smashed into it from behind and was now hissing steam from under its hood.

But the truck behind him, the one in which their most significant find was concealed beneath a heavy tarpaulin, was unharmed. In this moment, that was all that mattered.

And the Englishman, whose private little world out here had clearly been shattered by this abrupt accident, gave nothing but helpful suggestions, apologizing for the absence of his assistant, who might have been of further help but had gone into Cairo for much-needed supplies. And then the Englishman raised the car's hood, attempted to reposition the tumble inside without burning his bare hands. Dimitri doubted the man had learned these tricks in the region of Britain that had gifted him with his crisp, dignified accent. He'd learned them out here, no doubt. As a man of the desert. As an explorer.

When it was clear the most damaged of the two cars might take hours to repair, he introduced himself as Lawrence Stratford and invited Dimitri and his men to take refuge from the late-afternoon sun inside his tent.

It seemed the most gracious of invitations, and that's when Dimitri realized he might be seeing the man through rose-colored glasses, for he was so thrilled by his discovery a few days earlier, the world seemed joyful and limitless everywhere he looked. This grand voyage had been a roaring success, save for this one small mishap.

Using all the paper records he'd located inside his family's museum in Tomsk, he'd retraced every step of the expedition that uncovered the stones discovered there. In the process, he'd uncovered another piece of the great mystery that seemed just as significant, even though it did not in and of itself bring statues to life.

And so he told Lawrence Stratford he would only accept

his offer if the man allowed Dimitri's men to prepare for them both the best dinner possible under the circumstances, and only after they transformed the interior of his humble tent, strewn with worktables containing fragments of rock and the brushes and magnifying glasses required to study them in detail, into something suitably grand. Lawrence seemed pleased, but dumbstruck, watching wide eyed as the men unrolled Oriental carpets, set up and lit the tall golden oil lamps they'd purchased before setting out from Cairo. By the time they were finished, he was so impressed he withdrew his initial refusal of some of Dimitri's best vodka, allowing Dimitri's butler to pour him a thimbleful.

And then, so soon after their initial meeting, the two men were seated across from each other at a worktable that had been transformed into an elegant dining table by the swift removal of its tools and its thorough dusting and then the covering of a linen tablecloth and settings of silver Dimitri had insisted his servants keep polished and free of sand throughout the trip.

Once dinner was set, Dimitri dismissed his servants.

"You bring your world with you, Mr. Vasilev," Lawrence said in between careful chews.

"Some semblance of it," Dimitri said, "but these are mostly fine things I acquired during this journey. My own world, my own home, is of a different flavor."

"And what flavor is your home, Mr. Vasilev? As grand as the Hermitage, no doubt."

"No. No, good sir. Not the Hermitage."

"I've offended you."

"You've known me too briefly to know it's the Hermitage that offends me. This is easily forgiven."

"Surely you don't despise museums," Lawrence Stratford said.

"Of course not. My family has built several. Solid things. Strong walls. And the gold is within the displays, not on the façades."

"I see. So you think it crass for a museum to draw attention to itself?" Lawrence asked.

"I find it inconsequential is all. I speak of the buildings, of course. Most of Saint Petersburg is this way. A pale, swampy copy of an Italian city. As Russian as Yorkshire pudding."

"Is one of the great cities of the world so easily dismissed?" Lawrence asked.

"That's just the problem, isn't it? Saint Petersburg is too much of the world."

"Ah, I see."

"What? What do you see, Mr. Stratford?"

"You are a true Muscovite. A Slav."

"I cannot dispute this."

"And here you are in Egypt."

"As are you, my new British friend."

"Indeed, yet again. Although I must confess this time success has been in short supply."

"How so?" Dimitri asked.

"Museums. They are difficult to deal with. If you do not build them yourself, that is."

Dimitri laughed uproariously at this. He was not used to being spoken to as Lawrence Stratford spoke to him. So many were cowed by his presence, by the force with which his name entered rooms before he did. Lawrence seemed to think the evidence of his wealth an intrigue and nothing more, and it left Dimitri with the giddy feeling that men like them could remake themselves out here in the sands of Egypt.

They were soon lost in a discussion of Lawrence's career, which thrilled and delighted Dimitri. What a charmed life he led!

The profits of his family's shipping company, overseen by his brother, Randolph, had allowed Lawrence this life of travel and study. Allowed his daughter, his beloved Julie, to travel with him often, although she'd not been able to make this trip.

But he couldn't fund his work entirely from the profits of Strat-ford Shipping or else he'd bleed it dry, and so he'd established relationships with the British Museum, who'd promised fund-ing and supplies for this particular journey they'd not properly delivered. And, of course, there was always their insistence that all finds be swiftly brought back to London upon their discov-ery, a prospect which filled Lawrence with misgivings. There were museums and restorers here who could care for the items, and more fine scholars than the stuffy academics of the Brit-ish Museum would give Egypt credit for. These explanations, and the steaming plates of food Dimitri's servants delivered, left Lawrence in a placid, dreamy-eyed state. He had not had someone to talk to about these things for some time. Or, at least, not someone who had heard him say them all before.

"A long time ago," Lawrence began quietly, "I lived here. With a friend. In a houseboat on the Nile. We had great quarrels, but we agreed on one thing. Great mysteries of existence might be solved here. But solving them did not seem to be the most important thing. It was the seeking, you see. It was the quest that mattered. Now I'm not so sure. At the very least, after days of digging, I wish to uncover something of significance."

"This friend, where is he now?"

"Ah, Elliott. Elliott Savarell is his name. He's in London, with a life made of things that bore me to tears. Embassy balls, gentlemen's clubs. For him, Egypt was a phase. But for me, a life."

He smiled when he said this, smiled in a manner that chased away his painful longing for his old friend. Dimitri had seen something deep and moving in that longing, seen in it his own grief for all he'd seemed poised to lose before a cleaning woman of unrivaled beauty had made an accidental and momentous discovery at his family's museum, a discovery that had changed the course of a life once marked by the drudgery of extreme wealth and the social expectations it brought. But the forces that had sent Lawrence here seemed altogether more complex, and fascinating, and it was clear he mourned those days of living on the Nile with his friend in the same way Dimitri mourned the passing of the true Russia.

"I've upset you, sir." Lawrence had been studying Dimitri's expression for some time.

"No, you've inspired me. But tell me, sir, how do you define a significant find?"

"Anything that adds to the record. We know so little. Civilization existed here for thousands of years. *Thousands*, sir. It's difficult for a single mind to grasp that amount of time."

"And yet you try, don't you, Mr. Stratford? You try every day, I can see it."

Lawrence nodded, smiling.

"So it's the history that brings you here again and again," Dimitri said.

"Of course, sir," Lawrence answered. "Isn't it that with you? Why else make the journey?"

"The truth is, Mr. Stratford, I had no great obsession with Egypt, not until recently."

"I see. What brought about the change?" Lawrence asked.

"An unexpected discovery. In my family's museum."

"What sort of discovery?"

Lawrence Stratford asked these questions casually, with no sense of the great feeling swimming just beneath Dimitri's words. The fine vodka and the pleasure of the man's company were loosening Dimitri, conspiring with the magical little oasis they'd created here inside his tent, where the glow of the oil lamps flickered off walls shifting in the breezes, and the thick rugs underfoot conspired to convince him he was on a barge on the Nile and not atop a sandy mound.

Also, there had been so few he could discuss his discoveries with. No one, really.

But what would it be like to have an advisor, a companion in this, like Lawrence Stratford? A brilliant man whose eyes took on a dreamy cast when he discussed the thousands of years of discoveries to be made here. A man like Lawrence could comprehend the majesty of this. And they could spend long nights like this one, discussing topics that would bore their friends and relatives to tears.

"Vasilev," Lawrence said quietly. "I recognize this name now. A great Russian family."

"And how do you define *great*, Mr. Stratford?"

"Enormous wealth, a lineage that stretches back in history."

"And now," Dimitri asked, "how do you define *Russian*?"

"This is a trick question, surely."

"It is not. The term has been in dispute for some time. I am eager for your thoughts. As an Englishman."

Lawrence took a careful sip of vodka. "In some sense, Russia is much like ancient Egypt," he finally said.

"How is this?"

"They are lands of kings. Vast. Prone to fragmentation and invasion without strong central rule. For you, it was the Mongols. For Egypt, the Hyksos and others. This is a simplification, of course, but the themes are the same."

Dimitri was so pleased by these words, he had to suppress a smile. "You British have your own king."

"It is not the same. We don't believe he's an arm's length away from God. I don't, at least."

"What do you believe?" It seemed a casual question, and yet Dimitri felt Lawrence's answer might shape their shared destiny. Would determine if they had a destiny to share.

"Of kings, or gods?" Lawrence asked.

"Both."

After a brief pause, Lawrence said, "I like to think I'm too humble to declare there's nothing. After we die, that is."

"And yet the presence that might exist there?" Dimitri asked. "On this, you say nothing?"

"You mean God?"

"Your word, not mine." Dimitri smiled, sipped his drink.

"Ah, you are clever, Mr. Vasilev. You have tricked me, haven't you?"

"Goaded you. A little. But truly, Mr. Stratford, there must be something you believe. A mind like yours. An explorer's mind, an excavator's mind, I can't believe you are comfortable with an unanswered question."

"But didn't you hear, Mr. Vasilev? It's not the answers that have meaning, but the questions."

"When you were a young man, you believed this, yes. But now, Mr. Stratford. What do you believe now? Now that you are old and wise and easily frustrated when the sands around you do not cough up a looking glass into the thousands of years of history that so fire your imagination? Surely, the vastness of eternity must power your mind in a similar way. For what explorer would not want to journey into the mystery of death itself."

He had either frightened or entranced the man across from him; Dimitri could not be sure.

"Death itself," Lawrence whispered.

"Don't fear your answer. Don't fear my response. We are two men on an island tonight. Free from borders and nations, customs and conventions. Two men who might speak their minds freely without fear of consequence."

"But I cannot touch it, sir. I can touch the dead, but not death itself, and so I can't bring the tools I have to bear upon its true mystery. And so I have only my beliefs."

"And what are those? Tell me, Lawrence."

"When it comes to death, I fear I shall be met by nothing, but I hope I will be embraced by everything. Am I so different than most men?"

"But what would everything entail?" Dimitri asked. "The nothing I understand too well. But the hope for everything, that is where religions differ. Cultures differ. Nations differ."

It is where we might differ, Dimitri thought, *and in ways that might prevent me from bringing you into this.*

"Answers," Lawrence finally said, "illumination, insight."

"But do you truly believe the need for these answers will pass with you into the next realm? What if these needs are just petty human appetites that lose their hold over us when the heart ceases to beat? Once you step across the threshold, perhaps all concern and frustration and rage about the physical existence you just endured will leave you as the soul leaves the flesh."

"I've never heard it expressed so," Lawrence whispered. "The idea terrifies me. Especially as you've worded it."

"Why?" Dimitri asked. "Why does it terrify you? Yours is an expansive mind, sir."

"Yes, and you speak now of the utter annihilation of that which makes it so."

"No, Mr. Stratford," Dimitri said. "I speak of its transformation. Its transcendence."

"Into a thing that cannot be defined. And what is that but an annihilation?"

"Only if you are looking back, Mr. Stratford. Only if, upon stepping into the next great realm of existence, the afterlife itself, you insist on looking backwards, of turning away from the dazzling experiences that await you in favor of clinging to the physical past. Only then is it not transcendence."

He had captivated the man; Dimitri could tell. And this was good. A sign that this chance encounter was fated, fated just as the discovery of the stones had been fated. That the god which Lawrence Stratford was reluctant to name had truly placed Dimitri on a divine path.

"Mr. Vasilev, I must say I suspect you of something." Lawrence was smiling softly now.

"What is this?"

"Each time I ask you about Russia, you seem to plunge headfirst into my beliefs. And as much as I'm enjoying this conversation, I must confess, it does feel a bit one sided."

"Ha. Very well then. You call Russia a land of kings. You are correct. In part. But you speak of a Russia that's dwindling. We have suffered European intrusions, not at the head of a bayonet or an army. But in ways of governance and belief that are not suitable to our vast lands, to the true spirit of our people. And our tsar, Nicholas II, he is weak, a pale version of his great father, and he has proved incapable of holding back these tides.

"I simply mean to say I have beliefs, Mr. Stratford. Firm beliefs. I believe a single god waits for us beyond the dark. And I believe this god can guide us only through a single ruler. And when I look upon the expanse of my Russia and all its toils, I see the loosening of his hold and the ruin of all that which led it to rise up against the Mongols and the Swedes."

"God's hold?"

"Yes."

"A strange twist, then, that you have ended up in Egypt."

"How so?" Dimitri asked.

Lawrence smiled and raised his glass. "This is a land of many gods."

"But only one presides over the underworld, isn't that true? Only one waits for us in the land of death."

"Osiris."

"Yes, Osiris."

"True, but I'm not sure this Osiris would be a fitting guide for the fate of Russia itself. And I'm sure your Orthodox church would feel the same."

"Ah, so the costume changes over time, but the will of God remains as swift and resolute."

"The costume? You speak of the changing faces and names of gods over time as nothing more than costume? My good sir, ceaseless wars have been fought over the nature of what you call a costume. But it seems you would have them resolved rather easily."

"The will of a single god can be felt by all but those who are lost in delusion," Dimitri said.

"And how is it felt?" Lawrence asked.

"Through the ruin and grief wrought by those who depart from his path."

Lawrence flinched. "Not through divine guidance?" he asked.

"There is divine guidance in ruin and grief," Dimitri answered.

It seemed to Dimitri that he had truly frightened his new friend.

"I must ask, then." Lawrence spoke carefully now, as if he'd just glimpsed a great pit inside Dimitri and it was ringed by shadow and he was afraid of stumbling into it. "What of the other Egyptian gods? What becomes of them in the wake of your belief that Osiris is but one mask worn by the one true god?"

"Bit players."

At Dimitri's sly grin and dismissive wave, both meant to diffuse the tension, Lawrence erupted with laughter. "Bit players?" he exclaimed. "Hathor. Anubis. Bit players, you call them. I must say, I admire your confidence in your beliefs. It's far preferable to my own doubts."

"I cast them in no lesser role than the Christian archangels," he said, as if they were casually negotiating a business settlement. "But truly, who has greater power than the god of death?"

"But in much of the writing we've discovered, Osiris governs the land of the dead. He does not control death itself."

"I refuse to believe the god of the underworld does not decide who might enter his realm."

"Yes, but if he were to be the one true god, sir, then he'd have to control the granting of life as well. To my eye, at least."

The granting of life. Lawrence had said these words gently and casually, with no sense that they were precisely the admission Dimitri had been waiting for. The very opening he'd needed. For what had Dimitri discovered but the power to give life to that which had none—stone itself. And thanks to his most recent discovery, he'd traced it to the god once called Osiris. And this meant Dimitri could present this new friend, a possible companion on this grand journey, with exactly what he'd just asked for. Evidence of a god whose life-giving powers transcended the boundaries of the physical.

"Come," Dimitri said, rising to his feet. He picked up a glowing lantern, waiting for Lawrence to rise from his chair as well. "There's something I must show you."

His men, some lingering and smoking just outside the tent, parted nervously before them. Then Dimitri called several of them to the largest of the two trucks that were part of their arrested motorcade. He ordered them to uncover the enormous artifact in back. Then, with his free arm, he assisted Lawrence up into the truck's front seat.

It took Lawrence a moment to realize that Dimitri did not mean for them to travel anywhere in this truck. But to turn and watch as the men carefully drew back the tarp, revealing the giant slab of stone filling the cargo platform. As they did so, Dimitri raised the lantern in one hand so that its glow fell across the ridges of the carvings.

It wasn't enough light. When he called for more, more men appeared, holding more lanterns, standing all around the truck so that they were effectively lining the rough edges of the stela they'd unearthed days before. Now the detailed carvings, from the hieroglyphs across the top down to the dazzling marriage of figures—one small, the other colossal—were bathed in a golden glow.

Was it the image that captivated Lawrence now or the message written across the very top of the stela?

In the image, a great colossus towered over a man less than a third of its height. But the outfit of this smaller man, particularly his crown, made clear that, despite his size, he was, in fact, the pharaoh. And the colossus was crowned by the outline of an atef, the ovular crown of Upper Egypt lined with two matching ridges meant to indicate feathers, the crown of Osiris.

Wide eyed, breathing heavily, Lawrence took the lantern from Dimitri's hand, bent forward as far as he could without touching the stone itself.

He was studying the details, no doubt. Studying the little chip of amber stone embedded at the base of the tiny king's neck, a re-creation, no doubt, of the very necklace Dimitri now wore hidden under his garments. If Lawrence could accept the enormity of this, Dimitri would show him the stone, show him the Eye of Osiris and all he could do. But for now, he needed time to study the image before him and absorb its meaning.

Raising the lantern higher, Lawrence read the hieroglyphs.

"It depicts a ritual," Lawrence said. "The king stands before the colossus of Osiris, and the lines, the curving lines stretching between them, are meant to indicate a connection. A profound one."

"Yes," Dimitri said.

"A connection between Osiris and the king," Lawrence said, but he was talking to himself as much as Dimitri, translating the hieroglyphs under his breath.

And Lawrence fell silent, a silence that stretched on so long Dimitri grew impatient with it. Excitedly, Dimitri began to explain. "Look to his neck, the king's neck. See the jewel there? That's the source of the ritual. The hieroglyphs explain it. We've had them translated. The necklace is referred to as the Eye of Osiris. And the hieroglyphs say it must be hidden for all time, for Egypt has lost its way, and there is great corruption in the priesthood. They refer to the looting of the Valley of the Kings and cite this as proof that the priests can no longer be trusted to guard the Eye. They say that if Osiris should ever wish to place himself in service to kings once more, he should unearth the stone and this map and reveal it to whom he wishes to serve. We believe the rest are fragments of a map that might lead to the colossus."

Lawrence was silent for a very long time, and with each passing second, Dimitri's excitement turned to a strange kind of disappointment. For this revelation did not excite his new friend the way he hoped it would.

"This translation," Lawrence finally asked. "Is it yours? Did you do it yourself?"

"Not mine, no. I can't read hieroglyphs. A scholar is traveling with us. I'll bring him here and we can—"

"No, no," Lawrence said quickly, "I don't want to offend him."

"Offend him? Whatever do you mean?"

"He's wrong, my friend." Lawrence set the lantern down on the truck's passenger seat and stepped to the dirt.

Dimitri felt an almost-childlike disappointment at these words, and for an unbearable few moments, he couldn't bring himself to speak.

"Wrong, how?"

"The bit about the looting of the Valley of the Kings and the Eye of Osiris being concealed, all that's correct. But there is nothing there that says Osiris will place himself in service of the king. He's got it entirely backwards. It says the one who wears the Eye will be placed in service to Osiris."

It seemed, at first, a subtle distinction, but the gravity of its implications took its painful time sweeping through every fiber of Dimitri's being.

The colossus will command the king . . .

"The way your scholar's interpreted it, well . . . it makes it sound as if the colossus is some great weapon the rightful king might put at his disposal. But that's not the meaning. That's not the meaning at all."

Some great weapon. Just a bit of dismissive sarcasm in these words, but how they lanced through Dimitri. Exposing ambitions and motives he'd nursed in secret, without fully articulating them to anyone else. Now, hearing them spoken aloud with suspicion and a hint of disdain humiliated him.

"What is the meaning?" He'd not chased the anger and disappointment from his voice, but he had no choice but to continue. "In your view, Lawrence Stratford."

Lawrence clearly bristled at the sound of his voice, studied Dimitri briefly, and already Dimitri could feel the magical flame they'd nourished together over the course of the evening had started to gutter. Suddenly he felt very cold, and very alone.

"In my view," Lawrence said softly, "it's a legend, a ritual designed to humble kings."

"Yes, but what if it isn't a legend, Lawrence Stratford?"

Too rashly, he'd asked this, and in a way that might betray what was hidden beneath his garments.

"I'm sorry, Mr. Vasilev. It seems I've injured you, and I didn't mean to—"

"You haven't injured me. Just answer please."

Lawrence went very still.

"If my translation is correct, it speaks of a process by which a mortal man, a king, but still a mortal man, is placed entirely under the control of a god. The god of the underworld, the god of death. And the difference in size between the two figures suggests this control is absolute, abolishing any concept of free will you and I might enjoy as modern Western men. I must say, if it isn't simply legend or a bit of royal theater, I find that rather terrifying."

Dimitri could not hide his anger at these words, a frustration edged with despair. Nothing about Dimitri's experience of the Eye of Osiris thus far spoke of this kind of dependence, this enslavement. It had given him control, absolute control, and so when he'd traced its discovery to the location of this great tablet and its mysterious inscription, he had assumed the colossus of which it spoke was but the divine grandfather of all the other statues and figurines and dolls, objects carved in the shape of life which the Eye allowed him to place under his absolute command.

He assumed the Eye a gift from God, capable of tearing apart everything unholy in its path. Not a doorway for his absolute will.

But now this man, this undeniably brilliant man, had gazed upon the same carvings and seen something entirely different. Something that spoke of enslavement for the one who wore the Eye, not power. And it made Dimitri a hypocrite. For all his talk of single rulers channeling the pure will of a single god, he'd not paused long enough to entertain the possibility that the ruler might lose himself to God completely.

"This is a risk in my profession," Lawrence said.

"Quarreling over the vagaries of a long-dead language?"

"Are we quarreling, sir?" Lawrence asked softly.

"Just say your meaning, Mr. Stratford."

He saw it then, the little flash in the man's eyes that said whatever connection they'd established here was finished. Snuffed out like a candle before retiring.

Lawrence said, "Sometimes we are blinded by the translation we want to be true, and not the one that is correct."

Dimitri pondered then what it would mean to kill him.

Some of his men were mercenaries, but not all, and so he'd have to slay much of his own entourage to ensure their secrecy and silence. Perhaps if he continued his search, a search that would now focus on the colossus, he would travel with more hired killers to ensure secrecy and protection. But in this moment, he should simply count his blessings he'd not made the mistake of showing Lawrence Stratford the Eye itself and all it could do. For he had misread this man badly. And he could leave him now without entanglements.

Better to prove him wrong in time, he thought, *than to kill him.*

"You have been most generous, Mr. Stratford." In response to the wave of his hand, Dimitri's men began to conceal the stone beneath the tarp once more. "I am sorry to have wasted your time with legends."

"It's not a waste of time at all," he said. "It's a significant find, and congratulations to you, sir."

"I shall see to it that we are soon out of your hair."

Lawrence simply nodded at this, but there was a flicker of hurt in his strained smile, as if he too sensed that something had been lost here.

Both the shredded tire and jumbled engine had been repaired while they dined, but Dimitri's men were still shocked when he announced they'd be driving back to Cairo now, in the dark. They'd already begun to assemble tents for the night. One look at his furious expression, and they fell silent. No explaining to them that he had to get far from here at once, far from the seeds of doubt Lawrence Stratford had sowed in his mind. It felt now as if his great discovery and its elaborate carvings were all fragile things requiring swift protection from Lawrence's hard and unforgiving interpretation.

But was that truly an apt description of what Lawrence had said?

No, there was something far more significant in Lawrence's response to the carvings.

Fear.

And it was from that fear that Dimitri knew he and his discovery must make a swift escape.

19

London

The elixir made her mind perpetually sharp, but still, Julie wished she'd taken notes.

At times her father's narrative had wandered completely astray. Into halting reflections on the nature of the desert wind and little debates with himself about the particular smells of that evening; of how the oil coming from Dimitri Vasilev's lamps contrasted with the scent of motor oil drifting into the tent from his cars, of the food his men had served them. Discussions, it seemed, he was having with himself. As if his memories had been shattered into a million pieces across the hardwood floor at their feet, and he were being forced to identify the tiny fragments aloud in the order he encountered them during a search of the room.

But certain details emerged, consistent and clear. After a little car accident in the man's motorcade, her father had spent the better part of an evening in passionate conversation with this Dimitri Vasilev. And their evening had concluded with the revelation of a stela Vasilev had discovered that told the tale of the Eye of Osiris and the ancient ritual in which the priests had used it. Then their evening together had come to an end that was both abrupt and dark. As if Lawrence had failed the Russian's test by translating the hieroglyphs in the way he did.

The tale had taken some time, and during its telling, her father's perspective on it all remained warped. His new tendency to refer to himself in the third person persisted. Sometimes he even used his full name, Lawrence Stratford; moments that had her exchanging worried glances with Elliott, with Ramses. Even Osuron.

And so, did they not have everything they needed?

A connection between a Russian name—a famous one, whose vast fortune had left footprints throughout the world—and the Eye of Osiris itself. And so it had not been a wasted effort, a wasted effort that had pushed her to the very brink of sanity. For this alone, Julie knew she should be grateful.

"Thank you, Father," she said.

"I am not your father."

No anger or malice in his tone, but still, it felt as if he'd slapped her. He sounded as if he'd meant to correct some ordinary, pedestrian error. But the words, so clearly stated, and with so much less confusion than had marked every other utterance he'd made since his resurrection, caused her heart to drop. She found herself sitting up, as if she'd been insulted at a public gathering.

"These things you've drawn from me," he said, "I possess them as a thief might possess a stolen locket. But they are not mine." With such calm, he said this. Because it comforted him. Because he believed it. And it was the telling of the tale that had done it somehow, convinced him that the story he told was not his own.

"They are your memories," she said. "How could they not be?"

"Memories. Where I have been, they are nothing."

"What does that mean, Father?" It was deliberate, her insistence on calling him *Father*. This time he did not correct her, but he winced slightly, as if the name was a curse.

"Death is the collapse of time," he whispered. "These things you call my memories, I merely collided with them as you drew me forth from the dark. They cling to me like veils of dust. But they are not mine. They were there with me. But not of me. They were being taken from me in the dark."

"And that is over now," Julie said. "If that describes what was being done to you in the dark, then we've arrested it. We've stopped this process and brought you back. It will take time, of course. Time for your mind to heal but—"

"No," he said. "No, you would not say these things if you could see the shadows in this room as I see them. They have a substance. A weight."

"Father, you're simply trying to reconcile the—"

"I AM NOT YOUR FATHER!" he roared.

Never, not once in her life, had the living, mortal Lawrence yelled at her with this kind of rage, his eyes bulging and his mouth contorted in a snarl. They raised her to her feet, these words, propelled her with a combination of hurt and anger, which together seemed a force as powerful as the elixir itself. Ramses rushed to her, embraced her quickly. Gently, he took her wrists. Was this his preferred means of embrace, or did he truly fear she'd strike out at the man across from her?

Her instinct, she realized, was to do just that, and Ramses had felt it, anticipated it. She wanted to beat a new awareness into him.

Guilt over this urge swept like a crosscurrent into the other emotions coursing through her, creating a storm that shook her core. "I cannot be present for this," she whispered into Ramses's ear. His embrace was tender, but firm. "I have given all I can to this effort. But I cannot be present for this rejection. I have endured too much . . . I have . . ."

"I understand, Julie. We'll go upstairs and rest for a moment."

He guided her from the room, asked Elliott and Osuron to stay.

She dared a glance back. Lawrence had returned his grim

attention to the rug underfoot, with no second thought of her at all. As if his outburst had settled it. As if any evidence of pain or terror he'd seen on her face had passed through him like the memories he claimed were not his own.

She was fighting sobs by the time she reached the stairs. She had prepared for other eventualities, all of them dreadful, but not this one. Not this rejection. A creature of predatory appetites or a wild thing that could barely be controlled. But a being who looked just like him, who could recount his memories in a manner sprinkled with his old and familiar gestures, and then, in the next breath, claim with feral rage that she was not his daughter. That nothing connected them except the grotesque and jarring events of his resurrection.

Ramses tried to guide her to the bedroom where this had all begun. Then, realizing his mistake, he steered her towards their own bedroom instead.

Once the door was closed, her words rushed from her. "That I will live forever and still I craved things from this moment a child might."

"No, Julie," Ramses whispered, stroking her hair tenderly.

"I did. I was mad to suggest it. And yet, it's given us what we need. But the cost . . ."

For a while he held her as she bitterly sobbed.

Then there was a knock on the door. Such a shockingly ordinary and polite little sound given the night's proceedings. Ramses admitted Elliott, who had a tense set to his jaw, a rigidity to his stance, but his eyes swam with pain. With grief, she realized.

"Osuron and his men sit with him," Elliott said crisply. "He has no desire to speak to us, it seems. I asked him questions about his experience, made no claim to have known him. He waved me away and turned his back. He sits in the conservatory now, staring at the damage he's done."

"Oh, Elliott." She threw her arms around him. So much

easier for them to comfort each other now. Now that they'd both been subjected to the same casting aside.

"What do you make of all this, my king?" Elliott asked.

Ramses was silent.

When Julie pulled gently free of Elliott's embrace and sank into the nearest chair, Ramses still seemed to be choosing his words.

He moved to the window, to the view of starry sky above the rooftops.

"We have no real frame of reference for this," he finally said. "The situation of Cleopatra only compares to a certain extent. But I don't believe he's a mad creature. As his mind heals, he'll be more capable of using familiar ideas and constructs to dismiss the enormity of this experience. A healthy mind, a vigorous mind, can still deceive itself. Sometimes with speed and efficiency. They are well versed in this, our minds. Indeed, most of what they do for us is to blot out all that might overwhelm us. He's brushed up against something momentous. But he lacks the words for it. So he casts it as veils of dust and darkness and other things which only skim the surface of its reality."

Elliott shook his head. "I feel a fool. A complete fool. I'd hoped against hope that once we raised him, Lawrence, the Lawrence I knew, the brilliant man, could join us in this. Follow us to the end of this road. For we can't deny that a clock hangs over this entire affair. The terrible clock of when this Dimitri Vasilev, or whomever he answers to, plans to use this Eye in some way so significant he felt the need to first wipe out all who might have known of his meeting with Lawrence. But I can't conceive of the man sitting downstairs now joining us in any of this. And I was a fool to think that could be the result. Imagine solving a murder with the newly risen Cleopatra. She was too busy committing them."

"They are not the same, Elliott," Ramses said. "Not the

same people, not the same beings. Not the same creatures. Not remotely."

Ramses straightened, turned his attention once more to the window. "Bektaten has left the consequences and the risks to us, and so we must decide how to proceed."

"The fundamental nature of what we've done is unavoidable," Julie said. "It's the thing that ties Cleopatra and my father together now, no matter how different they might be as individuals. They were brought back without their consent. And it's possible this fact shapes everything about him, and how he will perceive this."

"We are all born without our consent," Ramses said. "Should it really be so thoroughly shattering to be reborn in the same way?"

Julie rose and moved to Ramses, took his hands in hers, and tried to avoid being distracted by the openness of his steady gaze.

"Speak to him, Ramses," she said. "Make use of the wonder that came into his eyes when he realized what you are. To him, you are a new manifestation, connected to something of his old, mortal life. But you bring a magic with you that's new to this one. Act as if there is no clock over any of us. Speak to him of what he believes, what he now perceives. And then"—she reached up and caressed the side of his face, knowing that by looking into his eyes in this moment, she would make clear her sincerity and that alone would ensure his loyalty—"ask him what he would have us do with him. For I can surrender him to his wishes, but not Bektaten's. Not yet."

She glanced at Elliott and saw that even with his eyes swimming with pain, he signaled his agreement with a small, polite nod.

20

At first, Ramses wasn't sure what to make of the scene that greeted him in the double parlor. Osuron stood facing the conservatory, and also blocking Ramses's view of it. When he felt Ramses behind him, he turned, gave him a look that seemed pregnant with meaning, then stepped aside to reveal Lawrence.

The man had sunk to his knees on the conservatory's floor, and when Ramses approached, he heard a sound that chilled his blood. It was coming from Lawrence Stratford. Long inhalations followed by two short huffing exhalations, and Lawrence performed each little set without strain or performance, as if this strange rhythm had been engraved in his lungs. The same sound he'd demonstrated for the convocation at Brogdon Castle the night before.

"You are breathing strangely," Ramses said.

Lawrence did not answer.

"Why do you breathe this way?"

He raised his eyes to Ramses. With a satisfied smile, he said, "It reminds me of where I belong. It reminds me of the dark."

The wind-tossed grove, the obsidian gates, the sounds of a god's breath.

It had been some time since Ramses had known total fear.

Guilt. Anguish. These things had been threaded through so

many of the events following his awakening in this new century. But this was the bone-deep fear known only to those who stood at the edge of a great void that might swallow them without explanation or remorse. For this suggested that the presence which had greeted Ramses thousands of years ago had made an impression on others.

Say it, Ramses. There is no sparing yourself this. Say it's the presence of a god.

But they were just sounds, he told himself. Just breaths. Just soil atop a stone floor. But the strange rhythm of them made it seem as if this damaged conservatory had become an ancient temple, the shattered glass ceiling above a roof left open so the gods could peer in. And watch. And judge.

For weeks now, he'd been bristling under the authority of a new queen. But now greater powers asserted their presence. That's what the pulse of Lawrence's breaths meant; it suggested gods he'd once feared, who had never made themselves known to him during his centuries of wandering, were closer than he'd thought.

Was this the last piece of proof he needed that the thunderous voice that had called to him from the colossus was not the product of drugged wine? Had it trembled with the power of other realms? Was it capable of speaking to him once more?

Death is the collapse of time, Lawrence had whispered, as if it were a piece of wisdom he'd garnered in the darkness. And so if he had heard the voice of a god so long ago, would it speak to Ramses again as if no centuries had passed at all?

Ramses knelt beside the man. "Lawrence, tell me what you remember of these sounds you hear in the dark."

"You've heard it too. You'd not be so frightened otherwise." Lawrence suddenly grabbed Ramses's collar, eyes ablaze. "You have been in the dark."

"I have not," Ramses whispered, but he did not fight Lawrence off or seek to pull away, for to do so would be to lose his chance to hear whatever mad truths, whatever visions, might bubble up from Lawrence's mind in this moment. And perhaps Lawrence was right. Perhaps this was precisely where that ritual had taken him. Not into a mad, drug-fueled dream. But into the dark.

Into death.

"I have never died," he claimed, even though it now felt vaguely like a lie. "You know my story. You read my story on the scrolls in my tomb."

"Another man," Lawrence said, "another man with these bones and this flesh read those things, but not me. I am not Lawrence."

"Who are you then?" Ramses asked. "If you are not Lawrence, then who are you?"

"I am . . . unfinished."

"And where is Lawrence?"

The man before him gazed into his eyes. "Finished," he whispered.

These were a child's answers. A child attempting to conceal confusion and ignorance before adults.

"What does this mean?" Ramses asked. "And how do these sounds relate? Tell me these things and you can help me."

He recoiled, this man before him, recoiled to the wall closest to him, leaned against it, encircling himself with his arms as if he were suddenly cold, staring skyward as if the shattered ceiling above might allow for his escape or the entry of his rescuers.

"'Help me'?" the man whispered. "You take me from him. He will be angry at you for this. And now you claim you'll fix the problem you have made?"

Ramses rose, his legs trembling. On the bookshelves of the adjacent library, he found a journal with scores of empty, blank pages within, grabbed a pen to go with it. Then, as gently as he could, he set the notebook on the conservatory floor, opened it to two blank pages, and set the pen atop as if it were a little gift.

"Draw for me what you have seen, please," Ramses said. "Draw for me his realm and all its trappings so that I may understand what I have done. I cannot repair what I cannot see."

Lawrence swatted the pen from the open pages. A gesture more dismissive than angry.

"Return me to it," he whispered. "Destroy this body if you need to, but return me to the dark."

His heart broke. Not for the man before him, but for Julie. How tempting to speed them past this moment, to pretend Lawrence had not spoken these words. To drown him in further inquiry and questions. But to do so would be to deny Julie what she had asked him for.

A direction, a resolution to the terrible burden the resurrected Lawrence Stratford now posed for them all.

But something else was present within Ramses. A desire to comply. A desire to obliterate all the questions the being before him now raised. To do so would be to cast the terrifying fragments of knowledge he'd brought with him back to the realm from which they'd been drawn forth. And perhaps to appease the being—*The god, Ramses; he speaks of a god!*—of which he spoke. But it wasn't possible now. It wasn't possible to destroy those rhythmic pulses of breath and their implication, to forever ignore how this pantomime had sprung forth from Lawrence's regenerating mind, which struggled to reconcile its passage from death to new life.

And Julie needed more than this. She was so wounded by her father's rejection, she might wish to hurry him back to the grave. But she'd regret this choice, Ramses knew. And, perhaps, even this man before him now would regret it.

A compromise. He could broker a compromise here, but to do so, he would have to lie.

"Your body cannot be destroyed now," Ramses said. "Not after what we did to bring it back."

Osuron might not know about the vials Bektaten had given

him but surely knew about the existence of their contents. Still, he did not interrupt Ramses, or even flinch.

The look of the man before him, the one who refused to be known as Lawrence Stratford, was one of intense personal injury, as if a terrible betrayal had just been revealed. The ultimate choice, the choice to obliterate one's self, the choice most humans shared in common, had been stolen from him. Or so he thought.

"You did not bring anyone back," Lawrence snarled. "You reached into a realm where you had no place and pulled forth but a handful of that which you do not understand."

"Perhaps it's you who doesn't understand it," Ramses said. But the words coming from Lawrence terrified him. They sounded like the words of a god, and the prospect that Lawrence had become an agent for whoever presided over this realm, this darkness of which he spoke so fondly, Ramses could not accept this. Not yet. "And there is more to you than a handful. More to you than a ghost even."

"And so what becomes of me now?" Lawrence asked. "I am your slave?"

"I cannot return you to the darkness you crave, but I can bring you close to it. Time will seem to collapse again. But it won't be true death. Is this the desire of the man who possesses only Lawrence Stratford's flesh and bones?"

Lawrence studied him with bitter anger. "It is what I wish," he said. "But you should fear what he wishes."

"Who?"

Lawrence smiled distantly, then returned to the pattern of breaths that shook Ramses to his core.

"Did you agree to this with him?" Julie asked, once Ramses had recounted the conversation.

"No, I simply said it could be done. It's you who must agree to it."

On opposite sides of the bedroom now, it seemed Julie and Elliott were both quietly wrestling with their reactions to Lawrence's wish. A wish made inside the confines of a lie.

"He asks this?" Julie asked. "He says go upstairs and learn the wishes of the woman who falsely claims to be my daughter, does he?"

"No," Ramses answered.

"Of course not," she whispered bitterly.

"If we do this, we set the stage for a terrible temptation," Elliott said. "To unseal his tomb and expose him to the sun at some later date and seek to rehabilitate him."

"The temptation was always there," Julie hissed.

"It will be different now," Elliott said, "easier, swifter. A future resurrection would be a simpler affair. He's already crossed the bridge between here and this place he calls the dark."

"Death," Julie interjected. "It is death he calls the dark, Elliott. Let us use our own words for it."

"Yes, of course, Julie. I simply mean to say that only sunlight will be needed to raise him now."

"And still he'll crave the dark," Julie whispered. "Over us."

"Perhaps," Elliott said, "perhaps not. If newborn babies had the power of speech, would they not beg to return to the womb? To its warmth and comfort and constant nourishment? Is that not what they seek to do with their wails, wordless as they are? And we, arrogant as gods, tell ourselves what they truly desire is our embrace? We train them to love our embrace, is all. We train them to replace the dark. With us."

"Is that what you wish to do?" Julie asked. "Train him to be Lawrence once more?"

"No," Elliott said. "It's a heartbreaking thought. His coldness when he looks at me. The absence . . ." They'd all seen it. Their collective memory of it seemed to fill the room now like a quietly menacing ghost content to glower from the corner.

"I would have preferred the same," Julie said.

"What do you mean, Julie?"

"To have been recognized by him at first. For a moment. Then, to see it go. It is a thing I will not recover from. I will endure. I will go on. But I will not return to being the same creature I was before his recognition of me faded from his eyes."

"Oh, Julie," Elliott moaned.

"Ramses," Julie said coldly. "What do you think we should do?"

"I cannot be trusted with this decision," he said. "My lie to him is proof of this. He terrifies me. In his current state, he terrifies me."

"You lied to him because you want to destroy him?" Elliott asked.

Ramses nodded.

"And so the decision is mine," Julie whispered. "Again it is mine."

"As it should be, Julie," Elliott said. "You are his daughter no matter what he now says."

She smiled at this, but it was a strained smile. An indulgent smile.

She rose and moved to the window, rested her hands against the sill. After a long and agonizing silence, she spoke.

"If he wishes to return to his coffin, let us return him to it."

There was another painful silence. Then Elliott stood. Ramses thought he might be about to protest. "I shall take care of it," he said, with his old stoicism. "We'll see if Osuron will leave his two men with me to assist. No doubt, you'll travel to confront this Vasilev by sea, and for this you'll need Osuron's vessel and much of his crew. But perhaps he can spare these two men."

"You speak as if you're not continuing in this with us?" Ramses asked.

"I'm not. I'm removing this burden from you, so that you both may continue. So that you may put a stop to this Dimitri Vasilev and whatever dire things he plans to do with the Eye of Osiris. That will be my contribution."

"Why?" Julie asked. "Why should you suffer the terrible burden of sealing him away?"

"You have shown such courage in this, Julie. That you would even suggest it to begin with shows courage. And it's yielded incredible results. I will not have you rewarded for this sacrifice by forcing you to endure another death for your father. This time, you may say a planned goodbye, on terms of your design. He will not be stolen from you by a scheming cousin. You will choose your final memory of him and then depart, and I shall see to it that he returns to the dark he craves above us."

It startled them both, the sound that ripped from Julie. A howl not unlike the one that tore from her father upon his resurrection. She spun to face the window behind her, and then there was a terrible crack as Ramses realized she'd brought her fists down upon the windowsill with such force that the wood tore free of the wall and the glass in the lower part of the window shattered.

Rage, Ramses thought. *She is capable of rage.* He had never seen it in her before.

Despair and anguish, yes, and a symphony of other piteous sounds made by grief's orchestra. But not this. Not this eruption. And because she'd turned her back to them as she'd done it, it was clear to Ramses—and to Elliott too, it seemed—that she did not rage at Elliott's plan, but at the terrible truths that had formed it. Ramses did not dare to throw his arms around her too soon, even though that was precisely his instinct. He knew this great surge of anger needed time to flow through her.

"It is already another death we endure for our dear Lawrence," she finally whispered.

Now she turned to him, extended her arm to him, beckoning

him, and drawing him to her. Ramses gathered her in his arms. "Hold on to it, Julie. Clutch it to your breast as one might a hidden dagger. We may well need it to see us through to the end of this."

She went still when he said these things, and he hoped that was because they quieted her within.

After a time, she slipped free of his embrace and crossed the room, gently taking Elliott's hands in hers.

"I will accept your offer, my dear Elliott. But I will need some time to prepare my goodbye."

"Of course, Julie," he whispered. "Julie, in whom Lawrence will always live."

Dim sunlight now outside the windows of the bedroom, and Julie, alone, freshly washed and smelling of the sweet perfume she'd dabbed across her neck and wrists. The perfume which, in Ramses's lustful opinion, always made a delicious counterpoint to the men's attire she now favored.

But she felt hollowed out by the thought of what she planned to do: her parting charade, as she'd come to call it. She'd not gone downstairs again since Ramses and Elliott had left her, lest she lose her nerve. All the while, as she'd run the words she planned to say back and forth in her head, she'd hoped against hope that her father, or the thing that claimed to animate his body, would come racing up the stairs in a storm of tearful apologies. A new awareness of himself rising with the sun.

Was it so far-fetched? He was surrounded by the familiar fragments of his past, each capable of firing memories through his regenerating mind, as Ramses had called it.

A regenerating mind that now sought to banish all traces of his daughter from it.

We shall see how this mind behaves when I am done with it, she thought. *We shall see how it withstands my goodbye.* She

had warned Elliott of what was to come. He needed to be prepared for it. But Ramses, she feared, might talk her out of it, so
she'd asked for solitude and privacy as she collected herself and
rehearsed.

And now the time had come; she could feel it.

She was dressed, and the sun was rising.

It was a new day in which her father lived again but had
chosen a sleep close to death.

A resolute departure once the deed was done would be
essential, so she'd asked Ramses to select one of her trunks and
load it into the awaiting motorcar, so they could drive back to
Cornwall as soon as she'd said her awful goodbye.

A goodbye, Julie thought. *Will any of us refer to it as one,
once I've said it aloud?*

The men were waiting for her in the foyer, all but Lawrence,
who hadn't left the conservatory. He sat on the floor in one
corner, arms wrapped around himself, watching dawn's first
light paint the stone walls now so shockingly visible beyond
the broken glass. Morning birdsong drifted through this new
opening, a crass invasion despite its suggestion of good cheer.
Everything about his posture seemed to say he had reached the
end of his ability to endure their presence, this house. Life outside his coffin.

He did not stir as she walked to him.

She made a little show of looking skyward as well, as if the
dawn made her curious. But to see the conservatory in this
condition—the stained glass shattered—tore at her heart. But
she banished all thoughts of these things. The other men, she
saw, had moved into the nearest doorway, listening closely but
also coiled with tense energy, ready to protect her even though
her father's physical blows could do no harm.

"It appears I owe you an apology," she said. "There's been
such a terrible misunderstanding. And it's all my fault, I fear.
I thought if we brought you back, you would be exactly as

you were before. But I see we've stumbled into something we don't understand. And what we've brought back . . . is not my father." She looked to him now. "You are not my father at all, it seems."

He looked up at her now. No joy in his eyes, no great relief that she had conceded the point he'd made so cruelly several hours before. Did he suspect this was a ruse? Or was his confusion greater, deeper?

"This is a good thing," Julie said. "For you. Whoever you are."

"I am unfinished," he whispered.

"Yes, I know. And so we shall give you the darkness you seek."

"You do not. You cannot. I cannot be destroyed."

"But you can sleep, and this will spare you from your unfinished fate. And it's a good thing, I realize now. A good thing that Lawrence only clings to you in little veils of dust, as you put it. For the hours I've had upstairs have allowed me to reflect on who he really was."

He kept studying her, his brow furrowed, his eyes wide and unblinking. Was she imagining it, the flicker of pain in his eyes. Some reaction to the coldness in her voice, to a rejection that mirrored in some small way the one he'd delivered to her hours before in this very room.

"Grief can blind us just as love does," Julie said coldly. "Surely, you remember this fact, or are you a being who has lost your memories of that as well?"

"I am unfin—"

"Yes, I've heard," she snapped. Then, controlling herself once more, she continued, "You are unfinished. Forgive me for expecting you to understand. So let me get right to the point then. What I mean to say is you are fortunate to only inhabit Lawrence Stratford's flesh and bone, to be shedding all other vestiges of him. He was a terrible man, you see. A weak man.

A dreadful man who drowned his sorrows in drink. Who flew into rages when he did not get precisely his wish.

"And now that I've gazed upon someone who looks just like him but is not him, I no longer have to explain away those terrible nights when he raised a hand to my mother, or when he stumbled drunkenly into my bed, claiming to confuse me with her until I was old enough to fight him away. And explained away these sins as symptoms of misery, you see. His life, it made him miserable. Plucking priceless artifacts from Egyptian sand and selling them to the highest bidder as if they had no real meaning, no history. By the time he died, he'd lost his love of everything. A mystery now that he didn't lose mine."

They were lies. Damnable lies, and she could see them ricocheting into the dark reservoirs within this creature before her, into the spaces where he claimed to shelter an unfinished soul. She could see a vague sense of hurt in his eyes, and there, in the past, a thread of the real Lawrence, the true Lawrence, the Lawrence this creature before her now claimed to be shaking itself free of.

"But he has now," she said. "He's lost my love now. Thanks to you. And the freedom you've granted me."

She had practiced this venom. Sharpened each line, each word, so that she could deliver this speech with utter conviction. And she was terribly proud of herself. Because it was wounding him. And it could only be wounding him if there was a part of him that knew her voice intimately and was familiar with the love that once inhabited her tone when she spoke to him.

She told herself she was not insulting him. She was insulting death and all the confusion it brought.

"You . . . ," the man before her whispered, but he could not complete the thought, and this seemed to cause him pain.

"Me?" she asked. "We don't speak of me. We speak of you,

whatever you are. But I thank you now. I thank you for making it so clear to me."

Startled, he looked to her. No telling if the hurt in his eyes came from her lies, and no choice but to redouble her efforts.

"A man like my father, a man so wretched and full of pain, whose mortal life was marked by such failure and so many dire acts, he should never have been brought back from the dark at all. We were fools to do it, and I was a child blinded by grief. You have freed me from this." She leaned forward now, summoning all the angry emphasis she could. "You have freed me from my love for him, and for this I thank you."

Even though she'd told herself she'd make a quick departure upon these words, hoping to drive their finality through him like a stake, Julie waited, waited for the shell around the man before her to crack, for sobs to begin and howls like the one he'd let loose when first resurrected. Instead his eyes left hers, and he seemed beset by a great strain, and nothing more. She had stirred things inside of him with this diabolical trickery. But these things were not yet set free, and as the minutes passed and the silence between them stretched on, the wait became unbearable.

She rose to her feet.

He flinched, but he did not look at her.

"Goodbye now," she said primly. "Goodbye, whatever it is you are. May the sleep we send you to now finish you, as you crave."

She wanted to look back as she left the room. But before the urge could claim her, Elliott reached out to her, kissed her on both cheeks, held her to him briefly. She couldn't look into his eyes. Or anguish would seize her again.

And then she was descending the steps outside, flanked by Ramses and Osuron, who did not say a word or move to touch her as they approached the motorcar at the curb. The sunlight on her face seemed like an insult. She'd just stepped into the car's front seat when she heard a thud above her, coming from the window. Ramses, behind the wheel, placed a hand gently on her shoulder, directing her attention to the front window, where the lace curtain had been drawn partly back, and there Lawrence stood, balled fists placed against the glass, gazing at her as if she, in the street below, were the impossibility, the confounding mystery.

She would go back. At the first sign of true recognition or misery in him, at the first sign that he'd begun to cast off his convictions, she would race back inside the house and take him in her arms. But she saw only a thunderous confusion stirred by her words, and nothing more. She had, it seemed, presented him with a great mental challenge, but he hadn't crested it. And he might never, she realized, and this shattered her heart.

"Julie . . . ," Ramses finally said, as if looking for a cue.

"He is in there," she whispered. "I can see it. He places himself inside a shell of his own delusions. If we are to send him back to his coffin, I deserved one chance to crack it."

"With lies," Ramses said. "They were all lies, weren't they, Julie? I hope they were lies."

"Every word."

"Lies to draw out the truth," Osuron said, "by sending truth into a rage."

"Precisely," Julie whispered. "Now let us go before what's left of my heart breaks entirely."

Her father remained in the window, gazing at her. Confusion. Pain. But not recognition.

Still, she held his gaze until the car had chugged off down the street and rounded the nearest corner.

"Leave us," Elliott said.

The men, who had yet to give their names, did not protest, and in a moment, Elliott and Lawrence were alone together in the front parlor, Lawrence bathed in sunlight where he remained at the window, watching Julie's departure.

She had meant to do it this way. To leave a crack in Lawrence's perception of himself as an unfinished creature, yanked haphazardly from death, and then depart so that he could not question her or quarrel with her or accuse her. And because he'd never recognized Elliott at all, he'd have no sense answers could be gleaned from him. And so he'd sit with this confusion and simmer and then maybe, maybe, he would rethink his choice. Or he would enter into his sleep, but this confusion would roil inside of him. Some war between his fundamental nature and the false version Julie had presented him with.

But now that they were alone together, Elliott saw an opportunity.

The possibility to level a second blow against Lawrence's now-fragile sense of self.

"Are you hungry?" he asked him.

Lawrence spun, as if the polite inquiry were a slap. It was an absurd question, intended only to draw Lawrence's attention away from the window. From the now-empty street, down which the woman he refused to believe was his daughter had just left.

"Perhaps a bite to eat before you return to your coffin?" Elliott asked.

Shaking his head, gazing at the floor. "You knew Lawrence . . . You knew . . ."

"Why would I tell you if I had? You're just a thing that's claimed his body."

"No, no, no. This is not . . . not the truth of this. I explained, I explained."

"She explained. Just now. Who you really were. Why do you have difficulty believing it?"

"It's a trick. She played a trick."

"How would you know it's a trick?" Elliott asked.

"It's not . . . He's not . . ."

"Not what? Lawrence Stratford is not *what*?"

"Not what she said."

"Ah, and how would you know this? Is it because you reach inside yourself, whatever it is you are, searching for some evidence of the man she just described? And you can't find it, can you? And what do you search? What do you rifle through, nameless creature?"

"A trick," Lawrence whispered. He was pacing the room now. "A terrible trick, all of this."

"Memories. You search through memories, looking for proof of the man she just described. You find none. What do you find instead?"

"Nothing! I find nothing." But the assertion sounded childish, the first stirrings of a tantrum.

"That is a lie. You would not be so disturbed if you found nothing. You find contradictions! You find memories that cling to you more powerfully than the veils of dust you describe. And they seek to assert themselves now, don't they? They seek to tell you who you really are."

"*Monsters!*" Lawrence roared. "You are all monsters that have done this thing. You take what is a god's and expect no punishment for it."

"Ah, so you will punish us, is that it?" Elliott shouted back. "Because your god does not come for you, does he? He does not seek to reclaim you. Not one bit. And so now you must admit that it is you who choose this. It is Lawrence Stratford who chooses the coffin now, and not this god of strange sounds and darkness. *It is you who choose the dark!*"

Hands to his ears, Lawrence tried to run for the front door. When Elliott caught him, hurling him against the wall, the roar that came from Lawrence had more anguish than rage in it, and then he was quickly seized by convulsive sobs.

"I remember everything of you," Elliott said. "I remember

your stubborn refusals, your dogged insistence on living exactly as you saw fit. I remember the disappointment and disdain when I left you in Egypt, when I returned to a life you thought trivial and meaningless. I remember exactly how you sound and the words that come from you and the way you stand when you seek to reject an idea you find abominable. All these things you do now, all these things prove to me that you are Lawrence Stratford and not a dead, unfinished thing as you claim."

Tears spilled from his blue eyes, and each breath seemed to cause him immense pain. Could it be working? Could recognition be dawning, and, just behind it, acceptance?

He released his powerful grip on Lawrence's shoulders, brought his fingers to the sides of Lawrence's face, to the tender spot just below the left corner of his jaw. And yes, Lawrence's eyelids fluttered, his lips sputtered with a breath strained by a sudden bolt of desire.

"But most of all I remember the map of your pleasure," Elliott whispered.

He traced the line along Lawrence's neck he'd traveled so often with the tip of his tongue, his special trick for making Lawrence's back arch like a cat's as he rose to receive him, their combined heat charging the air inside of that houseboat with a special electricity.

"And I see the map is unchanged," Elliott whispered.

Dare he lean in. Dare he progress this. He had no other choice. It was working. It was the tenderest of kisses. Even so, he expected to taste bones ground to dust. But it was flesh he tasted. Living flesh. And the lips were quivering with tortured hunger, with a desire that was all too human. And alive. And it was a body he smelled. A man's body flushed with heat and desire.

"Where is the death in this?" Elliott wasn't sure if he'd asked this question of himself, or of Lawrence.

Elliott sank his hand between Lawrence's robes. Lawrence's

cock grew thick in Elliott's palm. Desperate, hungry breaths flared his nostrils and stuttering little moans escaped his throat that were nothing like the terrible, agonizing sounds he'd made when they first raised him.

"I will show you who you really are, Lawrence Stratford."

Then Elliott crushed their mouths together as he began to stroke, delighting in the feel of life pulsing through Lawrence's body, life Lawrence could do little to contain.

21

Lake Ladoga, Russia

Ever since he was a young man, Nikolai Vasilev had paced like a wild horse, had blown into rooms like a storm, berating those who sat within with accusations that sounded as if he'd already begun an argument with them hours before crossing their threshold. All things he'd done since his arrival at the palace that morning. He was not a brutish or violent man, but his words could be venomous and quick, and now Dimitri wanted nothing more than for him to sit and enjoy the breakfast he'd had prepared for them. If only in hopes that the busyness of some formal ritual would quiet the storm within his son.

But had anything ever quieted this storm?

Nothing of Dimitri's quiet, thoughtful nature had been passed on to his only heir, and for Dimitri, this remained a great mystery. Perhaps it was because Nikolai had not inherited Dimitri's great size. He was a frail, willowy creature like his late mother who made up for it with a force of personality that was often his weapon of choice in the fierce verbal battles in which he seemed to thrive.

For what felt like an eternity now, Nikolai had refused to take his place at the table, had ignored his food altogether, even as Dimitri and Sergei ate with tentative bites, their eyes on their lecturer as if they feared he might suddenly strike out at them if they ceased to listen. It was all frenzied talk of what he'd heard in Saint Petersburg. Talk of the war, of course. And throughout the fevered recitation of portentous facts threaded with speculation and gossip, there was a persistent tone of accusation.

"Russia advances now to the German border!" he proclaimed. "If the Germans do not hold them back, they'll have no choice but to invade with horse-drawn supply trains they will soon outrun. Unless, of course, the Germans are foolish enough to leave undefended trains behind. Which they would not be! All this is because of the rail gauges, you see. We've always maintained our own to prevent an invasion from the Germans. Well, now, with our roles reversed, they work against us, you see? On foot and in miserable wagons, our troops will soon be stretched thin."

It was the moment they'd long discussed; the moment when the powerful secrets they harbored on this island could trigger the essential humiliation of a great nation gone astray—their own.

"I understand all of these things, my son." Dimitri could take no more. "Russia is on the march, as we feared it would be."

"The time is now, Father! Now is when we can shroud our actions in the chaos of war. Destroying the supply lines when the troops have moved so far ahead is key. When they're at the front, they'll have no idea what's taken place! None! When they withdraw, they'll discover their wagons destroyed as if by a giant fist. They'll be like ships at sea without sails or steam, with no choice but to surrender or retreat. There will be a reckoning throughout the halls of power in Petersburg and beyond. The collapse of our terrible involvement in this war will begin!"

"Sit, please, Nikolai, and eat," Dimitri said quietly.

In a controlled rage, Nikolai dragged his heavy dining chair from the table with a thunderous scraping across the floor. Threw himself down into it like an irate child.

"We wait," Dimitri said.

"For what?"

"For our men in Britain. The men you dispatched."

"Father," Nikolai whispered.

"I have always been impressed by the disdain you can pack into a whisper, my son."

"It's not disdain."

"What is it then?" Dimitri asked. "Was it not your idea to attack from the shadows? To avoid witnesses. Only then can we use the Eye's power again and again like the guiding hand it is. Your words precisely, were they not?"

"Yes, but—"

"That's why we have sent your best men to London." He injected a note of finality into his words, even though he knew it foolish to believe the matter settled.

"To kill a man who is already dead," Nikolai said.

"You know that's not true."

"Oh, so Lawrence Stratford lives again?" Nikolai sneered.

"I sent them to wipe out those who might make sense of the mystery surrounding our essential actions. And yes, I should have dealt with all this before now. You know the guilt I've suffered over this. Why torture me with it?"

"And yet you waited," Nikolai said. "You waited until *exactly* the outbreak of war!"

"A war I hoped would be avoided."

"Ah, is that it?" Nikolai asked in disbelief.

"Yes, my son. Killing doesn't come so easily to me. If it did, I would have strangled Lawrence Stratford in his tent."

"I don't believe that for a moment," Nikolai snarled.

"Nikolai," Sergei said quietly, voice full of gentle reprimand.

"What?" Nikolai asked, attacking his food with his fork and knife. "What have we been discussing for months except for murder? You think Russia's restoration will be achieved without loss of life? We've waited so long now, we've no choice but to use the war. Come, Father. None of us entertains the illusion you're a gentler man than you are. Would Anya tell us this?"

"You bring up Anya when you fail to persuade me of something, my son. Otherwise you have no concern for her at all."

"I have concern for our efforts," Nikolai said. "For the time we're wasting."

"We wait for our men in London to send word," Dimitri said. "Let that be the end of it."

"Another suggestion, then," Nikolai said brightly.

"Nikolai, I have spoken."

Undeterred, his son responded, "We approach the kaiser."

He waited for Nikolai to reveal this as a joke. Sergei gave him a look that made his astonishment clear. When no further words came from his son, Dimitri sat back in his chair. "On horseback or on foot?" Dimitri asked.

"I mean we send word."

"Announce ourselves as traitors?" Sergei asked quietly.

"We are already saboteurs in the making. What is the difference?"

"If I only could drive patience into you at the tip of a sword," Dimitri growled.

Undeterred, Nikolai rose to his feet again, bending forward over the table and the balled fists he rested against it. "We announce ourselves as loyalists to nations run by the divine hand of kings! By kings directed by God. Has our purpose changed along with our plan? Or are we now Parisians, ready to sing the nonsense of 'La Marseillaise' in the shadow of the Kremlin?"

"Our plan has not changed," Sergei answered.

"The kaiser, Nikolai," Dimitri said. "What are you proposing with the kaiser?"

"We give him the colossus and the Eye of Osiris. In exchange for protection."

Sergei withdrew his hands from the table, let them fall into his lap, then gave Dimitri a stunned look. He did not believe his own ears and needed Dimitri's expression to confirm Nikolai's wild suggestion. Nikolai, meanwhile, took a careful sip of his coffee, the bone-china cup steady in his hand, eyes averted, as if he'd suggested nothing more significant than a walk along the shore.

"You think I have great love for the kaiser?" Dimitri snarled. "I seek Russia's surrender to its eternal truth. Not its complete destruction at the hands of the Germans."

"Both require German victory in this war."

Dimitri's anger got the best of him, and he slapped the table's edge with enough force to send fiery pain racing up his arm. "They do not!" he roared. *"They require that Russia not join in it!"*

No one spoke for what felt like an eternity, but Nikolai now wore a muted but satisfied smile, as if pleased to have sent his father into a rage.

"Fine," he whispered. "So you won't deploy our great weapon in this war."

"The colossus is not a weapon," Dimitri managed, still struggling to regain his breath. "We do not know what it truly is."

"Because you will not let us test it, Father."

"Because you found it without my consent!" Dimitri roared.

"You would have had me abandon the search?" Nikolai asked, stunned. "All because of that foolish man."

"The power of the Eye was enough!"

"And we do not use it now either!" Nikolai roared. "You are not a man to be infected by words, Father. You're a man of action and achievement. And yet a casual translation of old hieroglyphs leads you to strike out against Lawrence Stratford's ghost!"

"This is not true," Dimitri said. "I've explained myself again and again."

But they were true, his son's words. In part. He'd thought

them to himself last night. As always, no one could injure him quite the way his son could. Oh, and wasn't that always Nikolai's terrible gift. To lance straight through to the truth no one wanted said and attach it proudly to his lapel.

"Because the explanations do the same thing as this plan," Nikolai wailed. "To delay! And delay!"

"You mustn't speak to me—"

"I must! I *must* speak to you this way. Your actions threaten all we've discovered. You've allowed that foolish man inside your head. And now you're so afraid to give life to the colossus that you invent the need for these assassinations. And in so doing you've cast vital fragments of the Eye to the sea—"

Rage sent Dimitri to his feet before he realized he'd stood. "You do not know what it is to be God fearing, my son. You never have. I remember, Easter night. Saint Basil's Cathedral in Red Square. You were sixteen years old. The candles all about us like a great river. Flickering off the faces of the weeping and the worshipful. All of us watched as the priest went to the door of the cathedral just as they went to Christ's tomb so long ago. Watching as he rejoiced upon finding the cathedral empty just as they found the tomb of Christ empty. For he had risen. And when the priest turned to us and proclaimed this and we in turn shouted, 'He is risen,' all the faces around us were joyous, tearful. But not yours! In yours, I saw calculation, as if it were all a spectacle you might someday use to your advantage. In the piety of others you saw only profit. In their reverence you saw something you might seize upon and move like a chess piece. And I knew then, I have a son who does not fear God. Believes in him, yes. But does not fear him. Believes he can be drawn upon like a current of electricity for profit and for gain."

"Why would I fear a God who has blessed us with the Eye and the colossus in turn? Why would I fear a God who grants us these momentous things?"

"Because you do not know why he grants them to us."

Like a snarl, these words had come from Dimitri, and the anger and the fear that danced through them brought sudden silence to the room. And for a moment, a precious moment, Dimitri thought he might have won the argument.

But then Nikolai laughed bitterly. "You don't fear God, Father. You fear failure."

"And what will failure look like to you in this, my son?"

The sound reached Dimitri first—the smashing china and the clattering silver—then he saw all of it smashing the stone floor. Nikolai had swept away his entire place setting with one arm. "This!" he roared. "It looks like this. This paralysis when we are pregnant with magnificent opportunity."

"Control yourself!"

"Control your fear, and allow me to rid you of it!"

Nikolai sped for the door.

"Nikolai, no!" Dimitri shouted.

"The colossus," Sergei said, rising to his feet. "He means to use the Eye on the colossus!"

They were running now, both he and Sergei, down the stone steps, towards the brief blast of light that came from Nikolai's flight into the courtyard outside. They burst through the door just as Nikolai raced past the towering *Bronze Horseman.* His son was young and spry while Dimitri carried great weight and was often winded after a long walk. There'd be no catching up with him on foot. The thought that Nikolai might reach the colossus before they did, that he might do what Dimitri had forbidden them all to do, sent Dimitri's hand to the stone at his neck. It came to light within the heat of his clutching fist.

When the bronze hooves of the great horse met the courtyard's stone floor, they sounded like the muffled tolls of great bells. And it all seemed so effortless suddenly, so effortless for the great statue and its rider to come to life and take off in pursuit of his son.

Just to stop him, Dimitri thought. *Just to stop him from reaching the colossus.*

But it was terror that drove Dimitri in this moment, and so it was terror that drove the horse and its rider. When Nikolai turned, Dimitri saw his son's hand grab for his own necklace, his own fragment of the Eye. In a blinding instant, the thought that Nikolai might be able to wrest control of the great horseman from him flooded Dimitri with panic. This chase was poised now to become a duel, with father and son already turned and aiming at each other. The horse's great bronze legs rose high into the air, slicing Nikolai with shadow as he gazed up at them in terror. Then, as if he were made of matchsticks, his son went down under the giant horse's trampling metal legs, torso twisting in two impossible directions at once, and even then, Dimitri told himself it was essential. That he had to destroy the stone at Nikolai's neck, and everything else was now incidental.

Dimitri was still assuring himself of these things as he commanded the horse and its rider to turn back to him, back towards the pedestal from which Dimitri had just caused it to leap.

Behind Dimitri, Sergei's anguished moans sounded like attempts to form prayers. The horse, it seemed, was staring at them, as if awaiting further instruction. Dimitri knew that if he were truly to bring an end to this awful moment, he should command it to return to its original pose, but he could not bring himself to. There was blood on its hooves, blood splashed across the front of the bronze rider. The blood of his son who was not wise enough to fear God.

He would not stop, Dimitri told himself. *I had to do it because he would not stop, and he would not stop because he had no fear of God. There was nothing within him that could imagine all the horrors he might have unleashed had he brought the colossus to life. We might have been enslaved to it, just as Lawrence Stratford said.*

When they reached his body, they found Nikolai's neck brutally twisted to one side. Blood bubbled from a mouth gone lax, and his slitted eyes were weeping. Perhaps with tears, or with fluids forced from him by the terrible impact of those bronze hooves. The necklace was still around his neck, but its stone had been shattered. Fragments of it were spread across his blood-spotted torso. The chain had also been split. When Dimitri reached down and tugged at it, the necklace came free, shedding its last little bits of broken, amber-colored stone to the dirt at Dimitri's feet.

How abominable that he felt only relief. Relief to be freed of his son's arrogance, and his brashness in the face of great mysteries. And that a key to what the colossus held in store, a key Dimitri had foolishly granted his son, had been destroyed.

Another man's key, he corrected himself. *Not mine, not the one I control.*

Sergei was paces away, bent forward, hands clasped in prayer, tears spilling from his eyes at the sight of Nikolai's broken body.

If there was ever a moment that could melt the iron bond between them, it was now. His brother reached up and gently removed the necklace he wore and extended it to Dimitri in one hand.

"You abandon me now?" Dimitri asked.

"No, Brother, no." Sergei shook his head, but he was still studying Nikolai's corpse. "Only you can be trusted with this. But we are brothers always."

But his son was gone, and he could only hope now that he was cradled in the arms of the god he'd never feared.

22

Cornwall

Angry clouds and pewter wind-tossed seas stretched before Ramses as he watched Julie and several members of Osuron's crew travel to the proud, dark vessel anchored just offshore. The vessel was a steam yacht, with the lines and rigging of a sailing ship and a slender smokestack in its center. The sails, which were down now, could be used to free the ship from reliance on coaling stations, allowing travel across great distances.

If the occupants of the rowboat bouncing towards it now had not been immortal, Ramses would have forbidden the journey. The seas were so rough, Julie was forced to grip the boat's sides to avoid being thrown free. But he'd sent her ahead on purpose.

He would await Osuron before boarding, out of respect, he said. It was a lie. In part. They'd sent their immortal captain into the castle alone so he could provide Bektaten with a full account of all that had transpired in London. It was a childish thing, he knew, this attempt to skirt their queen's potential disapproval. But if it worked, they could simply carry on, abandon themselves to a sense of purpose. What else could prevent them from being consumed by the terrifying implications of the past few days?

When he heard two sets of footsteps descending the twisting staircase carved out of the rocky cliffs, his heart sank.

His little trick had failed. In part.

He'd spared Julie a reprimand from their queen. Now he would endure it on her behalf.

So be it.

Beside Osuron, Bektaten approached across the sand, the wind catching her purple robes, turning them into banners behind her. Intensely she studied the departure of the rowboat across the waves. Ramses was once again struck by the myriad and subtle ways in which immortals moved differently through the world, against the wind. Because she was not as sensitive to the stinging blasts as an ordinary human might be, because she did not flinch and squint, Bektaten approached with stillness and authority, a steadiness that made the wild dancing of her wind-tossed garments seem all the more spectral.

"Forgive our speed," Ramses said. "To reach Dimitri Vasilev's estate on Lake Ladoga, we'll enter the Neva River from the Baltic. But it'll take some time. The northerly route is best."

"Is it?" Bektaten walked to where the line of seafoam spread slowly across the sand. The rowboat was now a white speck against the dark hull of Osuron's yacht. "Is it best?"

"It's safest. We can't skirt the coasts of Germany and France. Not in this moment."

She turned her back to the angry sea. Her pointed glare suggested she wasn't about to take this bait. "The vials. Did you leave the vials with Elliott?"

"I did not."

"I must speak with Julie," Bektaten said, turning to the sea, perhaps to hide her anger.

"You must not."

Silence now, except for the wind howling across the cliffs that rose overhead, the insistent slaps and gurgles of sea meeting rocky shore. As was her custom when impatience seized him, Bektaten appeared intrigued.

Did she expect him to retract his command, apologize for his impertinence?

He did no such thing.

"Her father has died for her a second time. The first time, the loss almost sent her to the grave. She must give herself to a cause that heals, that resolves and completes. Not be brought to heel by a queen. Not now. Not in this moment."

"You protect her from me."

"There's an anger in her I've never seen," he said. "I protect you from each other."

"I see, well. Since you will not permit me to speak to her, I will leave it to you to give Julie my parting message."

"Of course."

"That if it turns out Elliott has lost his hold on Lawrence, and if it seems you have once again resurrected another murderous creature and loosed it upon a modern city, I will destroy it."

He had angered her, it was clear. Angered her by leaving Elliott to contend with Lawrence alone and without the means to destroy him. But he had not angered her beyond her means to give a calm and rational voice to that, and he doubted he ever could.

He envied her this. Later, perhaps, should this urgent mission be brought to a successful close, he would admire her for it. But for now, he could only envy her.

When he nodded in response, she said, "Travel safe, Ramses, and see this through to its finish, no matter what's required. Of you and of her."

Part III

23

Lake Ladoga, Russia

There had been a death in the palace.

Anya heard the weeping for days afterwards, mournful and echoing, the timbres too familiar to be ghosts. She knew it could not be a product of her broken mind, for her visions never spoke or cried out. Dimitri; his brother, Sergei; the servants—she heard them all as she quietly roamed the halls, eavesdropping on the frightened whispers of the maids, spying on their tearful hand-wringing. A terrible accident, they said, preceded by an awful quarrel between father and son. It was Sergei who'd found the stallion, frightened and running loose from where it had thrown Nikolai to the stone next to the great statue of *The Bronze Horseman* in the courtyard.

Such injuries to have been sustained from a simple fall, they wept. And then quieter, and at the end of their lamentations, the servants spoke of a darkness that seemed to be spreading throughout the Lake Ladoga palace. What had at first seemed like a privilege—to be one of the few chosen by the eldest Vasilev to work in seclusion on this forested island—now seemed like a terrible curse. Could this be because the island housed a secret? The larger church had been well maintained, but the doors to the smaller, more private chapel and family mausoleum had been barred for some time now.

Was there something within that had invoked the wrath of God?

A funeral was held, but Dimitri did not come for her. Did not dress her in something beautiful and black with a collar of lace and strands of pearls, did not take her arm in his and guide her to the island's private church. She'd told him she'd need no public display of any union between them. But still, his absence on the day of his son's funeral came as a terrible rejection. She could do nothing to heal his grief; he would not even permit an attempt. And so it was as she'd feared for some time now. He was tiring of her. Growing frustrated with his inability to heal her broken mind.

Indeed, on the day of the service, she was forbidden to take her walk, to leave her room at all. A butler was stationed just outside the door to her room, a sign that she was to remain hidden. A secret. *Cloistered* was a word he'd once used to describe their arrangement, and it was the first time she'd heard it. It meant "protected," "safe." But if he thought he could protect her, his madness rivaled her own.

The demons were inside of her mind. The demons were cloistered within her, feeding off all she saw. No island or palace could shelter her from this. Her only solace was her occasional ability to believe there was a reality to the wild visions, that the life which sometimes animated the figurines and statues and dolls in her presence was as real as clouds and lightning, and others were simply blind to it.

Some days this was a comfort. But on others, she wanted desperately to believe they were pure illusion. That a stone had dislodged itself inside her mind, and her thoughts struck it as water might a rock in the center of a rushing creek, sending up wild and blinding spray.

Total madness would have been a blessing. Easier for the visions to grip her in every moment. She could have slipped entirely into the mad reality they seemed to govern. Given the statues names and personalities, treated them to tea parties, engaged them in long conversations. But she could not. For the statues did not always turn to stare at her, and the chubby little porcelain dolls did not always march towards her across the room, extending their arms to her like children demanding to be held. There was no sure pattern to when they'd rouse and seek to engage her in silent, tortuous little games.

How she hated the dolls!

But how wounded Dimitri had been when she asked him to remove them. They were meant to comfort her, he said. Their faces conveyed innocence and warmth, did they not?

He had been so generous and kind. How could she disappoint him!

And so she'd trained herself to hide the effects of the visions should they seize her when Dimitri was near. For if he thought she was improving, then he'd come to see her as a suitable bride. A secret one, of course, given her peasant background. But he never left the island anymore, and so they could remain together, a comfort to each other. And for a time after she'd made this decision, the visions had receded altogether, as if simply making the vow to conceal their terrible effects had beaten them back, leaving her on stable ground. And how overjoyed she'd been. And how desperate to present this progress as a sign that she could serve him more truly.

But then, no sooner had she expressed this wish than the dolls had come to life again.

No doubt he'd heard her tears over this through the walls. Maybe that's why he'd rejected her on the day of his son's funeral.

He would be rid of her soon, she feared. Especially now that he'd lost Nikolai. His grief would add too much weight to the burdens she'd added to his life. She clung to him whenever he was near, which was rarely now. She pleasured him at a moment's notice. How else to distract him from what a painful reminder she was of his failures? His failure to heal her mind, to rescue her from madness. In the end, his desire would not be enough, she feared. He would tire of her flesh as he became exhausted by her brokenness. And she would be cast out a second time. To an asylum, perhaps. To a place with almost no sun and no trees, where no one would dress her or care for her or call her precious and a treasure.

Her only moments of real peace were on her walks, and the reason for this was clear.

The pine trees had no faces. The trees had no hands or arms, or stubby little porcelain fingers. They never jeered at her or taunted her, but stood instead in orderly regiments well suited to catch the wind. They whispered to her, sang to her, but the song was gentle and heavenly, and when she walked among them, even though she was clad in the beautiful, lace-collared dresses he filled her bedroom with, she was Anya from Tomsk. A poor Siberian girl who marked the passage of time with the completion of ordinary tasks whose results were plainly visible to the eye—the sudden shine of a table after a thorough wipe, the glisten on a stone floor after it was thoroughly mopped. These, and the predictable desires of a young woman—for love, for food, for the occasional beautiful thing, if only to hold briefly during her late-night hours of work at the museum—had once been the substance of her life. But this orderliness had depended upon the lifelessness of stone and other solid surfaces. Now she was cursed with visions that suggested a force could move through them all, animating them at will, but only to her eye.

Days had passed since the funeral and the departure of the guests who'd come for it. Guests she'd glimpsed as she peered out one corner of her bedroom window. They'd arrived by boat, clad in mourning black. None had stayed the night. The boy's mother was long dead, and this was good; this was a relief. It meant that Anya was not a mistress.

Then, during one of her walks, she came across Dimitri.

He was seated amidst a circle of stone benches installed in a clearing between the trees. He rushed to her when he saw her. Seized her, and backed her up against a tree. His eyes were wild and bloodshot, and the scent of vodka rode each heaving breath. He clutched her face, ran his fingers drunkenly and sloppily over her cheeks and jaw. The sunlight streaming through the trees sent a latticework of shadows across his face. He was driven mad by grief now, weeping and drunk in the middle of the day. He looked at her as if she had changed shape. And she knew better than to see this drunken groping as true need, the need that would form a new union, a need that would secure her place here. This was wild and desperate and fleeting; it would recede with the first long sleep.

Guilt, she realized. *He feels guilt when he looks at me now. And it has been loosened inside of him by the loss of his son.*

"What we have both lost, Anya," he whispered, "what we have both lost to be here."

To be here. This choice of words did not make sense to her. It implied she had aspired to be brought to this place, aspired to be cast out by her family.

"I can give you back some of what you lost." She feared he'd remember little of what she said now; that's how intoxicated he seemed. "If you let me . . ."

Foolish to make this demand of him now, when he was in this state. Would he even hear her words? It didn't seem so.

"Walk me" was all he said in response. The request seemed absurd. He was such a large man and she a tiny creature. But still, he lopped one arm around her delicate shoulders, holding to her as he might a tree trunk. "Too much to drink . . . I need you . . . to walk me."

And so she did. She walked the man who'd cared for her. Cloistered her.

Protected her. Fed her. Sheltered her when her family had cast her out.

She walked him through the woods and back to the palace, as she'd never done before, hoping that when he sobered he would remember this support of him, how quietly she endured the great physical strain his body placed on her own. By the time they reached the palace, Dimitri's brother was waiting for them. He took the enormous man from Anya's awkward half embrace as one might collect a child.

They left her all alone. Standing outside in the sunlight by herself.

And so she continued her walks.

Dimitri did not come.

Neither did her visions.

She came to believe it was the sun that drove them away. That it cleansed and healed her.

And then, one afternoon, not far from where she'd discovered Dimitri crying miserably some days before, she looked up to see a new sort of vision. But this was not a statue come to life. This was a living, radiant being. A woman, she realized, but dressed in the smart clothes of a wealthy man, with a head of brown curls and eyes so startlingly blue Anya lost her breath.

There was something about the woman that was impossible to name. She was not a statue come to life, but there were aspects to her that were beyond human, and the expression on her face was full of something Anya had not seen for some time. Understanding.

But it was a trick, she knew. Perhaps a trick to send a woman at all.

The day had come.

Dimitri had tired of her, and these well-dressed strangers had come to take her away.

Anya, doomed by visions, was homeless once more.

24

When the woman before them did not recoil or cry out at the sight of Ramses and Osuron approaching swiftly through the woods behind her, Julie realized she'd borne witness to far stranger and darker things than the stealthy advance of two blue-eyed immortals. How else to explain the reserve with which she regarded them now. She didn't cry out for help, didn't cast a desperate look in the direction of the palace. Rather, she regarded all three of them in turn as if they were just the latest in a series of grim inevitabilities.

From the little rowboat they'd used to circle and map the island as best they could, Julie had watched the fragile, dark-eyed beauty for hours, marveling at her isolation and the pained stillness with which she'd sit for long stretches, staring out at the water. She seemed to live entirely in a world of her own thoughts, and these thoughts were quiet, ongoing torments. And in those moments when she'd gazed directly into the waters of the lake, Julie had glimpsed her old self, consumed by grief, staring hopelessly into the Mediterranean's chop before she leapt from the deck of that homeward-bound ship.

This young woman had lost something just as profound, it was clear. But she made no attempt to drown herself, this delicate creature. At least none they'd witnessed through the binoculars they'd used to watch her.

"You must come with us," Osuron said with polite firmness, "and you must not cry out." He spoke Russian, which Julie now understood.

A mind bathed by the elixir could acquire a new language within days, and during their voyage across the Baltic, she and Ramses had sat for hours, listening as Osuron conversed with his loyal crew in the guttural language of the tsars. The musical patterns alighted down passages in Julie's brain opened by the elixir's fiery magic. And indeed, it seemed magical, the way behavior, mood, and tone somehow endowed previously incomprehensible sounds with meaning, with weight. The process was dizzying. Gradually, she began to see herself performing the actions they described, as if this mental image of herself had become a puppet for Osuron's words. Only then did she realize these sudden visions were translations of the words they spoke. It was Julie's first experience of immersing herself in a new language and allowing the elixir's transformative power to do the rest.

"You will not be harmed." The Russian, new to Julie's tongue, felt sensuous and exciting.

From their stances, it had to be clear to the woman that Ramses and Osuron were ready to restrain her if she tried to flee. But now she walked willingly, if miserably, beside Julie, who guided her towards the rowboat they'd beached on the flat, muddy shore.

Swiftly, they rowed from the island.

Osuron's steam yacht drifted safely out of view from the shore on which the palace sat, its engine prepared to go full power should they elicit a response from whatever forces might be gathered there. But they'd watched the island for some time now, and there seemed to be no forces of any kind. The place was ghostly, haunted. Dimitri Vasilev's wife had been dead for years, they knew, so this young woman, who spent her days wandering the pines like a frail apparition, might be some sort of unwed lover or ward.

Once they were a good distance from the shore, the woman began to softly weep, her head bowed. Julie studied her, realized their captive was fighting an urge to look back at the island. When the woman lost this battle, looking back over her shoulder at the mound of pines bathed in the unrelenting sun, her tears intensified, and Julie felt her own heart break. They had no plans to harm her. To question her, to perhaps trade her with this Vasilev if it came to that. But the total resignation with which she'd given herself to them combined with the piteousness of her tears now raised terrible possibilities.

What has been done to this poor creature? Julie thought. *How has she been broken like this?*

In Saint Petersburg, after they first entered the Neva River, Osuron had briefly disembarked to meet with one of his mortal spies, to whom he'd sent word before they departed. He returned to the yacht with a startling tale. Dimitri Vasilev's son had been killed in a terrible accident, the Lake Ladoga palace plunged into mourning. But this accident was cloaked in suspicion. And there'd been no mention of this woman.

As they brought her aboard, the boiler came to life, sending tremors through the wooden walls all around them. Just as Osuron had instructed, the yacht was putting distance between itself and the island. But it seemed a useless gesture. No one had pursued. They'd just quietly raided an island in mourning and easily made off with one of its jewels.

They walked Anya belowdecks, into the luxurious private cabins with their mahogany furnishings. Because this was a vessel crewed by immortals with no need to sleep, the sleeping quarters were mostly sitting rooms; one had been turned into a little library where the walls were lined with low sofas containing dark blue cushions fringed with gold embroidery and, above the sofas, more shelves were filled with leather-bound volumes.

They hadn't restrained their new passenger, or even touched her. But she walked silently to the farthest stretch of sofa and sat down on it, head bowed. Her tears were quieter now, but they still flowed.

"I know nothing there is really mine," she finally said. "But there are a few things from my bedroom I would like to take with me if Dimitri allows it. If he won't let me return to my room, I can give someone a list, and maybe he will let these things travel with me. Is this too much to ask?"

So many implications in the woman's trembling, halting words, in the pleading look filling her generous dark eyes. It was clear she saw them not as invaders or abductors, but as figures of authority, dispatched by Dimitri Vasilev himself. Ramses seemed to see Julie's eagerness to take the lead with this poor creature, and gave her a small nod.

"What things would you like?" Julie asked.

"Several nightgowns. They're quite comfortable. And a silver locket he gave me shortly after he brought me here. It has my name etched on the inside. And the hairbrush."

"And when did he bring you here?" Julie asked.

"I have lost count of the days. But years, it seems. Dimitri knows. Ask him. If he wants you to know, he will tell you."

Such terrible submission, Julie thought.

"What is your name?" Julie asked.

"He did not tell you my name? Am I to have no name where I am going? No family, and no name."

"Where is your family?"

The woman shook her head. Her confusion seemed to replace her tears, and Julie thought this might be a good thing. It could focus her, even if it was tinged with growing suspicion.

"You ask me these things to see if I've forgotten them, don't you? You are testing my mind. Well, I can tell you, my mind's not entirely broken. Nor is it healed. Anya. My name is Anya, and my family is from Tomsk."

"Would you like to see your family again?"

Anya let out a shuddering breath. Her tears returned, bitterly now.

"You torment me with this question," she stuttered between tearful breaths. "Take me away as he wishes, but do not torment me. My visions torment me enough."

"We don't wish to torment you," Julie said.

"You're English. I can tell from your accent. Is that where you're taking me? To England?"

"Where would you like us to take you, Anya from Tomsk?"

Anya gazed into Julie's eyes as if the question was impossible for her to comprehend. As if the idea that she'd be allowed to plot her own course was a baffling impossibility.

"I wish to stay," she finally whispered. "I wish to be his wife. He cared for me, sheltered me after my family cast me out. I could not have asked for greater protection. But I have not been healed. I can pretend, but I have not. And I fear he needs me healed if we're to wed. I need no station or position. I'd be content to live here on his island for the rest of my days. But it's not to be. For you take me now. You take me far from where I can remind him of his failure. And whoever will care for me there will not be as kind as he has been, I'm sure of this."

"We are here to listen, not to judge. It seems you have judged yourself harshly enough. Speak to us of your visions."

"Surely he's told you everything of my condition," Anya whispered.

"The visions are yours, and so only you can describe them accurately."

"They do not speak. The things I see, they do not speak or cry out. But they taunt me. They challenge me. Silently. With gestures. They . . . come to life."

"What?" Julie asked as gently as she could. "What comes to life, Anya?"

"Things that should not live. Things that should not walk. Things that should not reach for me." At these final words, her voice broke and she raised a hand to her mouth.

Recognition swept through all three of them. Julie's pity

deepened. She felt fresh anger. For Anya, fragile Anya from Tomsk, was not a conspirator in whatever plot had been hatched on the island nearby. She was one of its victims.

"When did it begin?" Julie asked. "When did you first see these things?"

"In the museum," Anya answered. "I worked in a museum."

Osuron said, "The Academy of Science and History. Dimitri Vasilev's museum."

Anya nodded. "I lied to him," she whispered.

"To whom?"

"Dimitri, all this time, I've lied to him. There are things I haven't told him."

"The museum, Anya," Julie said gently. "Take us back to the museum. Where it all began."

"I was going to steal a jewel, perhaps two. Every night when I cleaned the archive, more fine things had arrived during the day. All from Egypt. From the expeditions the Vasilev family financed to build the museum's collections. And when I touched them, when I thought about placing one inside my pocket, that's when I saw the light."

"A light in the stone?"

"I thought so at first, but then it seemed to come from behind me. The statue's face. When I turned, it was . . . It was alive. It was glowing like its face was a mask atop fire. Anubis, they said it was called. Newly brought from Egypt, and before my eyes, it came to life."

When she'd witnessed the archangel come to life in Brompton Cemetery, Julie had thought of the appearance of the statue's glowing face in much the same terms: a mask atop a bed of flame. But Anya's assumption that the light she'd seen in the stone had come from the statue alone was proof she still knew little about the Eye of Osiris, despite having passed it through her hands. "It was alive," she continued, "it moved as I moved. It mocked me, it seemed, by mimicking my every gesture. I had no words for what I was seeing. I ran. I screamed and I ran."

"Did you take the stone with you?" Julie asked.

"What stone?" Anya asked.

It was answer enough. She didn't know the stone she'd held in her hands had been the source of the statue's animation. She still didn't know. There was much Anya from Tomsk did not know, and that ignorance, it seemed, had been used against her in terrible ways.

But the delicate woman did not believe herself to be ignorant. Or deceived. "It's my punishment, you see," she explained. "I plotted to steal something of great value and this madness has been my punishment. A curse. A terrible curse that only I can see."

Julie asked, "What happened after you fled the museum?"

"I confessed all to my parents. They believed I'd been possessed by spirits. Spirits that had been drawn to the museum by all the ancient items within. They recoiled from me as if I were diseased, as if I were not their own child. And then Dimitri, he heard the tale. He was visiting his holdings in the city. His family's mines, they'd built the museum and so much of our city. We loved him more than we loved the tsar.

"But my story had become a scandal. So he came to hear it for himself, and when I told him what I had seen in the museum, he promised he would go there to see if there was any truth to my tale. When he returned, he told me there was no evidence of what I had described. But since my family had cast me out, he would take me and protect me and heal me. Whatever had broken my mind had struck within the walls of his museum, and so I was his responsibility now. His to heal. But after all this time, he has failed, and I remind him of this, I know."

As the gravity of what had been done to Anya washed over them all, no one spoke.

Finally, in English, Julie said, "Bring me the necklace."

"Julie," Ramses said.

At the sound of English words she clearly didn't understand, Anya straightened, looked nervously between them.

"Bring me the necklace so we can show this poor woman what has really been done to her mind."

Next to her now, his voice a whisper in her ear, Ramses said, "Julie, we do not know this woman. This could be some sort of trick."

"This woman is no more suited to trickery than to flight."

She would fight Ramses on this if she had to. Fight him with words and fists if need be.

It was Osuron who relented, returning a moment later with the silver-plated box in which he'd stored the necklace Bektaten had allowed them to bring for their own defense.

Back to Anya, Julie slid on her leather gloves. "Bar the door in case the sight of it frightens her," she whispered. The men complied.

"Please," Anya said behind her. "I go willingly. I need no restraints. Please."

When Julie turned, the necklace's amber stone resting in one open palm, it was as she predicted. Anya cried out, drawing her legs up off the floor as if she thought it possible to crawl through the porthole window behind her. Tears sprung from her eyes. She believed it to be the same stone she'd touched that night in the museum. And it might well have been, given the journey it had taken since.

"What is this? What is this you've brought? What is it you seek to do to me?"

She bolted for the door. Osuron caught her, gripping her wrists as she tried to buck her slender arms free. But even amidst her terror and her attempt to flee, she could not take her eyes off the stone in Julie's hands.

"You don't just come to take me away. You come to punish. He knows, doesn't he? Dimitri knows I tried to steal it."

"Anya, you have been deceived."

These words quieted her, but they didn't chase the terror from her expression.

"Cursed," she whispered. "I have been cursed."

"Not by this stone, by men. One man in particular. You do not see this man for who he truly is because he's used this stone and its power against you. Nothing you've done, nothing you've thought, makes you deserving of the punishment you describe."

"It's not the punishment of a court. It's a punishment from a world beyond this one, disguising itself as a madness."

"No, Anya. No, this is not true. But for you to see this, I must ask you to do something that will require your courage."

"Conceal that stone from me and I will do anything."

"Anya, you must touch it."

Her wail turned into a piercing cry. "How can you ask this? It could invite worse judgment!"

"There are five stones just like this. I have seen what they can do. We have all seen what they can do. There is a power within them, and this power has been used against you, Anya. I believe Dimitri Vasilev has used this power against you. I believe the night you told him your tale he returned to the museum and found proof of everything you said. But instead he lied so that you would believe yourself mad and surrender to his so-called protection."

Julie's words silenced her. They also penetrated Anya's terror. Her breaths still heaved; her eyes still ran with tears. But she was listening, it seemed. Listening intently.

Quickly, Julie set the stone on the nearby table, reached up, and removed the jeweled dragonfly pin she wore on her lapel. She placed the pin on the table, picked up the stone again in her gloved hand, and extended it towards Anya, who gazed at Julie as if the last words she'd spoken still swelled from her like vapor.

"Who are you?" Anya whispered.

"If you touch the stone and follow my instructions, I will be the one who sets you free."

Anya looked to the men.

If they disapproved of this exercise, they were doing a fine job of concealing it.

Slowly, Anya extended her fingers towards the amber stone in Julie's gloved hand. The very tips of her fingers shook as they drew near; then, closing her eyes, she touched her fingers gently to the stone's surface. When the illumination grew within, she released a stuttering gasp, the terror of that night in the museum clearly returning.

"I see it," Julie whispered. "I see the light your touch has made. It is not a vision. It is real. It is happening to my eye as well as yours. Now look to the pin on the desk." Once Anya complied, Julie said, "Imagine it in flight, rising up from the table."

The pin did just that; its tiny, jeweled glass wings becoming a blur as it rose into the air. Once again, Julie was astonished at the completeness with which this power consumed the material of its subject. Comparing it to an electrical current was only partially accurate. Whatever momentous energy this stone channeled seized the very substance of the material itself, animating it, shielding it from the damage its unnatural contortions might leave. This stone yielded a life force as powerful and momentous as that which animated the cells of the human body itself.

So distracted was she by the dragonfly's flight, Julie had forgotten to study Anya's reaction. But Anya was watching Julie. She was watching Julie react to the little circles the dragonfly pin was making in the air above the cherrywood desk. Anya was watching another human react to what she'd believed to be a product of her broken mind.

"Land it on my shoulder," Julie said softly.

Anya did just that. Julie flinched slightly from the impact. Then, she reached up and removed the pin, extending it to Anya in one palm.

"Now higher," she said.

Anya complied. The dragonfly wheeled into a high arc. Anya watched with the same wonder a child might use to witness their first airplane. Julie realized what had calmed the poor woman. It was the act of stopping the dragonfly's flight, and then starting it again. It was the control. For the first time, she could direct and steer the impossible visions that had tortured her.

"Now, Anya, you can prove to yourself it's not madness."

"How?" Anya whispered.

"Make it stop."

The dragonfly plummeted. Julie caught it in one gloved hand.

How many acts like this had been used to terrify her? How many objects had been brought to life to menace her, to turn her into a prisoner of the island from which they'd just removed her? How many times had she tried to make the madness in her mind stop and failed? This time she had succeeded.

Julie handed the necklace to Ramses, who was careful to take it by its chain as he returned it to the box.

But Anya's stare remained focused on the fist Julie had closed around the dragonfly.

She walked to it, gently pried Julie's fingers open, as if the sight of the little jeweled beauty somehow focused and made real the implications of all she'd just witnessed, all she'd just done.

Julie caught the woman just as her knees buckled. The sounds that came from her were not piteous wails, but howls of rage. Anya clenched her teeth, balled her hands into fists, landing several blows onto the table before Julie was able to steer her towards the nearest bed of cushions and seize her in an embrace. The betrayal Anya felt convulsed her body with angry spasms in search of a brawl.

And, oh, how Julie envied her. Envied the abandon of her fury. She'd wanted to do as much when her father demanded to return to the dark. The strength with which she'd torn the sill from her bedroom window had been but a tease of the havoc she'd longed to unleash. And so now, she did not just cling to poor Anya to keep her from tearing this little cabin apart. It was as if the writhing energy of Anya's tantrum cleansed her, purged her, warmed her like a fire.

"You are free, Anya," Julie whispered. "You are not mad, and now you are free."

For a long while, Julie sat with her, cradled her head, and allowed her to softly weep onto her lap. Anya said nothing, but Julie did not need the fragile woman to speak to know the tumult within her. For Julie knew well that leveling blast of a belief system decimated, had known the dark hours it took for new knowledge, new awareness, to force out the old, which would continue to grope in vain for comfort unless it was excised. Once the process was complete, a terrible emptiness would seem to sit within the soul. But it was not an emptiness truly, but a barren field awaiting new seeds. This is what she hoped, at least.

This is what she had hoped for her father. But his fate, his dreadful choice, was too painful to contemplate in this moment, and so Julie devoted herself to Anya's care. The men came and went, of course. The expressions respectful but also searching and laced with anticipation. They were, Julie realized, checking to see that Anya had not summoned her old delusions. If so, she would not prove to be an ally, not provide the information they required about the structures, the human souls, and the threats that might await them in the island's forested depths.

But when Anya stiffened and rose, it was with purpose, and

she did not shake Julie off rudely as she did so. Instead, she walked to the nearby desk where a paper and pen sat as almost-decorative ornaments. And in her fixed expression and the glazed intensity of her eyes, Julie saw what must have been the hardworking peasant girl, who had braved chill winter winds to reach the late-night hours of labor awaiting her at the Vasilev Academy of Science and History.

Anya took the pen in her grip. "I shall draw you a map, so that you may do what you seek to do with no surprises."

And in her tone, it was clear she said these words as she might *I will give you all you need to destroy the man who sought to destroy my mind.*

But after more conversation, it soon became clear to Julie there was one secret on the island that had remained hidden, even to Anya.

She brought this news and Anya's hand-drawn map to the men. They awaited some sort of word in the spacious main cabin. A cold silence settled over the room. It was Osuron who first broke it. "If she's not glimpsed the colossus, then it might not be here. The Eye might be all they possess."

"But if it isn't," Ramses said quietly. "If it isn't, our plans could be tossed to the wind in an instant."

"The ritual you describe does not suggest this," Osuron said.

"It doesn't? How can you say this? Join it with our recent discoveries, and the ritual I describe suggests I was taken to another realm. You don't believe such a doorway could be opened on this island?"

"I trust us not to step through it," Osuron said quietly.

"There was no choice inside the Temple of Karnak."

"You were willing," Osuron said. "You stepped through it willingly. Under the guidance of the priests."

"This is a simplification. It's no matter. If there's the slightest chance the colossus is here, we must locate it and guard it before all else."

"We cannot, Ramses," Osuron said. "It's impossible without avoiding detection. The others on the island must be subdued first."

"It's true, Ramses," Julie said softly. "Anya has named seven servants, and then eight guards."

"And yet no one came to her defense when we took her," Ramses said.

"They guard the buildings above all else, and we came upon her in a remote section of the island," Julie said.

"Of course, because the structures are precisely where the colossus might be hidden." His jaw was tense; his hands rested on the table before him.

"All of it, Ramses. They guard all the structures. The colossus could be anywhere. Osuron is right. We can't just strike out and begin a search for it before we've subdued all who might stand in our way."

Osuron said, "And I've a tool that will help us do just that."

Startled, Ramses gave the man his full attention. "Dream rose," he whispered.

Osuron nodded, but it was Ramses's anger and not his words that held his full attention.

"I see," Ramses said, "and so our queen equipped you as she equipped me. Because she did not trust my judgment alone."

"Ramses," Julie whispered, "please—"

"It was not the age of the motorcar or the flying machine, but I was a king. And as king I knew well the approach of a threat which required an army, and even with mortal eyes and hands I could tell if a field was riven with stone that would tear the wheels from our chariots before the first swords met. And I know this now. To travel into the depths of that island with no clear sense of where this colossus might reside, it's as good as striking out to sea with great yawning holes in the hull of this very vessel."

"We will find the colossus," Osuron said, "but it will be

Dimitri Vasilev who brings us to it, once we have incapacitated all who might render him aid."

"This will only give him time to unleash it while we are busy sending each and every one of his servants and guards into a trance," Ramses muttered.

"We'll strike with greater care than that." There was a pleading note in Osuron's voice now, and he was slowly closing the distance between himself and the defiant former king. "And we will strike with greater precision than you suggest. Ramses, your plan, it would have us tearing through doorways and flailing madly at all we find in our path. Why? Why embark on something that would surely result in an orgy of killing when we have one of our queen's great secrets at our disposal? There will be less blood this way. There will be less death. And if the colossus is here, we shall discover it with patience and care."

Ramses considered this, then turned to her. "And you, Julie? Which path would you choose?"

"Oh, Ramses. I don't wish to close my hands around the throat of any servant who might bar our entry to a curious passage. Osuron is right."

"I don't suggest this," Ramses said, "I don't suggest this eruption of killing you describe. I merely insist that we must proceed with our focus on that which might rend the world in two."

"We will," Osuron said. "We are. But first, the residents of the island must be peacefully subdued. And we must shield their eyes from all that will be asked of us to diffuse this threat."

Ramses stared down at Anya's map.

But Julie knew he wasn't seeing its lines at all. Julie knew he was grasping within himself for a humility forced on him by these modern times. By this new immortal band.

She risked going to him, taking his hand gently in hers.

He did not recoil. But when had he ever recoiled from her? Still, his defiance was a brittle presence throughout his powerful body, his fear of the colossus a specter that drifted about the cabin.

"And so it is," Ramses whispered, "and so it shall be."

When he returned her grip, she was relieved. Then he straightened.

"I relent," he whispered. He kissed her gently, smoothed curls from her forehead, and added, "But I fear for us all."

Silent and swift, they emerged from the shadows.

The first guard barely had time to reach for the Luger at his hip when Osuron bent forward and huffed his powerful breath across the tiny mound of glittering red powder he held cradled in one palm. Like the ghost of a small dragon's fiery breath, the dream rose took to the air, releasing a little shimmer as it settled over the guard's wide-eyed face. At the very moment when the man might have sputtered and raised his hands to his face in a panic, his arms went limp, and he seemed to fall into a trance.

Osuron said, "You will do as we ask, for the safety of the Vasilev estate commands it."

"The safety of the Vasilev estate commands it," the guard replied weakly.

"To the other guards so they might join us," Osuron said.

It fascinated her, this aspect of the power as Osuron had explained it: each command must have the veil of a justification placed over it, otherwise the trance did not endure for quite as long.

The next strike was easier, quieter. There was no need to spring or hurry. For the first guard did their work for them upon the second, and after that, their subsequent targets, when greeted by their fellow guards, did not recoil in the quick moment before they inhaled this secret of Bektaten's garden.

Osuron and Julie fell back, allowing their captured men to walk ahead of them like silent sled dogs. They'd asked the hypnotized men to take them to the island's church, in which the funeral of Dimitri Vasilev's son had recently been held. Julie studied the pieces of it that came into view between the dense canopy of pine branches. Its fat and rounded walls were densely striped with bright white spines that seemed to soar up the red brick, past the surrounding branches, before terminating in rounded cupolas crowned with small onion domes.

Now there were footsteps beside them as well.

Ramses and one of Osuron's men off to her right, two of Osuron's men on the other side, each walking slowly behind a group of guards, all under the spell of dream rose. By Anya's count, these were all the armed guards of the island, the guards for the main house as well as its outbuildings and its boat dock. Only the servants inside the house were left to subdue, and they were most likely asleep.

Osuron instructed one of the guards to unlock the church's doors. As they stepped through, one after the other, Julie glanced back. Behind them, hidden deep within shadows and across several yards of forest, was the family's mausoleum, in the exact spot where Anya had placed it on her little map. This alone was a relief, a sign that Anya had not betrayed them. The building lacked the bulk and grandeur of the Greek Orthodox church into which they now corralled Vasilev's men. The mausoleum was small, and its single onion dome was a bulging thing atop a square column that rose from its flat roof. But its shadows called to her, and the cascade of heavy locks sealing its iron door suggested secrets within.

But it was not yet time. There were several steps left in the plan, and if she were to deviate, Ramses might as well.

Inside the church, Osuron directed the men into the pews. Like schoolchildren they obeyed. Only more mute and passive than any irascible child.

With her sharpened vison, she could see the frescoes covering the rounded ceiling overhead glittering in the weak light, the spindly limbs and figures of the Orthodox icons. No statues of any kind, she realized, and that struck her as odd. Perhaps not. Given what power might be sheltered somewhere on this island, all statues had been removed. That a group of their number could enter this place in near silence astounded her. Osuron stepped up onto the altar.

Then, in her ear, in a whisper, Ramses said, "And now, the master of this estate."

"Ramses, wait," she said quickly. "The servants—"

Osuron's commanding voice filled the church. He'd not heard Ramses's whisper. He was addressing the mute guards. "You shall sit in silence and reverence. No summons shall draw you. No sound shall call to you. Give your mind entirely to prayer and reflection until you hear my voice again." Momentarily forgetting that Osuron did not actually need these men to voice their agreement for this plan to take effect, Julie was startled when he quickly said, "Sit."

"I go now," Ramses whispered. "I've waited long enough. Proceed with your plan and I'll proceed with mine. There's only one man on this island who will know all its secrets, and we'd be fools not to secure him this instant."

He was gone before she could protest, and before Osuron could notice. Before she could tell him that there was only one plan, the one they'd agreed to together, and this sudden separation from her pained her as much as it alarmed her.

But all around her were the low rumbling sounds of the guards following Osuron's command. They sank into pews without the hesitancy or gradual settling one would expect of a conscious mind.

It was a horrifying little display, and once it was complete, Ramses was gone.

For days now, Dimitri had been alone, alone with his stacks of papers and his charcoals and his frenzied sketches and the smell of vodka oozing from his pores. They'd come to him in fitful dreams, these images he now drew with a fevered hand. Dreams of tall, dark skeletal figures marching along the banks of the Neva, boluses of orange flame guttering in the steel hands they held open in front of them, hands they'd then raise so they could hurl comets of fire at the façade of the Winter Palace. In his dreams, armies of these figures marched on Saint Petersburg, determined but faceless. What need did they have for sculpted eyes and mouths when it was Dimitri who drove them, Dimitri and the Eye of Osiris?

In his dreams, Saint Petersburg burned, and his son's angry soul was soothed.

The survivors of the holocaust would tell tales of the mad, metal army that walked with clanging footsteps, of how its soldiers could not be reasoned with or stopped. Of how they were driven by a power that could not be seen. After Saint Petersburg lay in ruins, the memory of *The Bronze Horseman*'s terrible footfalls would recede, and Dimitri would no longer see the blood gurgling from his son's lips, the dazed and helpless look in his dying eyes. And never, not once, would he be forced to lay himself before the dreaded colossus, the colossus his son had found against his wishes, triggering a war between them that had brought their grand plans to a halt.

So much could be done without it.

Dimitri could see that now.

They could make this new army in the Vasilev foundries. The ones they'd operated for years. The ones that had built their fortune. And this would become his family's legacy, and its redemption. All over Russia these figures would march, incinerating all attempts to bow before the West. In their ghostly hallways, Peter the Great could rage, and Catherine herself could rend her gowns and weep, but the degradation they'd brought would end, and the true Russia would rise once more. The Russia of Moscow, the Russia of piety over strutting, preening achievement. The Russia of tsars who were true fathers to their people.

But the sketch before him now was a smeared mess of charcoal. His fingers were as blackened as the page. His hands, he realized, had been moving without his direction for some time as his thoughts rampaged away from him. Throughout his bedroom, the candles guttered, some tilting dangerously low in their candelabras. He stumbled to his feet and blew out the ones closest to the drapes.

In the quiet between his heaving breaths, he heard footsteps outside, a snap of branches that sounded too careful and hesitant to be from a wild thing.

It wasn't Anya. She never went for walks this late.

The thought of Anya twisted his gut. How long had it been since he'd seen her? A vague memory of coming across her in the woods. But the days ran together. It could have been a dream.

He had dreamed of her during the night, he knew. But in these dreams, she possessed different qualities, malevolent ones. She would slither into bed next to him, taunt him with evil whispers. It was his fear that had killed his son, she'd tell him. His terrible, crippling fear. His unwillingness to act. And when he woke, he'd plunge his fists into the pillows where he'd imagined she'd lain, finding only sheets soaked with his sweat.

If he went to her now, the dream version of her would recede, he was sure.

If only he could go to Nikolai, and somehow be rid of the bleeding version of him that appeared beside the bed each night. But Nikolai was in the ground, and so it was entirely possible the staring, silently accusing version of his son that visited him now was truly his ghost.

Dimitri stumbled to the cord for the servant's bell beside his bed and pulled.

As he waited for a response, for the familiar hurried clops

of approaching footsteps in the corridor, he returned to the window. Dark came late this time of the year. The depth of it outside now meant it was near midnight or past it. He could see nothing through the branches but patches of star-flecked sky.

Minutes passed. No one came.

Again, he pulled the cord. Again, no one came.

He told himself that it was just his disheveled, unwashed state that made him afraid to leave his bedroom. Not the sudden ghostly silence coming from the entire palace. He moved through the fear, felt enormously proud when he found himself outside the door to Anya's bedroom. He pushed it open. The room was empty, the bed perfectly made, her silver brush resting neatly on the vanity.

He felt his pulse in his ears. Felt more sober suddenly than he'd been in weeks.

He turned to face the empty corridor, wondering if he had died during one of his binges, and his deathly punishment was an eternity spent in an empty palace. But as he descended the stairs, he heard a faint rustle coming from the great hall. The electric lights there were ablaze, bathing the deep red lower walls and the gold-filled frescoes that extended into the arches of the soaring, glittering ceiling. As he entered the vast room, he heard the faintest creak of wood, a familiar sound. The sound of a careful, hesitant footstep or someone very gently shifting their weight.

But he saw no one. Instead, he saw a little slip of paper resting on the seat of a high-backed, throne-like chair he'd had carved for just this room. Its construction matched the serpentine twists of the Solomonic columns that framed the outside of each of the palace's windows. It was a proud chair. Like so much of the room, it embraced the glittering and the serpentine; the lines that indicated humility before God. And the little slip of paper resting on its cushion befouled it.

Dimitri's first thought was that Anya, or the servants, or

even Sergei had abandoned the palace after sunset, leaving him this little note as an explanation of their parting. Perhaps they'd tired of his terrible grief. But Anya wouldn't do this. Not Anya. And for all of them to leave at once? The idea was absurd.

But the note was familiar. The words were familiar.

They were written in his own hand.

> JULIE STRATFORD
> MR. REGINALD RAMSEY
> ELLIOTT SAVARELL
> ALEX SAVARELL
> RANDOLPH STRATFORD
> SAMIR IBRAHIM

He felt a presence close by and turned. Nikolai's men, returned from Britain. The note was meant to be proof they'd completed this mission. And this would be a good thing. An emboldening thing that would set them back on the path of action after the loss of Nikolai.

But the man standing a few feet away, with one hand resting gently on the nearby chair, was not his cousin. He was impeccably dressed, the air of a British gentleman coming from him, but his skin was brown, his eyebrows dark, his eyes brilliantly blue. There was a steadiness to his gaze, and a general calm to him that seemed otherworldly. He did not project menace, but only because he seemed to have no use for it.

"Good evening, Mr. Vasilev," the man said gently.

"Who are you?"

"I am Reginald Ramsey, and I've come to find out why you sought my death."

25

Like a nearly drowned lion, this man before him. His long beard was matted, his hair a wild mane. His lustrous red velvet robe with its gold embroidery around the collar distracted Ramses from his disheveled state, but only briefly. With his thick beard and heavy robe, so long it puddled slightly on the floor at his feet, the master of this estate looked like photographs Ramses had seen of Russian aristocrats who'd dressed as Muscovite boyars for a costume party. But Ramses was sure this man did not believe it to be a costume. And so clearly wrecked was Dimitri Vasilev by grief for his son that Ramses felt something close to pity.

"You believe this note has something to do with me," Dimitri said.

Having expected this attempt to deflect, Ramses closed the fingers of one hand around one of the wooden finials atop the back of the chair in front of him. With a flick of the wrist, he snapped the solid wooden ball free, an effort that would have required a normal man to use a saw, at least. Clasping it between both hands he pressed on it from either side. Cracking sounds filled the room. Ramses parted his hands. Splinters tumbled to the rug.

"Let's not waste time on the petty games of ordinary men.

We're far from ordinary, you and I. Your problem, it seems, is that you sent mortal assassins to kill beings you do not understand."

"You're engaged to the wrong woman, Mr. Ramsey," he whispered. His smile looked like a snarl, but Ramses thought it might be the strain of exhaustion.

"And why did you want Julie Stratford dead?"

"Her father knew things, he'd seen things."

It was a shock to hear the resurrected Lawrence's fragmented tale confirmed in this way, by a living, breathing mortal. He'd thought it possible Lawrence's account had pointed them in the right direction, but its fundamental narrative was a distortion wrought by death and resurrection. Now, much of it seemed confirmed by this simple phrase.

"The stela," Ramses said, "the stela which told of the Eye of Osiris."

And the colossus, Ramses thought, but he held this thought back, determined to approach this topic as carefully as possible.

"Ah, I see. So my fear was justified. Lawrence told you all of what he'd learned."

It would not serve Ramses in this moment to let Dimitri Vasilev know just how they'd extracted this information from Lawrence, so Ramses gave the man an indulgent smile.

Dimitri laughed bitterly. "You were just a name on the list, Mr. Ramsey. That's all. The real target was your bride-to-be. But now I see . . ." Dimitri's gaze roamed Ramses's body as if he couldn't quite see him at all.

"What? What do you see, Mr. Vasilev?"

"I see I have roused something else I do not quite understand. You are yet another force from Egypt that shreds my understanding of reality."

"Perhaps that's a sign a man like you has no business in Egypt," Ramses said.

"Of course. My true business is here. In Russia. Accidents drove me to Egypt."

"Accidents? Like your encounter with a poor cleaning girl in your family's museum in Tomsk."

These words had served their purpose, driving the pose of weariness and confusion from Dimitri's face.

"Where is she?" Dimitri whispered.

"We'll speak of her in a moment."

"I answered your question. Now answer mine. Where is Anya?"

"We've not harmed her," Ramses said.

"I must see her."

"In time."

"She played no role in the plot against you," Dimitri said. "She must not be punished."

"Punishment is not the game. We have something of yours, and you have something that does not belong to you. Let us arrange a trade."

"And what is this thing that does not belong to me?" Dimitri asked.

"You know full well," Ramses said. "You thought it would make your men strong against us."

"And what became of those men?" he asked.

"They did not survive."

Like a blow across his chest, he received this news.

"I see, and so this thing you want, this thing you believe I've no right to, you have two of them in your possession already. What use do you have for mine?"

"I don't wish to possess this object for my own benefit," Ramses said.

"Why then?"

"So that you will not have it at all."

"I see."

"Do you? Do you see that we will trade you your precious Anya for this thing and then be on our way?"

Dimitri's expression had gone cold.

"But you would never agree to this, would you?" Ramses

asked. "Because without the Eye of Osiris, your precious Anya would no longer be yours to control. Her visions, which you create, would leave her and she would tire of you."

"You do not know my Anya."

"Oh, but I do, sir. We've told her everything of what you've done to her. She will never be yours again."

With a growl, Dimitri reared up from his chair, then, as if quickly remembering the strength Ramses wielded in his bare hands, he wilted. After a time, he said, "Who are you really? And don't give me the tale of you in the papers. You're not some Egyptologist who married into a passel of fine British."

"Tell me why you've done all this and I'll consider answering."

"What I have done? You speak of these events as if I wasn't chosen."

"Chosen? How were you chosen?"

"My intentions were basic, honorable. Our fortune came from the Urals. We've long been dedicated to the Siberian frontiers. Our museum brought culture and learning to the far reaches of our nation. I sought to build the collection in my family's museum, and so we contracted with archeologists who traveled to Egypt. That was all. I did not go in search of a power like this. This power made its way to me, don't you see?"

"It made its way to Anya. And when Anya's story made its way to you, you deceived her and hatched your true plot."

"What would you have had me do? Tell the world what the Eye was capable of. Put it on display and invite visitors to touch it and see for themselves how they could bring life to stone? You sneer at the prospect of a man like me exploring Egypt in search of these mysteries. What do you think would have resulted if this power had been written about in the newspapers? Hordes of men descending on your great land in search of magic just as those descended on the Americas in search of gold."

"You answer a question I did not ask, Mr. Vasilev. I asked why you used it to imprison a young woman's mind and assassinate strangers. What transpired between you and Lawrence Stratford that would result in all this?"

"It was well under way before Lawrence. The only thing Lawrence did was divide me from my son."

"How?"

"You know as much of the Eye of Osiris as I do. Perhaps more. You bait me. I should say nothing further at all. You've ruined Anya. She cannot be used against me."

"We've healed her. It was you who sought to ruin her. But this is what you must know. I will not leave without all fragments of the Eye of Osiris you have in your possession. This is not a negotiation, Mr. Vasilev. It is an announcement. How you accept it is up to you."

"How do you know so much of the Eye?" Dimitri asked. "Did you torture my men?"

"It's been thousands of years since I've tortured anyone."

"Thousands." Perhaps another man, a man who'd not seen what he'd seen, would have either cackled with derisive laughter or fled screaming from the room. But Dimitri nodded, trying to accept this information as one might a complicated set of directions through a dense, modern city.

"I recognized it," Ramses said. "I recognize it because I once wore it briefly. When I was king."

"Then you are as old as it is, I see," he said softly. "Yes, I see now, King of Egypt. You know the Eye because you wore the Eye. And if you wore it, you underwent the very ritual the stela described. And yet you circle the focus of this ritual like a shark preparing to take its first bite."

"As do you," Ramses said.

"Yes, but I see now. I see what you truly seek. You don't just seek the Eye." He leaned forward, an accusing finger raised. A malicious, triumphant light had come into Dimitri Vasilev's eyes, and his breaths were so strong now they brought spittle to the corners of his mouth. "You seek the colossus," he growled.

Ramses was as still as a man trying to avoid provoking a serpent's strike. But even this muted response satisfied Dimitri Vasilev, who laughed delightedly and clapped his hands together.

"It's perfect, then. Just perfect. The colossus is the reason for all of it, and this alone is proof there are no accidents in God's design. I returned from Egypt with the stela and Lawrence's terrible translation of it ringing in my ears, and I told my son the Eye was enough. That we could use the power of the Eye by itself. I forbade my son to look for the colossus and he ignored my request. And now his defiance has brought you to me."

"For what endeavor, sir, could you use the power of the Eye by itself?"

"To bring Russia to its knees before its head could be lopped off by the West."

"As I understand it, one kneels to prepare for a beheading, not to avoid one."

Dimitri winced and waved a hand dismissively. "This topic is too grave for me to engage in clever wordplay around it."

"Then be direct, sir. You have my full attention."

"I would rather Russia bow to the kaiser than a tsar who answers to England and France."

"Ah, so you're a simple traitor then."

"You have no knowledge of what it means to be truly Russian."

"And you sound like a German."

Rage lit his eyes at this. "I am more Russian than you will ever know. I am more Russian than the Germans who steamed their way into our royal palaces dragging Europe behind them. I am the Russia of belief. I am the Russia that rose against the Mongols, that made order out of chaos amidst the deepest winters the world will ever know. And if I decide that our fate is better served in an alliance with a nation whose ruler answers directly to God, without the intervening chaos of a human mob, then I am in alignment with God. And that is why God blessed me with the Eye of Osiris and all it might do."

"Is the colossus your blessing as well?" Ramses asked.

"I didn't think so. Until now."

"How so?"

"I feared it. I feared the enslavement Lawrence described when he translated the stela's words. I feared it so much I forbade my son to search for it. And when he disobeyed me, I feared it so much I ordered him to dispatch his best men to hunt down you and your fiancée like dogs, just in case Lawrence had ever told any of you of its possible existence.

"But now, all this, it has brought you here to me, and you have done something for me that no one else has done, and this is proof that you too, King of Egypt, were brought to me by God. The symmetry of it is perfect. I set out to have you killed because of my fear of the colossus, and now your desire for it has brought you to my doorstep. And now that you are here, now that you have taken the last thing I loved from me, you've also done what nothing else could. What my son died trying to do."

"Which is what, sir?" Ramses asked."

"You have removed my fear of it. You have removed my fear of the colossus."

Dimitri dug under his robe and pulled free the chain of a familiar necklace so that the amber stone attached slipped free of his robe.

"Do not do this," Ramses said.

"Oh, don't you see, King of Egypt? There's nothing else left for me to do. Nothing left but to bow before God and submit to whatever he asks of me."

There were no statues in this hall.

Which meant Vasilev was preparing to call to a distant one, one whose location only he knew.

As they corralled the servants into the chapel, it was Julie's turn for defiance.

She'd slipped through the shadows and gone quickly to work on the enticing spray of locks across the entry door for the family mausoleum. Now she was within, alone. Julie found a mad jumble of Egyptian statues—none of them larger than a person—crowded into the family mausoleum's little chapel, along with empty sarcophagi and crates of old jewels and stones. All arranged without regard for scholarship. These items stood before the altar as if poised to join in a mad chorus before an audience of curious Russians. And so it was just as Dimitri Vasilev had promised Anya; he'd cleared out his museum's Egyptian collection and transported it all here, no doubt in search of further magic.

Underfoot were family crypts placed beneath the stone floor.

But nowhere among the statues and crates of jewels did she find evidence of a giant. Nothing as large as the statue Ramses had described. But if it was here at all, and being kept secret, Julie doubted it would be whole.

Suddenly, the floor beneath her feet rumbled. Brilliant orange light shot up through various cracks in the floor which had been invisible just seconds before.

There was a presence below her. A shifting presence. The noises it made were steady, insistent; a clattering of large rocks that sounded like the gritting of massive teeth. While its rhythm was gradual, the sounds were made momentous by the sheer size of the components involved. Each click of stone caused her bones to tremble.

Not since she'd become immortal had any aspect of the physical world paralyzed her quite like this.

Worse, she did not have the Eye to protect herself.

Ramses did. At his insistence. He'd so feared its proximity to the colossus, he'd insisted on keeping it with him.

Julie stumbled backwards and watched. Watched as a great stone panel of floor rose impossibly into the air, rising and rising until she could see what was elevating it—a giant stone hand, almost the size of a normal man, its fingers chipped and rough-hewn, pressing up on the stone as a servant might carry a silver tray. Next appeared a giant face weathered by centuries of ruin. The same ghostly amber glow she'd seen radiating from the exquisitely carved faces of the stone archangels now illuminated features rough and ruined. It traced the outlines of the face as it must have once looked when it was newly carved, filling the chipped, cavernous eye sockets with the shimmering traces of a god's ancient gaze.

Higher the colossus rose. If this great statue was controlled in this moment by the Eye of Osiris, its captain did not have it within view, so this person was driving blind. This stone goliath might crush whatever was in its way as it freed itself from the chapel. She could survive such a blow, for sure. But an injury inflicted by a force of this size would test her capacity for rapid healing at a moment when she was desperately needed.

And so Julie had no choice but to back up to the doors behind her.

When the statue stood fully erect, it was still buried within the floor up to its stone knees. Its full height revealed, she saw her suspicion proved correct. It had not been concealed intact. It had lain beneath her in a tangle of disconnected limbs. And it was missing one now: its left arm. The statue reached down into the chamber from which it had risen and picked up its severed limb, lifting it to its own exposed shoulder. The top of the arm and the shoulder fused instantly. The golden glow was no longer confined to the face; it swept the statue's entire body. If the Eye of Osiris truly was the source of this awakening, it was like no other use of the Eye she'd witnessed.

Not the same, Julie thought, *what I'm seeing now is not the same as those events.*

The statue turned to look at her.

Riots of gooseflesh, unlike any she'd felt as an immortal being, broke out on her skin. Her powerful heart was reduced to a flutter. She was, for the first time, being coolly regarded by something from beyond the known world.

No human drives this, she thought, *no human mind drives this colossus before me.*

She couldn't finish the thought. Could only grip the wall behind her as the colossus stepped forward, walking with a fluid grace that now inhabited its rough stone. It reached up, held to one side of the open door as a giant man might, then it dipped its head under the chapel's entrance and stepped out into the night, footsteps shaking the earth.

It is alive, she realized. *Not a puppet for a human mind but a statue that lives.*

The approaching footsteps rattled the windows in their stone frames, shook the furniture on all sides of them. They gave music to the tale the priests had told Ramses so long ago, a tale of a statue sculpted by a god's hand, a statue that had risen to its stone feet and demanded a home be made for it deep within the Temple of Karnak.

Each thundering footfall shook Ramses down to his bones.

Wide eyed, struck by terror and wonder, Dimitri rose to his feet, the Eye glowing in his clutching fist. As the footfalls became louder, the man cackled with delighted, mad laughter.

Then he saw Ramses lift his own necklace from inside of his shirt, and his laughter ended abruptly.

"Oh, I see," he said, "a duel then? Is that what you propose? Shall we duel with a god?"

"You must stop at once," Ramses said. "You don't understand what you've done."

"But that's exactly the point, isn't it? I'm not meant to understand. I'm meant to awaken, to unleash, and to serve. This is my destiny. I've feared it and avoided it and killed my son for it. But no more. I must surrender to it. That is what your presence here means, King of Egypt!"

Dust shook loose from the ceiling, little chips coming free from the glittering frescoes. They dappled Dimitri's great mane of hair in snakes of yellow powder. But the wild man didn't notice. He gazed in the direction of the footsteps. Long corridors and rooms lay between them and the colossus's approach. Did he plan to command the god all the way through them?

"Stop this, Dimitri Vasilev!"

"You first, my friend!" the man taunted. "You've an Eye of your own, and you met this great stone beast during your kingly reign. Put your ancient knowledge to use. Remove this thing from my control if it scares you. But you will not stop me. I fear nothing now."

"Because you believe it to be under your control, and it's not."

"Nonsense! It comes as I command!"

"It's not like the others. It's not a simple statue. You've opened a door. Your fear was justified. You must stop."

"Raise your hand to the Eye at your neck and let us end this with a proper battle before the eyes of our awakened god if that's what you must do. Otherwise be silent and kneel!"

When Ramses reached for his necklace, his hand froze. He was seized by memories of a grove of wind-tossed trees beneath a bright but sunless sky, soaring obsidian gates, a sound like the breath of a god. Yes, it was fear that paralyzed him, fear that anchored his right arm to his side even as his fingers itched to touch the stone at his neck.

Silence fell. Dimitri smiled.

It was clear he thought he'd stopped the colossus's approach, commanded it to wait politely just outside the palace walls. He lowered his hand, releasing the stone, gave Ramses a satisfied smile.

"Come," he whispered. "Let us go to it and bow before it. Together. Perhaps it will guide the two of us to—"

Dimitri Vasilev's next words left him when he saw what suddenly held Ramses's attention. Dimitri's necklace. The stone still glowed even though no human hand touched it.

Before either man could address the implication of this, there was a sound that made the thundering footsteps of seconds before seem insignificant in comparison. A sound like a terrible storm, but with focus and purpose. Rending wood, shattering glass, what must have been chunks of ceiling crashing onto a hard stone floor.

Dimitri's breath left him in a strained moan; his jaw trembled.

In the next silence that fell, the man did not smile.

"You fool," Ramses whispered, "you mad fool."

The terrible assault came again. Louder, closer. Dimitri's eyes spit tears. He stumbled backwards several steps. This rhythmic maelstrom could mean only one thing.

The colossus, under its own power, was tearing its way into the palace.

It was coming for them.

Anya had never heard such terrible sounds outside of a storm, but the sky she could see through the porthole window was clear and star flecked. Still, it sounded as if some great and terrible force was tearing its way through the island. She knew then whatever made these sounds must be the true reason these strange and beautiful people had traveled here in this vessel.

She stumbled from the cabin where they'd asked her to remain. For her own safety, they'd said. And the tall, dark-skinned man who'd been standing outside her door moments before was gone. Then she saw the lower half of his body through the open door to the top deck at the end of this little hallway. His back was to her, his long plait of thick black braids like a layer of armor down his back.

As she moved to him, the sounds continued. An eruption of destruction echoing across still, night water.

The man, her guard, stared across the lake towards the mound of pines in which the vague lights of the palace glowed. Everything this man had done until now had seemed muted and restrained, but now there was alarm in his bright blue eyes.

It tormented him, it seemed, to be trapped on this vessel with her at a moment when his compatriots were being met by some ghastly terror amidst the dense pines.

"We must go to them," Anya said.

When the man grunted without looking at her, she realized he'd sensed her approach but had been unable to acknowledge it. What were these remarkable beings? Where did their unnatural focus and calm originate? Were they angels come to deliver truths and rescue? Or were they something altogether more mysterious? Whatever the answer, this man's strength, his wisdom, his powers, were no match against the fear the sounds brought from him.

"I'm to protect you here," the guard said quietly.

"I don't need protection, but it sounds like they do."

"They've taken all the boats," he said.

"Not this one." She was surprised by the strength in her voice, a strength that had found its way to her over the past few hours of solitude.

And then, just as there was another terrible crash—a rending of both glass and wood at once—the guard turned and gave her a long and probing stare that said he saw her as something altogether more complex than a patient. Or a prisoner.

After a moment of paralysis, Dimitri stepped forward. He summoned what seemed to be his last shreds of courage, approaching the doorway through which the terrible sounds came.

"I am ready," Dimitri said. "I am ready for whatever it brings."

"No, you're not," Ramses said quietly.

What Ramses saw next made him feel as if all of the elixir's power had been drained from him in an instant. Never before had his ancient mortal past and his immortal present collided with such clarity and force. It had been thousands of years since he'd felt so vulnerable, so humble. So afraid.

The colossus of Osiris bent its head as a giant man might so it could step through the doorway and into the glittering hall. Then it stood entirely erect as if presenting itself to them. Its body was chipped and close to broken in several places. The shell of Akhenaten's gold that had covered it all those years ago had long since worn away. But a radiant shimmer bathed and encircled it, pulsating with powerful, supernatural life, a shimmer that might well have been present during the ancient ritual, but which he'd dismissed as a trick of the eye played by the flicker of candlelight dancing across the layers of gold dust applied by the priests. Now it was as if this shimmer were the ghost of the priests' handiwork, and as Ramses beheld it, it felt as if the ghosts of the priests themselves had entered the room along with this stone giant. But that was an illusion, and if it had been true, Ramses would have bowed before them, begged them to share all they knew of this ritual he'd long dismissed, even if it had involved tugging at the hems of their white robes.

Stunning, the grace of the colossus's movements now, the ease of its power. It towered over Dimitri as the man stumbled towards it, arms raised in a wild gesture that could be seen as either supplication or some inane, hopeless attempt to deny the giant further entry.

Ramses felt heat at his neck, thought it might be fear. It was the stone he wore, the Eye of Osiris. It glowed as well. Just as all the stones worn by the priests in the Temple of Karnak had glowed during the ritual. When put to use on simple, ordinary statues, the Eye glowed under one hand to indicate a connection, but here it was clear, the glowing stone indicated the arrival of a momentous presence. This was not the diminished use of the Eye they'd worked again and again at Brogdon Castle; this was its true purpose, its intended use in full divine bloom.

He wanted no tether to its horrors. Ramses tore the necklace from his neck, hurled it to the floor. Still, the stone glowed. Still, the statue approached.

Paces from its great stone feet, Dimitri Vasilev fell to his knees.

"I kneel before you," he cried. "I give myself to you and your commands."

The head bowed, the giant regarding his supplicant.

Was it a god within the stone? Was this the vessel through which he'd chosen to regard the human world?

"Your awakening," Dimitri continued, confidence entering his voice. "It was not as I designed. Forgive me if I have disrespected—"

The colossus batted Dimitri Vasilev out of his path with the back of one stone hand. The blow, which had come quietly and instantly, was powerful enough to send the Russian crashing through one of the mica windows, leaving behind a jagged mouth of thick, shattered glass.

Suddenly there was silence.

And then a voice filled the great hall. It spoke with a power that seemed to course through every inch of Ramses's skin. It did not emanate from the statue. It came from every surface around him and on all sides, from the air itself. It was a voice that was everywhere and nowhere at once. It was a voice that could not be escaped. And it was not a hallucination wrought by tainted wine. With each thundering word, the shimmering gold wreathing the statue's entire body pulsed and danced. But it only spoke a single, terrifying word.

"Ramses."

Tears spilled from his eyes. Was it fear or reverence? Or was it grief? Grief for his mortal life, a life of limits and ignorance to true mysteries of the world, even amidst what had seemed like great power. Or was it terror? Terror at being known by this power.

He would not run, he vowed. He would not back up. He would not kneel.

When the colossus took several steps towards him, these vows became harder to keep.

In the ancient tongue, Ramses said, "I did not summon you. I sought to stop the plunderers who stole your form. Thousands of years ago I stood before you in an ancient ritual. A ritual designed in your honor. I was a king then, and the priests desired me to know your power. I commit myself to your protection now. We shall return your colossus to where you would see it hidden and shelter it for all time. Give the commands and I shall follow them."

"And so now that you have opened the door I built, you seek to close it."

"It was not I who opened it," Ramses said. "It was those who stole your form on earth."

"And now I claim yours."

The colossus lowered its hands on either side of Ramses. At the moment when he expected to be crushed, the statue's gold shimmer extended around him in serpentine curls. He had no words for what he felt next. It was not pain. It was a spreading absence, something close to what he felt when he walled himself off from the sun and descended into a sleep near death. He realized then he was rising above the stone floor, captured in some invisible force that pulsed between the statue's hands. Could this be how it had all unfolded during the ancient ritual, his transport to the realm of Osiris?

Impossible. He would have remembered this horror. It would take more than thousands of years to forget an experience this terrifying. To forget what it was like to look down at one's body as it began to disappear. For that was precisely what was happening now. Great snakes of shimmering gold poured off the statue's body, sweeping across Ramses's body in serpentine coils, and these particles joined with his very flesh, devouring it.

His body, indestructible for centuries, was disappearing.

And the last thing he heard before darkness claimed him was Julie's terrible screams.

She was screaming his name.

When he tried desperately to call out to her, he realized everything he might have used to speak had been claimed by a power that was now transporting him into another realm.

Julie's screams ravaged her throat, but she couldn't hear them over the terrible sounds filling the great hall, a gargantuan groan shot through what sounded like the howls of approaching, rioting spirits. It was what a storm's winds might sound like if each gust carried a fresh tide of human souls.

Ramses was paralyzed. Paralyzed and vanishing. His terror-filled eyes and grimacing mouth were the only physical response he could manage as he was consumed by the glittering tides of gold that swept from the body of the colossus. Her lover, her king, who up until that very moment had seemed to possess flesh and bone as resilient as steel, he was vanishing before her eyes. The colossus suspended him like a doll, high above the floor, frozen within some shimmering force that pulsed between its giant, parted hands.

She realized then that the glittering gold serpents devouring Ramses were reducing the statue's size as well.

A terrible union was taking place, the colossus shrinking as Ramses was consumed.

The implication of this sent her fear into a frenzy.

She felt pressure against her skull and realized she was poised to tear out her own hair.

A door had been opened, and now it had not just begun to

close. It would soon disappear entirely. The frame, the lock, the key. There would be nothing to pound her fists against. Nothing to pummel or break apart with any kind of power, no matter how momentous.

In seconds, Ramses would be gone. The colossus would be gone.

Hope would be gone.

When a force seized her from behind, she bucked against it. It was Osuron. He and several of his men had come running at the cataclysmic sounds coming from the great hall. He held her back now protectively as he watched the maelstrom with a terror that matched Ramses's. But to hurl herself into this storm might be her only choice. The only way to keep from losing Ramses forever. To join him in oblivion.

And then it was over.

They were gone.

Man and statue, immortal and god.

Both gone.

Layers of fine dust drifted to the floor of the great hall in a sudden, gentle ballet driven by the last breaths of the destructive winds. It blanketed the overturned and ruined furniture. For a brief moment, the dust shimmered with lingering gold radiance, then this otherworldly light left it, as if it had been finally released from the divine power that had fueled it. As it turned the color of sandstone, Julie's scream became a wail racked with sobs, and Osuron's restraint, a powerful embrace meant to console.

Roused by what felt like dozens of knives run through him, Dimitri woke, found himself kissing hard stone. His last memory was of the god's impassive stare, then an event that blotted out his senses and brought instant black.

He was lying facedown in the courtyard, several yards from the lake's gently lapping shore.

A brief memory of flight, of limbs leaving the earth.

He'd been cast out. By God.

A still-spinning part of his consciousness knew that if he rolled over, attempted to trace the path of his journey here, he'd set fire to the injuries racking his body. But then he heard a familiar sound, a sound that filled him with dread. A sound that had haunted his dreams for weeks now. Not the thundering approach of the colossus. This was the sound that had preceded his son's murder.

He had to endure the pain, had to see for himself if his fear was correct.

He forced himself to roll onto his back.

It was not *The Bronze Horseman* coming for him, just its rider. Taller than any normal man. It did not appear as fearsome as the giant who'd just torn his palace apart; it came with the same determination.

Dimitri tried to rise to his feet. His broken right leg crippled him.

And so he crawled. Through the mud and towards the moonlit water. Still the statue came. Nothing like the tsar himself, except, perhaps, for his height. Some classical Western version with a Roman nose and a small, determined mouth sitting atop a proud, rounded chin. Blank and expressionless, these features, even as they glowed with amber light. But still the statue came.

The water, it seemed, could be his salvation. He could float his broken leg and stroke with his arms. The statue might sink. The water would consume it, cover it, anchor it. They were desperate, these thoughts. Ill-considered, fearful thoughts, he knew. But what choice did he have left? He was a broken man, a man cast out by God, and he could not walk.

Only once the water consumed him did Dimitri come to know what a terrible plan this was. The weight of his suddenly soaked robes pulled mercilessly at his weakened body.

His arms weren't strong enough to propel him away from the statue's advance.

Sputtering, Dimitri rolled over onto his back, floating.

The necklace, he realized. He'd been so disoriented, he'd forgotten his greatest weapon. But when his hand went to his throat, he realized it was gone.

And then he saw its glow coming from the shore.

Its light shined on Anya's face, his beautiful Anya, his greatest treasure. But there was a coldness there he'd never thought he'd see.

"Anya," he cried.

But the golden light the glowing stone cast onto her face revealed an expression of malice and anger. And knowledge.

"Please, Anya," he begged. "There are no words. No words for what I've done, but if you give me time. If you give me time to heal I . . ."

His mind could not come up with a suitable finish to this sentence. And it was no matter. For Anya did not wait to hear it.

"No words, Dimitri," she called back. "No words indeed. Only this."

The statue placed one massive bronze hand on his chest and pushed him under the water and into the dark.

Julie could bear it no longer, these futile attempts. They had Dimitri Vasilev's necklace, the one Anya had stolen from him and the one they'd discovered on the floor of the great hall—Ramses's, no doubt, either cast off or thrown off in the chaos. And after searching the estate's rooms, they'd found a third. Osuron's men continued the search, but for hours now, she and Osuron had paced this hall. Again and again with their touch they brought light to all the necklaces at their disposal, but it failed to bring life to the fine layers of dust blanketing the great hall. Not a speck of it had moved or responded in any way. And should they have expected it to? The Eye of Osiris had never worked on anything that did not have the form of a living creature.

But now Osuron tried, clutching the Eye in one hand as he spun slowly in the center of the room, trying to remain stoic as he tried chants and whispers in dozens of ancient languages Julie didn't recognize.

Was this dust all that remained of Ramses as well?

This abominable thought drove her finally from the palace, out into the forested grounds beyond. She knew she was walking in a daze, would look mad to anyone who saw her. But she didn't care. Nights were still short here in August, and the first pale blush of a northern dawn kissed the sky above the treetops. She heard low conversation outside at the doors of the little church where Osuron's men stood watch over the captive servants. They'd soon exhaust their supply of dream rose, and the trances placed over the guards and servants would wear off, requiring they be treated as confined prisoners. Three of Osuron's men emerged from the chapel suddenly, walking a bound and blindfolded man by both of his arms in the direction of the mausoleum where the colossus had been hidden. They were separating this man from the others. What could this mean?

Perhaps they thought this man had something of value to share, and that's why they had not placed him under the thrall of dream rose.

Julie approached the chapel's open doors, listening to the men within.

The captive, she could see, was on his knees, still blindfolded. His beard was long and thick.

The men circled him as they questioned him, and the questions were all the same. What did he know of what had taken place here?

Their captive said nothing. His stubborn silence gave him away as a conspirator.

One of Osuron's men spotted her and approached. "We

recognized him from a portrait in the palace. We believe he's a member of the family."

She stepped inside. "What do you know of the colossus?" she asked.

The captive bristled at the sound of a new voice. And the men were surprised by the directness of her question, it was clear. No doubt they'd hoped to extract information from him without feeding him any prematurely. A wise move, perhaps, but Julie's patience had run out.

"Where is my brother?" he asked. "Bring me to him and I'll—"

The deafening crack that sounded next startled all of them silent. Julie had brought her bootheel down onto the floor with enough force to cleave stone. Their captive flinched and shuddered as if a gun had been fired.

"Tell me all you know of the colossus or the next sound I'll make shall come from your bones."

After a long, agonized silence, their captive finally said, "He raised it, didn't he? He raised it and he had no control of it, just as he'd feared. Is this what happened?"

"He'd never raised it before?" she asked.

The captive shook his head. "He was too afraid."

"You expect me to believe it simply lay here under the floor of this chapel."

"I expect nothing now but ruin."

"How long since it was brought here?" Julie asked.

"Months," the captive answered.

"And no one on this island has ever used it with the Eye?"

"Never." There was despair in the man's whisper. "That sound, that terrible sound. Was that . . . ?"

"How many stones did you discover?" she asked.

He was silent.

Julie approached him, each careful footstep meant to remind him of the deafening one she'd just leveled against the stone floor a moment ago.

"How many?" she asked in a voice that brokered no disagreement.

"Five," he whispered.

The very number Ramses had seen in the Temple of Karnak,
she realized.

"But one was destroyed," he added miserably.

"When?"

"Weeks ago, when Nikolai, his son . . . It was destroyed
when Nikolai was."

If the man's tale was true, then they'd secured every last
stone that had fallen into the possession of these mad men. But
further searches of the rooms would be done to verify this, of
course, and this revelation was not the comfort it might have
been mere hours before.

For Ramses was gone.

Gone or reduced to dust, and both possibilities were an
equal horror.

And this man had lived steps from the crypt in which the
colossus had lain hidden, and he'd never heard a maelstrom
like the one that had claimed Ramses. And so these men had
not tested this thing, not experimented with it. No one here, it
seemed, possessed any knowledge essential to Ramses's abduction, his rapture. And so they'd have no idea how to get him
back.

"Where is the colossus now?" their captive asked.

"It is destroyed," Julie said, "it is gone."

"And with it, my family. With it, my Russia."

"Your Russia? It's for Russia you've done all this? Did you
plan to use it as a weapon of war?"

"Our own war. To shift the balance of power. To bring Russia into an alliance with Germany even if it meant making us her
subjects. For a time. Nations of kings, run by kings. That was
our hope." His exhaustion and despair were such it sounded
like these words were something he'd memorized in a child's
lesson book years ago.

"And I, and those I loved, had to die because my father knew what you had in your possession?" Julie asked.

The captive raised his head as if he was trying to see her through the blindfold.

"Julie Stratford," he whispered. "Daughter of Lawrence."

"Yes, and it seems I've thwarted your plans."

"No. My brother's fear thwarted our plans. His fear of the god he claimed to serve."

"Now he's gone to meet this god. Your brother's dead."

The man before her did not sob or collapse. He bowed his head silently as if in prayer.

"I wish to join him," he finally said.

"You seek to avoid the consequences of your acts?" Julie asked.

"Isn't death the worst consequence of all?"

"That depends on the form it takes."

"We meant for yours to be quick, without pain."

"This is no consolation now."

"I understand."

"You do not," Julie said, a fight between rage and despair adding a quaver to her voice. "You do not understand."

"Very well, but I understand this," he finally said. "One war, our war against the Japanese, changed our great nation forever, weakened it beyond repair. Now we enter into a war we cannot afford on behalf of a tsar who cannot rule because he fears the judgments of nations who do not share our beliefs. What Russia will become after this will be unrecognizable and abominable. And so, Ms. Stratford, it is not, you see, the consequences of my actions I wish to avoid. It is my country's terrible fate I wish to never see."

"Very well then," Julie whispered.

She stepped forward and closed one hand around the man's throat.

Vicious of her to believe taking life would give her strength.

And misguided.

For even though her victim had not suffered or struggled, the act had weakened the last little filaments of her endurance. And so, when Osuron's men emerged from the palace, carrying alabaster jars she knew to be filled with what was left of the colossus, Julie turned from the sight, turned from the palace, and plunged into the woods. At first, her steps were careful and determined, then speed overtook her, and she ran. In flight from the very real fact that soon they'd have no choice but to depart. Fleeing, if only for a moment, the terrible prospect that the dust they'd collected into jars might be all that remained of Ramses.

She pushed branches from her path as she went, but her great strength caused her to tear them from their trunks without intending to, and she was forced to cast them aside as she ran. Finally, she came to a clearing where the bright sun washed the soil and sprays of fallen needles, and there she let her sobs take a rageful form they'd never taken in either of her lives, mortal or immortal. The wildness around her offered no comfort. The soil did not invite her to bury herself in its cold embrace; the trees did not whisper a response. How many glimmering miracles had lit up these past few months, but in this moment of despair there was no new and glittering revelation to push back the walls of mortality.

Despite being bathed in a substance that defied nature, she was just one more grieving soul standing atop unforgiving and impassive soil.

Was she now nothing more than a widow? A widow who would live forever with her grief.

Once she'd exhausted herself, she raised her face to the sunlight filtering through the branches overhead. Perhaps it was an attempt to dry her tears, or perhaps the hot blaze of the sun, which could not damage her eyes even when she stared into it directly, was so much like the great explosion of light that had claimed Ramses she found it a comfort, and assumed it might return her lover to her if she allowed its blindness to consume her.

It did nothing of the kind, and after a while she heard footsteps crunching pine needles. They were coming towards her. When she turned, there was Osuron. She thought at first he'd simply come to deliver more terrible news.

But the man before her now looked shattered. Tears shimmered in his brilliant blue eyes. All traces of the calm and reserve he'd displayed before were gone. As he moved to her, he fell to his knees, extended one quivering hand in her direction. It would have looked as if he was bowing before a queen, had he not landed on his knees with such sudden and terrible weight.

"It is I who have done this," he whispered. "It is I who've lost him for us."

"No!"

"If we'd yielded to his plan," Osuron whispered, "if we'd found the colossus before all else, it would not have been sprung upon us. But I doubted him. I doubted his belief in what it could do."

"Rise," Julie said, "please, Osuron, rise. I cannot bear to see a man of your wisdom brought to his knees like this."

"It is my fault, all of this, and I bring that truth to our queen." He raised his tear-filled eyes to her. "I bring that truth to you, Julie."

"If he'd remained with us," Julie said, "it might not have unfolded in this way. But he could not. He went to Dimitri before the servants had been subdued, and he went alone. He is a king in his blood, and a king cannot be contained."

She'd not meant to refer to the awful way in which Ramses had vanished before their eyes, but it seemed as if her choice of words had done just that.

"Not a one of us predicted this terrible spectacle," Julie said, "not a one. Even Ramses. I saw it with my own two eyes. Once it was risen, it could not be controlled or stopped. Not even by ones with powers such as ours."

At last, Osuron allowed her to pull him to his feet and clutch his great hands in hers.

"It is but one thing and nothing more," she finally said. "Only one thing explains it."

"What, Julie? What is this thing?"

"Death came for Ramses. And in a form we still do not fully understand."

He did not argue.

And after what felt like a small eternity, they turned, arm in arm, and abandoned the sunlit woods. And she was grateful suddenly that he'd come for her, grateful that she did not have to leave these woods alone.

The trees were more vivid than they'd been thousands of years before, the winds more powerful. He was not beholding this landscape through the golden skin of the colossus. He was within it, surrounded by it, pummeled by it.

Sand billowed through the air all around him.

Ramses went to spit it from his lips. But he no longer had lips. His tongue was gone, and so was the length of his throat. This desire to cough was an instinct triggered by the sight of the surrounding storm, but it had no body to go with it. Only awareness.

The tides of sand that swept across him were the same bright and shining hue of the golden snakes that had devoured him in the earthly realm. They came now in greater and thicker assault, their source unclear, for there was no sign of the colossus, just this familiar grove of wind-tossed trees and the glimpses it offered of the soaring obsidian gates filling the cliff face beyond.

When Ramses willed himself to stand, he experienced it as a subtle lifting of his spirit without the expected tensing of muscles, the instinctive attempts of his feet to find balance. The swirling gold dust clung now to his silhouette, a subtle effervescence of his spirit. This gathering sheen gave an outline to limbs he could not fully feel.

He had been broken down entirely, he now realized, so he could be brought to this place, this other realm. And now he was being reassembled, but only in part and in a form that was far from physical. Just enough of a gathering of his spirit so that he could have an experience of this place, this grove, these obsidian gates, and all that might lie beyond.

The great pulse came to him. A pulse like a god's breath or its heartbeat.

He did not walk; his desire to walk compelled him forward. And through the tossing branches he saw once more the towering obsidian walls in the cliff face above, the bright blue sky knotted with dark storm clouds that somehow blotted out the sun while still allowing its light to spread across the vault of blue.

There is no sun here, *he thought.* The light across the sky has a source, but how arrogant and foolish of me to assume it is the sun. For I am no longer on Earth.

The pulse drew him forward, and the towering black walls did what they had not done thousands of years before—they opened.

And then Ramses was ripped into the dark.

There was such force behind the attack, he assumed he'd become flesh once more. But he was still formless. Driven and tossed like paper on a fierce wind, but also seized by something that could command spirit. He rose high into a darkness which strobed with the pulses of light coming from below him. He saw in these great flashes carvings so intricate and detailed on the ascending walls of this chamber he knew he could spend a millennium trying to decipher them. He could not tell if they were the writings of an ancient language or sculptural renderings so intricate it was impossible to determine where one began and another ended.

He had the sudden sense these carvings were impressions left by whatever powered the great pulse that had drawn him

here, and the flashes of light—as white blue as lightning—
accompanied this pulse. He heard weeping and sounds of joy
and urgent rushes of conversation and argument. He saw then
that he was being pressed downward, his back towards the
great flashes of light, and knifing through him were bolts of
brilliant blue, gaining forms that seemed close to human. They
rose high into the chamber, past the carved walls, and towards a
void above. And it seemed then as if whatever force had seized
him was pressing him down into a chimney, but rising from the
chimney were spirits, and when they passed through his incor-
poreal form, he briefly merged with them, experiencing surges
of their loves, their deaths, their gasping moments of sexual
release, their graveside grief.

Their memories, *he realized.* They are the dead passing
through me and I am experiencing their memories.

And he remembered then the words of Lawrence Strat-
ford after they'd pulled him from the dark. His comparison of
memories to veils of dust the dead might collide with as they're
plucked from this realm, and Ramses felt this now. Experienced
it himself. And the fusillade of it was increasing, the memories
coming faster and more furious, no matter how much he tried
to roil and struggle against the force that held him. And he
realized then the force was not just holding him; it was press-
ing him farther downward, downward into the great flashes of
light, downward towards the throbbing pulse. And the memo-
ries came faster, not because they were rising into him. Because
they were falling; they fell as the spirits knifing through him
rose, and the more Ramses was pushed down into the center of
this chamber, the more he swam amidst these falling memories.
Discarded memories.

And even though it was terrifying and he felt as if what
remained of his mind might well shatter as it was swarmed with
the losses and loves of others, there was a great relief that came
with it. A sense of explanation. For those he'd pulled from death

had been tormented by memory—by the absence of it or the sudden appearance of memories that were not their own. And this explained it. Memory was fundamental to the process of death, and if his journey here ended in oblivion, then at least his awareness would wink out after having acquired this knowledge.

Not just the process of death, *Ramses realized,* memory is fundamental to the process of rebirth.

It was then that he saw the eyes of a giant. They glowed amber, but they were not made from stone. This luminescence was not of the earthly realm. The expression was fixed and unreadable but intense, for the giant's face had appeared through the streaks of spirit matter rising towards the dark above, and there was no denying that this great figure had inhabited the colossus, but in this realm, it floated free. And in this moment it was trying to press Ramses farther and farther down into the rising tide of spirits.

And it was failing.

*The face was three times the size of what Ramses's entire body would have been had he still possessed his body; twice the size of that of the colossus. Its skin was as brown as that of Ramses's mortal form, and one hand was opened wide. But despite the luminescence and the sheen of its skin, this spirit—*A god, Ramses, why can you still not bring yourself to call it a god?*—seemed as immutable and statuesque as the colossus that had allowed it to briefly walk in the mortal realm.*

Then, suddenly, there was release.

He was tossed free of the rising storm, floating through open darkness.

He willed himself to turn, saw the great luminescent structure into which the god had tried to drive him. At its center was a great, glimmering stone, the same shade and substance as the Eye of Osiris, and he knew then, instantly, that the Eye had been made from it, and that it had connected the impossibilities of this realm with the mortal world. The stone was the heart of this cavern, and through it, the spirits who entered this place passed. As they rose towards the stone's bottom, the spirits formed a teeming mass of brilliance that gained shape only after passing through the stone and rising above it.

The god had retreated. Into vapor or shadow, it wasn't clear. Did flesh of any kind exist here? Was this why he'd been reduced to nothing? Did he only see what this god wished him to see?

When, Ramses wondered, *are we willing to call a god by its given name? Is it only when it adopts the poses and behaviors granted it by human sculptors and painters? Is it only when it announces itself by the name we've given it? Or do we remain blind to it because we refuse to acknowledge its true form when it arrives without those trappings? Must every god in the pantheon exactly resemble its earthly depictions before we bow before it and say, "Yes, you have come to me from the infinite to remind me I am but dust before you."*

The god appeared. But it paid Ramses no attention. With its giant hands it held to the great stone, and as the result of this loving embrace, it seemed to gain greater physical form; the form of a great bald giant. As it placed its forehead to the shining amber stone, its glowing eyes closed, its expression beatific. Satisfied. Then its eyes opened again. The gold was gone from them, replaced by the same brilliant blue of the spirits passing through the stone. And it regarded Ramses with sudden calm.

And it was then that Ramses understood that this great stone truly was the engine of rebirth, and that the teeming masses of spectral figures rising into the stone were the newly dead, and what rose from the top of it were spirits destined to be reborn. But what to make of this enormous giant who clung to it lovingly, who pressed its forehead to the surface as if warming itself?

And then a new phrase to describe what he'd seen came to him, but he sought to drive it from his mind. For it seemed abominable. But he could not.

You feed from it.

The god laughed. Its lips did not move and its eyes did not change color back to gold, but the sound that filled Ramses's awareness was undeniable. And when the god spoke it was with the same voice that had filled Ramses in Dimitri Vasilev's great hall.

Yes, Ramses. I feed from it.

You bring me here to reveal this to me?

I bring you here to learn what you are.

You know my name.

I know you stood before me thousands of years ago as king. But your substance is not the same, your soul is not the same.

You did not seek to destroy me just now, did you? You sought to test me. By driving me into the rising dead. To see if I could be torn apart.

Nothing is torn apart here, Ramses. Nothing ends. Nothing is lost. All that takes form in this realm comes from the passage of those who briefly depart the mortal world before they return. When I depart the province of the stone, I am but spirit, as is all that is not mortal.

The province of the stone, was that its term for this cavern, this realm beyond a wind-tossed grove and gates, this place whose threshold he'd been brought to thousands of years before? He struggled to comprehend the god's words. Did it mean to say this place was illusion, or were the physical attributes Ramses could see here created by the process taking place within the great stone at its center? Had these carved chamber walls been created by this process like smoke stains upon the walls of temples where firepits and candles burned for years on end?

And what is mortal? *Ramses asked.*

It is not you, Ramses. That is what I have just learned. The very substance of your spirit rejects the cycle of rebirth.

How is this possible? How is it possible I can reject the actions of gods?

They are not the actions of gods. They are the actions over which gods preside.

You are Osiris, god of the underworld.

I am nameless, uncontained by human terms, and one of many. And you, Ramses, are a king who should not still live, whose soul is altered beyond what I clutched in my hand during your ancient ritual so many mortal years ago. All life seeks rebirth when removed from the mortal realm. All life, through its very nature, returns. Except for yours.

It washed over him, suddenly. Washed over him that this was the god of mortal death and rebirth, and so an immortal was unknown to it, an alien being inspiring confusion and fear. And it seemed to be the greatest miracle of the elixir, suddenly, that a quickly blended potion, consumed in several quick swallows, had now placed him in the position of being questioned by a being as powerful as this one. The elixir had not, he now realized, changed just his cells and organs and flesh. It had changed the very substance of his soul. And souls were the only currency of this god, and it had no experience with a soul that did not die.

He'd feared he'd been brought here to face judgment from drawing Cleopatra and Lawrence from this realm, but now it seemed quite different. He had been brought here not so that he could understand the god, but so that the god could understand him.

You know only that which passes through the stone, *Ramses said.*

All life passes through the stone.

Except for mine.

The god was silent, its massive face unreadable.

This is what you mean when you say you feed off the stone and the spirits passing through it. You obtain their memories, their knowledge, their lived experiences.

Yes, Ramses.

It would be the perfect recipe for an all-knowing, all-seeing god, *Ramses realized,* if it weren't for the complication of immortals. *The complication of him.*

But another, darker possibility was emerging.

If the god fed off memories and lived experiences, an immortal would be a treasure trove of such things. This meant Ramses had been brought here not just as a prisoner or some outlaw, but as a potential feast.

Why did you build the colossus? *Ramses asked.*

So that I might know the mortal world beyond what is revealed to me here.

Ramses thought of the deep-sea diving suits he'd seen in books after his resurrection.

Did you succeed?

I was more limited by the laws of the mortal realm than I'd hoped, but I was grateful for the priests and the work for which they used me.

You were cast aside, abandoned, left to history. This did not anger you?

The mortal realm presented me with few surprises.

You prefer this darkness?

This darkness, as you call it, is all that you can see of a world and a realm that moves beyond your ability to comprehend it. I learned this in the mortal realm. Most of you entertain delusions that your creators wish to move among you, love as you, and die as you. These are fantasies spun by those who cannot imagine the worlds I travel.

And so are you a god, *Ramses said,* and this an afterlife?

Do you see life here, Ramses?

I see, I hear, I feel, what I believe to be life passing through.

But does it remain?

I remain.

But are you life or some aberrant version of it exempted from the cycle of rebirth?

I cannot answer this.

Neither can I. Yet. And that is why you remain. But it is no afterlife, Ramses. Life is too strong to be contained. It is never destroyed. Divorced from the flesh, it moves through all matter and form to find flesh again.

The god approached him now, and as it did, it seemed to lose form, becoming vapor and a presence Ramses could feel drawing near in every suspended cell of his being. Ramses was tempted to cry out with a mouth he no longer had. He was being encircled by the god's presence, wrapped up first in its fog and then seized by its power.

Except for yours, Ramses. I have removed your spirit from the flesh, and it fights me. It does not plow headfirst into the invitation of rebirth that all spirits crave. And so you are a mystery to me, and you shall remain here with me, until the mystery of you is solved.

*Frozen now. He felt frozen. Not a tiny body gripped by a giant hand. Every molecule of him had been suddenly halted and seized by a force he could no longer see, a force that had lost definition. All traces of the cavern, the province of the stone, vanished, and darkness drowned his vision. With it came a sense of timelessness. He remembered Lawrence Stratford's words—*Death is the collapse of time—*and wondered if the god was making yet another attempt to subject him to the process it visited upon mortal souls.*

But the god's words had been direct, and fearsome, and what reason did Ramses have to doubt them? What need did the god have for deceit? The god had proclaimed him a mystery, and so he would remain with the god until the mystery was solved.

And so as darkness claimed him finally, as all sense of his physical presence was lost, Ramses realized he had become the prisoner of the god who'd claimed him, the prisoner of Osiris.

26

Brogdon Castle

There was a window in the stone corridor outside Bektaten's library, a window through which Julie could watch the sparkling sea as she listened to the low murmurs of Bektaten and Osuron speaking to each other in the lost language of their fallen kingdom.

During their time at sea, she'd said little, done little, eaten almost nothing, which had tired her and made her pale. Occasionally during their voyage, Anya went to her and held her without requesting attention in return, and this had comforted her. But as the journey wore on, Julie couldn't stand to remain belowdecks because belowdecks was where the glass jars containing the residue of the colossus traveled as well. The unchanging state of their sandstone-colored contents seemed to mock all hope that Ramses could be found, rescued. Retrieved.

And so, for most of the remaining hours of the trip, she'd stayed above deck, holding to the rigging no matter how angry the seas. Once, when a powerful storm swept the vessel, Osuron pleaded with her to go below. She refused, passing the hours by staring into the roiling waves. Daring them to swallow her. They were larger and more fearsome than the seas she'd gazed into before she'd tried to take her life. A moment that had ended with her cradled in Ramses's arms, then swiftly reborn. But Ramses's powerful arms might just be dust in a jar now. And she could not be drowned. Perhaps an eternity of drifting in solitude, weakened from hunger, gradually heal-ing from whatever injuries the open ocean brought, would be preferable to this return journey and its obligation to relive the terrible events that had taken Ramses from her.

Now, gazing at the sparkling seas off Cornwall, she wished she'd given herself willingly to the waves. That was how much she'd come to dread this inevitable meeting with her queen.

It was a mercy that Osuron had agreed to sit with Bektaten first. He would provide, he'd assured her, a full account of their actions on the island, so Julie wouldn't have to.

But what then would Bektaten ask of her? Julie couldn't know.

She knew only what she planned to ask of Bektaten.

It had come to her as she'd ridden the storm, as the rain had soaked and pummeled her. As she'd taken silent note of the thousands of ways in which her immortal body did not react or recoil or flinch or even tense at the storm's assault. The erup-tion of wind and waves and spray had assaulted her as if she were stone. But inside, she was a hollow ruin. This discrepancy had to be healed, reconciled. And only Bektaten could do this, Bektaten and the powerful secrets in her garden.

There seemed to be pity in Osuron's eyes when he stepped from the library. A sadness she had never seen radiate from him before. He gave her a small nod. Julie stepped into the room.

Bektaten stood beside the single window, lancing sunlight streaming in over one shoulder, the jagged profiles of cliffs extending to the horizon behind her. Her stance was erect and regal, her hands clasped in front of her, but when she spoke, her voice was as gentle as it had ever been in Julie's presence.

"Julie," she said.

Slowly, the queen moved to her, took her hands in hers, studied her face as if trying to determine whether she'd be receptive to greater comfort. "Julie," she whispered again, as if the very mention of her name made her grief a presence in the room which must be honored. "Sit," she whispered, and Julie did. Bektaten did as well.

For a while, neither woman spoke.

The question Julie meant to ask was simple, but its implications momentous, and so it paralyzed her.

Bektaten broke the silence. "What do you believe you witnessed? I have an account of the events, but what do you believe it was, Julie?"

"Rapture, my queen. There's no other word for it. A rapture."

For a while, they stared at each other. Such a simple, subtle statement, but the fearsomeness of it washed over them both. That a being eight thousand years old, who had wandered all realms of this earthly plane, recording millennia of observations and insight in her journals, had no frame of reference for this left Julie speechless, and it was an admission that left Bektaten weary and appearing as close to grief stricken as Julie felt. And it seemed that, like Osuron, she shared some measure of guilt over all of this as well.

"I will undertake a study of it. I will bring the full power of my labs and potions and tonics to bear on the remains we have. But in this moment I have only speculation, and I fear those things will not comfort you."

"I know what will comfort me, and it comes from your laboratory."

"Julie—"

"I don't wish to end it all. I merely wish to know there will be an end. I see how much of a comfort that is for mortals now, even if they don't realize it. To know that their pain will not go on forever."

"Your pain will not go on forever even if you do."

"Ah, yes, and so I'll live with the cold awareness that eventually my heart released him. I'll live with a dim memory of him, and then after centuries, perhaps I will forget him completely. An experience no mortal ever suffers. No mortal lives long enough to forget their great loves entirely, do they? This is the thought I cannot bear, my queen. That I might live long enough to forget Ramses. Please. I will swear loyalty and secrecy to you forever, but you must do this for me. Bring me your potion. Make me mortal again."

"I will not," Bektaten answered. "Not now, not in this moment."

Julie's lips parted and she took a deep breath to speak. But just then she heard her name spoken. The queen's lips hadn't moved. The voice wasn't hers.

The voice was familiar and it was male.

"Julie," the man said again.

She turned her head and saw him standing in the open doorway, having just stepped into the library's shadows without her notice. His eyes were vividly blue, but there was something else there that had been missing when last she'd seen him. Recognition. It was a strained and painful thing, as if he were struggling to maintain each passing second of it, but it was there. The coldness was gone.

Her father was seeing her; her father was saying her name.

"Julie."

Her legs trembled, but she rose to her feet regardless. Only then did she realize what she'd truly done on her journey home. Somehow it had seemed easier to imagine him sealed in his coffin, sleeping a sleep close to death by choice. Easier to grieve one great loss than two. And yet, this had added an insufferable weight to her grief. And now, at the sight of him, his eyes full of a curiosity and dazed wonder where there had once been only coldness, she felt suddenly lighter.

Softly, Bektaten said, "It was his wish that he tell you of his decision himself."

"A decision," Julie whispered, hearing the tears before she felt them stinging her eyes.

"Oh, Julie." Sympathy in his voice now, a recognition of her tears, and a sense that they were something he could stop. That he could stop. Because he was her father.

Was it real? Was it pretense? Would the terrible detachment return? Despite all the horrors she'd seen since, the pain of his last rejection was still fresh.

She could not go to him.

So he came to her, walking smoothly across the stone floor, without the frightened, catlike reactions of his newly resurrected state. He gazed into her eyes, and when he gently took her hands in his, she crumbled into his embrace, felt his arms assemble a familiar pose. He held her as he did when she was a little girl who'd injured herself, as he had during the funeral for her mother.

If it was not truly him, it was most certainly his embrace.

Through her tears, she glimpsed Bektaten's serene expression, and then Lawrence said, "Come. Come with me, Julie. Let us dance as we used to, for I have chosen the light."

Part IV

27

Again it was words that healed. Words and memory.

Her father's journals, the ones she'd retained, the ones too personal to give to the museum, had helped restore his mind. To hear Elliott tell it, he'd devoured them in the front parlor after she'd left. But the restoration was far from complete. In her presence, he suffered moments of disorientation and confusion that left him blinking and wide eyed and very much like a boy. Or a newborn bird. But they were balanced by surges of memory, moments when he'd grip her hand suddenly and begin describing an afternoon they'd shared together in the park when she was a little girl, when the sun had shined brightly and their kite had climbed ever higher. Or he'd erupt into tears over how coldly he'd rejected her in the front parlor of their home.

But the defiance was gone; the resistance to life was gone.

That had been a pose, it was clear now. A mechanism, marshaled by either his mind or the substance of his spirit itself, for shutting out the madness of his experience. A form of shock unique to the risen dead.

It seemed the cruelest of ironies that Lawrence, who had withered away inside a coffin for months, lived among them now, while Ramses, whose flesh had seemed as strong as steel but weeks before, was now gone. Claimed by an event to which their ancient queen's wisdom had yet to bring even the smallest bit of illumination.

But Julie sensed a gap in Elliott's account of all that had transpired in the front parlor after her agonizing departure, after her great deception. A sense that events within the walls of the house in Mayfair involved greater struggle than either man wanted to confess.

They would tell her, in time.

Still, their evasion seemed unjust, given how many times she'd repeated in excruciating detail all that had transpired on the island of Dimitri Vasilev in the days since their return. The terrible rapture of Ramses. In every room of Brogdon Castle she'd told the tale, to almost all who stayed within its walls.

With one exception.

And she was sitting now before one of the great soaring windows with its view of the cliffs, and in her regal profile, there was not a hint of the malice or outright fear Julie had grown accustomed to seeing there. An altogether-different emotion pursed her lips and gave a tense set to her chin that seemed to threaten a quiver. Julie recognized it. Tasted it.

Grief.

Cleopatra was grieving.

For a long while, Julie didn't move, simply stood within the doorway she'd just entered and studied the former queen before her as if she were an entirely new creature. Surely, Cleopatra noticed her presence, could feel it. But whatever tumult roared inside her now would not allow her to acknowledge it.

Go to her, a voice said inside of her.

As she approached the little table and chairs where Cleopatra sat, the being who'd once threatened to snap her neck like a reed slowly turned her attention to Julie, ashamed of her emotions but too weary to conceal them.

"Is there news?" Cleopatra asked.

"Belgium has fallen. The French will seek to flood the country with their own troops in hopes of stopping the German advance. And the Russians are now advancing on the Germans from the east."

And the world did not know, would never know, how close the Russian effort had come to sabotage.

"Not the war," Cleopatra said. "Bektaten, her laboratory. Her efforts."

"They're all at work now. She and my father and Elliott."

"And so there is no progress?" Cleopatra asked.

"We must hold out hope."

"For what?"

"That what we brought back will yield answers."

"Dust," Cleopatra said bitterly. "Is this what's so soon become of our new immortal band? Desperate for answers from dust. Are we now no different from the dying soldiers in the mud of Belgium? Clawing at the earth in hope of hearing God's voice."

"I may well have heard God's voice. I've no desire to hear it again."

Cleopatra studied her. Julie studied her back. It was, it seemed, the first time they'd simply regarded each other.

"Why do you linger?" Cleopatra asked.

"I've realized something about you."

"Oh?"

"You were mortal when you raised him. And so he was a miracle to you as he was for me. And I imagine you grieve him much as I do."

Something quieted within the former queen. Some persistent, gnawing hostility vanished from her, and after a long moment, she settled farther back into her chair and gestured with one hand to the empty chair across from her. A small invitation that was also momentous. Julie accepted.

And for a while they said nothing to each other. Which also seemed momentous, to sit so peaceably in each other's company when their past meetings had been defined by tangles and threats and rage. They watched the gulls wheeling in the winds outside and the strands of cloud that passed high overhead and they listened to the wind whistle through the little cracks of the window.

And then Cleopatra said, "The words in her letter. The one she wrote to you. They disturbed me."

"How?" Julie asked.

"I've spent hours with her now. She is a being of great power. I don't deny this. But her existence has been defined by the betrayal of one man, her former prime minster. And I fear this causes her to speak of passion and of love in a limited way. It doesn't weaken us as women, as immortals, to follow our love, even if it leads to a man. There is no crime in the devotion she describes. Only in devoting ourselves to that which would see us tear ourselves apart for its petty benefit. And this was never Ramses. Not to you, and not to me."

"Perhaps this is not what she meant."

"Perhaps not. But she said it nonetheless. And so I must say to you what I just said. There is no weakness in grief. There is no weakness in love. No one can rule without them."

She had, for the past few days, managed to keep her tears in check, but now they threatened to return. And when Cleopatra rose suddenly, Julie thought it was to avoid a likely display. But a moment later, she had settled back into her chair, carefully placing a gleaming chessboard on the table between them. Its pieces were stout and carved of ivory, and Cleopatra, last queen of Egypt, was carefully returning them to the proper positions with long and delicate fingers.

"Let us play, Julie Stratford," she said.

And so they did.

In her laboratory, they worked, Elliott and Lawrence on the frame for the statue Bektaten had tasked them to create, and

Bektaten at her examination table beneath the glow of oil lanterns and torches. This chamber, with its rugged stone walls, was buried deep within the tunnels that honeycombed the cliff beneath the castle. Smugglers' tunnels, Bektaten had told Elliott on his first visit here, discovered when they'd first moved in.

In various places, rivulets of sunlight poured over their ceilings, walls, and floors as they twisted and turned. Some corridors opened suddenly to the sea. In other places the light came through deep cracks too narrow for a human to pass through. If it were not for these light sources, drowsiness might have overtaken Elliott the deeper he went into impenetrable dark.

The mastiffs lounged about their feet as they worked.

On a great stone slab in the center of the room Bektaten had carefully sculpted the contents of the jars into the shape of a man, a faceless body composed of dust. But she had not touched it since, and she'd forbidden Lawrence and Elliott to do the same. Smoothed flat, thickly layered, enough to make a full-size man.

A man like Ramses.

He and Lawrence had devoted hours to the sculpture's frame they were building in the corner, using their incredible strength to bend the metal where a normal man would require several tools. Using the anatomy texts from Bektaten's library, they'd measured out the proportions so that they were roughly human sized.

And on a high shelf made of uneven stone sat the two Eyes of Osiris recovered from Dimitri Vasilev's palace, as well as the one cast off by Ramses during his terrible abduction, and the one Bektaten had kept after it had been stolen from the neck of a would-be assassin. The fifth one, apparently, had been destroyed entirely when Dimitri had murdered his own son.

For days now, Bektaten had tested the seemingly infinite number of tonics and potions derived from the secrets of her garden on the same little mound of dust. For days, she'd

scribbled notes in her ancient language in the same leather-
bound volume in which Enamon and Aktamu had recorded
details of their initial encounters with the Eye of Osiris and
those who had wielded it with malice.

Occasionally, Bektaten had risen from her table to give them
instructions on their sculpting of the metal. And Lawrence and
Elliott had taken these instructions willingly. Lawrence perhaps more so than Elliott, given he now took to waking life as
if he needed constant instruction from those around him if he
was to avoid being pitched back into madness and a desire to
return to the dark.

They knew better than to ask the queen what she was learning, discovering.

Days had gone by now, and Enamon and Aktamu brought
them great platters of food which they dined on constantly.
And they never slept. Occasionally, they rested, he and Lawrence. Withdrew from the lab quietly and without announcement so as not to disturb their queen. But this was only to cast
their eyes upon something different and new, however briefly.
To restore their minds so they could return once more to a
depth of focus achieved only by immortals. Immortals who did
not need sleep. Who could work for hours without tiring so
long as there was some form of sustenance within reach.

But still, there must be some cost, Elliott thought, some
mental toll.

But Bektaten did not warn them of any such thing. And her
other instructions had been specific. They were not to touch
the gathered dust atop the slab, the dust she had roughly shaped
into the outline of a human being.

Finally, one day, she rose from her table. Elliott looked up
from his work. The frame was not just the general lines of a
human body, but they'd fashioned an interior skeleton for it
that would hold whatever material they'd eventually apply
to it.

Don't deceive yourself, good man, Elliott said to himself. *The material will be the dust brought back from Russia. This will be a statue composed of all that remains of the colossus, and perhaps of Ramses himself.*

Lawrence also paused his work. But Bektaten did not come to them. She moved instead to the slab, rested her hands gently against its very edge, and stared down at the ghostly pile before her. For a while, she did not speak, but for the first time in days there was raw unguarded emotion in her eyes, replacing the analytical thoughtfulness which had defined her every action prior.

She had either just discovered something, or her days of analysis had finally brought her to an unavoidable conclusion.

"It does not change," she finally said.

"What doesn't, my queen?" Elliott asked.

"This dust. I have subjected it to every tonic in my possession. And it does not change."

Slowly, both men moved to her until the three of them were standing around the slab as if beholding an actual corpse.

He thought her despair shortsighted. She'd already assured them that no secret in her garden could give life to that which did not already possess some form of it. Was that really her plan? Elliott had assumed they'd fashion the dust of the colossus into the shape of life and then use the Eye against it once more, opening the door that had been so terrifyingly thrown open on the shores of Lake Ladoga. It was a laborious endeavor, to be sure, and one that would require great courage at its end. But it was achievable. Imminently achievable.

But their queen was in despair.

"I don't understand," Elliott said. "Did you truly think a potion would bring it back to life?"

"You don't understand, Elliott," she whispered, "it responds to nothing. Not even tonics capable of eating through yards of pure stone."

"And so it cannot be destroyed," Lawrence said carefully.

Bektaten nodded, but this was clearly not the source of her sadness.

"It remains dust," Elliott said, "but it is immortal dust."

"A small comfort, I fear," Bektaten said.

"How so?" Elliott said. Finally, she lifted her eyes to his, and the agony there knifed him. "It resists all substances applied to it. Including adherents. Including all we might use to sculpt it into a shape resembling life."

Once she was satisfied the full implications of this had settled over him, her eyes returned to the dust before her. For the first time, she reached into the pile and took up a handful of it. She let it drift through her fingers, her teeth gritted, as if she wished to pulverize it even further in her powerful grip.

"The door is closed," she whispered.

No one spoke for a while.

"Come," Elliott finally said, "you must rest."

"Sleep for centuries, you mean," she said. "Abandon this endeavor. All this, all this is the result of my commands. An immortal lost to a power we cannot yet comprehend."

"I mean you must place your eyes upon something other than this room, and this dust. If only for a moment or so."

When she extended one slender black arm in his direction, he was startled. She meant for him to take it. While she needed no help to her feet, she seemed to draw comfort from the warmth of his flesh, holding to his arm as if it were a tender thing in need of her comfort. When she extended her other arm, Lawrence did the same, and as they left the laboratory, the mastiffs rose and shuffled to their feet, following closely beside them.

He drew the door shut behind him with his other hand. The heavy iron thudding into place sickened him suddenly.

There was a terrible note of finality to it.

In asking the queen to abandon her work, if only for a short spell, was he not admitting some measure of defeat?

Just rest, he told himself, *I'm admitting a need for rest.*

But before he could stop himself, he said, "We mustn't tell Julie of this yet."

Neither shadow traveling the dark tunnel beside him protested.

Bektaten could not bring herself to address them, for to do so would be to give an air of finality to these proceedings. And while her despair was deep, she was not powerless, not without wisdom. Not without aid. She could summon all the Heralds of the Realms to this castle and begin a quest into the history of this colossus and the mysteries that surely marked its path through history.

Lawrence's account of his meeting with Dimitri Vasilev, as well as archival papers Julie and Osuron had brought back from the Lake Ladoga estate, made clear that a great span of time had passed between when Ramses had first bowed before the colossus within the Temple of Karnak and when it was finally hidden by the priests in response to the terrible looting of the Valley of the Kings. Perhaps the colossus had not spun off tools as powerful as the Eye upon its journey, but surely there were other clues.

Other doorways.

Some trail that might lead them to the realm where Ramses had been taken.

But the words that haunted her now were less ordered than these plans and designs, and they hovered close to her as she lay in retirement in her candlelit chamber, unable to return to her lab.

I have lost you, my king, these words said. *I sent you forth on this mission and now I have lost you. And it is my burden to retrieve you.*

And then, suddenly, the mastiffs at her feet stirred and rose. The ones who'd followed her to her chambers stood rigid and erect. Their movements were rarely this doglike, and so their skittishness startled her.

Then she heard it, the sound that had roused them.

At first, she thought it was the sea. But it was louder, and its rhythm distinct from the steady roar of waves. But it seemed to travel on the wind outside. And it seemed to be drawing closer. It had the same syncopation as the sounds Ramses had demonstrated for them in the great hall below, the sounds he'd heard outside the towering obsidian gates to the realm of Osiris.

And then, one by one, the dogs began to howl.

How strange that she would think it impossible given all she'd experienced.

But after the sound of the strangely familiar pulse drew her to the window, Cleopatra told herself that what she was seeing was merely fog. Or some illusion produced by it. But it was impossible to deny the gold in it, the shimmer. And it did not slide past the glass; it kissed it. Tasted it. Tested it. As if it were a luminescent snake in search of something.

She pressed her face to the windows and saw other snakes of shimmering gold just like it, slithering along the castle's great stone walls. Draped like tendrils from the roof before she realized those too were animate, searching. And they did not seem to find what they were looking for along these upper walls and windows, so they curled around the castle's sea-facing tower and vanished from sight.

And then came the terrible howling of the dogs. A mournful sound, for the mastiffs usually made no sounds at all. But they howled now as if in warning. And that's when Alex and Sibyl reared up in bed, looking immediately to Cleopatra, who only moments before had been watching them sleep, a sight that always comforted her. For they thought themselves her protectors, when truly, with each passing day, it was they who were falling under her care.

"What is it?" Alex said, quick fear chasing the sleep from his voice. "What's alarmed the dogs?"

Cleopatra paused to consider her answer. "Something is here."

Lawrence took Elliott's hand as they descended the stone stairs. His sudden need and urgency a reminder of how recently he'd been freed from the dark, from death. And how easily convinced he was it might try to reclaim him. Could that be the cause of this strange teeth-rattling sound and its accompanying flashes of golden light beyond the castle's windows?

If so, why did it allow the two of them to rush unimpeded through the castle. Why did it not strike them down where they stood?

By the time they reached the great hall, everyone was there. Bektaten in her purple robes and Sibyl and Alex and Cleopatra, and Enamon and Aktamu and Osuron. And Julie, wide eyed and terrified. But the quiet confusion on Bektaten's face was the most frightening element of it all. For she seemed to have no sense of what befell them now, of what shimmering force had embraced her citadel before vanishing. Leaving behind this terrible, growing sound, like some sort of great heartbeat given off by the cliff beneath the castle.

And the dogs. The dogs were all here as well, which was a shock, for they often split off into little lazy packs. But now they'd all gathered, and their howls were piercing and mournful, and they were all facing in the same direction, Elliott realized. They had all turned their attention to the passage that led directly to the smugglers' tunnels.

"It's beneath us," Bektaten said, "the sound is beneath us."

"The lab," Julie said. She tore a torch from its sconce. A sure sign she meant to pursue it into the tunnels, even if she had to go alone. "It's coming from the laboratory! It has to be!"

Without another word, she plunged forward into the shadows, holding the torch aloft. Elliott followed, searched its flickering light for some trace of the flashes of golden light he'd seen pressing against the windows earlier. Only when they turned a corner did it come, so much brighter than the torch, as if some sort of compact golden maelstrom had been lit within the twisting stone passages up ahead.

Julie hesitated for only a second, then plowed ahead.

Elliott grabbed her shoulder. "No," he said. "No, I'll not have you lost to this as well."

But she would not stop and he would not release her, nor would he abandon her, and when he looked back, he realized they were all here, all following Julie into the dark, even Alex and Sibyl, so precious and mortal and so very vulnerable.

The pulse became deafening now, and the light even brighter. It was no comfort to him that it did not flicker as a mass of flames might. For it had the fierce intensity of an electrical storm. Another corner turned, and there was no denying it now. All of it, the terrible sound and the blinding flashes of golden light, was coming from Bektaten's laboratory.

A new sound joined the tumult, a sound like the sudden sharp retreat of ocean across packed sand. A serpentine hiss with deeper undertones.

The dust, he realized, *whatever this storm, it works its magic upon the dust.*

He could only see a flash of it, so blinding was the light pouring from Bektaten's lab. But he saw the outline of a man taking shape. Saw the golden snakes that had kissed and probed the castle walls had converged here, a frenzy of activity around the slab on which Bektaten had tried to shape the dust into the form of a man. But the man was sitting up now. Elliott saw shoulders and a head, bare arms clasped around bent knees, and thick black hair forming out of swirling tendrils of gold.

Hope surged within Elliott for the first time in days.

Hope, he was sure, surged in them all.

And so this sound, these flashes of light, these golden tendrils, had all worked their strange magic upon the dust that had been Ramses, the dust that had been the colossus, the dust that could not be altered by a chamber full of secret potions and tonics. And this had to be a wonderful thing. So long as the man who took shape atop the slab continued to have a figure and features that were familiar to them all.

When she could deny it no longer, when it was plain to all of them, once the golden light had faded and the pulse that had shaken their hearts in their breasts finally ceased its terrible beating, that it was Ramses sitting atop the great stone slab in the center of the torchlit room, head bowed, his lustrous dark hair draping his face, Julie went to him, a wordless cry issuing from her. He was nude and shuddering, but she could not stop herself. She threw her arms around him, and when she heard his familiar voice say, "Julie," the sobs ripped from her and she embraced him more tightly.

He returned the embrace, but his shudders were severe, and there was a breathlessness in his voice that frightened her. She'd never heard him sound so winded, so weak.

"Julie." This time when he said her name there was concern in his voice.

She drew back, reached up and lifted his chin, brushed away the thick black hair that draped his face even though her urge was to gather it gently into her fist, to nuzzle her nose into it. To bless his return by savoring his scent and his flesh and all those parts of him made physical again.

When she gazed into his eyes, she was so relieved to see warmth and recognition there, nothing like the cold regard her father had shown her during those awful moments back in London, that she missed their remarkable physical transformation.

And it was then that the breathlessness and the shuddering suddenly made an awful kind of sense.

He was not just exhausted from an impossible journey.

Ramses gazed at her with eyes as brown as the ones with which he'd been born.

For Ramses, returned from the realm of the dead, was mortal again.

28

He was as cold as he'd ever been inside the walls of this vast
castle, as cold as Alex Savarell and Sibyl seemed to be, dressed
as they were in long, draping coats.

Mortal again. It made terrible sense. And he was so caught
up in the logic of it that he'd allowed himself little time to
absorb the reality of it, the implications. And if the others were
to understand his thinking, he would have to explain everything. And so he did, and they listened intently as he told them
of his otherworldly encounter with a giant, powerful figure
who had rejected the name and limitations of any god, of the
great stone through which all mortal spirits appeared to pass
and were subsequently transformed, shedding the memories
that had defined one mortal existence so that they could be
opened to another.

They were all attentive, their expressions open and free of
judgment. Even Anya, who was clad now in a brightly colored dress that bore little resemblance to the ghostly veils she'd
worn when they'd discovered her. Osuron held her close, her
protector now, it seemed. Ramses looked to Bektaten throughout his tale, bracing for the possibility she might dismiss the
things he'd seen as illusion and fantasy. But she'd witnessed
the impossible circumstances of his return, forming out of dust
itself. How could she not believe him?

And as he continued with his tale, he realized that she did, in fact, believe him.

They all did.

Their expressions were welcoming. Loving, even.

His abduction and his absence—days to them, but mere hours for him—had brought a unity to all of them that might have eluded them otherwise, that was new and faltering the first night they'd all gathered here but now strong and thriving. And this comforted him, comforted him even as he felt the first tremor of what he feared might be a fever. It had been so long since he'd had one, he couldn't be sure. But he was sure the little wounds he'd just inflicted on his palms with a hatpin of Sibyl's still bled, and he was sure that the room felt very cold, even though it was still summer and the fire was blazing.

"And why do you think he ended it?" Elliott asked. "Your confinement. Why have you been returned now?"

"And in this state?" Julie asked.

"Mortal," Ramses said for her, and she nodded.

"He could not inflict death upon me in his realm. He'd never encountered a soul like mine, and so he held me for as long as he needed to study me. But all souls who enter his realm die a mortal death in this one. This allows them to pass through the stone over which he presides. Only in this way can he acquire such a soul's memories and experiences. I believe he wants mine. I believe he sensed the expanse of my existence, but the only way for him to acquire it was to change my soul to that of a mortal and send me back here so that I might someday pass into his realm as all humans do."

"So that you might die," Julie said. "He sent you back here so you might one day die a mortal death."

"So that he might then consume you," Bektaten said quietly. "This being, this entity, wants to *consume* you."

"Yes," Julie said, "that is one way of describing it."

"He knows nothing of this world except what he draws

from mortal souls," Elliott said, "so he's not some all-seeing, all-knowing god who can take any form?"

"We do not know that he's any sort of god," Sibyl offered. "A spiritual entity of great power, perhaps, capable of creating intricate illusions even. But dare we call him a god?"

"I felt the memories of the soon-to-be reborn," Ramses said, "I felt them rising through me as he attempted to drive my spirit into the beating, luminescent heart of this process over which he is guardian. All I saw there supports what we have learned of the nature of death and rebirth. From Cleopatra to Lawrence to Sibyl, the elaborate connection between memory and rebirth has been made clear to us. And this place, this realm, it was as if I were inside a great modern factory where memories are removed from souls as though they are fuel for the universe itself. And only once this removal took place could the soul be reborn."

"And their life consumed by this so-called god," Bektaten growled.

The sound of Bektaten's anger sent a tremor through the room. It was not anger at him, Ramses realized, but at what she saw as the injustice of the vast system he'd described.

"There's another possibility," Elliott said. "If we're to believe that the time you spent in this realm was the time this entity needed to transform the very substance of your soul, then perhaps the minute he rendered you mortal, you were simply sucked back here before he could stop it. Because you had not entered his realm in the correct way, yet he could not inflict mortal death upon you, and your mortal soul, not having properly died, could not remain there in confinement. Because all of this, Ramses. All of this suggests the force of life, the force of spirit, never stops its motion, always seeks physical form, and so the very idea that he could confine you for any great length of time, it contradicts this, you see? And so this ... being, whatever he truly is, he did not send you back here solely so he could one day consume you. Perhaps he's not so avaricious. Perhaps he simply lost hold of you once the substance of your soul became mortal again."

"I cannot know," Ramses said. "When he ended our exchange, there was only darkness. Darkness and the sense that a thousand hands had reached into the very fibers of my being and were holding tight to everything they found there."

When Bektaten rose to her feet, the room prepared for a lecture. Instead, she walked to the table on which she'd placed the four Eyes of Osiris and brought her fist down upon them with all the strength she had. Everyone flinched at what sounded like the crack of bone.

Rage. That was what filled her. Quiet, focused rage, and the strength of the blow shattered the stones into dozens of fragments. Gently, she pushed these fragments into a neat pile, then raised her fist a second time, shattering those fragments into even-smaller ones. And again, and again.

"Whatever this being claims to be," Bektaten said, "its Eye is closed now. Forever."

Slowly, she walked from the room.

They were all stunned silent.

Finally, Osuron rose to his feet.

"You must understand what this is like for her," he said.

"Indeed," Ramses said, "she's gone eight thousand years without ever encountering a discarnate entity of any sort."

"This is not entirely true," Osuron continued. "You know of the vision she once experienced. She has beheld a spirit world. Once, during her travels, she sought to bring herself as close to death as she could. She lassoed herself to a tree before a great fire sweeping across the savanna, and as the flames consumed her, she saw spirits returning."

"The vision she experienced then suggested that the chain of human existence is a cycle of rebirth. My experience proves this. Why not rejoice that her vision's confirmed by all this?"

"Perhaps she did not wish her vision to be confirmed, Ramses."

There was more silence, and then footsteps.

The queen had returned, and when he saw what was cupped in her hands, Ramses realized she had not simply fled the room in a fit of anger. She had left with purpose, and she had returned with a vial of the elixir. The sight of it seemed to have calmed her.

"Eight thousand years I walked in solitude. I saw cataclysms that shaped the face of the earth, bore witness to human anguish on a scale mortals will never know. Not once did an angel appear to me, nor did a god make itself manifest in the trees or the storms or the crash of ice sliding from mountainsides. And it was an accident of nature that gave me the power to bear this kind of witness, but first, it stole from me my kingdom, my lover, my family. It leveled the world around me with war, plague, and famine. That I might endure these things solely so they might one day be plucked from me by a trickster spirit, that I might one day feed him or delight his otherworldly senses with my millennia of heartbreak, this is the only true abomination. I shall never endure it, and neither shall my subjects."

She'd closed the distance between them now. When she extended the vial, its contents glistened.

"Drink, Ramses," she whispered.

"My queen," Elliott said, a note of warning in his voice.

"There's no other choice, Father," Alex said softly. "He must return to being what he was. He is Ramses, Ramses the Great."

"We must be careful here," Elliott whispered.

"Elliott," Julie whispered. "You can't be serious. You can't mean for him to remain mortal."

"I only mean to say that Ramses is in this state because of the actions of a being we do not fully understand. A being capable of moving between realms of existence, exercising powers that boggle our minds and render our ancient and exceedingly wise queen mute with astonishment."

"Have I been mute during these proceedings, Lord Rutherford?" Bektaten asked. "I am not mute now."

"If we act rashly to change this," Elliott said, "there might be yet another thunderous response from a force we don't understand."

"You mean for him to die, Elliott?" Julie asked. "You mean for him to one day die and be taken from us all?"

"He was already taken from us all," Elliott said, "and I fear that if we act rashly in this, he'll be taken from us again."

"How?" Bektaten said. "The Eye is destroyed. Its fragments will be cast into the sea. Every speck of dust brought back from the scene of the colossus's destruction is gone now, reassembled into the man we see before us. We have sealed off our world, our realm, from the base trickery of this spirit, this being, who coyly rejects the name of the god Osiris even as he seeks to dazzle Ramses's spirit with all the spectacle of his realm. We are safe from him now. The world is safe. The war is safe."

Elliott's eyes met Ramses's. They were full of tears.

"I do not want you taken from us again," he whispered. "You understand that, don't you, my dear friend? That's all I want. Is for you to never be taken from us again. That is my only fear in this."

"I understand, my friend," Ramses said. "Do not fear. I understand you perfectly."

Julie clutched his hand, but there was fear in her eyes. Had she been infected by Elliott's doubts? He was about to ask when a new voice spoke, clear and steady and familiar.

"Drink, Ramses," Cleopatra said.

She stood just outside the circle, her hands clasped, an erectness to her poise that seemed new, fresh. Alive. At the confidence in her voice, and the unexpected intrusion of it, all fell silent.

"You do not wish to see me one day wither away as punishment for what I did to you?" he asked.

Slowly, she moved to him. "I wish for the miracle of you to always be somewhere in the world as long as I am in it." She had reached him now and tenderly cupped both her hands under the one in which he held the vial. Slowly, she guided it to his mouth. "Whether I have forgiven you or not is beside the point. You must drink, Ramses. You must drink and defy the gods."

He uncapped the vial and brought it to his lips, downed its contents and felt the delicious tingling sweep him from head to toe just as it had three thousand years before. But the rest of the experience was so different from his ancient theft in that Hittite cave. For now he consumed this accident of nature knowing full well all it might do, all it could bring, all it would make last forever, and all it might end.

And as he felt its rush for a second time, he knew once again the taste of eternal life.

Once a theft. Now a gift.

And there was no thunder, no shaking of the walls around them, no great assault against this citadel and its new inhabitants. Instead, Ramses heard only the little gasps of relief that came from the immortals closest to him when they saw his eyes were once more as blue as their own.

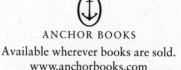

PRINCE LESTAT AND THE REALMS OF ATLANTIS
The Vampire Chronicles

In this ambitious, rich novel of vision and power, the indomitable vampire hero Lestat de Lioncourt, prince of the vast tribe of the undead, returns. Lestat finds himself at war with a strange, ancient, otherworldly form that has taken possession of his immortal body and spirit. It is through this perilous and profound struggle that we come to be told the hypnotic tale of a great sea power of ancient times: a mysterious heaven on Earth situated on a boundless continent in the Atlantic Ocean. As we learn of the mighty, resonant powers and perfections of this kingdom of Atalantaya, the lost realms of Atlantis, we come to understand how and why the vampire Lestat, and indeed all the vampires, must reckon so many millennia later with the terrifying force of this ageless, all-powerful Atalantaya spirit.

Fiction

ALSO AVAILABLE

Angel Time

Anne Rice's Vampire Chronicles: An Alphabettery

Called Out of Darkness

Christ the Lord: The Road to Cana

Of Love and Evil

The Wolf Gift

The Wolves of Midwinter

ANCHOR BOOKS

Available wherever books are sold.

www.anchorbooks.com